Tangled Reality

R. D. Chapman

Copyright © 2022 by Reneé D. Chapman
ISBN: 979-8-9906998-4-7

Editor: Ray Rhamey
Cover Design: SelfPubBookCovers.com/thrillerauthor

Shades of Fall Publishing
www.ShadesOfFall.com

A warm thank you to Amy and John for their insights into the corporate mindset, and to Chivi and Jack, my beta readers. A very grateful thank you to my editor, Ray Rhamey. Lastly, a very special thank you to the readers who are willing to give a new author a chance.

Chapter 1

Jem Wilmont risked a quick peek around the fat statue she hid behind.

Quick flashes of lights into doorways and under the few vehicles lining this backstreet marked the searchers progress. Crap. It wouldn't take them long to reach this spot. She didn't dare shift here, a security cam might catch it. She needed—*halleluiah*! An alley, about twenty meters down and on her side of the street. Thank the Universe this planet's gravity was Earth-like. Her heavier Midgard-healed muscles were the only reason she'd made the fast sprint to her hiding place before they turned the corner.

The crunch of footsteps on frozen snow drew closer. She bolted out of her hiding spot.

"There she is!"

"Get her!"

Jem felt the thump and warm tingle that signaled a stun shot in her back. A second one in her shoulder felt like jagged needles. *Owww!* She staggered, but kept running. Footsteps pounded behind her. She darted into the alley. Between the third and fourth step she shifted, rendering herself invisible to her ambushers. Her heart quit pounding. Her lungs no longer heaved. Her cheeks weren't freezing.

Wonderful. Maybe I should have shifted into ghost-mode sooner.

She watched her pursers slide to a halt at the alley entrance only seconds behind her. Wow. Now that was some heavy-duty cursing. They began searching the alley, two to a side. More cussing when one of them slipped on an icy spot. The leader stayed at the entrance, dividing his attention between the alley and the street.

Watching for Enforcers?

The four worked their way back. "Nothing, Yance. Not a damn thing. No prints, nothing. Where the hell did she go?" said a very frustrated male.

"I got her in the back and shoulder," the shooter said. "I'm sure of it. She must be wearing some kind of armor under her thermal suit."

Yance rubbed his chin. "She was expecting trouble or gave it a high probability. She's got to be ex-military turned freelance."

"Want to bet she also snagged a hover-belt on her way out?" the single female in the group asked.

Nope. Guess again. Jem watched, amused, as they scanned the alley's rooftops.

"All right," Yance said, "Spread out. Hit all the entrances to the tourist section and the hotels. I want that cash card."

"We *all* want that cash card," the female retorted. "She sold Jantze *three* J-crystals."

The short, squat guy blew out an explosive breath. "That's a frigging lot of credits. My split will get me off this ice ball."

"Then you'd better find her," Yance snapped.

Yay. Just a localized robbery attempt. No psycho stalkers this time. Jantze, the clerk-manager she'd conducted the transaction with, must have contacted this gang when he went into the office to download the money into the cash card.

"How, Yance?" the female said, jamming hands on hips. "We don't have a name and not much of a description."

Yance shot them an irritated look. "There shouldn't be too many women out alone at this time of night. She's from off-planet—you know the shortcuts back to the tourist sections. Get there first. Talk with your contacts about any wandering women or one that stands out. I'll check with Jantze, see if he has any more information."

They split up as light snow began falling.

Yance headed back toward the pawn shop that had a no-questions-asked sideline. Jem mulled things over as she followed along behind him. She'd landed in Valasia, Stromli Four's capital, yesterday. Its main tourist draws were year-round winter sports with toasty warm casinos and gaming rooms. It was just one more stop in a long string of planets she'd visited in the last five months, selling her Jaguide crystals.

She would have preferred to sneak them back into the vault they were stolen from. But a promise to use them in helping to rebuild a destroyed world had tied her hands. A shudder rippled through her, remembering images of the blackened and scorched landscape.

With each crystal worth a fortune, most pawn fronts dealing in the high-dollar black market could only handle one or two of them. But she'd figured the silent casino backers of the ones here could afford an additional crystal or two. After a few discreet inquires, she'd selected Abbot's Good Deals as the one appearing to be the safest.

Obviously, appearances were deceiving.

She phased through Abbot's door to find Yance browsing and acting like a normal customer until Jantze's customer left. Jem's mouth set in a grim line as she listened to their conversation. Her cash card hadn't been just a greedy grab. Evidently the group had their own murderous sideline going. Their victims weren't just robbed, but quietly disposed of to keep anyone from learning about their little enterprise.

She considered the best way to stop them. When Yance left, Jem trailed along behind the gang leader.

* * * * *

Detective Jerry Peklow stomped snow off his boots as he entered the small station's vestibule. He enjoyed the freedom and independence that working on the city's southern edge allowed, but not so much the weather's full and unimpeded power sweeping in from the open terrain. As his new partner had learned the hard way—newbie Detective Tony Feldman was currently out with a mild concussion from an icy misstep.

The duty officer gave Peklow a head-shake as he entered the main building. "It wasn't supposed to snow tonight," Officer Stahl said.

"Maybe they should have stuck their heads out and looked. That's twice this week they got it wrong. Especially about that wind." Irritated at the weather morons, he added, "It's a four-stepper out there." Meaning it only took four steps outside for nose hairs to freeze. He swatted ice off his cap. "Any calls?"

"No. We can probably thank the weather for that. Looks as if winter might be blowing in early."

He headed down the hall, pulling his gloves off. He was loosening his jacket when he stepped inside his office. Huh. There was a woman sitting in his visitor's chair. Odd. Stahl hadn't warned him he had a guest. On second thought, why had Stahl let her back into the office area at all?

He studied her as he hung his jacket on the back of his chair and seated himself. Young. Blue-eyed, fair-skinned. No noticeable scars or tattoos and appeared to be average height. A brown braid disappeared down the back of her jacket. Still wore her gloves. Hmmm. Something danced at the edge of his memory.

"Don't yell at your officer. He doesn't know I'm here."

It was *her*. Jem Seaborne Wilmont. Wearing contacts, since the Ghost had heterochromia eyes. He leaned back, hiding his shock. He'd never expected to meet her. Unproven rumors implied she was an accomplished and dangerous assassin, but her ability to penetrate both electronic and physical security systems was well documented. And just now demonstrated. Whatever was coming, it wasn't good.

He crossed his arms. "Can I expect a report of some kind of mayhem?"

Annoyance flashed across her features. "I'm making the report and the mayhem was already here. Abbot's Good Deals pawn shop on Twenty-Eighth Street…you know it's a front?"

"Yes."

"Do you know who's funding it?"

"Yes."

"Have you tried raiding it?"

"No."

"Lack of solid evidence or the gumption to do so?"

Gumption? "Yes, to the first." He didn't care who was backing it, he'd raid the place if he had credible proof.

"What about the murder gang operating out of it?"

He dropped his arms and straightened. "You're sure?"

"Two nights ago, an ambush was waiting for me after I made a high-level sale at the shop. Obviously, it failed. The comments I overheard afterward linked the gang with the shop manager. I snooped. Jantze, the evening manager, alerts his accomplices to customers leaving with a large cash card which they…retrieve, then split among themselves."

They hadn't recognized her. Only idiots would antagonize someone with her reputation.

"They pick their victims carefully," Wilmont continued. "Off-world, low-profile visitors mostly. Celebrities, high-profilers, and locals would be too easily missed and give away their pattern. Check local crematorium records. One should have a number of unscheduled late-night usages. One of its workers is either taking a cut or getting paid by the body. The victim's keys are used to access, empty, and clear them out of their hotel rooms. An accomplice in Port Authority slips their name on an out-going cruise ship's roster."

"Nobody would buy them disappearing off the ship."

"It's quite simple, actually, due to a cruise ship's multiple stops. They use *Starlight Five*. The victim's personal effects and a couple of fingers are given to another accomplice on the ship's crew. She works in housekeeping and makes it look as if the room is occupied until one of the stops. She sets the stage, leaves fingerprints in the appropriate places, and it appears the victim disembarked and never came back."

Peklow stared at her for several moments. Cold anger settled in his gut. If she was telling the truth… "You got all that in two days of *snooping*?"

Wilmont smiled. It didn't reach her eyes.

"Carl Holdbridge sold a high-value item at Abbot's three nights ago. *Starlight Five* left this morning with his bags. If you send an UPMS express message to its next planetary stop, they should be able to catch Louisa Steinway with the key to a room that has only her fingerprints and possessing a freeze-pack with some interesting contents."

All those inquiries he'd received concerning people that hadn't returned home. He'd reported them as leaving Stromli Four after a check of the port files. The bogus files. *Sonovabitch*. How many had there been?

Wilmont rose and began fastening up her jacket. "I suggest sending someone in with a high-ticket item and have a team waiting to ambush the ambushers. I'm sure the gang members would rather talk with your Enforcers than with the casino boss funding the shop. I assume his interpretation of 'spill your guts' will be different from yours as his manager's sideline brought attention to the shop and possible exposure to any other operations."

"Given that you're obviously pissed at them, I'm surprised you aren't taking care of it yourself."

She gave him a cold smile. "Not everything you read about me is true, Detective Peklow." She started to leave.

"Jem Wilmont?" When she paused in the doorway, he asked, "What did you sell?"

"Not relevant."

He was still digesting her words and that cold smile when he heard Stahl's confused *Hey! Hey, you!*

Stahl barreled through the doorway. "Who the hell was that? Where did she come from? There's not a frigging thing on security cams."

Peklow pinched his nose. Obviously, some of the things he'd read were true.

Chapter 2

"Morning, Mom. Granddad," Thane Baron said, heading straight for the sideboard. He skipped a small platter of bacon, filling his plate with an extra-large helping of fried shard. The meaty fish was one of his favorite dishes. Unfortunately, shard didn't freeze well so he couldn't stock it on his ship. He spooned steaming eggs on top and grabbed a couple of bread slices. He got warm smiles from his mom and granddad as he sat opposite them.

"Welcome home. We thought you'd be back a week ago," Reyna Stohlass said.

Thane grimaced. "The job on Thrallon took longer than expected."

"Thrallon?"

"Webster Two," Thane said, providing the planet's Galactic name. "Has anyone heard from Jem?" he asked, trying for nonchalance.

His mother shook her head. "No, and we don't know whether to be worried or not."

"You haven't heard from Jem? At all?" Gordon Stohlass asked, his fork arrested in mid-air.

Something curled tight deep inside Thane. "No. She's gone completely silent since disappearing on Euphrates Three."

Six months ago, Jem had delivered Joseph Beckett, a psychopathic pirate-rogue responsible for countless deaths, to Law Enforcement. After days of LE interrogation and news media hounding, Jem had vanished, leaving only a vid-message behind. He couldn't blame her. Not really. Still, months with no word?

Seeing their worried looks, Thane managed a smile. "Jem's pretty good at taking care of herself."

Reyna's gaze shifted. A small stab pinched his chest at the smile blooming across her face. Leroy Twobears came in, his dark eyes puffy, and went around the table to give Thane's mother a kiss. He then gave a "Morning all" and proceeded on to the breakfast buffet.

"Sorry. I overslept."

"Don't be, Lee," Reyna told her significant partner. "You only arrived ahead of Thane by an hour or so and I could tell you were exhausted."

Thane looked down at his plate. The federal agent was the first serious relationship his mother had formed since they'd lost his father over twenty years ago. Thane should be glad for her…he *was* glad for her…he just couldn't squash the uncomfortable feeling of his mother having a sig-ner.

He glanced over as Twobears settled beside his mother. Ah, that explained the bacon. Well, he was from Earth. Come to think of it, Jem preferred it over shard, too.

***

Thane maneuvered the *Stohlass Five* into Spine Ridge Fjord. The sails went limp, the northwest winds blocked by the steep tree-lined ridges around him. He fired up the boat's engine, leaving the sail in place for the return trip.

Slightly less than two kilometers in, he reached the Elbow. Some six meters high, and even broader, it was a massive granite protuberance similar to a slightly bent arm that jutted out of the tree-lined slope. A rugged, rough-hewed wall of the same material and nearly as tall framed a rocky beach from the arm's crook until vanishing into a fold of earth about twenty meters away.

Thane cut the engine to idle and gave the floating dock anchored there a disgusted look. He couldn't believe it. Sold. The *whole* fjord, all the way to Spinal Cove. He'd been flabbergasted when his granddad mentioned it at the tail end of breakfast. According to his mom, rumor had a large Earth investment group planning to build a private retreat for well-to-do off-planet tourists.

Great. An expensive vacation spot. Just what Midgard did not need.

Currently the area was empty. No people, no boats, no equipment. *Off somewhere making plans of how to ruin the place?* Thane wondered disgustedly. How did they plan on doing it? Terrace the slopes? Build into the hillsides? Fancy tree houses?

He let the *Five* drift slowly past the Elbow. A sea hawk briefly kept pace with him on thermals high above, its roughly four-meter wingspan distinguishing it from its slightly smaller river cousins. It flapped its wings and soared away when his engine revved up. Thane carefully navigated through the dangerous Scuttle, staying in its S-shaped center. There were flat areas on both sides of the passage that no one would want to walk across. Covered in foot-shredding rocks, they stretched out into shallow rock-strewn shelves beneath the water's surface. Get a boat too close on either side and the passage would live up to its name.

Would the owners dredge and widen it? Leave it as a challenge to those willing to risk it?

Twenty minutes later and happy to find the cove at the fjord's end empty, he dropped anchor. He leaned back, propped his feet up on a stack of rope, and let out a deep sigh. The peaceful quiet seeped into him, unwinding the tense knot deep inside. Eventually, his thoughts drifted toward Jem.

Where was she? Was she okay? Was Kurzvall still stalking her? Why the hell hadn't she contacted *someone*? Even Boyd hadn't heard anything from her, which was both strange and unsettling. Jem had met the man while working on Pappia, a moon mining colony. Her relationship with the middle-aged heavy-worlder had evolved into a father-daughter one.

Thane scowled at a couple of hapless pinal trees. Jem was making it plain she didn't want anyone's help. Given her ability, she probably didn't need it. But shit happens. To everyone. His eyes closed and the door to memories opened. *The crack of her ribs during the fight on Magnus. The pain-filled eyes from the drug they'd incapacitated her with on Pappia. How she'd felt in his arms as they bolted away from the kidnappers…*

Several hours later, the boat's rocking brought Thane awake. Stretching, he sat up and looked around. Then up. The lazy swirls of pink and green of early evening filled the sky above the fjord walls, but the incoming swells meant a storm was brewing. He eyed the trees lining the ridge top, bent over and waving their branches warningly. He probably wouldn't make it home before it hit. Thane grinned. What better reason to hang out in the fjord? It provided the best protection around, although he needed deeper water to safely ride out the swells.

The Elbow's shielding bulk would be perfect.

He reefed the sail, rolling it up and lashing it tight against the mast. Anchor up, engine started, he grabbed hard on the steering wheel when a wave almost tipped him out of the boat. *Whoa.* Was it a Blowhard? Storms from the northwest could get nasty this time of year.

The wind rose, howling through the tree tops. The swells grew rougher and wore whitecaps. He accelerated sharply through the Scuttle, fighting to keep from being driven onto its hull-shredding shoulders. Dark, boiling clouds filled the sky above and darkened the fjord around him. He snapped on his running lights.

Finally. The Elbow was just ahead. He was almost there.

A flash of light from the Elbow's crest. Pain seared his shoulder. His brain supplied *laser* as he dropped to the deck. Another flash. A course, burning odor from the wheelhouse behind him assailed his nose. A strong wave tilted the pilotless *Stohlass Five* on its side and Thane rolled into the storm.

Rain sheeted down.

Chapter 3

Nicholas O'Daniel entered the library quietly and joined the stare-a-thon out the large windows. The storm was more than three hours old and showed no sign of waning. A hard gust whipped trees at the yard's edge. "Captain Ames and her crew are on standby," the Stohlass Security Chief said. "Forecasters say it should be over before dawn. We'll leave at first light if Thane isn't back by then."

"He should have returned home as soon as the horizon clouded up." Reyna rubbed her arms.

Lee drew her close and squeezed her shoulders lightly.

Gwendolyn Williams shook her head. "I'm betting he was in Spine Ridge Fjord. He wouldn't have seen anything until it was on top of him and wisely stayed put."

"The fjord won't protect him from the waves, Mom. You saw the news. They're enormous." Worry colored Reyna's voice. "They'll funnel up the length."

"Thane may spend most of his time in space now, but he's Midgard raised," Gordon said. "He knows how to handle himself on the sea."

That didn't prevent an exchange of worried looks. Everyone in the room knew anything could happen, regardless of experience.

The Blowhard blew itself out shortly after midnight. No one went to bed, everyone hoping to hear Thane come stomping in the door. Or call. At dawn, Nicholas, Gordon, Reyna and Lee climbed aboard *Stohlass One*. The fifteen-meter cabin cruiser pulled out of the harbor as a red-rimmed sun lifted above the horizon. The hour-plus ride to the fjord was silent, everyone watching, hoping to pass the smaller *Stohlass Five*.

Captain Ames slowed the boat to a crawl as they turned into the Fjord. Binoculars were passed out. "People, take sides and start scanning the banks. Look above the waterline and into the trees. Miss Stohlass, what was he wearing?"

"I-I don't know," Reyna said. "He had on jeans and a white shirt at breakfast…but he could have changed."

"Let's hope not," Nicholas said. "A white shirt will stand out."

"Assuming it's not covered in mud," someone muttered.

At the Elbow they spotted a dock's remnants tossed up onto its rocky beach. Multiple sets of eyes examined it and the surrounding area. Nothing.

They moved slowly past the Elbow. The Scuttle's first bend came into sight.

"Something's sticking out of the water," yelled a crew member from the bow.

Binoculars trained forward. It was a broken mast.

Reyna gasped, clutched Lee's arm. "Oh, God."

"Anyone see Thane?" Gordon asked, his binoculars sweeping the area.

The boat came to a stop in the bend's center, the anchor rattling as it was deployed. The captain dashed down the steps. "I'm dispatching a skimmer."

Nicholas bolted for the stern in time to join the three crewmembers. They zipped toward the broken mast. The crew member in dive gear went down while the rest continued to scan the hillsides. Minutes later, the diver climbed back aboard and appeared to confer with Nicholas for about a minute. They returned to the *Stohlass One* and everyone gathered to hear the news.

"It's the *Five*," Nicholas confirmed. "No sign of a body. There are several large tears in the hull where the Scuttle got her." He paused, then said darkly. "There's also a couple of holes in the top of an otherwise intact wheelhouse."

His listeners stiffened. Holes on *top* when the rest of the wheelhouse wasn't shattered?

"Captain Ames, please take us farther in." Gordon strode back to the railing.

Worried faces lined both sides as the anchor was winched aboard. Captain Ames skillfully maneuvered the ship through the Scuttle. They moved forward two boat lengths at a time, holding position until the area was thoroughly scanned. The captain finally warned them they couldn't go much farther. The bedrock was shallowing as they approached Spinal Cove.

"*Over there.*" Lee pointed at a smudge of white curled around a tree.

"Thane!" Gordon leaned so far over the railing a nearby crewmember grabbed his belt.

The skimmer was relaunched, Nicholas poised in the prow.

Trees covered the sodden hillside right down to the water. A crewman grabbed a branch to steady them as the medic scrambled to the unconscious man. He carefully felt for a pulse and gave the others a relieved nod. He gently felt along Thane's spine and neck, then his arms and legs before motioning to the security chief.

Nicholas used his seven-foot-three height to gently tug Thane down as the medic unwrapped him from the tree's base. Then he simply sat down, holding him as the skimmer reversed and zoomed back to the ship, already turned around and facing outward.

Stohlass One raced away from the fjord at top speed.

Chapter 4

Jem watched from the safety of ghost-mode as the murder gang was arrested, cuffed, and stuffed into a vehicle. The Enforcers' ploy had worked well. The gang had thought they had it easy, ambushing an older woman. The retired federal agent enlisted to help had happily disillusioned them. They were further disabused when surrounded by local Enforcers.

Detective Tony Feldman closed his phone. "Maurice Jantze has been taken into custody. Maybe we can get him to give up some information on his boss."

"I doubt it," Detective Jerry Peklow said, a plume of warm air rising around his words. "No judge is going to give him a lighter sentence for multiple murders. Considering the mood his boss is probably in about now, he'll be lucky to survive to his court date. Agent Garcia, thank you for that excellent assist," he told the woman joining them.

Garcia gave him a broad smile. "My pleasure. Felt good to know I still had it."

"Want us to find you another undercover job?" Peklow asked with a teasing grin.

"Lord, no. My bones are past handling this much cold. I'm heading to my nice warm planet as soon as your commander clears me."

Peklow motioned to an officer standing off to the side. "See Agent Garcia gets back to her hotel after giving her statement at the Enforcement Center."

The woman waved and disappeared into an idling vehicle.

Agent Garcia isn't the only one getting off this ice ball. Jem had stayed for the three weeks it took them to set up the operation, watching the shop. She'd only needed to step in once when a young couple sold several items to cover a gambling loss. Jem had approached them out of sight of Abbot's, pretending to be heading back herself and told them she knew a shortcut back to their warm hotel rooms.

"What about Wilmont?"

Peklow gave his partner a mildly puzzled look. "What about her?"

Yeah, what about me?

"We have cause to search Jantze's records now. We can find what she sold and backtrack it. It has to be stolen."

Jem squinted at the detective. *Looking to make a name for yourself?*

"Looking for a career enhancement, Detective Feldman?" Peklow's voice was mild, but his censure was obvious and Feldman flushed. "You can check them, but I doubt Wilmont's sell went into the official records. I also highly doubt the other set is kept in the shop. Besides," he shrugged, "I've already checked for any active alerts or warrants out for Wilmont. There aren't any."

That's gratitude for you.

"Think she hung around?" Feldman blew out a huge plume of air. "Nobody has seen her. Believe me, they looked."

"Maybe, at first," Peklow said, shrugging. "Probably wanted to see if we were going to do something."

"Why do you think she turned them in?"

"My guess? She's trying to distance herself from all the rumors and hype about her."

"Not likely. Where there's smoke, there's fire. And it's pretty thick around her. Those around her are going to get burned…one way or another."

Jem shot Feldman a dirty look and left them to their conversation. Returning to the room she'd rented, she removed the contact lenses and rubbed her eyes. She hated the frigging things, but having one eye green and the other brownish—amber, Thane called it—made her noticeable. She hated that even worse. With Thane on her mind, she called up her email list on her hand comp.

Ah! Five files from Midgard.

She'd set up a postbox on Midgard and a subscription to the Azusa news network, primarily to stay informed about Thane and his family. Out of all the speculation crap swirling around her, the rumors of her ties to them were true. Which meant they could be used, or hurt, as a stepping stone to her. As others had tried. She'd sent a 'Forward' command to her box through the Universal Postal and Messaging Service network three days ago to get the latest news.

She scanned the files by date. Nothing outstanding in the two oldest. The next one detailed the family's newest Stohlass Entertainment Arcade that was opening on Copenhagen. Jem grinned, remembering Thane's 'three and a half continents' description when telling her about Midgard. He'd explained that Copenhagen was either Midgard's smallest continent or largest island…depending on your viewpoint and which continent you called home. Her grin lasted until she opened the fourth file.

THANE BARON SHOT!! IN SERIOUS CONDITION!!

Jem quickly read through the file, then the last one. He was in a coma. No further word on the shooter. The dates of the two files were three, four days old. Her chest tightened. Was he alive?

It took less than ten minutes to throw her things into a travel bag, don the contacts, and start jogging toward the spaceport.

Chapter 5

Gordon turned from where he'd been staring out into the late afternoon light as two men hurried into the room. Dane, his youngest son, and Reese Witt, husband to Dane's twin sister Jane, had arrived last night. They both captained ships for the Witt family's fishing fleet out of Port Seattle on the west coast of Copenhagen.

"How's Reyna?" He'd have received immediate word if Thane's condition had worsened. As if a concussion, a laser burn, nasty cuts, and a hairline fracture on one leg weren't bad enough.

"Worried," Dane said.

"Pissed," said Reese.

Gordon gave a tired chuckle. "Sounds about right."

"Why can't Lee look into it?" Dane asked. "He worked on that stuff last year, exposing Kurzvall's conspiracy."

Which they couldn't do a damn thing about, Gordon fumed. Reginald Kurzvall was an ultra-rich sociopath who'd used everything from bribery and blackmail to assassinations in his manipulations, ensuring the Consortium's plans for succession would succeed. The new four-system Consortium had then dredged up the old Earth rules of diplomatic immunity. The bastard was using it to freely come and go, attending to *business* in various Republic Systems. Reyna had practically vibrated out of her chair with indignation when she learned that.

"That was tied into a federal investigation," Gordon said. "Lee stepped on a lot of local Law Enforcement toes doing it, something he's trying not to repeat since he wants to move here. The guard is still there, right?"

Reese nodded. "Two of them. Only medical personnel and family allowed in."

"Gwen and I will be spelling Reyna and Lee in a few hours. A family member should be there when he wakes." Gordon refused to even contemplate an *if*.

"You didn't tell us he had a laser burn in his shoulder. What in Thor's name is going on, Dad?"

"No one knows. I'm not surprised Thane went sailing in the Fjord, despite knowing it had been sold. He loves it there." Gordon sighed tiredly. "Everything but the burn is probably from being tossed around in the storm. Sea Patrol brought the *Five* in yesterday. Nicholas has—here he is now." They all turned as the tall man strode purposefully through the doorway.

"Nicholas?"

"The boat was hit with at least two laser shots through the wheelhouse. The angle is high, the holes are oblong and rounded on both ends."

"Meaning?" Reese asked.

"Meaning a laser stream from the hillside above hit the boat as it rocked in the waves. Military issue for sure. Both I and the Sea Patrol investigator believe the attack happened either before or as the storm hit. The remaining damage is storm-related. Doesn't rule out more shots, just that the damage destroyed the evidence. We're also assuming the shooter either thought he'd killed Thane," his voice went even harder, "or left him for the storm to finish."

Gordon's fist clenched. "Think Kurzvall is behind this? I wouldn't put it past the bastard to get back at Thane."

Nicholas held up a hand. "While that's possible, Thane's a Tracker. A damn good one, which means he's made a number of enemies. Not counting the ones from this past year."

"Most of those are either dead, in prison, or hiding safely in the Consortium," Dane said.

"That we know of." Nicholas shook his head. "Who killed those five Azusa Enforcers last year? Who helped Richardson kidnap Jem? Is there a pissed off ex-pirate that escaped the military's net?"

"Thane didn't take down the pirates," Dane protested. "Jem did. Technically."

"Yeah, but no one knows where she is. As her friend—a rumored *close* friend—Thane is the next best target."

"Shit," Dane said.

"Damn," Reese said.

"Or," Nicholas added, "the next best way to flush her out."

"Shit."

"Double damn."

* * * * *

Reyna gave Dr. Zachary Blackwood a worried look when he entered the room. "It's been five days. Are you sure there's nothing else that can be done?"

"Positive. He wakes when he wakes. Go home. I'll call you when he does."

"There has to be something. Did you check—"

"We've checked everything, ma'am. Including all those black and purple areas. They're called bruises. Your son went head-to-head with a bunch of rocks and lost."

"You don't have to be so impertinent about it."

A weak voice piped up. "Maybe he's tired of repeating himself."

"Thane!"

"Ma'am. *Ma'am!* Please move back to the foot of the bed."

"I'm his mother."

"I'm his doctor and you're in my way."

"Why, you rude, impertinent—"

"Out-of-patience *doctor*. Move."

Katrina Stohlass laughed, rose from her chair. "Mom, let Doctor Blackwood do his exam."

"I highly suggest you listen to your daughter."

"Let's go, Mom. I'm sure the others will want to know Thane is awake."

Chapter 6

After three days of improvement, the doctor agreed to let Thane convalesce at home. Thane was aware of the doctor's careful scrutiny as he dressed slowly. Stiffly.

"Slow is good. You're still healing. Very well, I might add, according to the x-rays and scans we took this morning. The bruises and contusions weren't worrisome; the cranial swelling was."

"No list or lecture on what to do or not do?"

Dr. Blackwood snorted. "I gave it to your mother. The way she hovers, you'll be lucky to get out of bed next week. No doubt your family doctor and an in-house nurse are waiting for you."

Hovering wasn't normal for his mom. He must have really scared her. Hell, he'd been pretty scared himself, being batted around like a ball in the waves.

***

Hours later, Thane found how right Dr. Blackwood had been. He sat rigidly against a pillow-fluffed headboard, his arms crossed and glared at Dr. Richard Spratt. A nurse stood quietly off to the side, his face professionally blank.

"I am not an invalid." Dr. Spratt's eyebrows shot upward. "Okay, I am," Thane admitted. "But I'm not totally helpless."

Dr. Spratt leaned forward. "While I understand Dr. Blackwood and his staff's desire to get your family out of their hair, the agreement was for another two days' bed rest. Minimum. More if you insist on doing something stupid. Medic Swenson will help reduce the stupidity factor and administer the gel packs on the burn."

Medic Swenson gave him a bland smile and a wink.

"Fine. Two days."

Dr. Spratt slid Thane's shirt down his arm and scrutinized the burn's cauterized groove in his shoulder. "It's healing nicely." He carefully draped a gel pack over it.

Giving Thane's good shoulder a pat, he said, "The family is lurking outside the door. I'll herd them away for now. Rest."

Thane slid down under the covers, embarrassed the doctor had seen how much the trip from the hospital had worn him out. However much he might refuse to admit it verbally, they were right. He was weak, tired, and hurting. Two days, he thought, his brain slowing down. Maybe he could figure out by then who wanted him dead.

***

Thane held up both hands as his mother rushed out on to the terrace. "I *am* resting, Mom, and I've done the two days as decreed. Swenson walked me out here after I promised not to move from my chair. I'm going to obediently lounge here, bask in the sun's warmth, and digest breakfast."

Reyna kissed the top of his head. "I'm sorry. I can't help but worry about you."

His granddad stepped out. "Me, too," Gordon said.

Thane studied his mom as they settled in chairs around him. She was a bit paler than normal, tired-looking, too. "I'm sorry for giving you such a scare."

"Since you didn't shoot yourself, it's not your fault."

He grinned at the tart tone. That's more like it. Movement caught his eye. His pulse quickened at the sight of Jem Wilmont leaning against a tree. *She's here.*

Nicholas stalked out, glaring at Jem. "We have a visitor *inside* the gate."

Thane's gaze followed her as she crossed the yard. She shook her head when his granddad started to rise

"I'll stand. Thanks." Jem leaned against a trellis post and grinned sheepishly at Nicholas. "Sorry. Couldn't resist."

"Try harder," was his annoyed reply. He flopped down into a chair. It gave a protesting creak.

Jem grinned at Thane. "Good to see you up and around. Last I heard you were in a coma."

Thane waved a hand. "Old news."

"What's the new news?"

Thane gave a frustrated grunt. "Nothing helpful. Detective Wheeler called yesterday—remember her from last year? From what they've put together, the killer used a stolen jetpack to get there and back. He evidently rode out the storm in the fjord, then jetted back afterwards. Two people recall seeing a jetter about daybreak, but didn't pay him any attention."

"And we still have no idea who attacked Thane or why," Reyna said.

Brusquely Nicholas said, "We do have guesses."

Jem's expression became blank. "I can assume I'm one of them?"

"Yes."

Thane glared at Nicholas, who was giving Jem a narrow-eyed look. There was no reason to be so heavy-handed with her.

"Have you had any incidents?" Nicholas continued with the same tone.

Jem was silent for a heartbeat. "Nothing to speak of."

Which meant there had been, Thane fumed silently. Dammit. Why wouldn't Jem talk to them? He needed to get the stubborn woman alone.

"If someone had wanted to use Thane as a means to coerce me, they wouldn't have tried to kill him." Jem's voice was cool, factual. She looked to Thane. "It was a kill shot, right?"

"We're assuming so. Fortunately, the boat rolled right as I saw the flash."

"Jem's right," Gordon said. "He's no use to anyone dead."

"Dad!" Reyna said, appalled.

"I've also acquired a reputation," Jem continued, directing her matter-of-fact stare back at Nicholas. "If anything, it should keep certain...elements away from Thane and this family." She shifted her gaze to Thane again. "I've contacted Daniel Milhann. He's going to check with some of his old contacts on Palmyra to see if there's a contract out on you."

Thane nodded. He should have thought of that. Palmyra Two had established itself as the source for any and all mercenary needs. From anonymous postboxes to weapons to assassination. As a retired assassin himself, Milhann would know who to ask.

* * * * *

Jem wasn't sure how Reyna did it, but she'd been deftly maneuvered into agreeing to stay for dinner. Reyna and her mom had both vetoed any talk of assassins, so they passed the day in idle—if a bit stilted at times— conversation. She had congratulated Nicholas and Andi on their marriage. Andi had laughed, saying her gift—a case of Pounding J Aspric whisky—had lived up to its name. Thane gave a few highlights about his recent jobs, including a botched attack on Dakota Two by his quarry.

Jem knew she was the cause of the underlying stiffness, as she had deflected several questions about where she'd been or what she'd been doing. Thane, especially, hadn't been pleased, although, like the others, he had remained politely silent about it. At least for now. The sideway glances from the gray eyes beneath silver-flecked eyebrows said 'later.'

She sighed inwardly. *Why do they put up with me?* She should leave. If it wasn't for the dinner promise, she would. Damn promises. They were getting her in all sorts of predicaments.

Dinner, when it finally arrived, was excellent. Jem smiled, gave the cook the praise she deserved, and exited as quick as she gracefully could.

"Thank you for the meal, but I need to be going."

"Do you have a place tonight?" Reyna asked.

"Yes. I have a room reserved."

"Can one of us run you there?" Gordon motioned toward a window. "It's late and the fog is rolling in pretty thick tonight."

He wasn't kidding. The stuff had been coalescing since early afternoon. September was the start of their foggy fall, which led into an even foggier winter.

Jem gave a polite smile. "No, but thank you. Azusa has a great public transportation system. It's not that far to a transport stand."

She was halfway to the gate when Thane called her name, materializing out of the fog. Spooky. Probably how he felt about her ghost-mode. She'd been so relieved to see him sitting outside, shaggy black hair and all. He'd started wearing it longer to help hide the laser scar.

"How are you? Truly?" she asked. Jem doubted either his babysitter or his mom knew he was out here.

"Confused. Worried. Things happen when I'm working a job, but this is different. It's sobering to know someone wants me dead and I'm not even sure why. What about you? Why the months of silence?"

Her heart gave a sharp squeeze. "I needed time to think about…everything. How my life had changed. I just…drifted." And sold stolen crystals.

"Just…drifted?" he echoed. "Is that all?"

Silence. Dread filled her, certain of what was coming next.

"More secrets, Jem? Like what really happened at the Myerstone lab, why you won't give Kurzvall all their data, and the truth about this ghosting? I…we trust you. Shouldn't you trust us?"

Her mouth opened. Closed. "There are reasons…I can't…say." Her voice was strained.

"You mean, won't." Thane stood silent for a moment, then gave her a curt "Good-night." He turned and left without a backward glance.

Half of Jem wanted to call him back, to tell him everything. The other half, intertwined with her fear of what that would bring, throttled the urge. Tears pricked as he disappeared inside the house.

Chapter 7

"You agreed to meet with him, not me."

Thane had started the day in the same angry-hurt mood he'd carried from last night's foggy encounter with Jem. After his grandfather's breakfast-table announcement of a meeting with Helga Baron's lawyer, he'd spiraled down into grumpy and ill-tempered. Being called into the library as if he was fifteen again stung.

His granddad's brows drew in. "Beside the point. You will be there."

"Why'd you frigging agree to it anyway?"

"Markos Stephanos is the senior partner of Helga Baron's legal firm, not some flunky associate like they sent to Random Two. Besides showing him the courtesy he's due, I'm interested in what he has to say. As you should be."

"Why?"

"Because it's a good financial opportunity. Because we'll learn why she is so set on you taking over Baron Financials. So, stop bitching and jettison the damn attitude."

Thane managed to dredge up the proper amount of curiosity by the time the lawyer was seated across from them in his grandfather's library. Small pleasantries were exchanged and refreshments brought in. Stephanos declined coffee in favor of simple water.

"I've been asked by my client, Miss Helga Thornwild Baron, to personally make another appeal on her behalf. You've ignored or otherwise refused all her previous ones." He gave Thane a wry grin. "I must admit, I didn't realize we had several black holes in our part of the galaxy. Your list was quite…illuminating."

Thane ignored the pun. He'd told her to go hug a black hole during one of those refusals. "Found another one. I'll send an update."

"That won't be necessary. Miss Baron is willing to make several concessions, including the eventual relocation of BF from Milania to Midgard."

Thane and his grandfather exchanged startled looks.

"Ah." Stephanos rubbed the side of his nose. "Please keep that last bit confidential. My client doesn't want to upset her employees prematurely."

"Why is she so insistent on Thane taking over the company?" Gordon asked. "There are other Baron family members available."

Stephanos sipped his water. "Over the past year, my client has had to accept several truths. One of them is that you, Mr. Baron, are the family member she feels is acceptable to carry BF successfully into the future."

"After twenty-plus years of not being acceptable?" The woman had cut all of them out of her life after his father's loss.

"Ms. Baron now regrets those years of silence very much. She has, in fact, come to regret a number of things." He didn't elaborate. "Research into her sister Valeria's family on Rigellous Two has revealed that none of them have the necessary skills, aptitude, or inclination to run Baron Financials."

"Or the right *name*," Thane said. Valeria Baron and her husband, Travis Holtzclaw, had followed the standard naming convention of given, maternal, paternal for their children. Helga Baron had insisted the family names be reversed in her prenup with Jonathan Perlman. Which is why his father was named Gregory Perlman Baron.

Stephanos ignored his sarcasm and continued. "On the other hand, you and your mother's family have shown extensive business savvy. Stohlass Enterprises and the Valhallass Dance Troupe are considered leaders in their respective fields. And you are widely considered to be *the* Tracker."

Thane shrugged. "Finding people and things doesn't qualify me to lead a large business."

"On the contrary. You would not have such an impressive record without an innate grasp of how others think and how to handle their most probable response or action." His gaze flicked briefly to the scar that went from Thane's left eyebrow to his hairline. "That ability will be priceless in boardroom negotiations. Plus, I'm sure you'll have your family's extensive experiences to draw on."

Thane shifted uncomfortably in his chair. "What about her brother's children?"

"Alexis, Cassandra, and their mother live in Ladoga. That's a city several hundred kilometers from New Zagreb. They have no interest in Baron Financials. Katherine Jager Baron, the middle daughter, moved into the vice president position after your uncle's death."

"Has she said anything about wanting to take it over?" Gordon asked.

"Yes."

"Problem solved." Thane flung out his arms. "Katherine's welcome to it."

"Unfortunately for you, Ms. Baron disagrees." His annoyance was quite plain when he added, "Nor has she disclosed her reasoning."

"What's the hurry? She's what? Eighty something? She's got several decades to go, unless she has medical issues." Not that he cared.

"Helga Baron is seventy-nine and in excellent health. She intends to enact the Living Inheritance Statute. And that definitely needs to be kept confidential."

"The what?" Thane caught his grandfather's thoughtful expression.

Gordon rubbed his chin. "It's a special dispensation that allows a person to pass on an inheritance, pre-death. All inheritance rules apply, as if they truly were dead. The advantage is that the transfer is non-contestable since the person is physically handling the matter. The disadvantage?" He cocked an eyebrow at Stephanos. "They give up all claim-slash-control of whatever and that's why it's rarely implemented. I can't see Helga Baron giving up control of Baron Financials before that particular milestone hits her."

"Miss Baron is prepared to do just that. She wants to spend her last decades in a more relaxed manner."

Gordon folded his hands together. "What are you proposing, Mr. Stephanos?"

"That Mr. Baron comes to Romanique Three, along with you and/or any other family member he feels comfortable with. Look the company over, talk to people, talk to Miss Baron. Maybe in her campaign to win you over, she might even be more forthcoming with her reasoning."

Thane opened his mouth, closed it again at a sharp look from his granddad.

"We'll need to discuss it," Gordon said.

"Please do, but I can only stay for another week."

"I'm sure we'll have an answer for you by then."

They all stood. Stephanos shook hands with Gordon. He turned to Thane. "We all make mistakes. Please give Miss Baron a chance to rectify some of hers."

Thane waited until their guest left before exploding. "You can't be seriously thinking about it."

"Why not?"

Chapter 8

Breakfast the next morning was a quiet, tense meal. In a replay of the previous day, Reyna watched Thane shovel his food in with the obvious intent to leave the room as fast as possible, responding with grunts or monotone syllables when someone spoke to him.

"Really, Thane?" Her mother sounded as exasperated as Reyna felt. "I don't care how upset you are, you could at least be cordial to the family."

"Yeah, well my family could support me, not toss me overboard."

"Thane! Apologize to your grandmother!"

"Sorry." His sullen tone said otherwise. He pushed away from the table, leaving a troubled silence behind him.

Reyna found him later in the family room, staring into the unlit fireplace. She quietly took a seat across from him. Her patience was rewarded after several minutes when his gaze flicked over to her then skidded away.

"I'm sorry," Thane mumbled.

"I know. It's been a while since you threw a tantrum. *Ahhhh.* Those good ol' adolescent days."

His shoulders hunched.

"You feel as if you're being forced into something you don't want?" She got a confirmation nod. "You haven't been a child for some time now, Thane. You're more than aware that responsibilities sometimes compel us into doing something we'd rather not. I haven't seen you fight something this hard before. Why?"

He faced her. "I don't like the woman. I'll never forget the way she treated us. The way she treated *you*, even before Dad was gone. She said you were a plebeian upstart with grandiose designs on the Baron money and resources."

"*Pffft*. Sounds like her." She waved a hand. Hopefully that had been overheard and not directed at him. "I ignored anything she said as inconsequential. I hope you never overheard what I said about *her*."

Thane grinned and relaxed a bit. "I can imagine."

"I'm not sure why Mom and Dad are so set on this myself. It's not as if we need it. At least you won't be going alone. Dad and Erik will be with you and they plan on giving the company a very thorough look-over. If there's anything wrong with it, they will find it."

"I don't want to go."

Reyna simply raised an eyebrow.

"They don't need me."

The other eyebrow followed suit.

He scowled. "Fine. You'll be running Stohlass Enterprises while Uncle Erik is gone?"

The surrender wasn't graceful, but she'd take it. "No. Your Uncle Clint will step in as interim CEO. I won't be here.

"Huh? Where are you going—how long?"

"Where? Earth. How long?" She took a deep breath. "For the foreseeable future."

Thane stared wide-eyed. "What?"

"Lee's been recalled and I'm going with him." She spoke calmly. This would top off his day. "His transfer to Midgard's FBI office has been denied. They're too badly undermanned there."

All the Republic's agencies, Federal or otherwise, were digging deep and hard to find those compromised by Kurzvall's bribes and blackmail. Earth had been the hardest hit, undoubtedly due to his manipulation of the Federal Senate.

"But…but…"

"You and Katrina are grown. You have a wonderful, fulfilling life. Your sister will start hers after graduation this spring. There's more than enough family to continue the family business here. Lee is the first man I've cared for since your father. Greg and I only had a dozen years, Thane. Less, if you count all the times he was gone on survey missions. Those memories will always, *always* be treasured."

She leaned forward, grasped his knee firmly.

"I want this. I want him. Loneliness is insidious. It creeps up, skewering the heart and squeezing the lungs, even in the midst of a large, boisterous family." She smiled at her son's shocked look. "If the Universe smiles on us, Lee and I will have many years ahead. But the future is unpredictable and fate is not always kind." She patted his knee. "Something you and Jem should keep in mind."

Thane lurched to his feet. Grabbing her arms, he drew her into a tight embrace. "God, Mom. You…he…I don't…If he ever hurts you…"

She laughed and gave him a warm squeeze before breaking free. "There'll be a long line. Yes, I know." She gave an impish grin and added, "So does he."

"Does GG know?" Thane used the family term referring to both his grandparents.

She grimaced. "My announcement topped off that lovely breakfast."

"I'm sorry," he said again. "They'll get a proper apology. When will you go?"

"Lee has to leave day after tomorrow. I'll need a week or two to put a few things in order before following."

"I'm not leaving before you."

"Dad is going to inform Mr. Stephanos your trip will be delayed by a couple of weeks. I'm sure they'll count you coming at all as a win." Worry creased her face and she gripped his arms. "You'll be very, very careful, won't you? Do what Nicholas and your grandfather say and not go running off on some fool clue?"

Thane drew her into another hug. "I promise."

***

It was late afternoon and Reyna was in the kitchen when Jem approached her. The younger woman had been in a closed-door session with her father and son since her arrival several hours earlier. No doubt going over ideas about Thane's attacker. Hopefully, the exercise would also smooth out that tension between them. What had caused the stiff and strained air between them? It hadn't been there the other day.

"I hear you're going to Earth."

"Yes." Reyna returned Jem's smile. "I'm about to invade your old stomping grounds. Any suggestions?"

"A couple." Jem gave the cook a quick glance. "We could go over it now, if you have the time. I, um, also want to ask a favor."

After giving final instructions to Merle, she led Jem toward the family room. She paused, surprised when Jem cleared her throat and asked for somewhere private.

"Dad and Thane still in the library? The terrace then." Reyna changed direction at Jem's nod. Good thing the sun had come out. What kind of favor did the girl need privacy to talk about?

A big one, as it turned out.

***

Hours later, Reyna snuggled contentedly in Lee's arms as they sat propped up against the bed's headboard. One more day, she thought regretfully, then several weeks before they could do this again.

Lee gave her a gentle squeeze. "Are you sure you want to go? What with so much going on here, especially with Thane."

Annoyance briefly ruined her mood. She'd been getting that question all day from family and friends. Reyna took a breath, let it go, and smiled up at him. The man loved her and understood how close her family was.

"Yes, I'm positively, absolutely, one hundred and ten percent sure. Thane is going to have to work out his own issues with Greg's mother. As for someone trying to kill him?" She pressed her head against Lee's chest. "All I'll do here is sit around and worry. On Earth, I'll at least have something to help take my mind off it."

"Doing what?" Curiosity tinged his voice.

Reyna sat up, grinning. "That's right. You missed dinner, which is where

I told everyone else. I'm going to be working for Jem."

Lee's head pulled back and his brow furrowed. "Doing *what*?"

"Well, let's see. She wants to set up a full-service assassination guild. Members vetted. Contract hits scheduled and coordinated. Making sure clients pay up properly and on time. They'll be rules of honor, similar to Milhann's no-children rule and…"

Reyna threw back her head and laughed. "If you could see your face."

Lee managed to get his jaw closed.

"I'm sorry. I couldn't resist."

He shook his head and gave her a rueful grin. "You need to be careful throwing that out. There's enough swirling around her that someone else might believe it."

She sobered instantly. "People still think—damn."

"Given her reticence on explaining things, suspicion will stay with her for some time. Maybe for life. She *is* a mystery."

"Well, I for one am glad she's not going around teaching Bypassing Security Systems one-oh-one. What would happen if others knew how to do…whatever?"

"She's hiding more than security skills, Reyna. Hacking didn't sabotage those engines. Or explain how she can disappear in one system and reappear in another days, weeks later with no trace in between. Who does she morph into when she's not Jem Wilmont?"

"What do—"

"And they don't even begin to explain how she passed Major Markowitz's infiltration test. I inspected their set up. She should have tripped at least two alarms. *Two*, Reyna. Every Law Enforcement agent who reads his report wants to know how she did it. We *need* to know how she does what she does so it can be safely counteracted."

Reyna's eyes were wide in stunned surprise. Lee's hard FBI voice left no room for doubt. Or the implication that Law Enforcers were watching her. "I've heard people call her a ghost."

"Uh-huh. The Ghost. Thane's amusing nickname is becoming permanent. Markowitz even made a similar comment in his report summary."

Reyna's thoughts skittered between worried and irritated. "I'm worried about those who'd want her for all the wrong reasons, Lee. How often will she have to dodge someone like Kurzvall or Beckett? Those Federal Law Enforcement flyers certainly didn't help. Did they have to list her 'unsurpassed' ability of bypassing most security systems?"

"That will be a problem," he admitted. "Not just from those flyers, either. Markowitz's classified report was leaked. The *full* report. Fortunately, it's not in the public domain. Yet. Unfortunately, it's circulating in the less desirable circles."

"She's aware, Lee, and she's doing what she can to safeguard herself. That's why she stays so mysterious. Those disappearances are her survival mechanism. Can't use her if you can't find her." She was rewarded with a small smile flickering across his face.

"We could help with that if she'd provide her methods to the proper authorities. We'll safeguard the information."

Reyna's tongue briefly touched her upper lip. "Same as Markowitz's classified report?"

Lee grimaced. "Touché. So, what will you really be doing for Jem?"

"Managing a non-profit foundation. Yeah, it surprised me too." Her head bobbed. "It's called the Hands of Hope Foundation. Its founding goal is to help fund Magnus's recovery and you will not believe how much has already been donated. It's a good thing I was sitting down when Jem told me.

"Beyond Magnus, the Foundation's purpose is to provide help when the support needed is beyond normal resources and/or cost." After a moment's thought, she added, "I think significant consequences should be included. Anyway, she's already fielded several requests and told me the one from Traxia Three should be looked at next. It's a new colony. Everything was normal for the first seventeen years. Now, their crops are stunted and dying. Their animals are getting sick—including pets—and they're worried that whatever it is may begin affecting people."

"How will the foundation help?"

Reyna couldn't keep her excitement contained. "First thing they need is food supplies since they're afraid to eat their local wares. Second, I'll be soliciting and hiring the best medical and veterinarian personnel I can find. Everything environmental needs to be analyzed and researched, so scientists in those areas too."

She hugged him. Hard. "This is a good thing, Lee. Now and for the future. New colonies always face a risk. No matter how well Survey vets a planet, anything is possible. Hidden. Mutated. The Foundation will make things better by giving hope and a helping hand to those who need it."

"Excellent. You can start with me. I happen to have a problem that you can fix." With that, he rolled her under him.

Chapter 9

Jarrod Kline closed the file and leaned back in his chair. No, he hadn't misread it. It said the same thing as his first two readings. His mind spasmed, wanting to refute the ramifications.

The crystals they'd named after their system had revolutionized the laser and construction industries. Cut and polished, Jaguide crystals powered everything from medical scalpels to military weapons. Ground and melted, they increased the tensile strength of any material they bonded with. Mines on three of their eight planets were at full production. The fourth…

He pushed out of his chair. Two corridors down from his office, he turned into a door marked Marketing and Distribution. His boss's assistant was in a vid-conference and simply waved him toward the inner office. Entering, he closed the door firmly behind him.

"Have a seat, Jarrod. I'll be right with you."

"No problem." He was in no hurry to ruin his boss's day. Probably his whole year.

"There. That email should hold them for a while." Dave Catton sat back from his computer, stretched. "What can I do for you?"

"I've been contacted by Commander Allread Kohring, Space Fleet Acquisitions. They have some new designs coming off the drawing board."

"Not surprised. That new Consortium design caught everyone off guard. To tell the truth, I'm surprised no one thought of it earlier."

The Otanak Drive had an annoying quirk: the bigger the ship, the longer it took to go from point A to point B. This had predetermined a size-limit on the military's combat ships, with the largest battleships relegated to system defenders as it would take months for them to get anywhere. Kurzvall's engineers had designed a way around the limitation. Their battleship was composed of five frigate-sized units that could self-propel themselves independently, then relink back into a single, powerful vessel after arriving at their destination.

Personally, Jarrod found the idea of a rapidly deployable battleship disturbing.

"We're getting advance notice they'll be needing large quantities of both powder and crystals when they move into production. He's also requesting priority in shipments."

"Hmmm. I'll check. I'm sure we have sufficient in the vault to cover their needs."

"No, we don't." *Hold that surprised look, boss.* "Our current inventory is acceptable for weapons and incidentals. They want J-4 powder for the physical ship structure."

His boss frowned. "The Jaguide Four Complex won't be operational for at least another five months. It'll take another two months after mining starts to get the production pipeline going. They willing to wait that long?"

Jarrod paused for a moment, then said carefully, "Commander Kohring wants *only* J-4 powder for their hull plating because it will increase the tensile rating by *twelve* percent over the current crystals. With the uncertainty generated by the Consortium Systems withdrawing from the Republic, they want their ships as solid as possible."

Dave's brow furrowed. "Twelve percent? How do they figure that?"

"By calculating the increased liquefaction temperature and bonding factors." Yeah, Dave looked as surprised as he'd expected.

"How do they know *that*? We've only recently starting testing ourselves. I read the first lab report on them last week."

And here came the stunner. "Two raw crystals in their last supply shipment scanned different. When testing produced the impressive new figures, Kohring realized they must be from the new mine we're opening."

How and where did someone get J-4 crystals?

Dave sputtered. "Impossible. None of our samples have been released. They're all in the vault."

Jarrod simply held up two fingers.

Dave gaped for a couple of seconds before lunging for his comp. Flipping it to comm mode, he ordered the Head of Security to drop whatever he was doing and report to his office immediately. Terminating it, he immediately placed another call.

Yep, Jarrod sighed, a whole lot of days were spiraling down the drain.

<h1 style="text-align:center">Chapter 10</h1>

Jem watched Midgard recede in the *Lone Tracker's* viewscreen. The beautiful green-blue world was going to be her new home. The days were a bit longer, the years a bit shorter, and the gravity a couple of decimal points higher but, astrophysically speaking, it could be Earth's twin. Not counting the extra moon, of course.

Thane had insisted she and Reyna take the *Lone Tracker* since it was too small for the group heading for Milania. He, Gordon, and Erik would be accompanied there by a small contingent of bodyguards headed up by Stuart, Nicholas's second.

Thor will get you to Earth and return you to Midgard. Besides, Mom will love being on it again. She rarely used it after we lost Dad, and gave it to me when I got my Tracker license.

Thor was the ship's computer brain. More than a standard computer yet not quite an AI, it ran most of the ship's functions, including a fully navigable control system. This negated the need for a qualified human pilot, which neither she nor Reyna was. Just point and say go.

"Greg named the ship *Viking Lass* for me," Reyna said, breaking the silence from the co-pilot's seat. "He bought it to give us more time together. Thane was ten when we visited him that last time." Her words were quiet. Contemplative. "It was to be his last mission. Greg intended to resign when they returned to port and join me permanently on Midgard." Reyna gave a small laugh. "He didn't want to return to Milania. He and his mother were always clashing. Different plans, different goals. So, we celebrated that night and," she grinned at Jem, "I became pregnant with Katrina."

When she grew quiet again, Jem knew the woman was back in the past. A lump lodged in her throat for the man who had missed out on so much life. Never watched his son grow up. Never knew he had a daughter.

Reyna stirred. "They sent a drone with their last reports, said they were loading up for return. Six weeks later, when they hadn't made port, a small scout was sent to check on them. The camp was closed down per normal procedures, nothing out of order or unusual. They simply vanished."

Though rare, it still happened every now and then. There was so much they didn't know about the Otanak engines and whatever dimension they drove a ship through.

"They spent eight months scouring all the systems between the planet and the Coleman System. It's Survey's home base," she added, seeing Jem's questioning glance. "They finally declared *Survey 22* officially lost and all on board dead. They held a very nice memorial service for all the families. I have the Survey flag they gave me. I probably should give it to Thane now."

Reyna looked around. "Here I am, reliving the past while heading toward my future."

"Nothing wrong with that. Especially since you're traveling in a ship full of those memories. Is that why you stopped using it?"

"No, I didn't need it. I haven't left Midgard since Katrina was a baby."

"Not even for business?"

"Midgard has everything I need. Had," Reyna corrected. "Lee isn't there now. But I couldn't bring myself to part with it either. Clint and Gilida used it a couple of times, then I gifted it to Thane after he got his Tracker license. First thing he did was rename it."

"Well, *Viking Lass* wouldn't exactly boost his Tracker image," Jem said, laughing.

Reyna laughed along with her. "True. He converted his old room into a med-room and a storage area into a bunkbed holding room. Things prudent for his chosen profession. I have no idea when the laser cannon and extra engines were added, although I'm certainly glad he had the foresight to do so."

So did Jem. Both items had saved their butts when the pirates attacked them at Magnus.

"I think…I believe Greg's death was why Thane became a Tracker," Reyna said.

Jem leaned forward, the better to hear the soft words.

"He wouldn't accept it. For years he kept waiting. Just…waiting. The first two years, he only took jobs for missing people. Maybe he thought that if he looked hard enough…far enough, he could find his father. Or at least what happened. I've never asked, and I don't know if, deep down, it still drives him."

Jem had asked Thane about the memories the ship might stir. He'd paused for a long, long moment. *I think Mom came to terms with Dad's…death sooner than I did.* It was the first time she'd heard him use 'death' in reference to his father.

She gave Reyna's arm a gentle touch. "Thane has spoken to me of his father in a way that tells me he has finally found acceptance. Tracking?" Jem struggled to find the right words. "It's more than a profession…it's who he is. He cares about people, about right and wrong. His father's disappearance may have influenced him, but I don't believe he'd be happy doing anything else now." Like sitting behind a corporate desk.

"Good. Good." Reyna gazed at the planet's small image. "I'll miss it." She turned to Jem. "What about you? You bumped around the Republic for several years, hunted by a sociopath." She raised a hand when Jem smirked. "Thane doesn't count. My son was unknowingly hired to catch you by said sociopath. Will you go back to Earth now to stay?"

"Reaching transition point in one minute," Thor announced over their heads.

The *Lone Tracker* was reaching the limits of Midgard's planetary gravitational field. Otanak engines had a tendency to explode in strong ones. The larger the planetary system, with moons and/or rings, the further out a ship had to go before safely engaging them.

"I rambled around Earth after Granny died. It has so much beauty. So much history. Then I left and rambled some more. I've spent time on Earth these last few months, setting up the Foundation and taking care of various other things. It didn't…it didn't feel the same. Maybe because I healed under Midgard's heavier gravity. Maybe because I've changed in other ways." She paused, not yet ready to reveal her plans. "Either way, I felt like a visitor."

"Transitioning."

The ion engines shut down and the Otanak engine switched on. So did the dull throb at the base of Jem's skull. An annoying side effect of her change, it would be there as long as the O-engine was running. The viewscreen turned a solid black before automatically switching off.

Chapter 11

Thane stared morosely out a hotel window. Milania, Romanique Three, was one of the oldest settled planets. Its capital, New Zagreb, was huge. It climbed the mountains enclosing it on three sides and stretched out into the plain on the fourth. A little smaller than Earth, the planet had one moon and only a few shallow seas.

Seas? By Midgard standards they were ponds.

Their first day on Milania and he was ready to leave. He'd rather be anywhere than here. Earth would be interesting right about now. Jem and his mom should have arrived there. He grinned, thinking of the surprise in store for his mother's sig-ner. The look on Lee's face would be priceless.

Reyna's pregnancy announcement had been served with dessert at the family dinner the night before she left. Due for a physical, she'd elected to have it with her long-time physician rather than someone new on Earth. The news was totally unexpected.

"Did Dr. Bakken tell you when?" he'd asked, flabbergasted.

"You mean after she quit laughing?" His mother wasn't. *"Her exact words were 'Stohlass genes strike again.'"*

"Well, this explains why you've been so tired and your emotions all over the place lately. Will you be staying here now?"

"No, Mom. If I wasn't already going to Earth, I would be making plans to do so. We hadn't discussed having children—didn't think we needed to. I know Lee will be as happy as I am...after he picks himself up off the floor."

A lot of laughter and good-natured ribbing had followed until his mom finally threw up her hands and left to finish packing. He turned from the window, wishing he was with them.

***

Midmorning found Thane standing on one side of an impressive lobby. The floor was marble. The stately columns were marble. Even the reception desk his grandfather and uncle stood in front of was marble. Real flowers and midget trees bloomed in planters or pots strategically placed around the room. A bank of elevators lined one wall, a young woman in a wheelchair exiting the one on the far end. Several small sitting areas were spaced around the room. Baron Financials headquarters reeked of class and money.

Shaking his head at the architectural arrogance, he headed toward a comfortable looking chair.

"So, you're the great Thane Stohlass Baron."

Thane pivoted sharply at the icy comment to find the woman in the wheelchair studying him with cold blue eyes. He pushed down a spike of dislike. "Yes, I'm Thane Baron. Don't know about the great part."

"You must be, else why would my aunt prefer you over me in the CEO chair?"

This was Katherine Baron? Ah, yes, he should have recognized the arrogant, I'm-entitled-to-whatever-I-want attitude. CEO chair, huh? Apparently she wasn't aware of her aunt's full intentions. Another reason to keep it confidential? "I have no idea why she does."

"Didn't you state publicly a couple of years ago that you weren't interested in assuming control of Baron Financials?"

Her hostility rekindled his dislike and he didn't bother tempering it this time. "Perhaps I've reconsidered." The same far-end elevator spat out another woman, this one joining his relatives at the desk.

"What makes you think you're qualified?"

"Your aunt."

"Aunt Helga's decisions have been a little off since her son died."

As if his father's loss had been meaningless. "Does that include appointing you as Vice President?"

Her mouth opened, snapped close when his grandfather appeared beside him.

"My grandfather, Gordon Stohlass. Granddad, this is Ms. Baron's niece, Katherine."

The woman gave Gordon a single cool look before activating her chair control and rolling back toward the elevators.

"You do realize how rude both your comment and introduction were?"

"Better than what I got, Granddad. All I got was attitude and interrogation. She's Helga Baron recast." He glanced in her direction. "Did you know she was in a wheelchair?"

"No. Must be a recent injury."

"Permanent, maybe? Surely that's not a reason to pass her up?"

Gordon shook his head. "Even if it is permanent, Baron Financials is run with one's head, not the legs."

"I don't like her."

"I'd say the feeling is mutual," Gordon said, giving the closing elevator doors an amused glance. "Thought I was going to have to check you for frostbite."

Erik and the well-dressed woman joined them.

"I see you've met Vice President Baron," the woman said.

Thane heard an underlying disdain despite the polite tone. Not just him then.

"Thane, this is Helen Brinkman, Vice President of Public Relations. She's our guide today."

"CEO Baron told us to give you all courtesy and—with very few exceptions—open all files for your inspection. I suggest today be a high-level tour, showing you the offices and acquainting you with the people who'll be answering any in-depth questions you may have. This way, please."

She took them over to an open elevator.

"I have an overview prepared in the main conference room on the twenty-second floor." She pushed the button marked B1. "It'll provide a basic understanding of the interactions between BF's internal departments and the services we provide to clients. First, I'll take you down to Security. They have badges prepared that will allow you free movement within the building."

"Where does the elevator you and Miss Baron got off of go to?" Thane asked.

"It opens exclusively on the three executive levels."

Fortunately, it was a short trip to the large, bustling Security office as Ms. Brinkman chatted non-stop the whole way about people Thane had no desire to know. Their guide introduced them to the Security Chief Saylor.

He handed them each a badge saying, "Wear these at all times. You have access to all floors except twenty-three through twenty-five."

Brinkman gave him a sharp look. "I personally submitted *all* floors in the requests."

"It was countermanded," Chief Saylor said neutrally, "by VP Baron."

Helen Brinkman's anger registered for only a second, replaced with a practiced PR smile as she turned to them. "One of us will have to escort you to those floors for today. I'll see about getting your badges updated."

With a curt nod at the chief, she led them back to the elevator.

Gordon gave her a thoughtful look. "I take it those are the executive floors?"

"Yes." She stabbed the 'UP' button.

* * *

After enduring over an hour of boring statistics, Thane learned they were expected to lunch with CEO Baron in her Executive suite. *Hell, no.*

"Granddad, going through the company is your and Erik's expertise. I won't understand a tenth of it. I'd also prefer to lunch somewhere else," he told them bluntly, "then wander for a bit. I'll meet you back at the hotel."

"There's a nice restaurant not far from here," Helen Brinkman said. "Since I'm at your disposal, I'll be happy to show you around the city."

Twenty minutes later they were sitting at a table and snacking on chips.

"Can I ask a personal question, Ms. Brinkman?"

"Within reason. And please, call me Helen. We're not at the office."

"You obviously don't care for your boss. Why stay? There's bound to be other positions."

"I've had several offers but, the truth is, I got those offers by being associated with BF. Career-wise, it's considered the pinnacle company to work for. And the pay is exceptional."

"Perks and pay, huh?"

She shrugged, popped a chip in her mouth. Pushed the bowl toward Thane. "What about you? You apparently have as much enthusiasm toward becoming CEO as I do for my next personnel review. Why are you here?"

"Granddad says it's a financial opportunity. Good for the family in general and for me specifically. I think he's hoping I'll give up Tracking."

"Will you? It would be difficult to do both."

"No. What happened to Katherine Baron? We were unaware she was in a wheelchair."

"An accident about, oh, five months ago crushed her lower spine and severed the nerve bundle. She's currently using a back brace for support."

"They're not using regen?"

"Bone regeneration doesn't work on Miss Baron. Well, it works, albeit slowly. The theory is it's due to some of the blood issues her family has." Helen shrugged. "Time-wise, it'll only be three or four months shorter than natural healing. Once it's healed completely, the experts will start work on regenerating the nerves."

Thane's hand halted in the bowl. "They can do that?"

"It's a relatively new process. My understanding is that they'll coax the nerves to grow new ends and graft them together. She spent six weeks at a special medical facility on Orion Two being evaluated and having all sorts of tests done. According to VP Baron, she'll be walking again within two years. Well, about eighteen months now."

She leaned in closer and lowered her voice. "Most of us are hoping you *do* accept CEO Baron's offer. Personally," she flashed him a sultry smile, "I encourage it."

He gave her a considering look as he munched. "What's your opinion of Helga Baron?"

"Well, she's not the huggable type." She waved a chip. "CEO Baron follows an old-fashioned class hierarchy. She's a firm, no nonsense disciplinarian. I've never known her to go out of her way to screw someone or make them miserable."

Thane leaned forward on his forearm and said shrewdly, "But VP Baron does."

Her face blanked, then broke out in another one of those professional smiles. "I believe that's our food coming."

***

They shared information once they were all back in their hotel suite.

"So," Erik teased, "you coming back with us tomorrow? We'll actually be digging. Today was spent getting a general feel for everything and everyone."

"Nope. I've rented a car. Helen Brinkman is going to show me around."

Erik's eyebrows bobbed a couple of times. "I know what she'd prefer to show you."

Thane gave him a blank look.

Gordon snorted. "Don't tell me you didn't see the way she was eyeballing you? Prime fish fillet on a platter."

"Not interested."

"Yeah, well I think she's planning on trying to reel you in," Gordon said, flashing a grin.

"We only had lunch."

"You're rich and that scar on your forehead gives you that tough, manly look a lot of women seem to prefer." Erik grinned at his nephew's dark look, before adding in a more serious voice, "You're also being courted to take over as CEO of Baron Financials, with all the social and financial perks and privileges that go with it. She's looking to move up the social ladder."

Gordon nodded in agreement. "She won't be the only one, son. Especially if word gets out about the living inheritance. You need to be very careful and not make any promises that could be misconstrued."

"Taking VanCamp or Wilson with you should help hinder that," Stuart said.

"Why? Didn't take one of them today."

"That's because I erroneously assumed you'd stay in BF's building, surrounded by their security people all day," Stuart said, giving Thane a scowl. "You weren't supposed to be out, traipsing around in the open."

"Do you really believe it's possible my Midgard attacker would follow me here and then shoot me in broad daylight while surrounded by a crowd of people?"

There was a loud chorus of "Yes."

Thane gave them all a sour look. "Fine. Want to meet for lunch?"

Chapter 12

After spending the morning sightseeing with Helen, Thane met them at the same restaurant he'd eaten at yesterday. Helen couldn't join them, having been called into the office to take care of pressing matters. He assured his relatives he had gained neither sig-ner nor fiancé in the intervening hours. Of course, he'd added, having Wilson in the back seat might have dampened the mood.

"Bodyguards do tend to dampen things," Stuart said, as he and Wilson exchanged amused glances.

"Learn anything surprising this morning?" Thane asked, only half interested.

"Learned that there are actually two companies." Gordon swirled his tea. "Besides Baron Financials, there's Baron Properties."

Erik nodded. "Yes, that was an interesting split Helga's father did."

Intrigued in spite of himself, Thane asked what the man did.

"Hugo Baron, Helga's grandfather, founded Baron Consolidated Enterprises. Her father, Cesar Baron, sold off the odds-and-ends and split the remainder into Baron Financials and Baron Properties. The latter, naturally, is made up of a number of income-producing properties, including the building BF occupies. Ezra Baron, her brother, got Properties on their father's death and added to it during his lifetime. It was evenly distributed between his three daughters on his death. His widow got the balance of his estate and is BP's current CEO. They're all receiving a substantial yearly income, more than enough to support them in Ladoga."

"So Katherine is getting income from both Baron Properties and her VP position at Baron Financials?"

"Yes." Gordon's face turned thoughtful. "Maybe that's behind Helga's choice. Maybe she feels her niece doesn't need it."

"Well, Katherine obviously disagrees, and I don't need it either."

His grandfather's mouth tightened. Erik forestalled the impending argument by asking if he had any specific plans for the afternoon. Thank you, Uncle.

"No. We appear to have hit the highlights. Think I'll go back to the hotel and work on the files I brought with me. See if I can come up with a possibility or two who'd not only like to see me dead, but actually act on it."

"Can I borrow your rental then? Dad and I are going to split up. He's going back to BF and I want to visit some of their business associates personally. I want to know what their real opinions are, not what their reports say."

Thane gave him the keys and entry code. "It's the blue F420A sedan parked out back. Take Wilson with you," he added. "Showing up with a bodyguard will make you seem important."

"I am important," Erik said haughtily.

"We'll drop you off at the hotel." Gordon motioned for their check. "Jason can keep an eye on you there."

"I'll be reading files and don't…" Thane gave up. That level look from both Stuart and his granddad said arguing was a waste of breath. Jason VanCamp was in for a boring afternoon.

They separated. Erik and Wilson going out the rear door while the others headed for the front desk.

Gordon handed the bill and his card to the cashier. The cashier swiped it and handed it back. "Don't know how long—"

A loud explosion broke off all conversation. People looked around uneasily.

A man stumbled in through the door leading to the parking lot. "Call Emergency," he gasped. "A car just blew up."

Stuart bolted for the door, Thane and Gordon close behind him.

***

Wilson was dead. His uncle survived surgery but lost his left leg above the knee.

Thane knew his grandfather was sitting inside his son's ICU room. Waiting. Guarding. Maybe praying. He and Stuart were at the Law Enforcement office watching a security tape overlooking the parking area on a large viewscreen with Detectives Small and Trotmire.

A person in loose, non-descript clothing, cap, and sunglasses walked slowly between the vehicles. Apparently absorbed by his phone, chin tucked in at his chest, a casual observer wouldn't be surprised by his 'blunder' into a car and the phone dropped. Said watcher would undoubtedly be amused at the universal finger of irritation flicked at the vehicle before reaching down to retrieve it.

"Pause," Detective Thomas Small said as the individual began to bend over. "See the arm…it's not straight down, as if reaching for the phone. It's beginning to angle across his mid-section."

"He's reaching for something under his jacket," Stuart agreed.

"Yes. Continue, one frame per second."

The unknown person flicked downward slowly.

Small paused it again. "The body has shifted slightly, toward the car. He's attaching the explosive directly beneath the driver's position. Probably using some pre-applied adhesive."

"*Degenerate-spash-of-a-diseased-ridden-bastard*," Thane swore. It had been a small but powerful bomb. Minimum damage to everything except the car's occupants.

Detective Janet Trotmire coughed. "Is that the Midgard version of SOB?

Detective Small looked over. "Spash?"

"Space trash," Thane said, all but snarling. "How was the bomb triggered?"

"Unknown at this time. You said there was an earlier attempt?" Trotmire said.

Thane's jaw flexed. "On Midgard. We brought guards. I didn't think—" He broke off, anger and guilt choking him.

"Obviously, you're being watched. The rental gave him the method. He waited for the right time and place. When did you rent it?"

"This morning, but I made the arrangements yesterday."

"Plenty of time for a professional to prep," Small said.

Thane stared at the screen, a mass of emotion boiling in his stomach. Stuart had been right. He should never have gone roaming around. He might as well have held up a sign saying, 'Here I am. Hit me.' His uncle and Wilson had paid the price for his stupidity.

Stuart unclipped his signaling phone. "Yes sir? No sir. No sir. On our way." He snapped the phone back on his belt.

Thane bolted up from his chair. "Uncle Erik?"

"No change. Your grandfather wants us to meet him there as soon as we can."

"I'll send out a bulletin, do what we can," Detective Small said. "Unfortunately, we don't have much to go on." He gestured at the image frozen on the screen. "Clothing is loose, fully covering the body. The cap hides hair and half the face. Sunglasses and gloves hide the rest. We have nothing to go on except a bit of skin tone. And that," he said morosely, "may be as fake as his height if he's wearing lifts.

Chapter 13

Ahrymani Carpenter poured a glass of her lover's excellent brandy.

"How much fucking luck does Thane Baron have?"

She took a sip before turning to answer the annoyed question. She was damn well annoyed herself. "He does seem inordinately lucky. I'll get another shot at him. After all, I was trained by the best." She'd been applying for an opening on an elite military team when her accident happened. Suddenly, she hadn't been good enough. Her hand tightened around her glass, remembering her abrupt dismissal by her asshole commander.

"You do realize Thane isn't your only problem," Ahrymani continued. "His sister is majoring in Business and Finance, which would be a perfect fit at Baron Financials. In fact, I'm surprised your aunt didn't consider her first."

"Helga knows Katrina is being groomed as the next Stohlass Enterprise CEO." Katherine Baron frowned. "With Thane dead…it does become a possibility. Unfortunately, taking out both of them creates a problem, especially now. Control of BF would be the most obvious common denominator and suspicion would point to me."

"Then we have to make sure that doesn't happen." Ahrymani weighed a few options. "Do you still have that poison?"

"Yes. I couldn't find a way to administer it to my aunt without, again, becoming the prime suspect. Targeting Baron, with all the attacker possibilities due to his profession, was safer. You have an idea?"

"Maybe. Need to plan it out."

"We have time." Katherine rolled her wheelchair closer. "The audit is now on hold. Why don't you pour me a glass and we'll celebrate?"

Chapter 14

They fidgeted in a small visitor room down the hall from Erik's ICU room. The doctor had promised to give them an update.

They should have asked him *when*, Thane thought irritably.

His granddad and Stuart were working on a message for the family. Nicholas would be the one to contact Wilson's family and—

"Dammit." Gordon slapped the chair arm. "The man was with us for nine years."

Stuart nodded, his face grim. "Wilson was a good man, a solid worker. Nicholas was planning on moving him into third position."

"What about Mom? She'll want to know what's happened."

"Gwen will undoubtedly send the courier on to Earth. Now, any idea who the bastard could be behind these attacks?"

For over an hour they had discussed Thane's recent jobs and all the events from the past year. Which ones they were sure were caused by Beckett or Richardson, which ones might possibly, could possibly, have been someone else. They looked up when Detectives Small and Trotmire strode into the room.

"You have something?" Stuart said, rising.

"Yes," Small said. "The explosive was an expertly-built shaped charge. The blast was directed upward for maximum damage inside the vehicle and minimum damage to the surrounding area."

"That much was obvious," Stuart snapped. "What's new?"

Trotmire gave him a sharp grin. "It means a large chunk of the bomb's components survived. In pieces, but recoverable. We'll start looking at component purchases."

"Any idea who built it?" Gordon asked, tense.

Small shook his head. "*Expert* covers a lot of professions with demolition experience. Its precise destructive field and the remnants of its structure have us leaning toward advanced military training. Perhaps a Special Forces or Commando who decided to go private. Regardless, we've posted a guard on Mr. Stohlass's door. We'll arrange coverage for you while—"

"That won't be necessary," Gordon interrupted brusquely. "We'll accept the guard for Erik. However, I trust Stuart and his team. Thane and I aren't slouches either. This…person has made a very grave mistake. The family will not rest until he is caught."

"No taking the law into your own hands," Detective Small said.

Thane bared his teeth. "Wouldn't dream of it."

"Stuart, we need to finish the message to Nicholas and update the family. Have him start re-evaluating everything. Thane, we will need to go through all your case files."

"Hello. Law Enforcement here," Small said, holding up a hand, palm out. "We need to have those files turned over to us along with any other pertinent information *and* do the investigating."

Stuart barked out a clipped laugh. "You don't know the Stohlass family."

"Unfortunately, Detectives, most of those records are in my ship's comp brain, which is currently on Earth. I only brought the most recent ones with me."

***

They were halfway through a somber breakfast after a mostly sleepless night when a brisk knock sounded on the door. Stuart moved toward it, motioning for VanCamp to take up a position several feet away. He cracked it cautiously, then swung it open. Gwen marched in, pulling a suitcase behind her.

Gordon rose and wrapped his arms around his wife.

Thane heard her murmured *I'm here* as his granddad kissed her on the cheek.

His grandmother must have commissioned a UPMS courier pod as soon as she received the message they'd sent last night. She'd claimed there was only one reason she'd ever climb into one. Well, he thought grimly, watching them simply hold each other in a tight embrace. This would count as a life-or-death situation.

Universal Postal and Messaging Service's autonomous Class One drones took advantage of the Otanak's size-vs-time quirk. Averaging seven meters long from engine base to electronic nose, they transported their cargos to even the farthest systems in just hours. Compartments could be configured as-needed for any cargo, from physical and electronic packages to people to produce: anything needing to get somewhere fast.

"I am glad to see you, but what are you doing here?" Gordon drew her to the table.

"Did you really expect *everyone* to 'stay put'? You almost got both me and Lana." She took the chair beside her husband.

"How did you keep Erik's wife from coming?" Thane considered his aunt as stubborn as a blood-born Stohlass.

"I told Lana she needed to be there. For their children, and to make the medical and physical arrangements he's going to need on our return."

Thane's hand tightened around his fork. His fault.

"I'm here to take over Erik's audit of Baron Financials," Gwen continued. She raised both eyebrows when Gordon's mouth opened. He wisely closed it. "You do remember I gave him his first lessons in corporate finances?"

He'd better. Grandmother had founded Stohlass Arcades, which had grown into Stohlass Enterprises under her CEO leadership.

"I'll place your bag in Mr. Stohlass's room and call down for additional food."

"Thank you, Stuart. That's a yes to the first and a no to the second. I had supper before getting into that claustrophobic pod, but I'll take a cup of that coffee I smell." She yawned. "It's past my bedtime on Midgard. Thane, I don't know how you manage all these time differences. Oh! Stuart. Emily Barker came with me. She'll be by to get her assignment after getting a room, preferably as close to us as possible."

Nicholas wasn't taking any chances with Wilson's replacement. Thane hadn't met the new addition to the family's security team yet, but he'd heard about her. Accustomed to two Earth gravities, Barker had given Nicholas a challenge few could manage in their sparring matches. She'd also be able to accompany his grandmother everywhere.

"We've suspended the audit," Gordon said, refilling his cup. He handed it to his wife.

"Why? The family came here for a reason. We'll continue forward despite some asshole spash. We need to confirm whether or not BF is worth having in our future." Gwen took a swallow of coffee and smiled. "Excellent."

"I don't understand why you two are so adamant about it," Thane said.

Gwen took a second sip before saying, "When the Consortium separated from the Republic, they took some of the oldest and largest financial institutions with them. They were smart to announce that there'll be no change monetarily—a credit is a credit and ten makes a dollar. That hasn't stopped the confusion and growing distrust. People will be looking at alternatives for business dealings and other financial aspects. Potentially, Baron Financials is poised for an astronomical growth." Her eyes held an anticipatory gleam. "Especially with the right person at its helm."

He'd never even considered that aspect of the Consortium's secession. Thane leaned back and crossed his arms. "I am not the right person to helm it, Grandmother."

Gwen ignored him. "I sent the information about the attack on to Earth with a few addendums. Reyna is to keep her pregnant butt on Earth—there's nothing she can do here and we'll keep her updated. I imagine Lee will make security arrangements. I also asked Jem to join us as soon as she got Reyna settled into the foundation."

Thane's jaw set. Jem's refusal to trust him fully still rankled. "Think she can help with this? The detectives' last message said they had nothing new. No leads and no suspects."

"Are you kidding?" Stuart let out a snort. "She'll skulk around the Port Circle—Jem probably knows where to look and what to listen for. Might even have a few other contacts she can touch."

Like the seaports of ancient days, the areas that grew up around a spaceport were filled with hardened people that catered primarily to those who worked there or on its ships. They also provided many other services, both legal and not-so-legal. And regardless of whatever weird terrain-hugging shape it conformed to, Port Circle had become its standard designation.

Thane gave Stuart a considering look. "You sound as if you approve of her. She gives Nicholas fits."

"She gives everyone in security fits, even though she is unquestionably a very valuable asset. Maybe she's heard back from Milhann by now."

A patterned knock at the door signaled Barker's arrival. The raven-haired woman's gaze flashed around the room, assessing everything as she entered. Sturdy-looking, with a martial arts glide-walk. Nope, he did not want to mess with a 2-Eg powerhouse. He exchanged a polite nod with her before turning back to the table.

"Grandmother, if you take up the audit, you're going to have to deal with Helga Baron."

"Oh, no, my dear boy. If she is determined for us to take on Baron Financials, the bitch will have to deal with me."

Gordon broke out in a fit of coughing.

Chapter 15

Chris Rutherford, Repository Chief of Security, slid into the seat in front of CEO Brandon Sutherland's desk. He apologized for being late.

Sutherland waved it off. "I'm sure you and your department have been extremely busy. How positive are you that the theft occurred in the Repository?"

"One hundred percent. The raw stones were sealed into a container at the mine and weighed to the hundredths of a kilogram before shipping with a full complement of guards. It was reweighed in the processing room on arrival. It matched the value sent separately by the drilling supervisor. The container—about three cubic meters—wasn't unsealed until after being placed in the vault. We've reweighed it. It's short, about twenty to twenty-five stones, depending on the sizes taken."

"How can you tell? A number of them have already been removed for testing."

"Fortunately, weight and size measurements are the first part of any analysis. Those values were added in."

"Alright." Sutherland heaved out a long sigh. "We've been breached. What steps are being taken?"

"I have a team reviewing all our surveillance feeds. They will be looking for any discrepancies. Another team will be going over every inch of our security protocols. Sir, I want to add a couple of skilled civilians to each team."

"Why?"

"We've evidently missed something. A fresh pair of eyes and way of thinking may see something that's slipped past all of us."

Sutherland cleared his throat. "Could...could a Keeper have been compromised?"

The Keepers were the last line in the Repository's defense. Five persons of impeccable integrity held the operational and override codes to the Repository. Only one had ever been identified in their two hundred years of anonymous service. The elderly woman had stepped forward to deal with a crisis and then quietly taken her own life later that night. A new Keeper would have been selected by her peers.

Rutherford shook his head. "They'd still need to shut down security protocols to reach the vault, which would be recorded. There are no gaps in log entries or any of the security feeds. *None*."

Sutherland nodded. "Understood. Ensure any additions are sworn to silence. What else?"

"A mixed team from my department and Personnel will be reviewing everyone who works in the Repository or has visited since the container's arrival. They will be looking for any changes in behavior or circumstances. Lastly, I have several teams heading out into the field. They will backtrack the crystals Commander Kohring received and check out places known to deal with black market items. Hopefully, we'll get a good description of the person, or persons, who sold them."

"How many people do you think are involved?"

Rutherford looked thoughtful. "Not many, to keep it this contained. If the breach occurred from inside the Repository, no more than two as the stones had to be snuck out one or two at a time. If the breach occurred from outside—I'm not eliminating anything," he said, when Sutherland started to protest. "Some genius could have found a hole or a way to blind our security feeds. That team would also be small, maybe three or four at most to juggle equipment or whatever. Then someone had to receive the stones and sneak them off planet, and they'd need someone else who knows the black market."

"So, half a dozen—give or take—depending on how many hats each team member wore." Sutherland rubbed his neck. "How long till we know something?"

"If it'd been something simple, we'd have already discovered it and taken steps. With this level of planning and implementation…" Rutherford shook his head. "Weeks. Months."

Sutherland gave another sigh. "Dismissed."

Chapter 16

Jem sat silently, only half-listening to Thane and Gordon's low conversation. As soon as Gwen finished dressing, the four of them were headed for the hospital. Well, six, she amended, counting their bodyguards. The doctors were bringing Erik out of his healing coma today. Whatever pain medications Erik was on would be insufficient for the news he was about to hear.

She'd spent a good portion of the past two days prowling the city and its Port Circle while the others dissected Thane's records. Even when hidden in ghost-mode, she'd learned absolutely nothing. Not even a passing comment. It was as if the assassin himself was a ghost.

A hard double rap sounded on the hotel door. Stuart moved into position, his weapon pulled and pointing downward. Opening the door slowly, Barker peered out. Stepped back. Detectives Small and Trotmire entered, both guards getting nods of approval.

Gordon rose to greet them. "Detectives. We weren't expecting you. You have news?"

Both detectives' faces acquired the patented LE blank countenance as Detective Small said, "Information about an in-progress investigation is confidential."

Thane crossed his arms. "We're not going to announce it on the frigging news."

"What about your news?" Small gave Thane an irritated look. "We've made several requests for your Tracker records since your ship landed. This morning, we received *three* records from Mr. Stuart. I'm sure that does not comprise years of work."

"We've reviewed all of my records carefully and sent you the ones that showed the most potential. You don't need the others."

"We'd prefer to determine that for ourselves." Trotmire didn't hide her irritation either. "We may see something you've overlooked or dismissed."

"Even if you did find something, would you tell us?" Gwen asked, coming out of the bedroom. "And *we* might see something in your records *you've* overlooked or dismissed."

And they were back to two sets of blank expressions.

Thane gave the detectives a very shark-like grin. "Unless you can show me a reason—a credible reason—*my* records stay confidential."

Frustration came and went on Small's face. A silent message passed between the two Enforcers. Trotmire nodded.

Small said, albeit ungracefully, "We've sent out queries for the individuals named in the three files. Which may not mean much if the assassin was simply hired for the job." Small paused. "The names were all male."

"So?"

"The bomber was caught on external security cameras on several streets. We haven't ruled out the bomber being a slender male, but—analyzing the body movements—there's a high probability it's a woman. Female assassins do exist."

Not even a shifty glance in her direction from either detective. Jem was impressed. "One of my contacts states there is no general contract out on Thane," she said. Trotmire's eyebrow twitched. *Yes, I know assassins.* "His enemy either contacted a specific contractor directly or is quite capable on his-or-her own."

Small grunted. "Fine. Anything or anyone else? From all accounts, you've had an eventful year or two."

"No," Thane said.

"Patricia Keegan," Jem said at the same time.

Thane shot Jem a frown. "It's a long stretch between a frame and murder."

"Since you never learned the reason for the first, how do you know the second?"

Thane's mouth quirked in an annoyed, sideways twist.

Detective Small cleared his throat. Loudly. "Who is Patricia Keegan?"

Grumpily, Thane said, "Who the hell knows? The name's fake. She was behind an attempt to frame me for drug smuggling about two, two and a half years ago."

Small turned to Jem. "Why?"

"We never did figure it out."

"No. Why do you include her in this?"

"Similarity. Unknown assailant for unknown reason."

"She's right," Gordon said. "Maybe we should be relooking at that."

"To find what, Granddad?" Thane said. "We turned everything we could think of upside down back then. We found *nothing*."

"Which is why a different avenue of investigation is necessary for *all* your cases," Trotmire said.

"No. The ones we gave you fall under credible reason. But," Thane grudgingly added, "I will send a copy of what we have on the frame and Keegan,"

"If there's nothing else?" Gwen said. "We have an appointment at the hospital."

Chapter 17

Jem found herself boxed in by several reporters and their video drones.

"Jem Wilmont! Are you here because of Thane Baron?"

"Jem Wilmont! What is your relationship with Thane Baron? Are you his sig-ner?"

"No. I'm friends with the Stohlass family, so that includes Mr. Baron." She really, really disliked reporters. They were worse than mosquitoes.

"Jem Wilmont! Do you know who's trying to kill members of the Baron family?"

Dammit. She wasn't PR. "The attempt was targeted against Thane Baron. As a Tracker, he's made enemies over the years. Unfortunately, his uncle and his bodyguard became victims instead. The Milania Baron families are not in danger, other than that represented by the cowardly actions of some idiot. If said idiot has a legitimate complaint against Mr. Baron, they should bring it to him or file a court action." Great. Now she was a pseudo-Gordon.

One of the drones flew right up to her face. She grabbed it and twisted its wings.

"Hey!" squawked a man. "You'll have to pay for that." Jem gave him a cold look. "Maybe," he mumbled.

She turned. There had to be a less bothersome route to the spaceport.

"Are you here to assassinate whoever's trying to kill Thane Baron?"

She whipped around. "Who said that?" Everyone took a step back, except for a man with a cocky sneer.

Mr. Cocky said, "There's a lot of speculation about you, who the authorities—and a number of others—are calling 'the Ghost.' There are a number of incidents around the Republic that…" His voice melted away. So did several other reporters as the circle around her suddenly shrunk back.

"Are you implying something?" Jem pinned him with a cold stare. "I am here in support of my friends. When the authorities find this attacker, he or she will be processed accordingly by Law Enforcement." Her voice dropped a few more degrees. "I tend to ignore the *unproven* gossip and those that stupidly delve into my private life. Usually."

***

Thane cut the viewscreen off when the newscast rolled into a commercial. "That last was a pretty good answer. It would have gone down better if it didn't look as if you were about to add that reporter to your *unproven* hit list."

Jem slouched down in her chair. "I was pissed. I simply copied one of your expressions."

"That expression might have its place in Thane's profession. For you? That stony, hard-eyed, you're-about-to-die look is going to haunt you, Jem." Gordon shook his head. "For months we've tried to debunk all those assassin rumors. You just shot that in the ass. On camera," he said, exasperation coating his words. "Whatever you do…whoever you become in the future, those whispers are going to follow you."

Jem stared at the blank screen as the tiny dream she'd been nourishing withered and died. "I think that's already a given, sir, regardless of how much it's protested or by whom," she said quietly. *Where there's smoke, there's fire.* If uncertainty and a sullied reputation made her friends safer, so be it.

Chapter 18

Jem watched a historical drama on New Zagreb's early days while Thane worked on wearing a path in the carpet. She glanced over as he made another pass. The guy was not used to being cooped up. Unable to go anywhere without at least one bodyguard—even before the attack three weeks ago—wasn't helping his ego either. He was bored. No, she thought, he's antsy. He's not going to last much longer.

Thane stopped in front of her chair. "I'm leaving. Tomorrow. I'm not needed here. Not for security, not for medical, and certainly not financial wizardry."

Yep. That's what she'd figured.

Thane waved his hand. "I need to be out there. Tracking…hunting."

Yep. Figured that too. "Do you even know where to start?"

"No." His face took on a predatory cast. "I'll find her. Or she'll come to me."

He was going to make himself a target. "Bad idea. She favors death-at-a-distance methods. Think you can dodge the next laser shot?"

Thane thrust his hands in his pockets. "I'm on guard now."

"These attacks are driven by a cold, calculating mind, Thane. All she has to do is wait, pick her time and place. She's already waited more than two years."

"*If* it's Keegan," Thane rebutted, his jaw set in a stubborn line. "And even if it is, am I supposed to spend my life looking over my shoulder? Waiting for the next strike? How did that work for you?"

Jem winced.

"Sorry. Sorry. That was uncalled for." Thane ran a hand across his face. "I *can't* do that, Jem. I *won't.*"

She understood his frustration, having experienced it herself when she was running from Kurzvall. He was right, though. This could go on for years. If they could figure out the why, the person responsible should become obvious. Maybe it was the person behind Keegan's mask, and maybe it wasn't. Her guts said it was. In the meantime, she'd do what she could to help.

"You taking Stuart or VanCamp?" Jem sighed at the swift flash of mulish irritation. That was as loud a 'hell no' as a verbal one. "Well, then, can I tag along? I need to get back to Midgard, myself. I'll take the bunkroom," she said, then waited. Would he refuse? After several seconds of study, he gave her a clipped *okay*. Good. They needed to talk. *She* needed to talk, to try and smooth over the awkwardness that'd grown up between them. Maybe, if she explained—

The door flew open. Jem scrambled to her feet as Thane whipped around, his hands curling into fists. It was only his grandparents and their guards rushing in. After giving the room a quick inspection, Stuart and Barker withdrew, closing the door behind them.

"Uncle Erik?" Thane asked.

"Yes," Gordon said, "and in a good way. The doctors have assured us he's stable, his vital signs are good, and he can be moved with prudent care. We'd like to commandeer the *Lone Tracker* back to Midgard. It's got a med-room and Barker has medic credentials. It'll be a tight fit, but I want us gone before anyone realizes it."

And there goes any chance of a private conversation.

"When? I'll reschedule my outbound window. I, uh, was planning to leave tomorrow."

"What time tomorrow?" Gwen asked, a calculating look on her face.

"Eleven forty-five."

"That's doable," Gwen said, giving Gordon a nod. "I'll request his release for tomorrow morning."

"You and Grandmother can have the main bed." Thane was all business now, the edginess gone. "The rest of us can use the bunkbed in my restraint room or roll up on the deck. What about the audit?"

"It's done," Gwen said. "BF is in excellent shape and will be an outstanding addition to the family portfolio. I've given our terms to Helga for acceptance."

"What the hell am I going to do with it?" Thane snapped. "I'm a Tracker and, no, I don't intend to give it up."

"Turn daily operations over to one who does know what to do with it."

Jem didn't bother hiding her grin at Thane's suddenly suspicious expression.

"You meant to do that all along, didn't you?" he said. "Why didn't you or Granddad say so, instead of leaving me dangling on a hook?"

"Occasional squirming is good for the soul," Gordon told him. "You'll be happy to know Gwen insisted the Inheritance transfer happens *after* a BF office is established on Midgard."

"To minimize the investors' jitters, of course," Gwen said, giving them a jaunty smile.

"Wasn't moving it to Midgard in the plan anyway?"

"Yes, dear, a very *long* plan," Gwen said. "Helga meant to keep BF and you on Milania as long as possible. She probably hoped you would become so entrenched in things here, you'd forgo the inconvenience of relocating the company."

"Entrenched as in married and with a family," Gordon said. "Barker overheard a couple of BF employees talking in the bathroom. Helga has been quietly conversing with several prominent families with eligible daughters. She's still trying to separate you from our line."

Thane's jaw set. "Not going to happen. What happens if she goes around you and enacts the living inheritance first?"

Gwen and Gordon's lips pursed identically.

"I'll boot the woman out of the building personally," Gwen said. "The Midgard branch and transfer of Headquarters will happen so fast, she'll still be cleaning out her desk."

"It's doubtful she'll risk it," Gordon said. "The upheaval would cause a hugely negative impact to the company."

* * * * *

The following morning was a whirlwind of activity.

His grandmother oversaw clearing the hotel and getting everyone's bags transported to the ship, while Emily Barker insured no one slipped a bomb into them. An ambulance delivered Erik, Gordon and two burly orderlies, who helped Barker settle Erik and his medications in the med-room. Extra IV saline pouches were stored in the ship's cooler.

Thane remained in the *Lone Tracker* to prevent any last-minute attempts. He checked over the ship's preparations and last-minute supplies. He had Jem and Jason VanCamp purchase sleeping bags and stack them in the plazo, the open area just inside of the ship's hatch. Barker moved hers to the med-room.

Gwen received a call twenty minutes before their exit window. It was Helga Baron.

She was grinning broadly by the time the call ended. "Helga Baron has agreed to our terms and will start arrangements here. She'll send her niece ahead to Midgard to lay the groundwork there."

Thane snorted. "I bet VP Baron explodes when she hears that."

Chapter 19

Glass and brandy exploded against the wall.

"How dare she?" Katherine Baron practically screamed. "Of all the idiotic, asinine, unbelievable gall of the fucking bitch."

Ahrymani Carpenter eyed the woman. She'd waited until Helga Baron left before slipping into Katherine's apartment. While Katherine was often moody where her aunt was concerned, this was a bit more extreme than usual. Going to the hutch, she filled another glass with brandy. Walking over and handing it to the woman, she said, "Drink it."

Katherine glared at her, grabbed the glass and downed half of it.

Ahrymani sat on the couch arm. "What is it?"

"They're establishing a Baron Financials branch office on Midgard."

"So? Your cousin and his family can play with that one while you have the one here."

"No, I won't," Katherine gritted out. "Once the Midgard office is functional, my *dear aunt* intents to enact the Living Inheritance Statute."

Ahrymani's expression sharpened. "Meaning?"

"Meaning my cousin will inherit Baron Financials—immediately, and then he'll move the headquarters to Midgard. My *dear company-employee-aunt* will remain as CEO here to ensure a smooth transition and then retire after a year or so. I may or may not be retained with the company."

"Contest it."

"None allowed. Once Thane inherits, the company will follow *his* heirs when he dies."

"Then he dies before that happens."

Katherine glared at her. "When? How? You've not had much success so far." She downed the rest of her drink. "And Helga expects *me* to go and make the arrangements. To facilitate Thane Baron's inheritance of *my* company."

Ahrymani hid her irritation. Yes, she'd missed. Thane Baron's run of good luck couldn't last forever. In fact… She interrupted Katherine's ranting with a raised hand.

"*What?*"

"You'll need to take an assistant with you to help handle things. You know, travel arrangements, research, appointments, etcetera. Someone to help you work *with* the Stohlass family *inside* their security."

"You," Katherine said, a calculating expression replacing the fury.

"Me."

A slow smile spread across Katherine's face. "That has so much…potential. I suppose I could be accommodating."

Ahrymani shook her head. "They'll get suspicious. Be yourself and continue fighting to change your aunt's mind. They expect that. Who knows, you might even succeed." Her mind raced, plotting out several lines of assault. They needed information. "What was that alias you used when you framed Baron? We can use that. Make it look as if someone from his past is striking again."

Ahrymani gave a low laugh. Technically, it was.

Chapter 20

The Spine Islands were the tops of a long undersea mountain range stretching hundreds of miles southwest of Oslo toward the equator. The other end didn't stop at the continental shelf, instead marching right up it. The Spine Mountains wrapped a jagged wall around Oslo's western edge like, well, a spine. While the numerous fjords and bays among it were smaller cousins to Earth's Norway, their rugged beauty was breathtaking.

Spine Ridge Fjord, where those two halves met, was her new home. Or it would be, once completed. Jem had hired the highly recommended family firm of Nielson Architecture Designs to oversee it. Her unique requirements had snagged the attention of Grandpa Gustav, the company founder himself.

Jem closely watched the viewscreen in Mr. Nielson's office as he went over the final design for her home's interior. She smiled when he finished and said, "Your team has done excellent work."

"Thank you. We enjoyed the challenge."

The viewscreen projection changed to an exterior view. The beach and rock wall leading to her home were centered, with the Elbow on the right. She frowned at the large T-shaped dock superimposed on the image.

"I realize this is more substantial than you specified," Mr. Nielson said in an apologetic voice," but the excavation team—due in two weeks from Malver Two—has sent ahead their personnel and equipment lists. Mr. MacVay, the team leader, has specified a heavy-duty dock to accommodate both them and their equipment."

"Were there any problems getting an excavation team?"

"Not at all," Mr. Nielson assured her. "Entire cities are subterranean on some planets." He centered a pointer on the dock's flat T-head. "The depth here is over twenty meters, as the bedrock drops sharply. We're arranging for a tree harvester's flat trawler to transport them and their equipment from the Odinheim Spaceport to Spine Ridge Fjord. There'll also be room to dock the cruiser we're leasing to serve as their headquarters and residence for the duration."

The pointer moved to the T's stem and he smiled at her. "The dock will be a versatile asset. A boat house could be built in one corner for storage. Smaller vessels can dock on the inside with larger ones on the outside."

"I don't plan on doing a lot of entertaining," Jem said. "Most of the time I'll keep a vehicle somewhere in Azusa and jet back and forth."

Nielson blinked. Looked at the fog-shrouded window, back at her.

Jem grimaced. Right. Midgard had basically two seasons—summer and fog. Jetting in fog would be dumb. Boat purchase just went on her to-do list. "I concede both of your points. Can the dock be built in time?"

"I have a local construction team on standby. The Rockson Brothers is a reputable firm and does excellent work. They can start immediately once you give approval."

Jem stared at the image one more time. It was a finger, pointing straight at her home. Well, it wouldn't stay secret for long anyway. "Approved."

Wrapped in her own thoughts, she was several steps down the sidewalk before she halted in astonishment. Wow. The fog had been bad when she arrived, but this? This was a condensed atmospheric gray soup. Situated on Oslo's southwestern coast, Azusa rarely got snow. However, the Stohlass family had warned her, mid-December to early-January was the grayest part of winter. They'd hadn't exaggerated. The dim lights of shadowy vehicles appeared, slid past at a wisely sedate speed, and then disappeared.

They should simply call it Fog Season and be done with it.

The sun had only peeked through it three—four, maybe?—times since their return to Midgard three weeks ago. This wasn't the white-ish stuff of Earth, more of a steel-gray. Like Thane's eyes. Crap. *Stop thinking about him.*

He'd taken off on a job almost immediately after their return to Midgard. Partly due to the weather, partly to protect his family…partly because of her. She'd tried to draw him aside, to talk. He'd brushed her off. *And whose fault is that?* a snide corner of her brain inquired. *Yes, yes, I know. I keep throwing walls up between us.*

Great. Now she was talking with herself.

She began the one block trudge over to the nearest transport stand. At least it wasn't—*splat!* The large watery smack on her forehead was the only warning. She yanked her hood in place before its brethren followed. In a deluge. What visibility there had been was halved.

Make that the Foggy Rain Season. Jetting around in this stuff wouldn't be dumb, it'd be suicidal. She needed to be more cognizant of her new home's eccentrics.

She dived into a taxi, trying to bring in as little rain as possible. "The Thundering Falls restaurant," she told the driver, "if you can find it."

He flashed her a grin and pulled away from the curb.

It was almost forty minutes later before she could plop down in a chair across from Andi. "Lose many islands this time of year?" Jem asked, sourly. She draped her dripping raincoat over an adjacent chair.

Andi laughed. "You'll get used to it."

"Spring starts when…mid-February? Think I'll spend a couple of months off planet, see how Reyna and the Foundation are doing." Sell the remaining crystals. She had a few polished ones left and half of the raw, unprocessed ones.

"Coward. Have you decided on a place yet?"

There it was. Another poke. Andi had been fishing for her plans ever since she'd confided about changing her residency to Midgard. The temptation to tell her was brief. They were trying to keep it quiet for as long as possible. She was already dealing with stares and the whispers. Not to mention all the pesky reporters. It would become a media swarm once the news broke about their newest and—unfortunately for her—notorious resident.

"I want to stay near Azusa. But…I'm not comfortable living in the city."

"It's not fair," Andi said, with a half-frown, half-pout. "You were proved innocent of the Branson Fire and there is nothing, *nothing*, to substantiate those nasty rumors about you being an assassin."

Jem shrugged. "There's nothing fair about rumors or gossip."

"Well, I'm happy to hear you'll be living nearby. The family will be, too. Speaking of gossip, VP Baron will be here in March. She's booked a three-room suite at the Azure Regal Hotel."

"I can't blame her for refusing to come during this." Jem waved her hand toward a bank of windows. Lightening flashed, illuminating the rain cascading down. "Be kind of hard to get around—not to mention be able to *see* real estate in a wheelchair."

"Conditions outside a building doesn't stop one from looking inside it. It's another delay tactic. Want to bet Katherine Baron's trying to get her aunt to reconsider her decision?"

"Thane won't care if she does."

Andi played with her glass for a moment. "Baron Financials would be a good business investment—I can see that. But there are a number of great companies here already that could be expanded and, personally, I'm with Thane. I'd just as soon not have to deal with either CEO or VP Baron."

***

Jem endured the fog, the rain, and numerous questions from Gustav Nielson before leaving the following week. It took a couple of months to discreetly sell the remaining crystals across various systems. Earth was her final stop to deposit the accumulated credits into the Foundation account. Reyna had merely raised an eyebrow at the amount. She did have to weather Reyna's stink-eyed glare when she explained they were from 'donors wanting to help while remaining anonymous.'

Well, it was true. She couldn't exactly say how she'd gotten the funds. And Hopkins and the Kid did want to remain anonymous.

Jem had also arranged to have the last of her personal Earth account transferred to her Midgard account. The Hands of Hope Foundation was now her single remaining tie to Earth.

Happily, the Midgard spring was in full bloom by the time she returned, dominated by sun and turquoise skies. She found her home to be about three-fourths constructed. *Deconstructed?* she mused, stepping from Mr. Nielson's boat and onto the dock. The first thing she noticed was the flagstone walkway, about three meters wide and running from the dock to the large square opening about fifteen meters away in the hillside.

"Beautiful," Jem said. She stepped off the wooden dock to admire the close-fitted stones. The walkway rose in three wide tiers, each of them one step higher before reaching the entrance to her home. She gave Nielson a questionable look as it had been flat in their original plans. This also raised the entrance and everything else higher.

"Storms," Mr. Nielson said. "It raises the opening above the typical storm surge. It was simpler than building a seawall. We can do that if you want."

How long was it going to take her to start thinking as a Midgarder? "No. You're right, and thank you."

"Can't take the credit—it was Mr. MacVay's idea. It was a good reuse of the stone being cut out and he has two certified stone masons on his team. Ready to see the rest?"

Jem nodded and followed him toward three men standing in front of her new home, mentally earmarking bonuses for MacVay's team. Introductions made, they pointed out the various openings on the lower level. There were two storerooms, one large and one small, and a short hallway ending in a stone stairway. There was also a mechanical room for the large and surprisingly operational lift.

"It was a priority after we started on the upper level," MacVay said. "Workers and equipment up, debris bins down. It'll be replaced with a people-friendly elevator later."

Jem stepped on the spacious lift. One of the men hit a button and they rose smoothly upward.

***

It was late afternoon before Jem reached the door of her apartment, tired and happy. Her home was coming along nicely and she'd avoided the reporters waiting at the Azusa dock when she and Mr. Nielson returned. Nielson had kept the mangled remains of a drone one of them had flown through one of the upper floor openings. Fortunately, she'd remained unseen in another area and the quick reflexes of a team member had kept it from broadcasting much. Still, it was an invasion of privacy and Mr. Nielson intended to take it to the Enforcers.

Unfortunately, Jem grumbled silently as she inserted her key into its slot, the curiosity and speculation about the Fjord excavation was going to grow. Stepping inside, she spotted a piece of folded paper on the floor. It'd been shoved under the door. Picking it up, she went cold at the brief message.

Raven's Fist. Tonight. 2100. Need to talk. KID.

Her good mood ruined, she flung herself into a chair. What did he want? Blackmail? Surely, he couldn't have burned through twenty J-crystals' worth of credits this fast. She frowned at the ceiling. No…no, what little she knew about him, blackmail didn't seem right.

Actually, she didn't know a frigging thing about him. Impressions mostly.

She didn't even know his real name. He was always called 'the Kid.' He'd been one of the youngest of Beckett's pirates, if not the youngest, but his eyes had held the same coldness as the oldest. How old was he? Nineteen? Twenty? No one should be that hardened at that age. Yet, she'd found good hidden deep under that shell. Found some shades of honor. On the *Hidden Trove*, during the final confrontations with Beckett and his psycho second, he'd backed her. He'd even left several crystals behind for her donation pile. *Soooo,* maybe she should wait before panicking.

Whatever it was, she doubted it'd be good.

Chapter 21

The *Raven's Fist* appeared to be a standard combo of bar and restaurant, tucked away in what passed for Azusa's Port Circle. Azusa's private spaceport was a small offshoot of the main airport and had a rigidly controlled access. Though a microcosm of its big brothers, it provided *all* the same services.

Jem paused inside the door, finally spotting the Kid in one of the sound-suppression booths lining two walls. She felt the other patrons' veiled assessment as she made her way between the tables, which sheered away as she slid into the booth. Nothing to see, nothing anyone wanted to see, was the primary rule in these places. She folded her hands on the tabletop and studied the man across from her.

His fair skin appeared to have acquired a tan since she last saw him. The strawberry-blond hair she remembered was longer, shaggier, and mostly blond now. Bleached out by that same sun? But the cold blue gaze and the hard shell were unchanged. Seriously. What had this young man been through?

"How old are you?" she asked abruptly.

He raised his glass. "Old enough to drink this beer."

Fine. "Can I call you something other than Kid?"

Before he could answer—if he even intended to—a server approached, setting a dish down in front of him before turning to her. "You ordering?"

Jem eyed the platter. She'd been too wound up to eat any supper. "I'll have the same meatloaf platter and a glass of Moon Ale. Warm." She waved a hand after the server left. "Go ahead. Eat."

Her meal arrived quickly and they ate in silence. A passing server took his empty plate and another beer order. The silence continued as he settled back on his side of the booth with his fresh beer. She studied him discreetly in her peripheral vision. He'd never been what you'd call talkative. He'd get to whatever—*oh, crap*. He'd flipped the sound suppression on. Jem managed to calmly fork up the last bite of meatloaf and green beans.

"They're hunting you."

She choked when the food stuck in her throat. A couple of coughs and a sip of ale later, she asked who.

"Jaguide Enforcers."

"Oh. Well. We knew they'd eventually realize J-crystals were being sold on the black market."

"I've only sold a few of the polished ones and Hopkins dumped his before we left Tigres."

Tigres. Euphrates Three. The planet where Beckett's reign as pirate king ended. Where her media-splashed notoriety in his capture had turned her life upside down.

"They're not too worried about the polished crystals," the Kid continued. "It's the woman selling the *raw* stones they're after."

That was unexpected. "Why?"

"Because she's evidently working with whoever breached their vault. Which we know is one and the same."

"How did they determine it was breached?" Only three people alive knew what she'd done.

"Experts can match a crystal to its mine by its color and chemical signature. You've heard about the new Jaguide Four mine? One crate of J-4 samples was extracted and sent to the Repository on Westmoreland for initial testing. The mine was then sealed, so those were the first and *only* stones from that mine."

Jem's mind flashed to the three shipping crates near the vault's entrance. All the raw stones she'd taken had come from the one closest to her.

"Which means," he continued, "the raw stones being sold had to have come from the Jaguide Repository vault. They probably assume the polished ones were stolen at the same time."

"Oh." This was trouble. "How do you know all this?"

He took a couple of swallows, licked his lips. "I happened to be in a certain place planning to sell a crystal myself, until I overheard the manager being interrogated. Aggressively, I'll add. I shadowed them for a few hours and learned enough to figure out the rest. Good thing you kept your face and braid hidden. The buyers can't say anything other than an average sized, fair-skinned woman."

"They don't know it's *me*." That was too vague a description.

The Kid shook his head. "You're forgetting something."

She was pretty sure he and Hopkins, the *Hidden Trove's* pilot, wouldn't betray her. Reasonably sure, anyway. But if the ex-pirate king thought it would benefit him? "Beckett?"

"There's always that. It's those old FLEA flyers. How long do you think it'll take the Jaguide Enforcers to realize they describe the perfect suspect? Female. Stealthy. Mysterious."

Jem's heart sank. Those frigging flyers. Her name and description had been slapped in every spaceport facility and Federal Law Enforcement Agency office last year when they suspected her—erroneously—as responsible for Midgard's Branson Hotel Fire.

"Suspicions aside, they can't connect me to it. I don't have any crystals left." When his head cocked in question, she added, "I used them to establish the Hands of Hope Foundation on Earth." Look at that. She actually saw a glimmer of a smile. And his face didn't break.

But all he said was, "You kept your promise to Hopkins."

Hopkins had kept only one of his share of crystals, giving the rest to her and making her promise they'd be used to help others. "So, unless someone points a finger..." Jem gave him a suspicious look. His ice-blue chips went even colder. Her shoulders hunched. "Sorry. It's just..."

His gaze didn't waver. "I know. Trust is rare in our line."

"Which is?"

"Survival."

Wasn't that the truth?

"My name's Kaleb."

"With a K?" He nodded. Huh. Coincidence, or was his nickname more than a play on his age? "Well, Kaleb, I've already got suspicious rumors circling me." Resigned, Jem added, "What's one more? Thank you for letting me know about the J-Enforcers. I owe you."

Kaleb's eyes shifted, looked around the room. Ran his hand up and down his glass.

Jem's eyebrow arched. Fidgeting? Another first. She waited until the server swooping in for her plate left. "Something else?"

He hesitated. "Sometime…I'm not sure when…I may need help."

"Something from your past?"

"Yes."

His eyes were no longer cold. They held a raging firestorm. Whatever it was, it was the root cause of who he was now. What he'd become to survive.

"I won't cross certain boundaries," Jem said quietly, and reinforced it with a firm eye-to-eye look. "Otherwise, count me in." She gave him her Midgard contact information.

He nodded, finished his drink. Sliding out of the booth, he leaned back down, one hand planted on the table. "By the way, I know you didn't hack the *Hidden Trove's* computer."

Impossible. "How else could I have retrieved the crystals?" she said, bluffing.

The stolen bag of crystals had been locked in the pirates' clandestine ship's vault. When everything fell apart, Beckett had locked the vault with a passcode known only to him. To win the crew's cooperation with her against Beckett, she had retrieved the crystals by phasing through the wall and let them believe she'd hacked the passcode from the ship's computer.

"Easy. You either teleported in or walked through the walls."

Jem was left with her mouth hanging open. That and the bill for both dinners.

Chapter 22

Jem was trying to relax with a glass of white wine and an old Earth movie. Kaleb's parting statement last night had left her unsettled. She'd tried to find him afterwards, but he'd vanished into the night. Was he guessing? Bluffing? Why was he so sure? Even if he was, he couldn't prove it. And why had he seemed so…unfazed?

A knock sounded on her apartment door. She rose, wary. Andi was the only one who visited and she always called first. Had Kaleb tracked her down with more bad news?

It was indeed bad news at her door. Two Federal Law Enforcement Agents.

"May we come in?"

No warrant was good. She stepped back to allow them entry. "Please, have a seat," Jem said politely, proceeding to do so herself. "It's Agent Reis, isn't it? And Agent…Garner?" She'd met both Federal agents briefly last year.

"Gaines," the female FLEA said stiffly as they settled in chairs opposite her.

"Agent Gaines," she acknowledged and waited. Their move.

Reis cleared his throat. "We're aware of your change of residency to Midgard."

"Law Enforcement interviews all new residents?"

"No. Just those on Federal watch lists," Agent Gaines said.

So. Another one of those, judging by her tone. Was Reis too? His face wore the patented LE blank look. "You were both at the meeting last year." Jem kept her own voice neutral. "You're aware that my reputation is a result of the misinformation and lies Kurzvall and his people spread."

"Yes, he manipulated a few things."

"A few things? Agent Gaines, he manipulated *all* of it." Jem took a sip of wine, wrestled the irritation down. "So, why do I warrant a special visit?"

Reis spoke up, his tone guarded. "Director Vanderbilt wants to know why you relocated to Midgard and what your intentions are."

Really? "I have nothing and no one left on Earth. I've been drifting for some time, as I'm sure you're aware of. I want to settle down. I chose Midgard because I like the planet and I have friends here. My frigging *intention*, Agents, is to be an average, run-of-the-mill Midgard citizen, despite the rumors and insinuations."

Gaines snorted. "Hard to be a run-of-the-mill citizen when you're one of the richest."

"Let's not spread that around," Jem said, giving the agent an irritated look.

After several chain of events and years of compounded interest, she'd ended up with billions of credits. So much so, her Earth bank had transferred the electronic credit file to her Wotan Bank account in Azusa via an armed courier, instead of the standard UPMS mail pod. And that didn't take in account another—unintentional—chain of events that had swollen her Azusa account by more billions.

"Oh, it's going to get around," Reis said. "You might want to consider moving elsewhere that has guards and gates."

"I'll think about it. Anything else?"

Reis shook his head. "We're done."

Jem escorted the two agents to the door.

Reis motioned for Gaines to continue on and turned toward her. "Your presence here has generated a lot of…discomfort," he said in a low voice.

It was a warning. Was that why he'd come?

Jem dipped her chin in thanks and closed the door. She leaned her forehead against it wearily. Two warnings in two days. Wonderful.

* * * * *

It was a long hallway and Reis felt every one of his partner's sideway glances down it.

"What was that about?" Gaines jabbed the elevator's down button. "Vanderbilt did *not* send us."

He shrugged. "I wanted to hear her answers. See her reaction."

"You expected truth?"

"Yes."

"Do you really believe she's going to be a model citizen?"

"I believe she wants to be, and will be if others leave her alone." Reis caught and held her gaze as the elevator doors slid open. "I'd prefer Vanderbilt didn't learn we were here."

Gaines followed him into the empty car, wearing a puzzled look. He pressed the lobby button. "If anyone does ask," he continued, "You can honestly attest I asked her a couple of questions."

It took three floors before she finally asked, "What's going on, Rafe?"

"I don't know," he said, watching the floor indicator. "Simply moving here shouldn't have caused the churning that's going on at the higher levels." The car settled and the doors dinged open.

He strode out of the building and into the dark. Gaines was almost jogging to keep up, asking him to slow down. He didn't. He needed to distance himself from Wilmont. He needed to distance himself from overheard comments he'd never expected to hear from any Law Enforcer.

Chapter 23

"Thane! Wait up!" Andi yelled.

Thane turned, waited as she rushed toward him.

She plowed to a stop, glared at the pack in his hands, and fisted her hands on her hips. Nick was right. "You're leaving *again*? You just got home last night and you've been gone for *months*."

Thane shrugged. "I seem to be in demand."

"Well, you can put the current one on hold. At least for a couple of days."

"Why?"

"Jem wants to learn boating."

"Boating?"

"And sailing."

He nodded. "Makes sense. I heard she's been staying here."

"She *moved* here, Thane. Even changed her official residency to Midgard."

His eyes widened. *Surprise, surprise.* "Maybe if you'd bothered to check in with the family occasionally, you'd have known that." Didn't like that, huh? Tough. "Anyway, I thought you could take her out on one of ours. Take a picnic basket and a nice bottle of wine. Enjoy a relaxing day on the water."

"Sorry. Can't. Someone else will have to teach her."

"*Thaaaaaaaane!*"

He gave her a lopsided grin. "Got to go. LE has a prisoner transfer." He turned and headed for the security gate.

One day. It couldn't have waited one day? "Guess we know where we stand in your priorities."

His steps faltered, then resumed his normal stride.

"Andrea Stohlass Sullivan."

Andi whirled around. *Ohhh, crap.*

"That was unkind of you."

Her grandmother's angry expression said she was about to receive some unkindness, too.

* * * * *

"I'll have the Reuben on wheat, not toasted. Earth fries with ketchup and a large tea."

Jem handed the menu back and studied her friend as the waiter left with their orders. Andi had been unusually quiet since she'd sat down. Her red-headed friend didn't do quiet on a normal day. Something was wrong. Was that why Andi had called and asked her to meet for lunch? Jem didn't push; her friend would talk when she was ready. She let herself relax and basked in the warmth of her new home world.

A warm breeze played with their hair and the fringe on the umbrella shading them. They were on the open veranda on one of the many restaurants perched around the harbor. The city rose behind them, the Spine Mountains to the west. She smiled inwardly. The cartographer plotting this system must have come from Earth's Scandinavian region, considering he'd reused so many of their names. Many of Azusa's founding families had come from the same region, entire villages migrating away from the Earth's sea level's flooding rise.

Thane had told her a number of the founders felt it was preordained, between the topography and the system naming. They had carried that influence forward, in the naming of towns, businesses and physical features. The Longboat Shipping Company. The Valhallass Dance Troupe—a blending of Valhalla and the Stohlass family name. The numerous Fjords along Oslo's west coast.

"We can take one of the family boats out tomorrow," Andi said, drawing Jem's attention back to the table. "Or any other day if you already have plans."

As if her days were so busy. "Andi, I can hire someone and their boat. When I mentioned I wanted to learn boating, I didn't mean it had to be you."

"No, no, that's all right. Actually…I asked Thane to do it."

Jem straightened. "He's home?"

"And gone. He left again this morning. I was so mad when he refused, I said something not very nice. Maybe…something about him not caring about the family?" She made a face. "Grandmother overheard and we had a…conversation."

Jem hid her grin. Yep. That would do it. Gwendolyn Holms Williams's 'conversations' were legendary. Not only inside the family walls, either. Andi's ass had been handed to her on a low-keyed, frostily-polite platter.

Andi looked up from fiddling with her silverware. "I hurt him, Jem."

"It was your mad talking. Thane and I have said a few things to each other we probably shouldn't have, too." Or didn't say when she should have. "Send him a message apologizing and offer to give him a Nicholas-sized hug when he gets back."

"After what Grandmother said, I should get a Nicholas-sized kick in the butt."

Jem blinked. Hesitatingly she asked, "Can you say or is it a family thing?"

"You *are* family," Andi said. "Thane needs to stay home long enough to do something about it."

Jem's ears turned warm. Subtle wasn't in Andi's makeup either.

"Grandmother said the boy—boy? Thane is thirty-two. She said he's running from himself and distancing himself from us because of what happened on Milania. But he's *not* responsible, Jem. Can't he see that?"

Jem absently tracked a light blue sail as its boat followed the wind out of the harbor. She understood Thane's position. She'd done the same for several years. "He knows that, Andi. Intellectually. Emotionally, he still carries the weight of it. As I carry hundreds of—"

"You are not responsible for the Branson Fire," Andi interrupted hotly.

Her attention swung back, and she was unable to hold back a fierce glare. "No, but they died *because* of me, Andi. Because Beckett needed an incident brutal enough to generate a Republic-wide manhunt for me." Images of the fire climbing up the hotel's side and of the engulfed South Wing occasionally visited her at night.

Andi's mouth opened. Closed.

"Thane's afraid that if he's here for any length of time, someone else may be injured or killed in his stead. It's a valid concern," Jem told her grimly. "I thought long and hard before deciding to move here. My association with your family put you and several other Stohlass members at risk last year. I may be doing it again. I've fielded a number of *requests* from both individuals and criminal organizations. Everything from robbery to assassination." Thanks to the notoriety of the past year and those frigging Law Enforcement flyers.

Their lunch arrived, the waiter deftly depositing her sandwich and Andi's salad in front of them.

As soon as he left, Andi waved a hand and said, "Our family is already at risk due to our social and political standing. We know to be careful." She began spooning dressing onto her meal. "Don't worry about us."

"This can't just be waved off, Andi," Jem said, exasperation leaking into her voice. "Remember Richardson holding you at gunpoint? What about those that won't take *no* for an answer? Like Beckett. He threatened to destroy Azusa with a Delgado if I didn't do what he wanted me to."

Andi gave a startled gasp.

Oops. She hadn't told anyone what had happened when she was the pirates' prisoner.

Jem waited for the questions she couldn't answer. After several heartbeats, Andi picked up her fork and began to eat her salad. After another couple of heartbeats, Jem picked up her sandwich and took a bite. Warmth as well as relief filled her. When Andi did ask a question, it wasn't what she was expecting.

"What was the deciding factor in relocating here?"

Jem swirled a couple of fries in her ketchup and chewed them slowly. She thought of the years spent drifting. Of the empty days and lonely nights. Peering out from the shadows and watching life as it could be. Should be. No friends. No one she could count on. Until Thane strode into her life. Until his family had stubbornly dragged her into their circle. They'd given her their trust, despite her inability to fully return it.

But she was working on it, gradually scraping off the layers of fear and mistrust. She had hope, now, for something resembling a normal life. She could eat lunch with a woman she openly called friend. Despite all the problems bound to come, they were worth it.

Jem swallowed and simply said, "Your family."

"*Our* family," was Andi's response.

Jem finished the rest of their lunch in a warm glow and they parted ways outside the restaurant. Andi took a taxi home while she strolled down the street. Instincts honed in numerous Circles told her she was being followed. Couldn't be the same eyes she'd felt while they'd eaten. No one had exited the restaurant behind them. A partner then. She glanced in several display windows, stopped to admire an outfit in another one. She didn't bother trying to spot her tail. He was good, she'd give him that.

Jem exchanged a grin with her reflection. He was also outclassed.

She strode past three more stores before turning into an alley. Going several feet inward to avoid any street-level cameras, she shifted.

He walked past the entrance, giving a casual 'I'm not really interested' glance down the alley. A double-take had him making a sharp turn and sprinting past her to where it ended at a service lane behind the stores. After quick head-turn to the right and left, he disappeared to the left.

Jem sauntered behind him. A Federal Law Enforcer of some kind she guessed. He didn't look local. The man was about six feet tall, with dark hair clipped short and a medium skin tone that could be either natural or a tan. The casual clothes wouldn't have gotten him a second look, although his well-toned physique probably had.

By the time she reached the alley's end, the Fed was poking in the nearest garbage bin. *Really?*

Dropping back down, hands on hips, he looked first one way, then the other.

Yep. Lots of service doors and garbage bins back here.

He pulled out a phone, pushed a couple of buttons. "I lost her," he said in a clipped voice. "Alleyway about two blocks down—next to an ice cream place." Snapping it closed, he strode toward two men unloading a van two doors down on the other side of the alley.

Jem eyed the woman who stepped out of the alley a short time later. Same non-descript clothing and professional air. The woman—or at least her parents—had to be Earth-born. If she wasn't full-blooded Japanese, she'd eat her belt.

"Nothing," the man said, stopping next to her. He scanned the lane again. "No telling which—"

"Why'd you let her get so far ahead?"

His gaze snapped back to her. "I wasn't more than ten, twelve seconds behind her. When I crossed the alley, she was already out of sight."

Both turned. Jem knew they were mentally calculating the alley's length and going *no way*.

"There wasn't any mention in her file of being a striped andwarg."

"Andwarg?" the woman repeated, echoing Jem's silent question.

"Small and fast. Look it up."

"She couldn't have made that distance in that short a time."

"Then you explain it."

"I don't have to—you do. To Colonel Tungrove. He's not going to be happy."

"Have you ever seen him otherwise?"

"Okay, he's going to be very unhappy."

Shit, damn, crap. Military, not Feds. *Sounds as if their Colonel is a real winner in the personality department.*

The man shrugged. "I warned the Colonel this wouldn't work. The woman hasn't survived this long without fine-tuned instincts. She probably felt your eyes on her in the restaurant."

The woman's phone pinged. "Car will be here in five," she said after a quick look. "We'll pick her back up at her apartment."

The guy snorted. "Want to bet?"

Better not, Jem thought smugly. She trailed invisibly behind them as they headed toward the main street.

"If this is a simple case of surveillance, why aren't the locals doing it?" the woman muttered.

"I don't believe the Colonel has disclosed our full orders."

The woman gave him a sharp look. "Schmidt wouldn't have brought us in half-prepped."

"Unfortunately, Colonel Schmidt isn't running the team anymore. And," he said, anger filtering into his voice, "she certainly wouldn't have neglected to inform the Midgard authorities we're here."

"They don't know? Hell. They're going to be pissed when they find out."

Jem stayed close, but they fell silent. A car pulled up; they climbed in. She mentally replayed what she'd heard as it sped away.

She wasn't surprised the military was watching her—*hell, everyone probably was*, she grumbled, remembering Reis's warning. The fact it was an off-world team doing it, and hiding it from the local authorities, bothered her. That smelled of an ulterior motive more than just surveillance.

She bet it would bother a couple of others, too.

* * * * *

Agent Reis disconnected the phone call and stared nonplussed at Gaines.

"What?" she demanded.

"There is a military unit from off-planet performing covert surveillance on Wilmont. Or trying to." He laughed. "She slipped the two following her and turned the tables on them. Their commander is a Colonel Tungrove, who doesn't appear to fully trust his team *and* has not notified any Midgard agency of their presence or their intentions."

Gaines sucked in a sharp breath. "How many protocols does that break?"

Reis's phone pinged. "That should be the tag number of their car. Mr. Durand's interview can wait. Let's head back to the office. I want to run this plate before calling Sergi." His cousin was going to be furious.

General Sergi Kowalski, Commander of Planetary Defense, should have been informed of any military operation on or around Wotan Two, including who, how many, how long, and for what.

"You'd better tell Director Vanderbilt before calling General Kowalski," warned Gaines over the car's top. "In fact, it will look better with the call coming from him."

Reis made a face, nodded. Was there any federal job that didn't require a political dance?

"And then," she drawled, "you'd better have a creditable explanation ready for why the Ghost called *you*."

Chapter 24

"Miss Jem Wilmont," the aide announced, shutting the door behind them.

The aide had introduced herself as Lieutenant Lisa Corrigan before ushering her into the General's office. Escorting Jem to the seat in front of the general's desk, she took a seat at another desk off to the side

"Thank you for coming so promptly, Miss Wilmont."

"Your aide did request as soon as convenient. I'm guessing this is related to my surveillance. Naturally, I'm curious as to what's going on." She'd booked a shuttle flight to Odinheim right after receiving her call last night.

The general folded his hands on the desktop. "Colonel Tungrove and his team left Midgard this morning. I have filed a complaint with his superiors."

"Was the complaint about the surveillance or you being uninformed?"

"Both. I'll be frank, Miss Wilmont. Reports of your capability have been circulating among the Command structure. Colonel Tungrove's report of you besting his commando squad will enhance that reputation. There are two sets of opinions about you."

"A tool to use or a threat to eliminate," Jem murmured.

Kowalski leaned back in his seat and flashed a quick glance at his aide. "I wouldn't have put it quite that way but, basically, yes. The team that left belonged to a Special Operations branch specializing in the investigation, infiltration, and resolution of threats to the Republic. Which I was not supposed to tell you."

Oh? "Why have you?"

"I believe you'll only become a threat if forced in to it," he said bluntly. "You can infiltrate level seven security. If you wanted to threaten Midgard, or the Republic in general, you would have already done so. I stressed that fact in my report to Tungrove's superiors and that there is no credible evidence to the contrary.

"I also have the advantage of knowing most of the rumors and innuendos surrounding you are bullshit. The one item that isn't—the engine tampering—you've explained. My aide is fully cognizant of all the facts," he added when Jem shot a sideways glance. "She has read both Major Markowitz's report and last year's Stohlass meeting minutes. Speaking on behalf of all of Wotan Military Command, we will not facilitate any adverse action against you—against any of our citizens—unless they can prove beyond a doubt there is a good reason for such an action."

Jem gave him a warm smile. "Thank you, sir. That means a lot to me."

"That said, is there anything I should be aware of?"

How did she answer that? "If there is anything in my past, sir, there was a reason."

Kowalski's eyes narrowed but all he said was, "Good enough. My aide will see you out. Welcome to Midgard."

Jem rose. "Sir? I would like to extend the offer of my assistance if you ever believe there is need of it."

An eyebrow rose slightly, then his chin dipped in acceptance.

In the outer office, Lt. Corrigan turned to her. "We can't stop Earth Force from running, umm, we'll say harmless training missions."

Jem estimated the woman to be late twentyish—close to her age, which was bit old for the rank. Must have enlisted late, she decided, as she couldn't envision the general taking on a screw-up. And she had a firm, competent manner Jem liked.

"Meaning there'll be others?"

"Count on it. They're offended and embarrassed that a civilian beat them at their own game. It's a challenge now, both against you and each other. Who is 'the best?'" Corrigan's fingers did the air-quote thing.

Bragging rights? Jem rolled her eyes.

The lieutenant chuckled. "I second that. My money's on you. Those snooty *specials* need taught a lesson." She winked. "For their own good, of course."

Jem laughed and left with a light step. Midgard had changed her life in so many ways. And now her new home was wrapping itself around her protectively. She would give whatever assistance it needed. As for the others? Let them play their games. She'd show them how it was really played.

***

Jem spied a familiar face lounging at the bottom of the escalator as she rode it down to the main Azusa airport concourse. There were a number of reasons why Agent Reis would be here. Maybe meeting a relative or another agent? That hope died when he fell in step beside her.

"How was your flight from Odinheim? I heard there was a bit of weather on your route."

"A bit of turbulence. Nothing the pilots couldn't handle," Jem replied politely, continuing on toward the exit. "It's following behind us and will probably be here by midnight."

"I'll ensure my windows are closed. A business trip?"

"Yes." Interesting. They knew she'd left though not why.

Walking out into Midgard's twilight, she moved away from the main pedestrian traffic and halted. Turned. "Why are you here, Agent Reis?"

"A couple of agents have some questions they want to ask you. I was tasked to request your presence at our office tomorrow."

Jem studied him for a moment. "Do I need to bring a lawyer?"

"If you will feel more comfortable, yes, but this is only a question-and-answer session."

"Then what's got a burr up your britches?" If the man got any stiffer, his back would snap.

"Will 0900 be suitable?" he asked, stone-faced.

"Yes. I'll be there."

He gave a curt nod, strode to the curb, and climbed into the car Gaines had pulled up in. Gaines shot her an unfriendly look out the driver's window before pulling away.

***

Jem greeted Seth Sullivan outside the Federal Law Enforcement Center early the next morning, "Seth. How's the law firm working?" The family law firm of Stohlass & Sullivan had been in business for several months now. She'd called them as soon as she'd reached her apartment.

"It's going great," he said, giving her a huge smile. "In fact, we'll be upgrading the name soon. One of Jane's brothers-in-law wants to come in with us."

"*Ooooo*. Witt, Stohlass & Sullivan has a nice ring."

Seth laughed. "Granddad would have a fit if we voted that in. Last come, last mentioned. Granddad had some unpleasant business to deal with this morning and couldn't be here. In fact," he rubbed his nose. "Granddad has asked me to take primary on anything you need."

Jem tilted her head. "Are you okay with that? I heard tell you got pretty angry on Tigres." Worried about future legal ramifications for both her and the Stohlass family, he'd wanted to know everything Boyd and Thane knew about her. They'd refused.

He studied her for a moment. "My cousin says there's a reason for all the secrets. I have to trust him. I also trust you'll give me advance notice of any incoming."

Trust, trust, trust. Dammit, she needed to do better. "I'll do my best. As for today, I have no clue as to why or who wants to talk to me."

"Then let's go find out."

Building security vetted them. The ground floor lobby receptionist vetted them.

When the twelfth-floor receptionist demanded ID, Seth looked at the woman and said coldly, "We have been identified in more ways than I've ever experienced. You were undoubtedly notified of our presence as soon as we entered the building. If this bullshit is intended as an intimidation tactic, it's failed. If it's a delay tactic while they deal with other matters, call me to reschedule. My client and I are leaving. Come, Jem."

They didn't make it three steps before a door popped open and Reis stepped out.

"That won't be necessary. Come this way, please."

The neutrality of his voice and expression was briefly marred by the flash of a smile. Hah. They had tweaked someone's nose and Reis was enjoying it. They followed him down a short corridor and into a conference room. Three men waited within.

Reis motioned to the man sitting at the head of the table. "Mr. Sullivan, Miss Wilmont. May I present my boss, Director James Vanderbilt of Oslo's Western Federal Law Enforcement Division."

Dark hair, dark eyes, dark expression. *What a sourpuss.* It was his nose they'd bent.

"And these are Federal Agent Irvin Feyerherm and Security Specialist Chris Rutherford…both of Westmoreland, Jaguide Three."

Seth had to have felt her muscles tighten. His hand was on her arm, directing her to one of the chairs opposite the two men. He didn't even glance at her until they were both seated. Then it was a veiled, we-are-so-going-to-talk look. A minuscule lift of her shoulders was the only apology she could offer at the moment.

Shit, damn, crap. They can't know, not for sure. The worst she'd expected was someone paying her a quiet, unofficial visit to air their suspicions. This was as official as it could get. No way was this going to end well.

"Dismissed, Agent Reis," Vanderbilt said curtly.

In the process of sitting, Reis froze. His jaw flexed but he said *yes, sir* and left.

Apparently Vanderbilt was the burr in Reis's pants.

"Before this goes any further," Seth said to Vanderbilt, "I want to know why you are here and just dismissed a regular field agent. The FLEA Director doesn't normally deal with cases personally."

"This isn't a normal situation. The nature of our guests' information is both serious and sensitive."

Seth raised an eyebrow. "You don't trust your own people?"

"There are a few agents whose choices and associations I find questionable. I will be overseeing these men's investigation while they're here."

Jem's lips did an involuntary curl at Vanderbilt. Just what did he have against Reis?

Agent Feyerherm asked, a bit impatiently, if they could begin. "Thank you. Miss Wilmont, a number of reports indicate you have the means to bypass security measures all the way up to, and including, level seven. You have even successfully navigated extremely well-crafted military countermeasures."

Major Markowitz's report was certainly getting around.

"We have been unable to ascertain, from any source, what methods you utilize. Methods that by their very nature are perfect for committing various crimes, especially theft."

"Do you abuse your badge? Bullying others and throwing your Federal weight around?" Feyerherm stiffened. "Simply because something can be done doesn't mean it will be. Yes, I can be stealthy, Agent Feyerherm. But, like you, I do not abuse that potential. I have been approached and offered a various assortment of…" she pursed her lips, "opportunities, especially theft. You'll be happy to hear I've turned them down." Except for the one she couldn't.

"How do you explain the exponential growth of your Earth bank account, which you've since transferred to Midgard?"

"She doesn't have to," Seth responded smoothly. "That is classified under Federal statutes."

Both men shot Vanderbilt a surprised look.

"A classified meeting was held on Midgard last year that included Midgard LE and military representatives, Earth LE, Wilmont and her lawyers," Vanderbilt said. "I'd send you a copy except even I can't get one."

Was that his problem? His underlings were privy to something he wasn't?

"Why were you, a supposed drifter, included in what appears to have been a high-powered meeting?" Rutherford asked, speaking for the first time.

"I had information pertinent to the topics being discussed."

"Are you an undercover Federal agent or informant?" Feyerherm asked sharply.

"No."

"Was that information garnered by clandestine or illegal means?"

Jem did not like Rutherford's tone. "By overheard conversations and/or personal experience."

"Spying," Rutherford said, flashing her a smug smile. "Which means you *have* performed illegal acts."

Jaw set and side-stepping the issue, she said, "Can you turn off your hearing? Haven't you overheard conversations when sitting at a bar? Walking down a hallway? Urinating in the men's room? Just *being* somewhere isn't illegal."

"Depends on where you're at and whether or not you're supposed to be there," Rutherford tossed back.

"Is that what you are afraid of, gentlemen? That my client will be somewhere she isn't supposed to be?"

"No. We think she already has been," Rutherford said.

Jem hoped her new and improved poker face was working. "Where?"

"The Jaguide Crystal Repository on Westmoreland. A number of crystals of varying size and condition were taken from there."

Jem angled her head. "From my understanding, the Repository's security measures are on an entirely different scale from most security arrangements. Impossible to breach."

Rutherford pounced. "So, you're familiar with the Repository's security measures?"

Jem couldn't help it, her eyes practically rolled on their own. "A lot of it's been released as general knowledge. Part bragging and part warning, I assume. You might want to know that one of those job offerings I mentioned came complete with not-so-general details about your security." Had the guy gotten the information from the same place Beckett had? "It's not as tight as you believe." Rutherford flushed. "I will also state, categorically, I do not have any J-crystals in my possession."

They were all sold.

Seth tilted forward. "From *my* understanding, that's an enormous vault containing tens of thousands of crystals at any one time. How can you even be sure that 'a number' are missing? Do you actually count them? What is your proof that one, there's been a theft, two, my client may be responsible, and three, justifies you tracking my client's financial accounts?"

"We can determine which crystals originated from what mine," Rutherford said. "We've traced nineteen questionable sales so far. Eight of them were raw Jaguide Four stones that could only have come from the Repository vault as the mine itself was sealed after their removal. We're assuming the remaining crystals were also stolen from there by the same thieves."

Well, Kaleb did warn me.

"Investigation has found polished crystals have been sold by both a man and a woman. That same woman—blue-eyed, fair-skinned, average-height— sold *all* the raw J-4 stones."

Seth's expression morphed into disbelief. "That's your best description? Do you know how many women that describes?"

"She's hidden her eyes with contacts before," Feyerherm said. "There's no physical or electronic trace of an intrusion. She's called 'the Ghost' for that exact reason. It had to be her."

"You're basing your accusations solely on someone's gossip-fueled reputation?" Seth's voice vibrated with incredulity. "Gentlemen, unless you have something that's even close to approaching proof that my client is responsible for the missing crystals or their sale, this meeting is over."

"It's over when I say it is."

Both their heads snapped around to Vanderbilt.

"Reis said this was a question-answer, not a frigging inquisition," Jem said.

"It's whatever I make it."

Of all the—She opened her mouth, closed it when Seth's hand rested on her arm.

"Director Vanderbilt, you are about to create a very embarrassing situation for your department and you personally," Seth told him coldly. "My client came willingly to answer questions—which she has. This is a farce of an interrogation about something for which these men have no shred of proof to back their accusations. If you try to detain Miss Wilmont solely based on these men's desperate grasp for a resolution, you will end up more than embarrassed.

"And I want it stated for the record—I'm sure this meeting is being recorded although you weren't polite enough to mention it—Miss Wilmont is highly respected in many circles, including the military, for *not* using her knowledge and capability for ill or personal gain."

"Then explain that Earth bank account," Rutherford shot back.

Ignoring him, Seth stood and motioned for Jem to join him. "Any further requests for interviews or verbal beatings are to be made through my office."

Jem grinned at him when they reached the sidewalk. "Verbal beatings? I liked that."

"Good. You're about to get one. My office. Now."

Resigned, Jem followed him to his car. He had a right to be furious. The drive to his office was made in silence, which thickened as the elevator whisked them to the fifth floor.

"Please hold any calls, Liana," he told the middle-aged receptionist in passing.

Seth closed his office door behind them, tossed his briefcase onto a couch, and dropped into the chair behind his desk.

"I'm sorry. I honestly had no idea." Jem paced in front of the desk. She wished Kaleb's warning had come sooner and with maybe a few more specifics. "Reis didn't say anything about off-planet visitors."

"You did it. The Jaguide Repository." Seth's tone was scathing.

"Yes."

"Why? You certainly didn't need the money."

She stopped in front of him. "Azusa."

"What?"

Guess Andi hadn't said anything. "Beckett promised to drop a Delgado on Azusa if I didn't. He wasn't bluffing." Not after killing hundreds in a hotel fire. Not after immolating over two million on a planet he'd scorched with three of the highly destructive bombs.

Seth's hot glare melted into hardened determination. "That's why Beckett had you kidnapped." No need to make it a question.

She nodded, sliding into a chair. "The Jaguide System is too well defended for brute force. He needed sneaky."

"How many crystals and what happened to them?"

"A backpack full?" She received a very unimpressed look. "Forty-seven total, with seventeen of them raw stones. I ended up with twenty-six, twelve being the raw ones."

"You didn't try to return them?"

Jem gave a humorless laugh, then described the tumultuous events on the *Hidden Trove*. The greed and deaths. The surprising honor of two whose names she refused to say. "I divvied up the crystals between the two of them, as agreed. The pilot, who had been forcefully conscripted from Kurzvall's shipyard, kept only one of his. The rest were donated on my promise to use them to help others."

Seth crossed his arms. "Legally, the crystals weren't theirs to donate."

Jem gave him a level look. "It was a complicated situation and I'd given my word. I established the Hands of Hope Foundation and every one of those crystals were used to fund it. Hop—the pilot specified helping the Magnus survivors in rebuilding their world. The Foundation is currently doing just that."

"Is Reyna aware of all that?"

"No." Jem shot Seth a sour look. "I expected the black market sales to eventually get the Jaguide authorities' attention, but I figured they wouldn't be able to pinpoint where they came from. Those J-4 stones kind of screwed that up."

Seth took several minutes to mull it all over. Jem could almost see his brain whirling.

"We can work with this. You've not profited personally and, in fact, that money is being used for good. Beckett's obviously not said anything yet. Does he know how you—okay, that's good. *Hmmm*. He's probably holding onto the theft information to make some sort of deal."

"Think he might try to negotiate his freedom with it?" Jem asked. She'd worried about that since his arrest.

"Got news for him. The best deal he's going to get for *anything* is a softer bed. No way is he ever going to see the outside of a cell again. Although, he could attempt to blackmail you into freeing him by threatening exposure of your theft."

Jem's chin came up and she said firmly, "As your family would say, 'I'll raft those rapids when I have to.' I will not let that monster loose on the universe."

"Good. Let's preempt him." He leaned forward. "The Jaguide authorities obviously want to keep this quiet. We admit to them—under a privacy seal—that you did it and why. Any idiot trying to prosecute you under those extenuating circumstances would probably have his license revoked."

"No. They'll hound me…demand to know how I breached their security."

"Can you blame them? You did something that, theoretically, was impossible. Naturally they're going to want to know how, so as to prevent any future repeats."

Jem remained silent.

Seth huffed out a breath. "You know, I got the same silent treatment from Thane and Boyd. I realize—and agree—your 'secret' should be kept out of the wrong hands. But the limits you three are willing to go to? What is so special, so *critical*, about what you can do?"

Jem crossed her arms. Impulsively she said, "You tell me," and shifted.

He stared at what to him must be an empty chair. He cleared his throat. "That's…impressive."

Surprised at the calm reaction, she rematerialized.

"Very impressive. I didn't even see you activate it. It's along your arm somewhere, right? Where did you get it? How does it work? Andi would love to see it."

She blinked. Oh. He thought… Jem held both hands up, palms out. She graced him with one of her slow fades into invisibility for a full ghostly effect.

Held it for a moment, then *poofed* back. She wiggled her fingers at him, lowered her hands, and simply said, "No device."

Silence.

It continued to lengthen as he stared, wide-eyed and slack-jawed. Finally, without taking his attention off her, Seth reached over and activated his intercom. "Liana? Would you retrieve that bottle of whisky Granddad's got squirreled away in his desk? Thanks."

Chapter 25

Jem relaxed on a park bench. Eyes closed, her face turned upward to soak in the sun's warmth. The abundance of green spaces was one of the best things about Azusa. They were scattered throughout the city in various sizes. She'd made a beeline for this one immediately after leaving Seth's office, three blocks away.

After a half hour and two shots of whisky, Seth knew as much about her as Thane and Boyd did. Which meant, she sighed inwardly, not everything. She was simply delaying the inevitable, and her insides twisted at the thought of others having that last bit of knowledge. How long could she keep it to only the invisibility aspect? The first time she phased through a wall, once they fully realized the ramifications…complicated wouldn't begin to describe it.

Would she become the Republic's freak?

Would she become the target of the Republic's criminals? Of Law Enforcement?

She ignored the person sitting down on the other end until he said, "I know you did it."

Seth had spent the last fifteen minutes arguing for admitting to her deed, promising to have some kind of agreement drawn up where they would leave her alone. Jem had flat refused. She'd argued back that even if he could get the officials to agree to and sign that document, others would ignore it. Unofficially, of course.

The way Security Specialist Rutherford was now.

"No, you don't," Jem said, not bothering to open her eyes. "You and Agent Feyerherm are on a fishing trip. You're grabbing at anything that looks possible, as my lawyer said. I believe he also stated future contact should go through him."

"You're hiding behind legalese bullshit. He'll do and say anything for whatever large amount you're paying him. Maybe you pay him in other ways. How many cases has he won after you provided otherwise unavailable information about his opponents?"

Rutherford just nose-dived into her shit pile.

"You're the only one with the skills to have done it."

"Are you sure?" Jem turned an angry, derisive look on him. "Maybe there's someone else out there who's well versed in stealth. After all, knowledge about me was unknown until it was blasted across the Republic a year ago. If you don't know how it was accomplished, how do you know what skills were used? How do you know mine are even good enough to infiltrate the Repository?"

Doubt showed briefly in his face before it hardened again.

"Do you even know *when* the theft occurred?"

"Sometime between when the cargo bin arrived at the Repository and the first raw stone was sold."

What a snot. "Go home, Mr. Rutherford. Look for your answers there." She resumed her sun-worshiping posture.

The bench creaked as he stood. "I'll find the proof."

His footsteps crunched off down the path.

Jem gazed in the direction Rutherford had gone. The man was relentless and he'd set his sights on her. He was going to be trouble. He'd already ruined her afternoon. She might as well head home.

***

Jem was unlocking her door when her phone rang. It was Andi's number.

"Jem? Are you home?"

"Yes. What—"

"You got any of Thane's whisky available?"

"Sure. What—"

"I'll be there in twenty minutes." The call disconnected.

Okaaay, someone else was having a bad day. Jem checked her cabinet and found two bottles of Pounding J's Aspric whisky. She'd divided most of the case Boyd sent her among Thane's family members. Would Jansom be offended if she had it relabeled? They kept referring to it as 'Thane's whisky.' True, he had brought home the first bottles.

Jem met Andi at the door with a ready glass. Andi had it half gone before she got the door closed. Jem gaped pop-eyed as the woman flung herself into a chair and drained the remainder. What in the universe had happened?

"Andi? Want me to hand you the bottle?" Jem waggled it as she settled across from her friend.

"Maybe later." Andi held out her glass. "Katherine Baron showed up at the house this morning."

Jem winced. That was why Gordon hadn't made this morning's meeting? Unpleasant, indeed. She made a mental note to send a whisky reorder to Boyd. They'd need several cases. Filling both their glasses, she set the bottle on the table between them. "No prior notice?"

Andi shook her head. "None. First thing she complained about was nobody meeting her at the Odinheim spaceport and having to make all the travel arrangements to here."

"She should have sent warning—I mean word."

Andi snorted out a laugh. "That's what Grandmother told the bitch. Then Grandmother added that she evidently didn't have any problem getting from Milania to Midgard. The bitch just wanted to bitch. Besides, the bitch wouldn't be the one doing it—her aide undoubtedly handled all the details for the bitch, both to Midgard and Azusa."

That was a lot of bitches. "Aide?"

"Oh, yeah. She's got an aide named something-Carpenter. The woman looks competent. Nick is sure she's had military training, so maybe, she's part bodyguard, too. Anyway, the bitch then complained about GG not having ready a list of available sites for her to 'evaluate.'" Her air quotes were followed by a large swallow of whisky. "Complete with footage, amenities, price—you name it. Granddad said that was what she was here to do.

"Then Katherine Baron—I can't stand calling her that. Baron is Thane's name. I usually call her a bitch, but that's her grandmother, too. Got to find some way to keep them apart. Big and little bitch?"

Andi had really taken a dislike to the woman. Jem gave her friend a wicked grin. "Helga Baron is grand-bitch. Why not make her cousin-bitch?"

Andi's face lit up. "Cuz-bitch it is. Cuz-bitch then complained about Thane not being here. She expects him to accompany her, daily, so she can instruct him on what it takes to be a proper CEO and a *proper* Baron."

Jem stared, speechless. "How fast did that wheelchair get rammed out the door?"

"Not fast enough. When Granddad stepped forward, Nick said Carpenter assumed a guard stance, whatever that is. He should know, hence the bodyguard assumption."

"The woman isn't even trying. Unless it's trying to get everything canceled."

"I'll place a large bet on that. To rile things up even more, she started making demands. Appointments with local realtors, introductions to appropriately influential community leaders, and a twenty-six-hour security detail lead by Nick himself for her entire stay."

Jem was boiling mad now. The woman's audacity knew no bounds. She was even worse than Kurzvall.

"Well, cuz-bitch miscalculated." Andi's expression took on a predatory gleam. "GG is not about to let some self-entitled, antagonistic crude piece of trash run over them. Granddad informed her that realtors were listed on the Azusa Community Network, as well as several security firms. And if her aide was incapable of handling it, there were agencies listed for that, too. Best part coming up," Andi said, taking another swallow.

"Grandmother laid into her, telling her there were two reasons she'd not be introducing anyone. The first—and I loved this—was that *they* would be handling things after the Midgard BF office is established and *they* already had good community relations, so *she* was inconsequential."

"Oh, that was a good shot. She turn purple?"

"Reddish-purple. Secondly, Grandmother refused to introduce friends and associates to such a…" Andi's nose wrinkled. "Unfortunately, she paused there or I would have learned some new insults. She finished with 'a rude child.'"

Jem leaned forward and held her glass up. Andi bumped hers against it. Then it was bottoms-up. Jem refilled their glasses. "That's great. Although, the aide probably didn't deserve to be insulted, even indirectly."

Andi shrugged. "She knew by interview's end what kind of person her employer would be. Carpenter is either getting paid very well or she's a masochist. I do believe she enjoyed seeing her boss get slapped down. I spotted an odd sort-of-smile on her face when they were leaving."

"Which was immediately after the rude child comment?"

"You bet. Cuz-bitch whipped that chair around so fast she nearly knocked the aide down."

They laughed and drank, trying to see who could come up with the best unflattering description of either BF Baron.

Andi waved an empty glass "Oh, Granddad said something about you and Seth being interviewed by fleas this morning. How'd that go?"

Jem giggled at Andi's unflattering pronouncement of the Fed's acronym. *Giggling?* "About as well as your meeting with cuz-bitch."

"What happened?"

Jem scrunched her brow, then realized lying wasn't necessary. "A couple of enforcers from another system have a problem. They have an unsolved theft, don't know who committed it or even how it was done. Therefore, I must have done it."

Yep, she'd have to remember that. She tilted her glass up and finished off the last of it.

Andi rolled her eyes. "You're going to get a lot of that, aren't you?"

Jem shrugged. "Probably. We demanded proof, they didn't have any, and we left. We were blindsided…ambushed would be a better description. Seth was not happy."

"Nope. My big brother hates going into anything unprepared." Her phone rang. She pulled it out, squinted. "I think that's Nick. Hello? Is this Nick? ...I wasn't sure. Sometimes those nines and threes look the same... What? I'm at Jem's place. Jem, say hi." Andi held her phone out.

Jem leaned forward. "Hi, Nicholas. She's had a glass or three of whisky."

Andi pulled the phone back, paused. "Yep, the good stuff. We need to stock up on it. Especially with cuz-bitch in town. It might keep us from killing her. Wait. We could say it's a mercy killing. The whole universe would probably thank us."

Jem could hear his laughter from where she sat.

"What? Wait." Andi pressed her phone against her shoulder. "Nick has to go do something. Is it okay I stay a while longer? Yep," she said into the phone. "I'll be here. Love you." She disconnected, fumbled and dropped her phone. It missed the table. "Well, shit." Andi reached down...and tumbled after it.

Jem started laughing. She fell back on the couch, laughing even harder when Andi's befuddled eyes peered at her over the table top.

Andi maneuvered herself back into the chair, sans phone. "Nick can find it when he gets here. How much is left?"

Jem looked over at the bottle, surprised to see it nearly empty. That explained the giggling. "I think we can squeeze out another shot for both of us."

***

Jem woke the next morning, happy and hungover. When was the last time that had happened? Years. She and Dani used to have similar nights. A sad pang passed through her. Dani had died in the same out-of-control lab experiment that had changed her life. The sharpness of the loss had softened, and it had been months since the nightmare of that day had haunted her.

She smiled and hugged herself. It had to be the new life she was building here, a solid foundation for the goals and dreams she'd once given up as lost. Granted, both were a bit different than she'd once envisioned. A different life would mean different dreams. Right, Mister Universe?

Jem stretched slowly, careful not to jog her head. Andi would be feeling even worse than her this morning since she could claim some tolerance for the strong drink. Still, one and a half bottles of Pounding J's whisky were a bit much. Her head appreciated Nicholas arriving when he did and saving that last half. The man had taken one look, shook his head, and thrown his giggling wife over his shoulder.

He'd also told her…something. Jem's face squinched up as she tried to remember. Something about Gordon. Crap. What was it? After several painful minutes of trying to remember, she decided it was best to just call him. Could she reach without—it wasn't on the nightstand.

After several deep breaths, Jem swung her legs over the side and waited until her head settled before slowly shuffling into the living room. No phone. No phone in the kitchen either. Bathroom? More shuffling. Nope. What in the frigging blue blazes did she do with it?

She shuffled back to the bedroom. Contemplating vague memories, she lowered slowly to her knees, then to a prone position. Yep. She'd kicked it under the bed. Rescuing her phone, she rolled over on to her back and found a waiting text message. It was from Nicholas.

In case you don't remember, Gordon needs to see you as soon as possible. Wait. Better make that, as soon as you're able. (;p)

Did the bird have a text symbol?

A text message pinged. This one was from Gordon, asking her to meet at Seth's office at fourteen hundred. Okay. She could do fourteen hundred. She'd just lay here for a while.

***

Pleasantries exchanged, Gordon said, "Seth has briefed me on what happened yesterday and the underlying issues involved. With Beckett's threat, you really didn't have a choice."

Jem glanced across the desk. Seth's barely perceptible head shake told her what he hadn't shared. *Yay!* Client confidentiality.

"Rutherford requested another meeting this morning," Seth said. "I declined when he couldn't confirm any evidence acquired in the past twenty-six hours."

"Only Rutherford? A dog chewing on a bone," Jem muttered after Seth nodded.

"Unfortunate, but apt," Gordon said. "He's a civilian, so we can't do anything until he steps out of line. Then we can complain to his superiors. I did send a strongly worded message to Director Vanderbilt. Any requests coming through FLEA offices had better have some legitimately based questions and/or concerns in the future. 'It had to be her' is a windless sail."

"So, Rutherford is a wimp noodle?"

Seth coughed a couple of times. Gordon shook his head, unable to completely hide the smile.

"There's undoubtedly a number of LE offices at all levels that would love to use me to clear their caseloads. Post a memo saying 'The Ghost did it. Evidence unobtainable. Case closed.'"

"They want to sweep things under the rug internally? Fine," Seth said. "But they better have a good reason to do so publicly or bring it to our house."

Gordon cleared his throat. "Are there any other items we should be made aware of, Jem?"

Jem thought of how she'd sneaked about Kurzvall's home. On Tardon, she'd sneaked *and* 'rearranged' hidden evidence, making it easy for Enforcers to find what the crooks thought they'd hidden. Did Stromli Four count? Looking up, she saw both lawyers had acquired a pensive look.

"Does sneaking and eavesdropping to help enforcers catch crooks count?" she asked.

"Not in my book," Gordon said.

"Ditto," Seth confirmed.

"Then, no sir. Jaguide Three was my single walk on the dark side."

Both men heaved a visible sigh of relief.

Chapter 26

Thane studied the rundown house carefully. He'd approached on foot, his rental parked a block down the street. His quarry's vehicle was parked in the yard on the side, the driver's window rolled down. The man's rental company was going to be pissed as it was currently drizzling an icy-mush mixture.

He circled the house. The back porch contained one chair, three humongous, dirt-filled pots with long dead bushes, and a back door. No footprints in the mush. He chanced a quick look in a darkened window. A kitchen, its counters buried under stuff. He wedged the three pots against the door and continued on around to the front door. A light filtered through the tall, narrow, and very grimy window beside the door.

He knocked. A face appeared in the window. "John Rudd Albright?"

The face disappeared to the tune of running footsteps. Thane pulled his stunner out, shouldering the door open and giving chase, confident he'd get to him before Albright could get past the blocked door.

A screaming maniac dropped on his back as he passed a staircase.

"Don't touch my brother! Don't touch my brother!"

Thane staggered, dropped, his arms breaking his fall and his weapon flying somewhere. Caught between two opponents in a narrow hallway was bad. Then bad went to worse when the maniac plunged a knife into his shoulder.

Adrenaline surging, he reared up and twisted, slinging the knifer off. Albright was racing back, swinging a rolling pin. Thane dropped back to hands and knees as it whizzed overhead, Albright grunting with exertion when it slammed into the wall. Thane gathered himself and launched headfirst into Albright's groin. They both went down, Albright on the bottom. Thane immediately heaved himself to his feet, felt a slash in his right arm as he whipped around.

He's naked!

Thane blocked the nudist's next attempt with his arm and punched him in the jaw, knocking him back several steps. It gave Thane enough room to bring up a kick that sent him sprawling back down the hallway. Thane's gaze ricocheted. Searching.

Stunner. Where. *There*. Thane raced toward the kitchen, snapped it up—

"You're dead, dead, dead!"

—wheeled around.

"Dead, d—" The maniac collapsed mid-scream, his knife clattering on the floor. His brother lurched to his feet, obscenities spewing. Thane stunned him, too. Simpler, easier. No fuss.

Panting, blood dripping, shoulder throbbing, he stared at the two men on the floor. Well, shit. There had been nothing in Albright's file about a brother, much less a maniacal twin. Disgust flared and he kicked the small pocket knife away. Disgust for the moron that gave him an incomplete file. Disgust at his own arrogance and carelessness. A first-year trainee would have proceeded with more caution, would have verified his quarry was alone in the house.

Old Man Gundersen would be smacking him over the head with the Tracker's Manual if he'd been alive. If there were a manual. Hell, maybe he ought to write one. It might remind him of how he was supposed to act.

What in the frigging hell was wrong with him? Taking a risk like this? This was unacceptable. It was as if...his thoughts froze as the shocking truth hit him. Tonight's fiasco. Nearly getting rundown by a quarry on Tarus Three. Chasing another one—without backup—into the middle of an armed family compound on Hanmark One. Would getting hurt, or worse, bring back Wilson? Erik's leg?

He sank back against a counter, exhaustion hitting hard. The combination of blood loss and adrenaline withdrawal wasn't helping either. He holstered his weapon and rubbed a hand across his neck, his shoulder expressing its unhappiness at both movements. If he wanted to atone, this wasn't it. He needed to catch the SOB responsible for the attacks. Which meant it was time to go home. Time to start hunting logically and professionally instead of bouncing all over the Republic and expecting his nemesis to face him honorably.

He looked over at the twins. The local Enforcers were going to love this. They could have the naked maniac. Albright the First was headed back to Kettleman. Right after he visited a MedCenter. At least he'd only need to favor one side for a while. Thane reached for his—where was his phone?

He found it. Underneath the naked guy's—*ugh*.

Gingerly rolling the guy over, he retrieved it and dialed the universal emergency number.

Chapter 27

Jem gave Andi a wave as the woman left the restaurant for home and her computer. Her friend had been contracted to design a new engine for some local company. At six-feet-two-inches and built like a Valkyrie goddess, Andi didn't have the look of a mechanical-genius. Didn't act like some stuffy genius either, for which Jem was grateful. She looked out the window next to her. A light drizzle had sprung up after they'd docked, keeping them from enjoying their usual veranda table.

At least the lessons were over.

Andi and Nicholas had helped her pick out a nice cabin cruiser. It was medium length with both engine and sail capability. Andi had been determined she understood all the ins-and-outs and techniques of sailing. For two whole days. While Jem knew it certainly behooved her to know the how-to, if the engine was operational, she was motoring.

She was bored. As soon as the excavation team finished up a couple of requests she'd made that weren't on the blueprints, she'd be going over the next stage with Mr. Nielson. That included installing wind turbines and running power lines into the generator room. Its winds were Midgard's primary energy source, as it was a rare day there wasn't a breeze of some kind. With her wind pylons catching the sea breeze on the ridge top, she wouldn't need tall ones. In fact, they were to be discreetly hidden among the trees. Which meant she needed to decide on one of the two generator models Mr. Nielson had recommended.

So bored. She was tempted to pull out her Sadie Longstrate ID and eye contacts and go drifting. Work a few bar jobs…find another criminal boss to expose. It was her worry for Thane stopping her. Andi had told her he would be home in six, seven days. They had no leads, no idea who or why he'd been targeted. Worse still, if and when there'd be another attempt. Especially now that he was taking a break and remaining on Midgard. Thor, his ship's comp brain, would send the "Unavailable" response to all job inquiries until further notice.

So very bored. Which was why she was sitting here, waiting to see what their watcher would do. Andi had unobtrusively pointed out the blond-haired woman sitting across the restaurant and half hid behind one of the room's fancy pilings. Jem had felt her watchful gaze on-and-off while they ate. Was Katherine Baron's aide between tasks or finally getting a day off? According to Gordon and Gwen, the woman had been kept busy since their arrival two weeks ago. Appointments with realtors, previewing sites, driving her boss to view 'possible' sites and a few outings to eat.

According to Nicholas, they'd made no arrangements with any of the local security firms. He'd checked. Which had Andi steaming. Katherine Baron had intended to use the Stohlass Security Chief as a pawn in her throw-me-off-the-planet campaign.

Ah! She was coming this way.

"Hello. May I join you? I'm Ahrymani Carpenter."

Jem motioned with her hand. "Did you finally get a day off?"

"Half a day," she said, taking the seat opposite Jem. "Thought I'd stop in for a quick bite. I was wondering, will Mr. Baron be returning soon?"

"If you had come over after finishing your meal, you could have asked Andi before she left." The woman's left brow twitched. *Yes, we saw you.*

"Yes, well, my employer, and by extension me, isn't very welcome. I thought, as a friend of the family, you'd know."

Jem had to give the woman credit for not making the innuendo she normally got. Still, she erred on the side of caution. "I understand he'll be returning home after he finishes his current job."

"Good. Ms. Williams has taken point in his absence and they…don't get along very well."

Jem grinned. Thane's grandmother wasn't taking any of Katherine Baron's attitude. "You mean they butt heads."

Carpenter nodded. "Hard and often. With him taking over the negotiations, hopefully things will improve and—I take it by that stare it's not?"

"No. Thane is good with middle-level management, such as his Tracker business. He is totally out of his depth at the corporate high-end and is not about to jump into it unprepared." Or at all, if he could help it. "His grandmother, if you don't already know, built and ran the Stohlass family business until his uncle took over as CEO a few years back. She or his Uncle Erik will remain at the forefront…at least until things are settled."

"I see."

The woman appeared to be contemplating future head-butting, yet Jem's internal radar stirred. Why did she have the feeling she was being evaluated? Assessed?

"Thank you for the information. Perhaps we can meet after Miss Baron and I return."

"Oh? You're heading back to New Zagreb?"

"Not yet, although Miss Baron is anxious to do so. Rumors about a possible realignment already have some investors moving their assets elsewhere. Almost twenty percent so far, I hear. She is undecided whether to remain with Baron Financials or start up her own finance company with those who are pulling out of BF." That last was accompanied by a condescending smile.

The stirring became a tingle. The woman was being awful free with information.

"Maybe Miss Baron should be a bit more cooperative with Miss Williams. From what I've heard, your employer seems to go out of her way to antagonize the Stohlass family."

"Is she? Maybe you've only heard one side."

And her BS meter just pegged. "Perhaps."

Their gazes locked for a second. Both smiled. Neither was fooled.

"So, then, the two of you are taking a vacation?"

"No. Miss Baron wishes to scout out some properties in Odinheim. She believes Baron Financials will be better situated there. Being Midgard's capital, it has larger, more diversified resources and population." Carpenter rose. "Guess I better get back to work. I need to make our travel and accommodation arrangements."

Jem's thoughts churned as she watched the woman walk away. Absently, she noted her odd step as Carpenter turned a corner. What had been the woman's true agenda? The poke about BF's loss of clients and Katherine's plans? About Odinheim? Since Andi hadn't said anything, she was guessing they didn't know. One thing for sure, whatever Katherine Baron was plotting, her aide was fully onboard with it. Why? What was in it for her? A fat bonus?

Well, that took care of the boredom.

And if she wants me to light the fireworks, glad to oblige. That way she'd be there when Gordon and Gwen heard the news.

***

Jem was mildly disappointed at the lack of any fireworks.

Gwen merely shrugged. "I'd be ecstatic to expedite that woman off Midgard. For someone in a hurry to leave, she's certainly going about it the wrong way. We have final say on any real estate. She also knows we intend to anchor Baron Financials in Azusa and it's too early to look for additional branch offices."

"We expected some loss in clientele," Erik said thoughtfully, "although twenty percent is a bit high. We'll recoup it with the gains here on Midgard and elsewhere once the new, improved, and restructured Baron Financials goes operational."

"Think Katherine could be the rumors' source?" Gwen said, her irritation plain. "Trying to destabilize the company to where Helga Baron has to postpone things?"

Erik shrugged. "I wouldn't put it past her. It would give her more time to try and change her aunt's mind on everything."

"Are others aware Katherine Baron isn't authorized to sign any papers here?" Jem asked. "What if, as a *representative* of Baron Financials, she signs a lease, or an actual purchase, that the other party signed in good faith? She *is* a VP of the current company. Would it be valid?"

Everyone looked at Gordon.

"That is an excellent question. Helga Baron agreed we had final say on location and her niece has to know that. Unfortunately, we didn't get it in writing. So…it would be binding." He tapped his desktop. "Unless the other signee agrees to void the document, we'd have to argue it in court on the premise she wasn't authorized and knew it. We probably would get a favorable ruling. Eventually. In the meantime—"

"Everything else is at a standstill," Gwen interjected. "That damn woman. She intends to make this as miserable as possible. Erik, you and I need to make some calls to Odinheim. Gordon, would you send a message to see if the grand-bitch has changed her standing?"

Okay, Jem thought with a grin, she did get a small sizzle and *pop*.

Chapter 28

"I'll meet you onboard," Dane Stohlass said, stopping at the dock office. "I need to go in and give Jenny a hand. That new customer is an obnoxious pain. Besides some ridiculous complaints, he now insists on only discussing it with 'upper management.'"

Dan, his first mate, grimaced. "Better you than me. I'd drop him."

"Believe me, I'm considering it. We don't need his account."

"I meant to the floor," Dan said drily.

Dane hesitated, then shook his head ruefully. "Unfortunately, he's a not-distant-enough cousin of the Witt family. I shouldn't be too long." He glanced at the sun peeking over the horizon. He'd much rather be boarding the *Witt Three* with his crew, the ship he captained for his wife's family's fishing fleet. This obnoxious idiot would make them late leaving port.

Instead, he turned into the office as Dan headed toward their boat.

Witt Three pulled away from the dock thirty minutes later.

Halfway across the harbor, it exploded in a ball of fire.

* * * * *

Jane Stohlass took her usual route along the coastal highway. Her mind half on the scenic cliff road, the rest on the pile of paperwork waiting for her at work. Strange, she mused. It was still called that, despite almost all of it was digital files on her computer. She spared a quick look to her right. The sun sat on the horizon. *Witt One*, her husband's boat, would be preparing to drop nets somewhere. Her brother's boat, too.

It was going to be a beautiful day. She loved living on Copenhagen with its wild, rugged beauty. She lowered the passenger window to better hear the ocean's lyrical heartbeat pounding some distance below her.

She noted the heavy-duty work truck behind her accelerating to pass.

Hmmm. Maybe I can get away early enough to take the twins to—

The truck slammed into the left side of her vehicle.

* * * * *

Susi Taft sighed and leaned against her husband's desk. "Is there anything worse than *three* grumpy, sleep-deprived, teething toddlers?"

Her husband ran a hand up her arm. "How about a triple dose of teenage antics?" He laughed, she grimaced. His comp signaled an incoming vid-call. "My nine-thirty appointment is right on time." He gave her a quick kiss and settled into his chair.

Susi started for the door. Behind her a female voice inquired, "Cliff Stohlass?"

"Yes. And you—"

The wall behind them exploded inward.

* * * * *

Seth Sullivan exited the parking garage and walked briskly down the sidewalk, his brain already turning toward work. He needed to review his notes for the two clients coming in this morning. It was still early and the sidewalk wasn't crowded, so he was mildly annoyed when a woman bumped into him. And traveled on without an apology. *No manners a'tall*, as his mother would say. He suddenly became aware of a throbbing pain in his side. Surely he wasn't that badly out of shape. It'd been—he nearly doubled over as the pain blossomed into a burning fire.

He pressed his hand against it. Warm. Wet. Pulling his hand back, it bore bright red streaks. He didn't realize he was swaying until a man grabbed his arm.

"Sir? Are you alright?"

Seth blinked at him. That was a dumb question. "I'm bleeding." Then he was sitting on the ground, the man pulling up his shirt.

"My husband is calling the medics. I'm a doctor and you've got a nasty stab wound between your lower ribs."

Stab wound? "Woman. Bumped into me." Fire spread along his ribs. "It burns. Bad," he managed to say before blackness took him.

* * * * *

She leaned against the alley's recycle bin in her borrowed mechanic's coverall and cap, a rag dangling from a pocket. Waiting silent and unmoving as she'd been trained, her nose crinkled at the fumes wafting from the nearby garbage bin. This was risky, a block away from the airport and its constant traffic. But her shuttle to Swansea left in forty-five minutes and there was one last task to complete. Besides, the background noise was kind of comforting with engines revving or throttling down. She missed flying. Once this mission was done and Katherine's inheritance assured, a huge chunk of credits was putting her back in a pilot's chair.

She straightened when her hapless accomplice turned into the alley, a travel bag in one hand. The man she'd hired to do the two assaults on Copenhagen would have melted back into the local population. Even if he was somehow discovered and captured, all he could provide LE with was a masked Patricia Keegan. That old identity of Katherine's was quite handy. Unfortunately for the one she'd hired for here, she couldn't risk him being captured alive.

She glanced around after he reached her before saying, "Katrina Baron is alive."

He shrugged. "You insisted on time, place and method. After watching the news for the past hour, I understand why. And I warned you a four-story fall wasn't always fatal."

"Then maybe you should have been more precise in where she went over. Everything below you was concrete and fast-moving traffic, *except* for a strip less than two meters wide. Where does she land?" Carpenter flipped her hand, palm up.

His eyes narrowed. "Maybe you should have warned me she'd had defensive training. By the time I got a good-enough hold, a couple of would-be heroes were converging on me. I tossed and ran. Her injuries have to be bad so you'll probably still get what you wanted."

The report she'd paid for hadn't detailed any training. The girl must have done so privately with her family's security people. "Can anyone identify you?"

He gave her an irritated look. "I couldn't keep my head tucked under my cap while we wrestled. I knocked people down in the stairwell, which delayed the heroes chasing me long enough to get to the street. So…maybe. From a composite by multiple people."

"It's a good thing you're leaving then." She stepped toward him, pulling a cash card from her pocket. She held it out to him.

"The remainder of your fee. You have your shuttle ticket?" She looked around again.

"Yeah." He activated the card's read-out.

"When you get to the spaceport, go to Cargo Dock Three West."

"Dock 3W," he repeated, looking down.

Fool. Never take your attention off a possible hostile.

Her slender tactical knife was made for one thing and did it extremely well, the blade locked and lethal by the time it reached his skin. He probably had enough time to register the card's zero balance before her knife penetrated the abdominal aorta beneath his sternum. Carpenter shoved his collapsing body between the two bins, a small weeping wound the only sign of his demise. She moved quickly now. Blade swiped clean, knife folded and back in a pocket, along with the empty cash card. Bag tossed onto its owner after a hasty search of his pockets for his initial payment.

She was shoving that card into her pocket as she fast-marched toward the alley's far end. She needed to get out of here before—*shit!* A service door opened ahead of her. A gangly boy of about twelve or thirteen exited with a large bag of trash.

Her hand flexed around the knife.

Chapter 29

The *Lone Tracker* had landed at Azusa's private spaceport. The ship was locked and everything except Thor powered down for an extended stay. Thane started across the ramp, travel bag slung on his shoulder and looking forward to a quiet evening before his extended, nosy family heard he'd arrived two days earlier than he'd told them.

Except that's not going to happen. A grim-faced Nicholas and another guard met him at the entrance to the main concourse. Both wore stunners.

"Nicholas? What's wrong?"

"Roberts. Have Loftus bring the car to the front."

Roberts took off at a fast clip.

Nicholas grabbed Thane by his—fortunately—good arm and began hurrying him through the building. "We managed to keep your arrival quiet. We need to get you out of here before any reporters spot you and start yelling questions."

Thane was almost jogging to keep up with Nicholas's long stride. "Questions about what?"

Nicholas ignored him, continuing to rush him out and to a sedan waiting at the curb.

Roberts held the back door open as Nicholas shoved Thane and himself in. He jumped into the front passenger seat and Loftus sped them away from the reporters rushing toward the car.

"We're going to Azusa Memorial Hospital."

Thane's heart seized. "Who is it? Who's hurt?" His grandmother? Granddad?

Nicholas shook his head. "I'm sorry, Thane. There's no easy way to say this. Jane and Clint are dead. Seth, Susi and Katrina are in the hospital, all badly injured."

Thane stared at him, stunned, his mind a blank.

Nicholas continued. "Jane's car was forced over a fifty-foot cliff. A bomb exploded underneath Clint's office window, which partially caught Susi, and Seth was stabbed by a poisoned blade. Katrina was thrown off the Johann Overpass skywalk. Luckily, she landed in the median strip which was soft and squishy from recent rains."

"When…when did all this happen?"

"This morning…within minutes of each other. Dane is our second stroke of luck. He's alive because he sent his boat on out while he remained behind in the shipping office to deal with an antagonistic customer. Unfortunately, most of his crew were killed when the *Witt Three* exploded."

Thane leaned his head back. He'd thought by staying away he was protecting them.

A hand smacked his leg. "Snap out of it, Thane. Don't even think about this being on you. Even if it is connected, going after you for some reason is one thing. Going deliberately after your family members is a seriously warped mind."

He straightened. "Clint and Susi's kids?"

"Unharmed. Clint's office was on the opposite side of the house. Susi's assistant was with the triplets—she got them out and to the neighbors, who'd already called Emergency Services. Marcus had already left for school. They're all at GG's house now. The estate is locked down. The *family* is locked down."

"Mom! What about Mom?"

"Everything appears to be directed here on Midgard, so we believe she's safe. I've sent Stuart by courier pod. No way am I letting her read this in a message. He'll also be her guard and escort her back, although I expect Lee will be coming too. I've sent someone else to brief Seth's parents and escort them home. I've also sent word to Janice's Command HQ."

No telling when she'd arrive. Clint's oldest daughter commanded a Border Patrol ship. Messages, official or otherwise, wouldn't be received until the ship checked in with headquarters during a planetary stop. Seth's parents owned, managed and often performed in the Valhallass Dance Troupe. The family knew their itinerary in case of… Thane swallowed.

"Katherine Baron called, ranting about *her* safety. Told her—not what I wanted to—she probably didn't have anything to worry about."

Thoughts whirled through Thane's mind until one finally screeched to a halt. He jerked around. "Jem! Has anyone heard from her? Is she on Midgard?"

"Yes, to both. She called Andi shortly after the newscasts started blasting. Gave her condolences and said she'd be in touch. No word since."

Relief flooded him. Given her connection with his family, with the gossipy speculation to him, she would be a prime target. Still might be, and invisibility wouldn't help her if caught off guard.

"Think she'll find the bastard?"

Thane's blank look turned into a feral smile when he understood what Nicholas meant. Jem had gone hunting. "She might be able to flush someone out, but this wasn't a single-person operation." Not with simultaneous events on two continents.

Nicholas nodded and they stared out their respective windows.

*　*　*　*　*

"Welcome to Swansea," the loudspeakers announced cheerfully. "Hotel shuttles are available outside the main airport entrance for those without pre-arranged transportation."

One weary first-class traveler grabbed her single suitcase off the conveyer belt. Halfway down the concourse she rolled it into a bathroom. She ignored the other two women and stepped into a stall. They were gone when she emerged a couple of minutes later.

The weariness vanished, replaced by calculating sharpness and quick movements. A 'Closed for Maintenance" sign was plucked from a corner and set just outside the door.

Ahrymani Carpenter stripped out of her mid-level business suit and black wig. They went into the suitcase, next to the fake boobs and other disguises. Jeans, a previously-purchased Swansea-themed shirt, brown wig with ponytail sticking out a cap, brown contacts, and cheek inserts came out.

Redressing swiftly, Ahrymani studied her appearance. Good. She washed her hands, the sink edges, and did a quick check to ensure nothing was left behind. She put the sign back in place and casually, as benefits a well-rested tourist, she rolled her suitcase down the corridor and into the main airport, where she purchased a ticket to Odinheim with a cash card.

Nothing unusual. Nothing rememberable.

She headed back down the concourse and turned into a small restaurant.

Placing an order for a large salad and tea, she leaned back and evaluated her day. So far, so good. *Except for that fiasco in the alley*, she thought crossly. The coveralls and cap were stuffed in a restroom toilet tank back in Azusa. Any possible DNA should be washed away by now. At least her plans for preventing anyone tracking her were progressing smoothly.

The ticket to Swansea had been purchased several days before she and Katherine left Azusa. An egg-shaped island off the southeast coast of Stockholm, its spas and beaches were popular vacation spots. The geothermal spas were a year-round destination, as they could be enjoyed even when shrouded by fog. Midgard's largest continent was currently experiencing the Southern Hemisphere's winter, so her lack of a tan wouldn't draw any curious attention.

Her flight to Odinheim on Stockholm's west coast left in two hours. Another long, boring shuttle trip. From there she'd take public transportation to Star Town, an hour's ride to the south. After another clothing and disguise change, she'd return to Odinheim via the same public transportation. It'd be after midnight before she got back to Katherine's suite.

Hopefully, the woman had managed to keep her absence unnoticed. It helped that there was no one else in the suite to say she wasn't there. She smiled, remembering Katherine's epic verbal lashing at her personal aide that had resulted in the woman quitting and booking immediate transport home to Milania.

Salad and tea arrived, accompanied by the latest news on the Stohlass family attacks on the large vid-screen against the far wall.

Well, well, look at that. She couldn't have timed it better if she'd tried.

Welcome home, Mister Baron. Sipping from her glass hid Ahrymani's smile.

* * * * *

Thane strode into the ICU waiting room, grim-faced and prepared for the worst. He wasn't prepared to see his grandparents looking so haggard. So *old*.

"Thane!" His grandmother jumped up and they enfolded each other in a tight hug. "You're home."

Granddad gripped his arm. "Good to see you, son. This is a miserable homecoming."

His grandmother stepped back, her hug replaced by one from Gina. *He's going to be okay*, Seth's wife whispered in his ear. He gave her a grim thank-you smile. She patted his arm and returned to her seat. He turned to face the other two people in the room, Clint and Susi's next two oldest kids after Janice.

He took a deep breath. Did they blame him? "How is your mom?"

"Stable," Kevin replied, his hard gaze meeting Thane's. "She has a concussion and they've already started bone regen on her shoulder and collar bone. They're keeping her up here for security reasons. Her parents are with her now."

Good. Keeping everyone in one place made it simpler. Safer. Roberts had joined the Azusa Enforcer posted at the ICU floor's elevator doors. Nicholas himself was currently posted beside this room's doorway. Thane could see the edge of his shoulder.

"Your dad...I'm at a loss. I don't know what to say..." Guilt pounded through him. "I'm going to miss him."

"Say you'll find the bastard that did this," Shiloh spit out.

Thane nodded, unsurprised by the fury that was undoubtedly for Katrina as well as their parents. The two girls had grown up together. They shared ages, attitudes, and a propensity for attracting trouble. They were more sisters than cousins. "Count on it," he promised before turning to his grandparents. He steeled himself and asked, "Kat?"

Gwen gave him a watery smile. "Still in surgery."

Thane let himself be led to a chair and collapsed into it. "How bad?"

He listened numbly as his granddad listed the injuries. Concussion. Punctured lung. So many broken bones. Those were the preliminary? "She will live, right?"

Gordon hesitated, shared a look with his wife, and squared his shoulders. "Your sister is a fighter. If there's a way to come through this, she will."

They weren't sure.

Footsteps rang down the hallway and two older people stepped into the room.

"Kevin, Shiloh, your mom wants to see you," the man said. As the two younger ones hurried past them, his gaze landed on Thane. "You!" He took a step forward. "This is your fault."

Gordon surged up. "Edward. This is a difficult time for all of us. Don't let your emotions make you say something you'll regret later."

"What I regret is letting Susanita marry into your psycho-magnet family."

Gina was suddenly between the two men. "That's enough," she said sharply, pushing Edward backward. "You seemed quite happy when she did. In fact, you have unashamedly mined their social and political connections for years to win and keep your Planetary Representative seat. If you're that bothered by us, we can drop you from the next family reunion list."

There was a dismayed flicker in Susi's parents' faces. Both social climbers knew what that could do to the social and political connections they depended on.

The Stohlass family's three-day reunion was held every few years. Its last night was always an open celebration. Extended family and friends. Business and political relations. Getting an invite was considered a social and political coup. Being excluded? Less accessibility would be the least of it.

"No one here is at fault," Gina continued, anger coating her voice. "No one did anything to deserve this. At least *your* child is alive." She flung her hand out. "*They* have lost *two*." Her hand dropped, the anger replaced by tiredness. "Go home, Edward, Brittany. This is neither the time nor the place for emotional and unwarranted recriminations."

Edward shot them all one final glare before stomping out. His wife hovered for a moment before following.

"Wow, I'm impressed." Thane gave her a wan smile. "You're a match for Seth, all right."

"Who do you think proposed?"

Bursts of laughter provided a much-needed release and dropped the room's tension down to a simmer. They waited. A nurse fetched Gina to take her to Seth's room. They waited some more.

A man entered quietly on soft-soled feet. Sixtyish, green scrubs beneath a white jacket, tired face. A doctor. Everyone surged to their feet.

"Everyone here for Miss Baron? Good. Sit, sit. I certainly intend to." He plopped into a chair and stretched his legs. "That feels good. I'm Doctor Joseph Elser, primary surgeon for Miss Baron. She made it through surgery and is being settled into a room down the hall. I have to say, I don't think I've ever worked on a worse case."

"How bad?" Thane asked, his shoulders tightening His grandparents clasped hands.

"As you're aware, her skeletal structure on the left side took the brunt of her fall due to Miss Baron curling into a fetal position. A basal skull fracture caused intracranial hemorrhaging, which we've relieved and will monitor both concussion and swelling. Multiple broken bones aside, the ribcage fracturing caused serious damage. Her lacerated spleen, left kidney, and appendix—she was a lefty—were removed. The pneumothorax injury to her lung has been repaired, but her breathing is being assisted until the chest region becomes more stable.

"We've aligned and latticed the bones as necessary to hold the pieces in place until we can start bone regeneration treatment. The shearing force on impact caused a spinal lumbar transverse process fracture—which means a couple of disks were forced sideways. The spinal cord itself appears undamaged…as far as we can tell. There's a lot of swelling. That same pressure wave also damaged her ovaries, liver and right kidney, but they're salvageable. She got to keep them," he said, giving a wry grin.

Elser's attempt at levity failed. He cleared his throat.

"Right. Despite all I've just said, the most serious injury is to her left hand. While Miss Baron's fetal position did reduce the damage to her head and neck areas, it also resulted in a double whammy between the terminal impact force and the crushing force between ground and skull. To put it bluntly, it's a well-tenderized piece of flaccid meat."

Thane's teeth clenched. His grandmother's hand flew up and covered her mouth.

"We can rebuild bones but, in this case, her entire cellular and vascular structure from the wrist down is ruptured. Considering the extent of her other injuries, with the potential of infection and tissue necrosis, I seriously doubt the hand is salvageable and I normally would have already performed an amputation. However…" Elser paused, studied them for a moment before continuing.

"I contacted Dr. Aline Giovannelli at the Kontos Medical University. She is the leading small bone specialist, both podiatrist and orthopedic, and is developing a new procedure. She arrived a short time ago and is assessing Miss Baron now. If anyone can save the hand, it will be her." A shushing sound reached them. "I believe that's her now."

A woman rolled into the room and maneuvered her motorized wheelchair next to Doctor Elser. Fortyish looking, she radiated a confidence Thane immediately trusted.

"People, this is Dr. Giovannelli. Doctor, Mr. Stohlass, Ms. William and Mr. Baron."

"Can you save my sister's hand?"

The woman paused, giving each of them an assessing glance. "I can't promise that as the damage is extreme. I do believe there's a chance, although not without risk. The cellular regeneration serum my team has developed is in the experimental stage and there are unexpected issues that occasionally crop up that could be detrimental to her recovery."

Gordon leaned forward. "How detrimental?"

"Considering Miss Baron's overall condition…the loss of her spleen and the additional system stress by bone regeneration? Potentially fatal," she told them. "Therefore, I would need permission from the closest family relative before starting. As her brother, that would be you, Mr. Baron."

Thane gave her a wide-eyed look. "Our mother will be here in a couple of days."

"I'm sorry. The longer we wait to start, the less chance we'll succeed and necrosis will likely set in. Once that happens, amputation will be the only recourse. We need an answer from you tonight."

Weight settled heavily on his shoulders. How do you make that kind of decision? Amputate now? Risk her life for the sake of a hand? Prosthetics weren't uncommon, but they limited one's abilities and flexibility.

"I assure you," Dr. Giovannelli said gently, "she will be monitored constantly. At the first indication the procedure is failing, or that there are adverse side effects, we will immediately discontinue and perform the removal."

Silence as they waited for his answer.

Thane stared at the floor. Debating, arguing with himself. Finally, he took a deep breath and looked up. "My sister would take this as a challenge. Please begin your procedure, but keep us informed."

"Of course. Dr. Elser, I left a file with the necessary authorizations at the OP station. If you would help him with that, I'll change and get started. If you don't mind lending some of your mesh lattice, I'll work on piecing the metacarpals and phalanges together until my team arrives. They're on standby and can be here in two hours with everything else we need. Thank you, Mr. Baron. I'll be in touch."

She gave his grandparents a goodbye wave and wheeled her chair around.

She was over halfway down the hall before the rest of them stepped out of the room. *Wonder what the speed rating on that chair is,* Thane wondered absently.

Chapter 30

Kenneth Brower flipped on the lights and walked with his head enforcer into what he'd always thought of as his unassailable fortress. That belief was proven false by the very large knife pressed under his chin.

"Close the door," the knife's wielder ordered.

Brower glanced sideways into bi-colored eyes as his tense guard complied. Well, shit. Wilmont. The Ghost. If it was a hit from a competitor, he'd be bleeding out by now. He went with bravado.

"If you want a job, you could have made an appointment. Although this is a pretty good demonstration." She ignored him.

"An informant provided the Stohlass family's routines to the assassins. It's the only way those coordinated attacks happened."

He swallowed. "It wasn't me and I didn't authorize any hits against the family." That's about all the newscasters had been reporting on since it first broke yesterday morning.

"I know. You're going to help me find the informant."

"Ah…can we discuss this in a more comfortable…manner?" With less-pointy objects?

"I'm comfortable. Your little organization has fingers in almost all of Azusa's pies."

He didn't know whether to be insulted at her calling it little, or worried about how much she knew.

"You're going to put out the word," Wilmont continued, "that you want that person's name. Then you're going to give it to me."

That's all she wanted? He could work with that, maybe even leverage it to his advantage. "We can work a deal. I do that for you, you'll do something for me?"

The sharp point pressed a bit tighter. The up-till-now bland voice turned cold. "How about I not slip back sometime and cut your throat? Or not give Law Enforcement details about your business interests, including the two Planetary Representatives in your pocket?"

He cursed silently. She evidently knew a lot. "Deal. I get you the informant, you leave me and mine alone."

"Deal. Until you or one of yours does something stupid or crosses certain boundaries."

"What boundaries?" he asked warily, as she stepped away from him. The knife disappeared somewhere under her jacket.

"Mine. I recommend discontinuing negotiations with that new drug distributor."

How the hell did she know that?

Wilmont flashed him a smile that was all teeth. "There's a paper with an email address on your desk. I'm sure Joe here will be happy to escort me safely out of the building."

Brower collapsed into his expensive chair behind his custom-built desk. His doubts about Wilmont's stealthy reputation had just been soundly demolished. Vaporized. The ease with which everything he'd built could come tumbling down shook him.

"No one had an inkling she was here," the guard reported on re-entering. "You should have seen their faces. I have the techs going over all our security feeds and sensors."

Brower nodded. Prudent, though he doubted they'd find anything. He looked down at the slip of paper in front of him. The other rumors were true, too. You don't mess with the Ghost, and you don't fuck with her friends.

*　*　*　*　*

Jem's teeth ground as she rode the elevator up to the ninth floor. She hated using the local crime lord. Hated using an intimidation tactic that solidified her reputation in the disreputable circles. But she'd been forced into that unwanted option because she'd turned up nothing herself. Just like on Milania. Whoever this frigging psycho was, she was good.

She stepped out on the ICU floor, identified herself—needlessly—and waited patiently for the guard to finish his call.

"Mr. O'Daniel has vouched for you and ordered you added to the authorized visitor list. Full name, please?"

Jem provided it, gave the young Azusa officer a nod, and glided silently down the hallway. This wasn't her first visit. She'd come once before, in ghost-mode, and had been pleased at the security around Thane's family.

She spent several minutes talking with a groggy Seth before wishing him well and taking her leave. A quick peek in Susi's room showed the woman sleeping. Then she was standing in front of a window, looking into an isolation room.

The machines surrounding Thane's sister insisted she was alive. She lay unmoving, her skin colorless…what Jem could see of it. Most of her was buried under bandages and the old-fashioned cast that entombed her from waist to toes. Her left hand poked out of the heavy swaddling to lay submerged in a small vat of liquid. A nurse was positioning what appeared to be a magnifier over the vat. He sat on a stool beside the bed and began slowly moving her wrist back and forth, watching through the lens.

Jem watched for another couple of minutes before turning away. It hurt to know someone would deliberately cause such devastation to a family. The deepest hurt? Knowing Thane would blame himself.

Just you wait, you daughter-of-a-bastard. Just you wait.

Chapter 31

Thane stared out into the darkness. Neither moon was up, so the stars shined crisp and clear. These past days had stretched more like years. Yesterday, he'd stood watching through the plate glass as Dr. Giovannelli's team worked on Katrina. She'd looked so small and helpless, with thin cables and tubes linking her to a multitude of blinking, beeping machines and her left hand immersed in some kind of tub.

His thoughts wandered to Jem. Was she sky-watching as she used to do? Was she skulking through Azusa's dark alleys hunting the ones that had attacked his family? Worry contracted his stomach into a tight knot. No one had heard from her since her last message to Andi three days ago

I'll be in touch.

As usual, she was off in the wind and he was clueless as to where or doing what. He absently rubbed the scar above his left ear. Jem was Jem and no use worrying about her. Or being pissed when she wouldn't share whatever information she was guard—he drew in a sharp breath. *That had to be it*. The information was dangerous, either in itself or to the one holding it. She was protecting them as well as herself. Dammit. He was a testosterone idiot.

Voices in the hallway.

He ignored them…until he recognized one as his mother's. His grandparents had picked her and Stuart up from the airport three hours ago and immediately taken them to the hospital. A UPMS courier pod had brought them from Earth to their terminal in Eastport, a three-hour shuttle ride from

Oslo's eastern coast. Lee would follow as soon as possible, unable to leave right away.

Thane and his mother embraced in the center of the room. Thirty-two or not, the arms encircling him were comfort and security. He gave her a tight squeeze in return and held her out at arm's length. "How is everyone?"

"Seth and Susi are both progressing well. Seth's blood pressure and cardiac rhythm have been stable for the past two days. They'll both be released in another day or two if they promise to take it easy. We'll bring Susi here, help her with…" She enveloped him again, tears streaming down her face. "Dammit, I should be wrung dry by now."

They stood that way for several minutes, simply clinging to each other.

Reyna pushed back and rubbed her face. "Mom is having Merle put together something simple. Which you'll eat. They tell me you haven't been eating or sleeping. I'm going to clean up, visit with the kids, then I want you to tell me everything you've got."

Thane watched her march out of the room. A small smile tipped the corners of his mouth up. Yep, Mom was home. The smile slid away. She hadn't said anything about Katrina.

It took a while before his mom rejoined them at the small, informal dining table, Andi trailing in behind her. Eat first, Nicholas counseled, as everyone dug into the platters of sandwiches and cut fruit.

It was the quietest family dinner Thane could remember.

The table was cleared. Merle left them pitchers of water and tea and a carafe of coffee.

Thane plunged forward. "Katrina's hand, Mom…I'm risking her life for a hand. The procedure can be stopped if you believe it's wrong."

"No, Thane. You made the choice she would have wanted you to make. Regardless of the odds, Katrina would want that chance," Reyna said. "If it doesn't work, then it doesn't. She'll adapt. She'll fight to play the violin again, as hard as she's fighting to live."

Weight lifted. Thane felt almost dizzy with relief, then the full impact of his mother's words hit. He sucked in a breath. "What's happened with Kat?"

"They've found more damage."

More?

"She has a major brach…brach…" Reyna's mouth opened, closed. Her eyes glistened with unshed tears.

Her mother reached over and clasped Reyna's hand. "A brachial plexus injury," Gwen said, speaking quietly. "The nerves for her left arm were torn away from the spinal cord. They didn't find it earlier due to the swelling. Katrina's arm is paralyzed, which," Gwen squeezed Reyna's hand, "is a small matter at the moment."

Nerves. Like Katherine. "That can be fixed, right?"

Gordon's head jerked once in affirmative. "Although it'll have to wait for now. She's in a coma and it's not an induced healing one. The brain swelling hasn't gone down."

Dammit to hell! How much more could his sister's body take?

His mother took a deep breath, steadying herself. "She's only received a small, localized bone regeneration treatment, primarily in the chest region to get it stabilized. It's to put minimum stress on her system."

"Or interfere with Dr. Giovannelli's treatment," Gwen added. "Additional treatments will be introduced as she improves."

How long would it take for all those bones to heal at nature's rate?

"All right, we have plans to make," Nicholas said. "Susi and her kids will stay here for now. Seth's parents are arriving sometime tonight. They'll stay at his home to help Gina when he's released. Guards are already posted around-the-clock there. The same for Erik, Dane and Jane's families. Armed escorts will accompany anyone who ventures out for any reason. The same goes for anyone leaving here." His gaze switching between Gordon and Gwen, Nicholas added, "You should have taken guards with you tonight. Stuart is good, but he can't cover everyone."

"Who would do this?"

His grandmother's voice held tiredness and something he'd never thought to hear: despair. Anger clinched his fists. Whoever was responsible for this was going to pay.

"Joseph Beckett is in prison. Does he have an equally psychotic sibling? Parent?" Gwen turned to Thane. "Have you heard anything more from the Law Enforcers?"

Thane's "No" was coated in disgust. "They haven't talked with me since we came back from New Zagreb."

"Well, you have been hard to get hold of," Andi said. "This is the longest you've been home in months."

"I thought staying away would keep you safe. Evidently, I was wrong."

"Thane Stohlass Baron. You stop that thought right now." Anger sharpened Reyna's tone. "If you believe, even for a second, that you're responsible for some psycho nutcase's actions, I'll bend you over Nicholas's lap."

Nicholas's right cheek twitched. "Now don't go volunteering me for anything."

"Mine is occupied." Reyna pointed at her large baby bump.

"Think of it as practice," Andi said, her eyes sparkling.

"Practice? Why would…" Nicholas's voice trailed off as Andi's grin got bigger.

"Yeah, I am. I was going to tell you later tonight, but," she shrugged, "I figure everyone could use some good news." Nicholas reached over, lifted her into his lap, and they hugged each other.

"That's definitely good news," Gwen said. "Now, Reyna, don't you think Thane should know the other good news?"

"Boy? Girl?" Thane asked, grinning. His mother held up her left hand. "*Married*?" He'd just gotten adjusted to their sig-ner status.

"We were planning on it next month, so you all could be there. His granduncle is a registered shaman and insisted on doing the ceremony." She sighed. "Then Stuart arrived and, well, I didn't know how long I'd be here, so we had it the night before I left." She smiled. "He also sent a blessing for the family."

"Prenup?" Gordon asked.

"Oh, we did that shortly after I arrived on Earth. Seems most Earth couples in stable relationships sign one, whether or not they plan on taking that last step."

Gordon's expression turned thoughtful. "Huh. Maybe we can get that trend started here."

Thane was staring at her ring. Conflicting emotions clashed, then froze when he heard his name. The worry in his mother's face had him forcing a weak smile. "Sorry, Mom. It's caught me off guard. Congratulations."

The conversation turned to Jane's memorial. It would be in three days, on Copenhagen. They decided—Nicholas insisted—they go in one group. A servant appeared in the doorway.

"Mr. Baron? There are two Azusa LE at the main gate requesting to see you. They say it's important."

Thane rose. "It's about time. I'll meet with them in the family room."

"So will I." Reyna pushed herself up, one hand balancing her swollen belly.

There was a chorus of "Me, too" and everyone trooped to the den. They found Marcus Stohlass already there. Clint and Susi's fifteen-year-old son had obviously been eavesdropping.

He glared at them defiantly. "I want to hear."

Thane saw himself in those angry eyes and clenched fists. "He has the right," he told the others.

Relief flashed across Marcus's face and he took a seat in a corner.

"Lieutenant Wheeler and Detective Minsky," Ella said, escorting the two Enforcers in.

"Lieutenant? Congratulations on the promotion. Please have a seat." Thane indicated the small couch everyone had left open. Several additional chairs had been dragged in front of it.

"Thank you." Wheeler motioned to the man beside her. "I don't believe you've met my partner, Detective Dillion Larson Minsky. He's a recent transfer from Ord, Copenhagen." Minsky gave everyone a friendly smile. "Although Captain Kelding has expressed condolences for our entire department, I wish to express my personal one for your losses."

Detective Minsky added his, too.

"I realize it's kind of late, but I felt you…" Wheeler looked around, "and your family wouldn't mind."

"We have been wondering," Gordon said, "as you've interviewed both Seth and Susi at the hospital."

"Mr. Sullivan and Ms. Taft could provide first-hand details. We didn't feel you would be able to add any useful information."

Is that frigging so? Wheeler appeared impervious to the roomful of ruffled feathers.

"We, and the Copenhagen Enforcers, have been working hard on the attacks against your family."

"Is that why Detective Minsky transferred in?" Gordon asked. "To liaison?"

"Uh, no," Wheeler said. "He was already in place before the attacks took place."

In place. That was an odd way to phrase it.

"As it's obviously related," Wheeler continued, "the attack on Romanique Three is being added to our investigation here. We've put in a request for all their case information."

"Well? Any progress?" Gordon said abruptly.

Yep. Grandad was ruffled.

"Yes. The truck used to force Jane Stohlass off the road was found dumped in the ocean—where was that?" The lieutenant turned to her partner.

Minsky accessed his hand comp. "Stonehaven. It's a small town about fifty kilometers south of Port Seattle."

"We believe the man responsible for that is also the one who planted the bomb in Dane Stohlass's boat. It was probably rigged sometime the night before and set with a timer for 0930."

"Which is when all the other attacks were timed to happen," Detective Minsky said. "It took a great deal of planning to put this together."

"Obviously," Thane snapped. "Have you—"

"Please allow me to finish, Mr. Baron," Wheeler interjected. "The bomb killing Clint Stohlass and injuring his wife was also probably installed sometime during the night. His wife remembers hearing a woman verifying her husband's identity right before the explosion. The phone number, an Azusa airport temporary kiosk number activated by cash card one week before the attacks, was disengaged two minutes later."

No way to trace the phone used, Thane thought bitterly.

"Lieutenant?" Marcus spoke up from his corner. "Why didn't the kiosk record the phone's primary number?"

"There's a limited amount of phone numbers available, and the same numbers are used on phones across the Republic. Visitors obtain temporary numbers so as not to interfere with the matching local one. Granted, a local phone could also get a temporary one since the kiosk wouldn't know the difference. It's impossible to match a kiosk number to a specific phone and person unless they use a credit bank card to pay the rental fee."

It was a condescending explanation in a condescending tone. Really? Was she intentionally pissing off the family?

"I'm not stupid and it shouldn't be impossible," Marcus said, glaring. "The phone has to connect to the kiosk to receive the temp number. Why not have it record the primary number when it does? Also recording the make, model, and serial number should uniquely distinguish that phone, as it would be highly improbable all three would match on multiple phones."

Utter stillness. Something so blatantly obvious, so blatantly overlooked until spoken by a boy shoved into an early adulthood.

Wheeler said stiffly, "I'll bring that up to my superiors." She glanced at her partner, who was making a rather lengthy entry into his hand comp. "Seth Sullivan was attacked by a woman, who may or may not be the one on Cliff Stohlass's vid-call. We're going on the assumption she was as his attack occurred only minutes after the bomb's remote detonation. A third person, male, is the one who assaulted Katrina Baron on the skywalk."

"So," Gordon said, "three people for sure. Anything else?"

His granddad's sharp tone apparently made the lieutenant aware of her missteps.

Wheeler visibly relaxed her shoulders and attempted a placating tone. "Four people, counting the one who provided your family's routines and made the planning possible. Have you heard from Ms. Wilmont lately?"

"Heard, no, but she was at the hospital last night. Your guard called and we added her to the visitor list."

"Ms. Wilmont has been busy. We responded to a call from her this afternoon, asking us to meet her at an address on Eighty-Third Avenue. She found the individual who did the surveillance."

"Who?"

"Where's the bastard?"

"What's he told you?"

Wheeler held up a hand, their questions cut off. "Donald Sharpton was hired mid-December to watch and report on as many of the Stohlass family members as possible in two months. He doesn't remember all the names…there were over twenty on his list."

There were several sharp inhales of breath.

"If it's any consolation, he was instructed to focus on adults. His report was emailed in February to an anonymous Palmyra mailbox," Minsky said. "No telling where or to whom it went to from there."

"Mr. Sharpton undoubtedly claims he had no knowledge of what the information was going to be used for," Gordon said, derisively.

Wheeler shrugged. "He probably didn't, although he had to know it wasn't for magazine subscriptions. He's being very cooperative at the moment, even if the only other information he can provide is the name of the person who hired him and to whom he mailed the list to."

"Which is fake, of course," Minsky added. "However…"

Thane cocked his head at the Enforcers' intense looks.

"The name may be fake," Wheeler said, "but Miss Wilmont says you'll recognize it. Patricia Keegan."

"*Son of a bitch!*"

"That's a yes," Minsky said dryly.

"The woman was instrumental in a drug-running frame attempt against my grandson about three years ago on Random Two," Gordon said, his voice grim.

"Why?" Lt. Wheeler asked.

"I don't know." Thane jerked to his feet, unable to sit still and began pacing. "We've gone over my records—I've gone over my memories—I can't tell you how many times. I couldn't come up with anyone I pissed off that bad. Still can't. And this?" Thane threw out an arm. "What did I do that warrants this much anger?"

"Hate, not anger."

Thane turned. Jem stood in the doorway. There was a muttered expletive from Nicholas's direction.

"Hate," Jem repeated. "This is a deep, soul-twisted hate."

"I agree," Wheeler said. "And you can't think of anything that would have generated it?"

Thane shook his head. He motioned Jem in, watched her take a seat in the corner next to Marcus. *With them, yet keeping herself apart.* As she always did. Still, something inside relaxed at her presence. It was the first he'd seen her in months. She looked…good.

"I think soul-twisted says it all," Detective Minsky said quietly. "Whatever sprouted it originally, it grew in unhealthy soil. From whatever slight to a revengeful frame, to murder, to wholesale slaughter, she's escalated. Keegan, whoever she is, has more than one screw loose."

"Wouldn't that make it easier to find her?" Gwen asked.

"No. They can appear to be normal in everyday interactions, especially if they're fixated on a specific goal." Wheeler exchanged a glance with Minsky. "And that makes her even more dangerous."

"Because there's no telling how far she will go to achieve it," Gwen said unhappily.

"We need to determine that goal." Nicholas rapped his knuckles on his leg. "Is she going after Thane or his whole family? If the first, why these attacks."

"To hurt me? To bring me home?"

"My, God. It is Beckett all over again," Andi muttered.

"There are similarities," Minsky agreed. "The woman is an excellent tactician and strategist, as these coordinated attacks demonstrated."

"Military-trained?" Stuart said. "The New Zagreb detectives determined a shaped charge was used on the vehicle."

"One was used on Clint Stohlass's house, too." Wheeler paused, while Minsky made more notes. "That lends credence that she is the same bomber there and here. The Romanique Three file should arrive soon. Maybe they've learned something new since you left."

"You believe it's only those four?" Stuart asked.

"And that this 'Keegan' is the woman actively participating?" Nicholas added.

"Yes, to both. Limiting the number of those involved lessens the risk of leakage."

Thane plopped back down in his seat. "So, whoever Keegan is gets the report, analyzes it, notes some similarities timewise, and comes up with a plan to take out several at one time. Then, what, hires a couple of mercenaries?"

"Yes. The attacks were professional. We know nothing whatsoever about the assassin on Copenhagen. LE is doing the best they can, but he is completely in the wind. In fact, we're only positive it was a man because a driver coming from the other direction got a brief glimpse of the truck driver. We do know quite a bit about the man who assaulted your sister.

"Skyler Jones Harden of Palmyra Two arrived on Midgard six days ago. He stayed at a Port Circle transit dorm in Odinheim for three days before arriving in Azusa. Several of the witnesses to the skywalk struggle and subsequent stairwell chase positively identified him. He's a known mercenary. A loner, not affiliated with any particular group."

Gordon straightened. "Tell me you have the SOB in jail."

"Oh, yes, we've got him," Minsky drawled. "He's in the morgue."

"Morgue?" Gwen echoed, along with a couple of "*Shit.*"

"He was killed in an alley close to the airport several hours after Miss Baron's assault. Stabbed in the abdominal aorta, with a trace of the same poison used on Seth Sullivan in the wound. Keegan probably always intended to dispose of him. The odds of getting away with such a public attack was miniscule and why she didn't do it herself."

Nicholas grunted. "Also why she selected a loner."

"True, and even professionals can have a stroke of bad luck," Minsky said. "In this case, a second body with a witness to his slaying."

Thane straightened. "You have a description?"

"Sort of." Wheeler shared an amused glance with Minsky. "She must have just finished with Harden and was on her way out. A thirteen-year-old boy exited a service door, taking out the trash from his father's store. He didn't pay any attention at first to the person in coveralls and cap since airport workers often cut through there to the nearby transport stop."

"Then a large pair of breasts passed at about eye level," Minsky said with a smirk.

"Thirteen? Uh-huh. That's about the right age to notice that particular feature," Stuart said.

"If this wasn't such a serious subject, Stuart, I'd roll my eyes at you," Gwen said.

"I *am* rolling my eyes, Grandmother," Andi said to several chuckles.

"Could he provide any other description?" Nicholas asked, grinning.

Minsky held up his hand comp. "Quote. 'A woman with big boobs, short black hair, big boobs, taller than me—oh yeah, really big boobs.' Unquote."

Pressed lips. Eye Rolls. Head shakes. And a snorted "He noticed the hair?"

"Okay," Gordon said. "The second body?"

"Ricky Brown McRae left work for a medical appointment and, as usual, he went through the alley. Unfortunately, he probably looked higher than her chest when he turned into it. Plus, I think the kid's presence rattled her. No finesse this time. She simply grabbed the unsuspecting guy from behind and slit his throat. The kid had found Harden, turned to get his father and witnessed the throat-slitting at the end of the alley. She was too far away to see anything other than to confirm the hair and boobs."

"How is the boy?" Gwen asked.

"Shaken. Scared. So are his parents. He and his mother have left on an undisclosed vacation."

Stuart rubbed his chin. "The video image on Milania was very undescriptive—hair hidden under a cap, plain sunglasses, loose clothing on an otherwise slender frame. They did find security footage that leans toward it being a woman. It could be her with tightly wrapped breasts, assuming they're not false."

Wheeler frowned. "We have even less to go on. What can you tell us about Keegan?"

"As I said earlier, nothing. The name is false. Everything she told me was false. She was very careful to keep from providing me any physical description. She arranged our meeting in a dimly lit bar and wore a hooded cape and a mask that covered everything except her eyes, mouth and chin."

"Mask? Cape?"

"With the hood up and pulled slightly forward. Yeah, I know," Thane said, seeing the Lieutenant's skeptical look. "I figured she was someone locally important and couldn't afford to be recognized. I have a file that's got everything we've put together about the frame. I gave a copy to the Milania detectives and it should be in the file they send."

Gordon raised a hand. "Lieutenant Lundgren mentioned the frame when he was interviewing us after the Branson Fire. He may have something in his notes."

"Thanks, I'll check his files and match it with your file. In the meantime," the two Enforcers stood, "stay vigilant, stay careful. If she's that determined, she will strike again. If you learn or see anything suspicious," Wheeler flashed a quick glance at Jem, "please contact us immediately."

* * * * *

"I should be going," Jem said, standing. "I didn't know the lieutenant was here and wanted to make sure you were aware of the surveillance," she lied. She'd wanted to see Thane. Needed to see he was safe.

"No, wait." Reyna struggled to get up. Gordon and Nicholas jumped to either side of her and helped her to her feet.

Thane eyed her stomach. "Are you sure there's only one in there? You're what? Six and a half months?"

"Yep, but your brother is lumberjack-sized."

"Brother?" A smile split his face.

Jem watched the hugs and touches. Listened to the warm, happy exchanges. Life amongst death in a universal cycle. As it should be. A sudden deep ache throbbed as she once again stood on the sideline looking in. She attempted to slip away.

"Not so fast, young lady."

Jem froze at Reyna's words behind her. Gwen appearing in the doorway in front of her blocked her exit.

"Get her back here, Mom," Reyna ordered.

Gwen looped her arm around Jem's and pulled her into the center of the family huddle. Despite the baby belly, Reyna still managed to wrap her in a warm hug.

"Thank you," Reyna said simply.

"I'm not going to bother asking how you found him," Nicholas said.

He was still miffed. Seriously, she needed to stop tweaking his nose.

Hands on hips, Andi declared, "Well, I want to know. Spill it."

Jem shrugged, embarrassed warmth threading through her. "Someone had to know. I put out a, uh, request and kept an ear cocked."

Stuart's eyes crinkled. "The Ghost prowled the streets? They probably couldn't hand him over to you fast enough."

Jem's checks flamed. "Ummm…*weeellll*…" She cast a 'help me' look at Thane.

He reached out and gently laid a hand on her arm. "Thank you. Even if it's false, it gives us a name to focus on. We know—sort of—who we're dealing with now."

Hopefully, her burning cheeks hid the rising blush. "You're welcome."

Thane cleared his throat and stepped back. "Although you probably didn't help your street reputation."

Jem made a face. "I'm learning to live with it."

"You shouldn't have to," Reyna said. "By now, people should realize you're not…" her hand waved, "whatever they think you are. You're the same as everybody else."

"No, Mom, she's special."

Jem's gaze jerked to Thane.

"A special friend to our family," he continued. "I'm surprised Keegan didn't target you."

"I don't have a regular routine." *Don't frigging scare me like that.*

"Doesn't mean she won't take advantage of an opportunity."

"I'll try to not give her one."

"You do that."

Jem broke their stare-a-thon, aware of the gazes bouncing between them. "Good night to all of you."

Reyna held up a hand. "Promise you'll be back tomorrow? There's so much I want to tell you about the Foundation."

"Tomorrow," she agreed. Maybe she'd have better control of herself by then.

"I'll walk her out, Mom."

"Then you walk yourself right back here," Gwen told him, hands on hips. "I need to check your bandages."

"Bandages?" Reyna yelped. "I didn't know he was injured."

Gordon laughed. "Neither did anyone else until Nicholas happened to give him a shoulder tap."

"That wasn't a tap," Thane muttered, glaring at a snickering Andi. "And it's a small wound. Nothing to worry about…I've had worse."

Jem gave him a sideways look. He'd claimed the same thing about a laser-scored skull on Pappia.

"Thane!"

"I'm okay, Mom. Honest. It was a small pocket knife." This time it was him giving Jem a beseeching look.

Jem grinned. "Sorry. You're on your own. Although, maybe you should stop saying 'I've had worse.' The Universe might take that as a challenge."

"Fine, fine," Thane said to laughter. "Let's go."

They walked out in silence. The night was dark, although a hazy wash to the east meant Embla would be peeking over the horizon soon. The gate entrance loomed in front of them, soft light bathing both columns.

Jem stopped and turned to him. The gaunt, thin face was so different from the one she remembered. It'd be useless to tell him not to blame himself. In time, the weight of it would lessen, though it'd never fully go away. She should know.

Jem gave what she hoped was an encouraging smile. "Keegan will slip up somewhere and we'll get her."

"Before or after others die?"

She understood his bitterness. Understood having someone that demented focused on you. "We're prepared now, Thane. On alert. The level of difficulty in striking again, as well as the odds of making a mistake, have increased. In fact, she's already made the same mistake Beckett did."

Silence. "She's pissed off all the Enforcers?" Thane half-said, half-asked.

"Yep. This is a black mark on their reputation and they will be digging hard. I know for a fact there are regular patrols around your homes." She'd spotted them while doing patrols of her own.

"This…waiting, it's not me. I feel as if I should be doing something. I *need* to do something."

Stepping closer, her hand on his arm, she cautioned, "Don't let pain and bitterness push you into something rash or ill-advised."

A hand came up to cover hers. Her pulse quickened at its calloused warmth.

"Would kissing you be rash or ill-advised?"

Jem licked suddenly dry lips. "I won't tell if you don't." She heard a soft laugh, right before his lips closed on hers.

The Universe stopped.

When it restarted, she was pressed tight against Thane, caged in his arms. No, not a cage. A refuge. A safe haven. One she wanted to stay in forever. Reluctantly, she stepped back, his hands sliding up to her shoulders. They cupped her face. Gently, he kissed her forehead.

"Take very, very good care of yourself, Jem Seaborne Wilmont," he whispered.

Then he was gone. He paused briefly on the threshold to give her a wave before disappearing inside the house.

Wow. Just…crap.

Security was waiting to close the gate. Watching. *Recording.* Blushing furiously, she retained enough dignity to walk—not run—out the gate. Its whispered closing sounded like a snicker. Would it be too much to hope her face was a normal color by the time she reached the transport stop?

Chapter 32

Chris Rutherford collapsed into the seat in front of CEO Sutherland's desk. Was he being fired? Replaced as chief security officer due to his failure to resolve the Repository theft? Dammit, was he expected to pull a miracle out of his shoe? His instincts screamed Wilmont was the culprit. How the hell did he prove it? Was the guy standing beside the desk his replacement?

"Chief Rutherford, this is Sean Browning. He's one of the experts you brought in to do an independent evaluation of the Repository's sensor and security feeds."

Rutherford's attention sharpened. "He found something?"

A screen hanging on the wall to his left clicked on. A chart appeared, depicting a sequence of electromagnetic readings according to the legend beneath it. Rutherford recognized it and the wildly distorted band in the middle. It was from the new EM field installed around the Repository's vault.

"Yes, we saw that. It was the second weird occurrence in the three weeks the field was operational. The first was tracked to an imbalance in the settings and corrected. Given that the second one's power level itself didn't drop, and we couldn't find anything else occurring on sensors at the same time, it was recorded and passed off to a junior tech for research. Did they find the cause?"

"No." Sutherland motioned to Browning.

"My expertise is in electro-mechanical engineering. I've seen this kind of scrambled reading twice before."

Rutherford leaned forward. Browning was practically bouncing on his toes.

"Both times it was caused by an *external* interference to the field."

The grin splitting Rutherford's face matched the other two men's. "We have the *when*."

Chapter 33

The morning was cheerfully sunny, same as his mood. The eggs with fried potatoes and shard tasted great. And he felt…great, Thane realized as he ate his way through breakfast. Their problems hadn't gone away, but the black cloud that had weighed him down had burned away. His mind was clear, his thoughts sharp instead of clouded by the haze blanketing him for the past days.

Was it knowing now who the enemy was? Was it the family, which he now realized he'd pushed away, drawing together around him? Or was it last night's kiss? His next bite halted in mid-air as a surge of elation filled him. Jem was not as uninterested as he'd believed. He hastily shoved the bite in as his grandparents entered.

"You're up early," Gordon said, following his wife to the sideboard.

Thane chewed and swallowed. "I managed to get a good night's sleep." Was that a snort he heard as Nicholas and Stuart came through the door? He took another bite as his mother stumbled in, yawning and mumbling a 'good morning all.' Had everyone coordinated their arrival for breakfast?

The line formed at the sideboard. Full plates and cups later, everyone was munching heartily around the table.

Thane went back for seconds and returned with a full plate.

Gwen eyed his plate. "It looks as if your appetite has come back."

"Got rid of the thunderhead expression, too," Reyna said, sipping her tea.

"A good night's rest will do that," Stuart said. Then he asked Nicholas, "How's security?"

"Tight," Nicholas replied. "Guards make physical rounds on a non-routine schedule. Sensors have been upgraded and every inch of the grounds is fully integrated. Those new night cameras have an exceptionally sharp focus."

Thane's ear tips grew warm. *Damn. Night cameras.* "So, no unexpected guests?"

"No unwanted ones, at least," Nicholas said.

Ear tips went even hotter at the amused gleam in his eyes. His mother unwittingly—he hoped—came to his defense.

"Nicholas, is Andi sleeping late? She needs to eat."

"Nope, and not at the moment. It's your fault."

"What is?"

"The two of you spent an hour last night discussing pregnancies, right? Including all the *ailments* you went through when carrying Thane? Andi is in the bathroom and has been for the past half hour."

There was a round of grimaces as everyone understood his meaning.

"It was bound to happen," Reyna said, defensively. "Especially this being her first."

Thane seized the chance to poke back at his tall cousin-in-law. "Technically speaking, you're the one responsible for her," he coughed, "condition."

"Yep." Gordon scooped up a forkful of eggs. "Personal experience has proven she is going to let you know about it, too. Loudly and often."

Laughter erupted around the table.

It felt good to laugh. When was the last time he had? His mother gave him a smile and a brief nod. Laughter was good. They would need it to carry them through the darkness.

"Oh, Gwen." Gordon swallowed. "A reply from Helga Baron came in this morning. A vid-message."

"Finally. What did she have to say?"

"No idea." Gordon scraped up more eggs, stabbed a large piece of shard. "I didn't want to spoil breakfast."

"True." Gwen poured herself another cup of coffee. "Leave unpleasantness until later."

* * * * *

Gwen knocked briskly on the suite door. She was so looking forward to this. Not only had Helga Baron been surprisingly pleasant—if stiff—her message had been a welcome relief. A man answered the door. From his stance and hard expression, a guard.

"Yes?" he said bluntly.

"Gwendolyn Williams to see Katherine Baron."

He looked over her shoulder. "And you?"

"Go where she does," Emily Barker replied, just as bluntly.

"No weapons." He obviously recognized a fellow bodyguard.

"Plan on leaving yours out here?"

The door snapped shut.

Gwen was suddenly glad Barker was there. She'd protested the assignment, saying Reyna should have the highly competent woman as her personal bodyguard. Nicholas had replied that any strike against Reyna would be opportunistic since *her* routines weren't marked. Then he added—with a perfectly straight face—two men would be needed to cover Reyna when she did leave the grounds.

"Think she'll refuse to see me?"

"Nope. Too curious as to why you're here."

The door opened and the guard motioned them in. Gwen gave him a courteous nod in passing, comfortable in the knowledge that Barker could move very fast from her position beside the door if the need arose.

Katherine and Ahrymani sat next to each other. Well, as close as a wheelchair would allow. Data disks and papers were scattered on the small table between them. A comp terminal—now blanked—sat in front of Ahrymani. The atmosphere in the room was stifling. *Dangerous*, some instinct warned, although Gwen couldn't say why. After all, Baron's hostility wasn't unexpected. And exactly what she got.

"Why are you here?"

Ahrymani glanced sideways before saying, "Please have a seat. Would you care for something to drink?"

Gwen declined and took a seat facing the two women. "I see you've finally hired a security service."

"All the violence you people attract made it necessary."

As if they were responsible for it. Gwen kept her voice even. "I don't think you have anything to worry about. Our family members appear to be the ones targeted."

She noted Ahrymani settling back in her chair. Getting out of the line of fire?

Katherine's jaw flexed. "You're here for a reason. Let's hear it, then leave."

As gracious as ever. "We have been in contact with Helga Baron concerning your appalling behavior and received a reply this morning. According to your aunt, *assisting* us in researching real estate was secondary. Your primary purpose was to provide in-depth training on the company's internal structure, the various services available, the agreements and alliances with other companies, and whatever else we ask about. What we received at the time of the audit was rudimentary."

"I intended to discuss that with my cousin, as he supposedly will be at its helm. We both know that will be a wasted effort. What my aunt fails to realize," Katherine said, words drenched in scorn, "is that while Thane Baron may sit on the throne, someone else will be wielding the scepter."

Is that how she views it? Does she picture herself as a queen?

"Then maybe you should be briefing his management team," Gwen said. This obnoxious child was about to be taught a lesson. "You'll be pleased to know that task is no longer yours. Helga Baron is not as clueless as you think. She has appointed an interim Midgard CEO to plan and coordinate BF's establishment here and will arrive in a week or so to personally do what you appear incapable of doing."

Katherine's jaw tightened. "You."

"Me. You will immediately cease doing whatever you're pretending to be doing. You no longer have the authority to agree to—much less sign for—anything. That's now in writing. I will make all decisions from now on."

Katherine's mouth was a hard-pressed line. She looked ready to explode.

"And," Gwen continued, "if you attempt to ignore her directive again, or interfere in any manner, you will be shipped home like the churlish child you are. You are done." Gwen stood. "Leave. Go home. We've had enough of your spite, insults and deliberate disruption."

She walked toward the door, stopped and turned back. "By the way, your aunt expressed her condolences to the family and wished Katrina and the others well. That's more than we've received from you."

Katherine all but spit at her. "As you've implied, I'm not part of your family." She leaned forward in her wheelchair. "And I don't fucking care."

Gwen marched down the hallway toward the elevator. She couldn't leave fast enough. "I thoroughly detest that woman."

Barker studied the suite's closed door as they waited for the elevator. "That woman hates your family, and you especially. She will screw any and all of you if she gets half a chance. So will that so-called aide of hers."

Gwen's head swiveled around. "The aide?"

"Carpenter was unguarded for a couple of seconds when you were verbally thumping Baron into the floor. She was furious and it wasn't a don't-mess-with-my-boss fury, either."

The elevator doors opened. They stepped in.

Gwen shrugged, cast a last look down the hallway before the doors closed. She couldn't care less what their relationship was. "We'll have to make sure neither of them gets that chance."

* * * * *

Seething, nearly incoherent in her rage, Katherine dismissed the guard. A string of curses started as soon as the door closed behind him.

Ahrymani thought over what Williams had said while waiting for Katherine to wind down. That took a couple of minutes. "Are we leaving? Do you want to go back and start a new company?"

Katherine gave her a baleful glare. "Hell, no. It'd take years, decades to build up to match what Baron Financials was—is, even now."

"Good. Helga Baron coming here can work in our favor."

"How the hell how?"

What would the woman do without her? "If there is another attempt on Thane or any family member, your aunt could become an unfortunate casualty. Blame would fall on Patricia Keegan."

A wicked gleam lit Katherine's eyes. "I would be appalled—simply appalled, by the volatility represented by the Stohlass family and the death of my aunt. I would immediately take control of Baron Financials and terminate proceedings."

Ahrymani laughed with her, then grew serious. "How much fight can CEO Williams bring?"

Katherine's brow scrunched in thought. "On Milania? Very little, as I'm considered the heir apparent. Here, she's a fledging CEO of the budding Midgard *division*. And if the bitch keeps her mouth closed, I might let her keep it." Spite lit her face. "Make her dance to my whim to keep it. Yes. Yes, I'd enjoy that."

"What about the inheritance claim?" Ahrymani frowned. "Does anyone else know about the living transfer she's planning?"

"Just her lawyer."

Katherine's right thumb and pinky began alternately tapping on the tabletop. A habit Ahrymani had noticed whenever the woman was frustrated or thinking hard.

"My sisters were never in contention. Gregory's kids were disowned after his Survey ship was lost. When Stephen and his family were killed, that left me and I grabbed it. I moved into his VP slot and started learning all I could."

"Why did she disown them? They would have been potential assets. Profitable marriages, if nothing else."

"Reyna Stohlass refused to give up custody or move to New Zagreb, where my aunt could ensure they were raised properly—meaning her way. Having another son, she wrote them off."

"Until she didn't. I imagine her overtures to your cousin were unexpected. Enter Patricia Keegan."

"Very unexpected. That drug frame should've worked—would've worked if the drug distributor's girlfriend hadn't turned on him. Baron Financials was to be *mine*. Now?" She slapped the table. "Given Helga's recent decisions to reconnect with her Midgard grandkids…" Katherine spit out several more obscenities aimed at her aunt. "That lawyer husband of Williams would make a very good case for Helga's line-of-inheritance preference. Maybe even for her entire estate."

Which meant all this would have been for nothing, Ahrymani thought. Unacceptable. She planned to retire on that estate and its bottomless credit account. "Then we have to finish what we started."

"Any ideas?"

Ahrymani shrugged. "Blowing up the house would take out a lot of our problems. But it's doubtful we'll be able to get explosives past their security. It's very tight, which is why I had to plan external to it."

Katherine frowned. "Car?"

"All cars are thoroughly checked prior to use and a driver remains with it at all times once off the estate grounds."

"Hmmm," both women said simultaneously.

Chapter 34

They watched the sun sink toward the horizon. The ferry's deck was crowded with family and close friends of Jane and Clint Stohlass. Everyone who was able came, down to Jane's twin two-year-old toddlers held tightly by their grandparents. Voices were kept low, conversations kept short. Thunder rolled, and in the distance a rain band hid the southern horizon. It was if Midgard itself mourned their loss.

The sun touched the horizon and the murmurs stilled. Dane Stohlass and Reese Witt stepped to the guardrail, an urn in Reese's arms.

The ship drifted with the waves in silence. Thunder grew closer.

As the sun's rim edged below the horizon, Reese held out the urn. Dane took hold of a handle and, together, they slid the ashes of their beloved wife and sister into the water. They stepped back, Susi Taft and Kevin Stohlass taking their place. Clint's memorial wouldn't be held until after Janice arrived home, but Susi had said there was no sense in holding off his Ash Ceremony, especially since the family would all be present.

The ashes of husband and father joined his sister in the waves. They stepped back.

Jacob Witt, Jane's father-in-law, stepped up to the rail and faced the slowly sinking sun. He spoke in a deep, solemn voice.

> *The time has come and you move on*
> *To whatever waits for us beyond.*
> *While in our midst you no longer stand,*
> *We know you'll always be close at hand.*

You'll dance with the rain and all its kin.
Your whispers will sail astride the wind.
We'll feel your caress in the warm summer light,
And know you stand watch thru darkest nights.
A part of you will live in us,
And continue on till all is dust.

The flow of Jem's tears grew heavier when the throng joined in on the last two lines. It was part affirmation, part promise. This, her first Midgard funeral—Ash Ceremony, she corrected herself—was one of the most beautiful things she'd ever experienced. She hadn't expected to be here. Andi had dragged her from her apartment and now she silently thanked her tall friend.

The engines fired up and the hydrofoil raced back toward Port Seattle.

Jane's memorial had been held earlier that afternoon. Jem found the number of people who had visited to pay their respects humbling. Jane Williams Stohlass would be missed. She glanced at Jane's fretting son and daughter, now held by their father and uncle. Sorely missed.

The lights of Port Seattle broke the darkness off their bow. Twilight was rapidly being snuffed out by the approaching storm. Good thing they planned to spend the night here. The mass memorial for Dane's boat crew was tomorrow. Gordon and Gwen would attend with him to represent the family. After that, back to Azusa and the worry and pain it held.

Thunder rumbled. The breeze became a moist-laden wind tugging at her braid.

Jem clenched the guardrail and stared out into the dark. She knew, down to her bones, that Patricia Keegan wasn't finished. But when? Where? Who? She also had the nagging feeling they had overlooked something. Something important. Everything needed to be gone over again. And again. As many times as necessary.

Eyes closed, face raised to the sky, Jem made a plea to the Universe. *Help me. Help us, so no one else lies dead or broken, and I'll owe you unlimited favors.*

Lightning split the night. Thunder assaulted eardrums. Wind-lashed rain drenched them.

Was that a yes or a no?

An hour and dry clothes later, they gathered in the hotel's restaurant for the late supper Gwen had arranged. Catching a break in the conversation, Jem asked the table in general, "What was that beautiful poem Mr. Witt recited?"

"*The Liturgy of Passing*," Gilida said. "It was written by one of Midgard's founders, Sigurd Olsson, for his wife. Others began doing something similar, saying some kind of passage or farewell. They took the custom with them as the colony spread. About, oh, a couple of hundred years ago, a librarian formalized it. He took Olsson's original ode, massaged it a bit and replaced the last part about his wife with the current stanza. Somewhere along the line, everyone started joining in at the end."

"Drifting, I saw different places and people," Jem said. "I liked seeing what they'd done and what kind of world they had created. There is a lot of sameness, naturally, yet each planet has managed to evolve something unique to it. A certain dish, styles of architecture and speech, or, as here, a tradition."

"Those differences will undoubtedly increase," John Sullivan said. "With pieces of the Republic breaking off, diversification over time will be inevitable."

The entire table stared at him.

"What do you mean, 'pieces'?" Gordon said.

Gilida lightly touched her husband's arm. "It's been a whirlwind since we left Azusa this morning. Interest in whatever the newscasters are blithering about today is at the bottom of our lists."

"Oh. Sorry. I caught a news flash right before we left the house. The Tamarian and Euphrates Systems have voted to secede from the Republic."

Flabbergasted and dismayed expressions dominated the stunned silence.

"What? Euphrates thinks joining the Consortium will improve their mining sales?" Seth said.

"No. *They* are going Independent," John corrected, waving his fork at his oldest son. "Tamarian is the one joining the Consortium."

Chapter 35

The family cautiously restarted their lives over the next two weeks. Gordon said it best when accosted by a reporter outside his office.

Yes, the family has been hurt, which was obviously the <bleep> <bleep> intent. But if the <bleep> expects us to be cowering behind guarded walls, I have news for the <bleep>. Are you listening? I hope so. The Stohlass family is not cowering, we're pissed. We will utilize every resource to track you down. The war you <bleep> <bleep> have declared on us is reciprocated and we don't plan on losing.

Janice Stohlass was home on extended leave. A prior commander, now an Admiral at Command Headquarters, had personally taken a small scout craft and rendezvoused with the *Shining Star*, Janice's ship, and brought her to Midgard. He'd stayed for Clint's memorial service before taking his leave, after telling Janice to let him know if he could help in any way.

That caused a number of raised eyebrows and speculative looks.

Susi had left yesterday for the family's vacation home, situated on one of the Spine Islands. A nurse, nanny, and a number of guards had accompanied her and the children. Among her many decisions to make was where to live. Her house was unsalvageable. Did she rebuild or move somewhere else?

Seth returned to work, half-days to start. A driver and security guard provided transportation to and from the law office, with the guard shadowing him wherever he went. His parents reluctantly left at his insistence to rendezvous with the Valhallass Troupe, currently playing on Betelgeuse Two.

Reyna's husband finally arrived from Earth. Lee Twobears explained the delay was his new boss refusing to grant him leave, saying he was needed on Earth and that Midgard LE could handle whatever was happening there. He'd finally resolved the issue by resigning. He had shrugged off the family's dismay, saying he didn't expect difficulty in finding employment when they returned.

Katrina woke from her coma. The doctors immediately ran a battery of tests to pinpoint any brain damage and then placed her in a healing coma. Surgery to reattach her spinal nerves was being delayed until her healing was further along. Dr. Giovannelli warned them that, even though Katrina's hand was responding to treatment, there was the potential of long-term weakness and/or numbness in the arm or hand due to the spinal injury.

"That can be lived with," Reyna had replied with a relieved smile.

Helga Baron was in town, staying two floors above her niece in the same hotel. According to scuttlebutt, Katherine had welcomed her aunt with a rant about how no one would want to invest or work with a company where violence could break out at any time. Undeterred, Gwen, Sophia Lutz and two of Erik's children, William and Stacy, were learning BF essentials in Helga's suite.

The Stohlass family drama had finally been superseded in the newscasts. The Euphrates and Tamarian Systems' secession and speculation on how it would affect other systems were currently the top news. But curiosity and speculation about the Spine Ridge Fjord construction were rapidly gaining on it.

Which is why Jem had decided it was the time to let the Stohlass family in on her secret. Not just about her home, either. Her trust had withered in the dark for long enough. Time to stretch it, starting with the two who already knew a few things about her. She sat in front of Seth's office desk with Thane, having asked him to meet her here. Both men were waiting for her to speak. Both wore wary looks.

Jem cleared her throat. "That Spine Ridge Fjord construction? It's my home."

"You bought the Fjord?" Thane started laughing.

"What?" Jem's brows scrunched. Not exactly the reaction she'd expected.

"Way back, when I was tracking you? I wondered why you were working all those jobs when you had enough credits to buy a large chunk of a planet. Now you have."

"You could have bought something closer," Seth said. "It's an hour-plus trip by boat."

"Yes, well, I wanted a safe place. One that's secure from the curious, the paranoid, and the greedy. It will get worse as others learn about me."

Thane crossed his arms. "*We* haven't learned all about you."

Seth's gaze cut sharply to Thane then back to Jem.

Jem glanced between the two men, chewing the inside of her cheek. Her resolve wavered. She fought the fear down. *I need to do this. Think baby steps.* The phasing, the core of what she could do, she'd keep hidden for as long as possible.

"How much has Thane told you?" she asked Seth.

"The Myerstone Laboratory on Earth was trying to create an instantaneous transfer system based on the same Otanak principles the O-drives use. An experiment went haywire; you were caught up in it with resulting DNA-slash-cellular changes that allow you to become invisible. That it?"

Yep, that was the basics. She took a moment, gathering her thoughts. "The lab had set up two testing stations—one directly behind the lab and the other in a field about a hundred meters from the lab. That's what they were trying to connect to."

"That makes 'caught up in it' more sense," Thane said, nodding. "I couldn't see you wandering around the lab. They should have considered the possibility of someone getting between the lab and test base and set it closer."

Jem gave him a wan smile and didn't correct him.

"Everything went…crazy. The feedback to the lab was horrendous, destroying all their equipment. The test stations were demolished, blown apart. They found me in the debris." Jem stopped, reliving the nightmare. Sucked into a twisting, black hell that spit her out at the Myerstone lab…her friend's severed hand in the debris next to her. Months of—she was jolted back to the present when Thane took both her hands. Squeezed them gently between his.

"It's all right," he told her softly. "It's over…it's in the past."

He was wrong. For her, it would never be over. She took a deep breath. "On reviewing their data and talking in scientific tongues, they came up with a new theory. One very different from their goal and a very disturbing one. Think of what would happen if the lab's energy generator, stable and error-free, was on a spaceship and 'aimed' at another spaceship."

It took a few seconds. "Oh, my, God." Seth sucked in a breath. "An O-field cannon."

"There'd be no defense against it," Thane said, equally horrified.

"No, there wouldn't be. The energy field is interdimensional. My friends postulated it only needed contact with an O-engine—*like the one she'd been next to*—in space or on a planet's surface. It wouldn't make a difference. Imagine it sweeping across a fleet or a space dock or port."

Thane's face was as grim as his voice. "Kurzvall knows. That's why he wanted the data on the hand comp so badly. Why you refused to give it all to him."

"Yes. His spy in the lab was very chatty. The last six months of their data contained their final experiment results. It was the period during which they made major theoretical breakthroughs, leading to equipment modifications. All of which led up to the disaster."

"With those six months of data, he could develop an unbeatable weapon," Thane said.

"Yep."

"And now he has a highly mobile battleship and his own realm to defend," Seth said.

"Yep."

"*Any* military command would do anything for that kind of weapon," Thane said.

"Yep."

"Or keep it from being used against them," Seth added.

"Combine that with Jem's capability and her home will be hotter than a supernova."

"She'll need sensors," Seth said. "Ground, sea and air."

Thane nodded. "Nicholas or Stuart can do an evaluation and lay out a plan."

"I can file a legal restraint, have the Fjord listed as restricted airspace."

"Or I could just destroy the hand comp," Jem said.

Thane shook his head. "You wouldn't do it before because it was your friends' legacy. Properly utilized, it would be beneficial."

"That's the key, isn't it?" Jem said, gloom settling over her. "Even if an ethical laboratory worked on it, Grathen—Kurzvall's spy—proved the data will eventually leak to others less ethical. And once one is built, others will race to build their own. No, I think it's best I destroy it. As Boyd once said, the Republic works just fine as it is."

Thane tilted his head. "Except the Republic isn't the same now, is it? New political entities…new battleship configurations…anything's possible."

Seth gave him an appalled look. "Are you thinking war?"

"You had Old Earth history in school, same as me. There'll eventually be conflict over a system containing valuable resources—maybe something similar to J-crystals. Or things break down enough to where pirates such as Beckett roam freely. Or some idiot develops delusions of grandeur. With the mobility these new designs allow…" Thane shook his head. "Jem holds what could be Midgard's—the entire Wotan System's ultimate defense." He turned to Jem. "Kurzvall is the only one who knows about the O-data, right?"

"As far as I know, yes." She shrugged. "But he could sell the information to someone, hope they succeed, and steal it from them."

"Yeah, that sounds like him." Thane rubbed his neck.

"Jem's invisibility will become more problematic as the knowledge spreads," Seth said. "There's always going to be those who'll keep after her."

"A tool to use or a threat to eliminate," Thane said in a resigned tone.

"Yep, that's me." That was becoming her default catch-phrase. Maybe she should have it chiseled above the entrance to her home. "The military already has me on their worry radar." That got their attention. "We've been playing games for a couple of months. They send in a covert team, I identify and report them. They leave, next team comes in."

"Seriously?" Thane said. "What do they plan to do and who do you report them to?"

"I report them to General Kowalski's office. It's for surveillance…mostly." Which would they go for on learning how she did what she did? Tool or threat? "I prefer to think of it as training on their part."

Seth's expression turned calculating. "What's the status of your home?"

"It's fully constructed and the framing of doors and windows is finished. The wind turbines, power generator, and storage cells are on order. Wiring will follow once they're in place."

"Then this is the perfect time to get those security additions added. Thane, how soon can you get either Nicholas or Stuart out there?"

"I'll talk with them tonight." Thane looked at Jem. *We'll* talk to them. They need to know about this."

She started to protest. His very serious expression stopped her.

"It will make a difference, Jem. You need top-of-the-line security. Planning for wayward civilians and professional criminals is one thing. They need to plan for experienced and well-trained teams. Nicholas and Stuart are already sworn to secrecy on all aspects of family security. We'll make this a limited need-to-know information, even within the family."

She cleared her throat. "Tell them everything?"

Thane looked to Seth. "Energy weapon should be sufficiently heart-stopping."

"About stopped mine," Seth retorted. "I agree, ghost-mode should remain secret as long as possible."

Okay. Baby steps.

Chapter 36

Katherine was frowning over a document when Ahrymani jumped up from her chair.

"We have another chance at Thane."

The sheet crumpled in her fist. "How?"

The receiver Ahrymani pulled out of her ear was linked to the transponder she'd smuggled into Helga Baron's suite. "Thane's going with Wilmont and one of the security guys to her new home—it's that fjord place they keep talking about on the news. I have to change clothes." She practically ran toward the bedroom.

"Wait." Katherine rolled her wheelchair after her. "I thought you said it was too risky to buy a laser."

"It is." Ahrymani pulled on a pair of plain pants. "I'm going to improvise. Where did you hide the poison?"

* * * * *

Stuart stood with hands on hips and turned slowly, taking in the dock, the beach, everything. Jem and Thane remained quiet and out of his way.

"Approach is limited—that's good. A couple of sensors on the Elbow and a few underwater will cover that." He studied the hillside. "How much of this is yours?"

"I own from the foot of the land-side ridge to the ocean on the other. No sense on letting someone spy from the top."

"Excellent. Sensors on top will cover anything approaching from air or sea. I can barely make out the window openings from this angle, but they'll be visible further out in the fjord or on that hilltop." He looked back at Jem. "Their status?"

"All glass will be Jaguide reinforced, including the terrace doors. Not blast-shield level, though close. They're in a warehouse right now. Installation is scheduled for next week."

He started up the walkway, Jem and Thane trailing him. They stepped inside the entrance and Stuart poked at the frame. "Door here needs to be heavy-duty and watertight."

"On order. All the other doors will be ordered after the interior walls are finished, as they'll need to be custom fitted."

"Excellent."

Jem pointed to the openings in her…lobby? Foyer? "Those two on the left are storerooms. The one just past the elevator is its machine room. I opted to keep the large, heavy-duty one the workers used." She pointed down a short hallway on their right and before the elevator. "Stairs open up in the living area. Shall we go up?"

They took the elevator instead of the stairs. Jem gave them a quick tour of her very linear home. All the main rooms faced out, their windows providing natural lighting and keeping claustrophobia at bay. All the supplemental rooms—closets, storage and such—were on the interior side. A wide hallway ran between them connecting everything in a smooth flow.

She showed Stuart the rooms that would hold the main computer and supporting equipment. A small vault room would hold valuables, such as the hand comp with the lab's data. The generator room was down a short corridor and away from the main living area.

Stuart's gaze shined with approval as he looked around her future living room. "I like the way this is laid out. I need a copy of the blueprints."

"I'll get you one." Jem waved her hand. "In the meantime, feel free to look around."

Stuart pulled out his hand comp and headed toward the generator room.

"Well, he appears to be happy," Thane said.

Jem was about to reply when something scuttled across the floor. At least it was, until Thane's foot connected. "What is that?" She squinted down at the squished mess.

"Granite beetle. Like an Earth roach," he added, seeing Jem's blank look.

"Roaches?" Jem whipped around, looking into all the corners. "I have roaches?"

"Well, that depends on whether it was a female and she's had time to lay eggs." He shrugged. "Kind of hard to tell right now."

"I can't have roaches." Jem's voice rose in pitch. "There's nothing here."

Thane propped himself against the opening out to a narrow terrace. "Jem, this will be a nice place when it's finished. It'll be even nicer when you add all the home stuff. But it's still a cave system. There's probably a number of critters that would happily call it home, too."

That thing had been a good two inches long and—she froze. Two-inch-plus roaches. Five-foot-plus hawks. She swallowed. She hadn't seen any, but… "Thane? How big are the spiders?"

He appeared to think about it for a moment, then held a hand out with his fingers cupped. Bounced it a couple of times and spread his fingers a bit more. "About that."

Jem stared at his hand in horror. How fast could she sell this place? She'd renew her apartment lease in Azusa and—

Thane threw back his head and laughed. "You should see your face."

"It's not a laughing matter!"

"They're good small, furry pets. You don't even need to carry them. They hang onto your leg."

Whatever horror she'd been displaying morphed into irritation when she realized he was kidding. "How about I show you my knee? It is *not* funny."

Thane kept on laughing.

"Thane! Stop it. How big are they really?"

He took a couple of deep breaths, got it down to a light chuckle. "You're in luck. Midgard doesn't have spiders."

"None?" Jem asked, suspicious.

"None." He grinned and lifted his foot. "Just big bugs."

"Which you can spray for," Stuart said, rejoining them. He shook his head. "Thane, you should know better than to tease a woman about bugs. Or didn't your cousin teach you that lesson?"

"Oh, yeah? Who and what?" Jem asked.

"One of Erik's daughters and a two-by-four, from what I heard."

"Not Andi?"

Thane acquired a mortified look. "Nobody teased Andi."

"Well, if he got clobbered in the head, I guarantee it didn't take. Skull's too thick." She smirked at Thane's scowl. "What?" she said, innocently. "Didn't you say something similar when you shrugged off that laser burn to your scalp?"

"That is not what I said."

Stuart waved his hand "I've seen enough for now. The single issue I see is there aren't any escape routes if the primary entrance is compromised."

She wouldn't need it as she'd just shift into safety. *Although, if I have guests...*

"We'll need to look at expanding later."

Thane gave Stuart an incredulous look. "The whole front is her primary entrance. Anything else would have to be drilled straight through the ridge. Pick a direction."

Stuart looked thoughtful. "Yeah. It'll be a challenge. For now, I'll go over my notes with Nicholas and we'll annotate our updates to the blueprints. Which you'll get me no later than tomorrow. Yes? Good. If you two are finished flirting, let's go."

They were almost to the dock when a loud whistle sounded from behind. They instinctively turned, and a large dart *thunked* into Thane's chest. He stumbled backward.

"*Down!*" Stuart yanked on their arms.

"Burns," Thane said, swaying sideways on his knees.

"Shit, shit, shit." Stuart pulled the dart out. "Poison."

And they were way out here.

"Jem." Thane's voice was already thick. "I..." Stuart grabbed him as his eyes rolled back.

Noooooo. Jem pushed Stuart aside and snatched up the dart. Embracing Thane from behind, she snapped, "Hospital. Explanations later." She shifted. Everything stopped for them. No beating heart. No inflating lungs. No blood flow. The poison should be in stasis with everything else. It was his only chance.

No weight or friction in this phased-out non-existence either, as she dragged Thane into the boat and waited impatiently for Stuart to catch up. She'd never understood how her brain maintained some kind of spatial link to the real world, keeping her where she wanted. However it worked, it kept her from dropping through staircases, floors, or a boat racing toward the open sea.

* * * * *

Stuart broke free of his shock. He bolted for the boat, not worried about another dart. He hadn't been the target. He jumped in and just sat there for a moment, hands gripping the steering wheel. Damn. Teleportation. That answered a *lot* of questions. He grabbed his phone, then let an expletive fly. The fjord's walls would block any signal. A frigging relay needed to be installed ASAP. Firing up the engine, he raced full throttle for the fjord's entrance. As soon as he passed through it, he called his boss.

"O'Daniel here."

"Thane has been poisoned by dart. Jem is getting him to a hospital. I'm heading there now."

"What? I can't hear you. Where are you?"

Stuart slammed the throttle to idle and repeated it.

"Which hospital?"

Stuart blanked for a moment. "Azusa Memorial." He hoped. She'd been there.

"Where are you?"

"Outside Spine Ridge Fjord."

There was a brief pause. *"How then—"*

"Call Agent Reis. Have him meet us at the hospital. We're going to need some Federal weight to keep this quiet."

"What? Why would—"

"I just learned Jem's secret—her other secret, and it's a doozy." Stuart took a deep breath. "Trust me." He disconnected. Throttle back to high, he barreled along the coast and hoped he still had a job. A glint of sunlight caught his eye. Squinting, he made out a jetter rapidly disappearing in the distance. The bastard would get back to Azusa long before him.

* * * * *

Jem hung onto Thane's unconscious form and fretted. Even at the boat's top speed, they were at least an hour from Azusa. Then getting across town to the hospital…thirty minutes, more? Too long, too long. Despite practicing for months, her phased tolerance was still barely an hour. She was dimly aware of Stuart calling Nicholas. Some kind of arrangements. Reis? Right. The Feds would involve themselves once she shifted back in the middle of the Emergency Room.

Memorial Hospital. Too far. *Shit, damn, crap.* Forget the time. She would hold as long as necessary. An hour, two hours, whatever it took. She would hold the frigging shift or die trying. Could she die in this state? Would Thane exist in a form of death with her? Or would her body return to their universe on its own? Then Thane would die.

No. Not happening.

Jem pictured the hospital, focusing on the door they went through when visiting Seth and the others. Willed them to be there in time. *We will make it, Thane. I will hold*—pain. A searing, blinding, twisting agony, as if every cell in her body was exploding in flames. She threw her head back in a soundless scream as the world went black.

A second? An eternity? The black released her and she fell.

Everything hurt. She forced her eyes open despite the pounding behind them. She stared through a watery haze at Azusa Memorial Hospital's eastside door. Impossible, but…she could see it. She could feel Thane's body beneath—*they weren't phased. The poison would be active.*

She pushed herself up, falling back on one knee as a new assault speared down her spine and into her legs. Gritting her teeth, she rose. No one around. *Have to get to the main entrance. People there.* Five steps and she was back on hands and knees, back arched. *Oh, God, it hurts. It hurts.* Forced herself up again. Swaying, jaws clenched, she lurched toward the building's front. *Almost…* Knifing pain and nausea drove her back to her knees. She crawled the last few steps.

Entrance…there. People…*yes!*

She swayed on trembling arms, unable to go any farther.

This way. Please…please…look this way.

Fuzzy forms ran toward her. Shouts. Words? Her brain refused to interpret them.

Jem lifted a shaking arm, pointing back. More unrecognizable sounds. More fuzzy people. Her heartbeat fluttered, darkness crept into her vision. She struggled to draw a breath.

Was she in time? *Live, Thane, live.*

Hands clasped her arms. She looked into crystalline blue eyes and forced her mouth to move. "Pooo…zzznnnn," she gasped before falling into a blessedly numb blackness.

* * * * *

Stuart wasn't surprised to find both Reis and his partner waiting with Nicholas in the emergency room when he barreled through the entrance. "How's Thane?"

"In ICU. They've finally got him stable," Nicholas told him in clipped tones. "Were you really in the fjord?"

"Yes. Reis, Gaines, we need to get to the hospital's security room. Get their security recordings."

Reis folded his arms. "Why?"

"Later. You there," Stuart called out to one of the orderlies. "Where did Wilmont and Baron come from?"

The orderly shook his head. "Don't know. We saw her first, at the building's corner. She pointed back toward the east parking lot before collapsing. That's where we found him."

Close enough. Walking rapidly, he turned down the corridor leading toward security. His boss and Federal Agents hard on his heels. "Where's

Jem?"

Nicholas grabbed his arm and yanked him to a stop. "In ICU."

"What? Why?"

"They don't know why. No sign of poison, yet she came in nearly as dead as Thane. What in the frigging hell happened?"

Stuart's mind whirled. Not simple, not easy. Was it the distance she'd had to cover? "You won't believe me unless you see it. Reis, get us in the security room and them out."

Realizing that, whatever it was, it was serious, Reis took over. His badge got them in and access to the recordings before ordering the protesting security guards out.

Dammit. He hadn't checked the time. "Nicholas. When did I call you?"

"A minute or two after twelve-thirty."

Stuart started the recording at twelve twenty-five. He doubted he'd lost more than a minute to shock. The others gathered on either side of him.

"You going to start explaining?" Reis asked, watching the monitor.

"Watch," Stuart said.

A car pulled in. A man and a woman walked toward the door. Several people walked past and disappeared off the recording. Blank video except for the front view of vehicles.

"What are we—" Nicholas started. He and the Feds jerked forward, Reis nearly falling out of his seat when Jem and Thane popped into view.

Jem fell on top of Thane. She got up, fell, pushed back up. The shear effort of moving evident in the way she staggered. She fell to her knees again after a few feet, her back arching.

"That," Gaines said quietly, "is pure agony."

Jem staggered toward the building's front. Fell to her knees. Crawled a few steps. After a moment, orderlies swarmed around her. Several ran toward Thane. Two burly orderlies grabbed each end of him and ran. Another grabbed a strip of bright red. They disappeared back around the corner.

"Wait. What happened to Wilmont?" Gaines asked.

Stuart backed the recording up. They watch Jem point back toward Thane, then collapse into an orderly's arms. She was placed on a gurney and they raced off-screen. Stuart stopped the recording, rewound it all the way back to where they first appeared and halted it when she rose off Thane. Stuart zoomed the image, the dart and its red fletching now easily visible beside them.

Silence. They stared at him, the screen, each other, and back again with shocked expressions. Stuart said what they didn't want to. "She teleported Thane here. He was failing fast and would be dead otherwise."

They all stared at the image of Jem on her knees.

"She's never appeared distressed before," Nicholas finally said. "The distance, you think? The hospital is, what, a hundred-fifty, sixty kilometers from the Fjord?"

Stuart nodded. "But no problems for a short distance, say, into a nearby building?"

"If I hadn't seen it for myself..." Reis rubbed his forehead. "This woman is more dangerous than the Consortium's battleship," he said, voice grim. "At least we'd get some warning before it hit. This," he waved at her image, "is a security nightmare. I'll impound the recording. Gaines? Start checking nearby buildings. Confiscate any that caught it from another angle."

She gave a nod and was gone.

Reis rubbed his hands across his face. "This is going to be a supernova of a shit-storm if it gets out."

"At least one other knows already. The shooter was watching, wanting to verify Thane went down. I caught sight of a jetter hell-bent back to Azusa."

"Keegan?" Reis asked.

"Probably."

"Definitely," Nicholas said. "It was the same poison as used on Seth."

The three men stared at the frozen image.

"Director Vanderbilt is already paranoid about Wilmont and her ability to bypass security. Once he learns *how* she does it...I'm not sure what he'll do."

Nicholas gave him a side-wise look. "Are you implying he'd do something inappropriate?"

Reis met his gaze. "I can't say how anyone would react in this situation. I will say there's a lot of unhappy people in my department, especially at the higher levels."

"Don't tell him."

Reis gave a sharp laugh. "He's going to want to know why we confiscated the security disks. Now, if you'll excuse me, I need to get started. Would you send the guards back in? I need to know if there are any other cameras covering this area."

Nicholas and Stuart stepped out and motioned the two guards hovering in the hallway to go in.

Stuart's face got a double hand-rub. "What do you think?"

"I think we need to maintain tight security around Thane *and* Jem." Nicholas huffed out a deep breath. "Energy weapons. Teleportation. What other secrets does this woman have?"

"No idea, but let's hope none of them tops this one."

Chapter 37

Ahrymani pulled up to the valet station. Smiling at the attendant, she retrieved several shopping bags she'd hastily bought, handed her keys over, and sauntered into the hotel. She kept the serene mask in place until safely enclosed in their suite. The bags hit the floor and she headed for the small bar.

Katherine wheeled her chair around. "They're saying Baron is alive." She waved her hand at the large vid-screen behind her. It displayed a video of the Azusa hospital and a reporter blathering on about the latest attack against the Stohlass family.

Ahrymani finished pouring herself a glass of their strongest whisky.

"Dammit!" Katherine smacked the chair arm. "They were supposed to be at the fjord, away from any medical help. Where did you find them?"

She took several swallows before turning around. "At the fjord."

"Impossible."

Kathrine's disbelieving glare was understandable but annoying. In fact, she was beginning to find a number of things annoying about her. "When did the news break about the attack?"

"I don't know…at least an hour ago. They—"

Ahrymani stopped her with a hand motion when the video zoomed in on a man jumping out of a vehicle in front of the hospital's emergency entrance. "Look. That's Stuart, O'Daniel's second-in-command. He went *with Baron and Wilmont* to do the security assessment for her home *in the fjord*. It's taken him an hour-plus to race back to the hospital after I shot Baron *in the fjord* with enough poison to cause death within minutes."

She took another swallow. "If Thane's still alive, it means he's been here, under medical treatment, for most of that time."

Katherine's expression was almost comical. "But, but, I don't understand. Did they have a jet pack?"

"No, he'd still be dead. It took me over twenty minutes to jet back to where I'd left my car." Another thirty-plus to dump the dart gun and stolen pack in a river and do some fast shopping for a cover.

Ahrymani refilled her glass and poured a second one. She walked over to her wide-eyed, confused lover. "Jem Wilmont is a teleporter."

Katherine blinked. "A *what*?"

"Teleporter."

Katherine looked at her, at the screen, grabbed the glass from Ahrymani's hand and took a large swallow. "Damn."

"Uh-huh. Wilmont is a huge problem. With a few seconds of warning, she can transport a target away to safety or attack a sniper's position. This changes *everything*." She collapsed into a chair.

"Maybe we'll be the lucky ones for a change and she'll die too," Katherine muttered.

"Say what?"

"They're both in critical condition, according to the latest reports."

"I only shot Baron." Ahrymani replayed the scene mentally. Wilmont had grabbed the dart right before they vanished. "She must have snagged herself on the dart."

Katherine's phone rang. Pulling it up from a side pocket, she muttered an expletive at the display. "Yes? We're watching the news now. I didn't know anything about it," she lied. "Ahrymani heard about it while she was out shopping." She glowered at the vid-screen.

"I don't care, Aunt Helga. You've refused to listen to me about the danger surrounding them. We should go home before…" Katherine's eyebrows shot up. "You don't mean that… Fine. Ahrymani goes with me." She disconnected.

"Well?" Ahrymani said, impatient.

"I have been instructed by my aunt that I *will* remain on Midgard. I *will* show the proper concern for my cousin's health, and I *will* provide any support the Stohlass family requires of me."

"Or?"

"Or I will lose my vice presidency at Baron Financials." Katherine gave her a tight smile. "First duty on the agenda is to attend a 'show of support' with my aunt at the hospital."

Ahrymani's smile was all predatory. "Excellent. We have our reason for remaining here. One or two more family members need to be targeted. Live or die doesn't matter, it'll keep Law Enforcement's focus wide."

"It's going to be tough. If they were vigilant before, they'll be ultra-paranoid now."

"True." Ahrymani tapped her fingers on her arm. "We'll use this sham-show to see who's in town and what plans they might have. And it'll give me a chance to check out the hospital's security."

* * * * *

"Untenable."

"Sir, nothing in Miss Wilmont's background indicates she would use this ability improperly."

"Tell that to Jaguide Security."

Silence. "They don't have proof it was her."

"Once this leaks—and it will," Director Vanderbilt ranted, "everyone who *will* use it improperly—and I include those Consortium bastards—will target her. Her family and friends will become pawns in an effort to control her. That may, in fact, already be happening—pressuring her into something."

"No, sir. The recent attacks are aimed at Baron by someone from his past. Besides, Wilmont wouldn't allow things to go that far." Reis heaved a heavy sigh. "She'd capitulate."

"Exactly!"

"And Thane's assailant is now aware."

"The first leak. Untenable and unacceptable."

Chapter 38

"Welcome back to the land of the living."

Thane blinked groggily at his grandmother. It took a few seconds for her words to penetrate. "Where?" was followed by a dry cough.

"Azusa Memorial," she replied, activating a control to raise his head. She held a plastic cup to his mouth. "Jem barely managed to get you here yesterday morning in time for treatment."

He took a couple of swallows and laid back, unbelievably weak. His memories of those last minutes trickling back…the fjord, a whistle. Shit, he got hit by a dart.

"Where's Jem? Stuart? Were they shot too?"

"No. You were the only one shot with a highly poisonous dart."

A burning pain had taken him down fast. Too fast. "How did Jem get me back here in time?"

"You don't know?"

"I was unconscious," Thane muttered. The intense look he was getting made him wary. Something was up. "What's happened, Grandmother? Where is everyone?"

"Stuart and Nicholas are currently working up a security plan for Jem's home. Reyna is in the maternity wing."

He jolted upright. "It's too soon. The baby?"

She pushed him back down. "When you went into your third cardiac arrest, she went into labor. The baby is fine. Perfect." She laughed. "In fact, I think Reyna is secretly pleased. Your brother is already birth-sized. Another three weeks or so of growing and it'd be like passing a small boulder."

Thane winced, grateful to be male. "Guess I owe Jem big time. Okay, Grandmother, stop with the hawk eyes. Spit it out. Where is Jem and how did I get here?"

She leaned forward. "Jem is in an ICU room, two doors down. What she did to get you here—to be discussed later—nearly killed her." She cocked an eye at the machine monitoring Thane's pulse when it began beeping at the sharp increase. "That's what I thought. You and Jem have been dancing around each other long enough. If you really care for her, as she obviously does for you, you two need to work it out. Resolve whatever issues you have before fate steps in and leaves nothing except regrets."

What had happened to Jem? What did she do? Before he could ask again, raised voices sounded outside the room. Barker stepped in.

"There's a couple of FLEAs ordering our guards away from Miss Wilmont's door. They say they're taking charge of her."

"Call Lee. He's downstairs with Reyna." Gwen sailed out of the room.

Thane ripped the monitoring lines off his chest and pushed out of bed. Slid out of bed would be more accurate, as his legs appeared to be mimicking sea sponges. A death grip on a rail was all that kept his ass off the floor. Dammit. He needed to be out there but—*yes*! The chair his grandmother had been sitting in had wheels. He more or less fell onto it and forced the limp sponges to push it out the door.

"—to move," the older one was saying. "You're obstructing Federal Agents in the performance of their duties."

His grandmother stood with her back to room 904's door, spine straight and head held regally as she faced two Federal Agents. Dr. Blackwood stood with crossed arms beside her. Barker and the other Stohlass guards were poised to the side.

"We're taking Miss Wilmont to a more secure facility as she is stable and capable of being moved."

"That is *not* what I said and she should *not* be moved." Blackwood glared at them. "Stable, yes, but her vital signs are still weak and thready. Nor has she regained consciousness. She requires constant monitoring."

"She will be monitored at the facility. Please stand aside."

Gwen crossed her arms. "You are not taking Jem Wilmont anywhere."

Thane glanced over as Lee came around the corner. He frowned at the sight of his mother beside him in gown and housecoat. Should she be up? Her brows drew down at the sight of him sitting in the hallway. She was probably wondering the same about him.

"We have our orders, ma'am."

"From whom?" Gwen asked.

"Director Vanderbilt personally."

"I'm confused. Your director feels that a woman who pushed herself to physical limits needs a 'more secure facility' than my grandson, who has survived his *third* assassination attempt?"

"I was not given his reasoning, only his orders. Which I'm following."

"Were you given a lobotomy at your swearing in?"

"No. Were you given a double dose of curmudgeon at birth?" the agent snapped, obviously at patience's end.

"Triple. Which I made sure to pass on. Right, dear?" Gwen said, her attention on the agent.

Reyna grinned. "Yes, Mother." Lee wrapped his arm around her waist and pulled her close.

"You two buckets of barnacle waste can crawl back to your degenerate, egg-sucking spash of a director."

Everyone's eyes went wide.

Gwen continued in the same politely scathing tone. "Tell him that if he feels the need to put Jem Wilmont into 'protective custody' of some kind, he needs to provide the justification for doing so. In writing. And why that's more important in his myopic opinion than the assaults against my family. In writing."

"Director Vanderbilt does not have to justify himself to civilians," the younger Fed said stiffly.

"Then the boneheaded fool can provide it in court, because if he tries something this asinine and unreasonable again, there will be legal and public repercussions."

Thane grinned. Bonehead was a slur usually reserved for heavy-worlders, as it implied one had a smaller, less cognitive brain due to gravity-thickened skulls.

Reeking of anger, the older one jerked his head at the younger one. Turning, they stomped away. The silence lasted several seconds after they turned the corner.

Blackwood looked over at Gwen. "Do you have any unattached granddaughters by chance?"

"There's a couple left. Look them up."

"I'll have my son do that. I want to thank all of you for—you!" He pointed at Thane. "What are you doing up?"

"I'm sitting and I wouldn't have missed this for anything."

"Show's over. Would one of you gentlemen roll him back to bed? Thanks. I'll come and check on him in a minute."

A Stohlass guard rolled him back to his room and assisted him into bed. Family surrounded him, his mother even tucking him in. "What trigged that out there?" Thane asked.

"Jem, of course," his mother said, smoothing out the sheet. "Director Vanderbilt has obviously decided she's an unacceptable threat to his organized world."

Un-oh. "Threat?"

"Don't give me that," Reyna scolded. "You've been keeping her secret since you met her. The hawk shredded that cage when she used it to bring you to the hospital."

That didn't make sense, considering the distance. "How could invisibility keep me alive for—"

"Invisibility?" all three listeners echoed.

"Uh, yeah," he said, confused at their confusion. "You said you knew."

"Thane," Lee said. "Jem *teleported* you here."

Thane blinked. Blinked again. "Teleported? Seriously?"

Lee's jaw dropped. "You didn't know?"

Doctor Blackwood bustled in. He turned to the others after hooking Thane back up to the monitors. "I realize you're all family and happy to see him awake. Not up," he said, slanting a look at Thane. "He needs a good night's rest and there's too many people in here for that."

Gwen raised her hand. "I'm going. I need to brief Gordon on a few things." Giving Reyna a quick hug, she collected Barker from the hallway and left.

Reyna gave the doctor a small smile when he tilted his head at her. "Just a few minutes more, then we'll leave."

He gave Reyna a professional up-and-down and told her "to get off her feet, too" before he left.

His mom and Lee exchanged silent looks before both turned to him. "Thane, I believe there needs to be a very forthcoming discussion in the near future that includes *all* parties."

"Director Vanderbilt is only the first." Lee said, worry lines in his forehead. "Once Jem's, ah, capabilities filter through the various departments—that's why she's building her home out in the fjord, isn't it? An isolated, secure fortress."

Tiredness washing over him, Thane's head fell back on his pillow. "She's accepted it. Jem has decided to help others, regardless of the consequences. Even told General Kowalski to call on her if needed."

Lee looked startled. "Kowalski knows?"

Thane gave him a lopsided grin. "Not exactly. Teleporting will be a bit of surprise."

The silence stretched as each thought their own thoughts. A nurse pushed open the door.

"I'm sorry. Dr. Blackwood has prescribed medication and rest for Mr. Baron."

Reyna nodded. "We were leaving." She gave Thane a quick peck on the check. "I'll check back with you again tomorrow." They left with their arms around each other.

Thane took the pills, swallowing them under the watchful gaze of the nurse. She made a few adjustments to the equipment and dimmed the lights before wishing him a good night. Things were moving too fast, becoming too complicated. Time for secrets was past. Way past, as far as he was concerned. But if he pushed too hard…well, he'd found her once before.

His last thought as he drifted off? What did they name his new brother?

* * * * *

Lee sat in on a strategy meeting in Gordon's library that evening. Stuart and Nicholas were huddled together, quietly debating the technical and security aspects of teleportation. Nobody had even mentioned the I-word. Mental overload, most likely. Most definitely in his case. He was still trying to wrap his brain around the first. At least, he now understood the reasons behind Jem's secrecy. Was there anything else?

Andi marched into the room and plopped down next to Nicholas.

"I'm representing Jem and her interests," she said. "Not that I don't trust any of you," she added, when her husband aimed a raised eyebrow at her. "Where's Grandmother?"

"She, Sophia, and the others are meeting this evening to discuss BF board members. With the expansion plans she has, BF can't be run by a single person, as Helga Baron has been doing. We'll brief each other when she gets home. Nicholas, did you learn anything from Reis?"

"Not a thing. Seems he's been suspended for insubordination and assault."

"Assault?" Gordon echoed.

"Want to bet it was the Director?" Andi said.

Nicholas nodded. "You'd win. It occurred during the loud insubordination."

"Not good," Gordon said. "It means Vanderbilt's intentions are murky. Lee, how far can a FLEA director go?"

"It depends on the situation, although they do try to stay on the legal side." He hesitated, decided on honesty. "There are recorded cases where a director felt a situation was critical enough to warrant," he paused, made a face, "stepping over the ethical line."

"We can assume Director Spash has made that determination," Gordon said.

"There's not too many ways to control a teleporter," Andi said. "By the way, have you all seen the video Nicholas got from the ICU floor? Grandmother's Fed trashing is a winner."

There were grins and nods.

Gordon rapped his desktop. "Serious, folks. What do we do about Vanderbilt? Or any other Federal Law Enforcement Agency? Their badges supersede everyone else's. They have the power to go anywhere and do whatever they want."

Lee's memories flashed back to his friend and fellow agent, killed by their traitorous peers when Jason uncovered the Consortium's conspiracy. Of himself, bloodied and broken, in their effort to prevent him from passing on Jason's findings. Yes, it was a devastating power when used wrongly.

"They can legally press charges against someone for obstruction, which is what Gwen and Dr. Blackwood did earlier." Worry etched lines in Gordon's face.

"Do you think Vanderbilt will do it as a slap at us?" Andi asked.

Gordon's hand toss was a frustrated 'who knows.'

Stuart spoke up. "There is one category federal agencies don't supersede. Military."

"But would the military treat Jem any better?" Andi said, doubt in her voice.

"She's already offered to help General Kowalski," Lee said. "According to Thane, she's coming out of the shadows. She's decided to use her talents to help wherever and however as needed."

"I know the general," Stuart said, surprising them. "He was Major Kowalski when I served under him during my military hitch. He's a decent man, loyal to those who deserve it and has strong ethical boundaries. I can't say how he'll react, but I'm positive he won't go down Vanderbilt's path."

The room was quiet for several minutes.

"Do we reveal Jem's secret and ask Kowalski for protection? What will the military want in return? Do we do this? We're deciding Jem's future here," Gordon said, his voice thick with emotion. "Is this a betrayal?"

"No," Andi said firmly. "Jem has already made her decision and is building a secure home to protect herself from both users and abusers. And paranoids a la Vanderbilt. Since she expected to eventually tell Kowalski, we will be doing it for her…just not in the way she imagined it would be made."

Lee watched the others as gazes met and heads nodded. His included.

Gordon turned to his desk comp, switched it to comm mode and did a quick search. An icon blinked softly for a few moments, then turned steady.

"Gordon Stohlass. To what do I owe the pleasure?"

"Evening, General Kowalski. Please excuse the late call but…" Gordon looked around the room one more time. "We need your help with something that cannot be discussed over a comm link. Could you come to Azusa? Soon? It's rather urgent."

"This has something to do with the recent attack on Baron and Wilmont?"

"Yes."

"I'll contact you with my arrival time tomorrow."

"Thank you." The light blinked off. "May Jem forgive us if we're wrong."

Chapter 39

"Now, you listen to me young man."

Dr. Blackwood's serious voice drew Thane's full attention. He'd mostly ignored the doctor as his vitals were checked and places were thoroughly poked that didn't hurt until afterwards. Then he'd rolled up next to the bed in the visitor's chair.

"Your system has taken a very bad toxicology beating. You were going into cardiac arrest even as they ran you into Emergency."

"I had three of them?"

"Correct. Quite frankly, I'm amazed you're alive. But you're young, healthy, and evidently well versed in healing. That scar across your shoulder wasn't the first. You're a tough bird, same as your grandmother." He gave Thane a wide smile. "It was a pleasure watching her take those fleas down to their starched shorts yesterday." Dr. Blackwood's countenance flipped back to serious. "You've also been exceedingly lucky so far. I'm betting that laser burn across your chest and the one above your ear were skin-of-the-teeth survivals. This time, you were minus the skin."

Thane swallowed. That close?

"Aconitum is a potent cardiotoxin and neurotoxin agent. The dose you received is usually fatal in under ten minutes. You're recovering well but, while there are no indications of it, there is the potential of future cardiovascular or neurological depredation. Now, now, don't tense up so." He glanced at a beeping monitor. "As I said, there's no indication of any.

However, we couldn't perform a system flush until you were stabilized, meaning your organs were stressed in the meantime. Your body needs time to recover or you could have future problems. For the next two weeks, minimum, you need to keep things easy and light. Rest often."

"I, uh, had a bit of a problem walking to the bathroom this morning."

He nodded. "Pronounced motor weakness is common in severe cases. I'll have a wheelchair brought in. Be careful until it passes. I'd hate for you to fall and break an expensive piece of medical equipment with that hard head."

"Ha, ha. How is Miss Wilmont doing?"

The doctor frowned. "Not sure. What did I tell you about tensing up? That monitor is going to need recalibration at this rate. Not sure doesn't equal not good. It simply means there are things going on with her I don't understand. She has all the symptoms of someone pushed a light-year past physical exhaustion, plus a few others that don't normally go with that condition. And her MRI scan is a bit odd."

Odd probably wasn't the right word.

Blackwood rubbed his chin thoughtfully. "It doesn't make sense. You couldn't have been very far from here or you'd be visiting Doctor Kellermann down in the lower basement. Extreme exertion for only a few minutes would not cause her nearly going into cardiac arrest. There you go again. Want me to stop talking? That's better. Now, I said nearly, not that she did. That was you. Anyway, if someone could tell me exactly what happened…" he trailed off suggestively.

"Sorry. I was unconscious at the time."

"*Hurrmmph.* Anyway, her vitals are improving and she is showing signs of response to external stimuli. I anticipate her regaining full consciousness by tomorrow at the latest."

A wave of relief washed through Thane. "Thank you. For what you've done for both of us."

Dr. Blackwood stood. "You behave yourself for the rest of the day and I'll release you tomorrow on the condition you continue to behave at home."

"I'll behave."

"I'm sure you will, as I'll be informing your mother and grandmother of your physical restrictions. Yep, that usually wipes the kids' smiles away."

***

"I need to see her, Mom."

"Thane, you can hardly stand. Dr. Blackwood says—"

"I know what he said," Thane said impatiently, then realized he'd cut his mother off. "Sorry." He'd been waiting all morning for her to visit. She'd arrived a few minutes ago, dressed in street clothes. She and little Samuel Stohlass Twobears were being discharged.

His mother looked him over carefully. Evidently he passed inspection as she brought the wheelchair over to the bed. Thane gave her a happy grin and managed to get seated without too much help. Reyna pushed him down the hallway. One of the guards at Jem's door held it open for them. They came to a silent stop beside her bed.

Jem was attached to the same machines he'd been, their beeping a soft background noise. Her skin tone naturally on the fair side, an unnatural paleness now outlined stark features. She was thinner. As if it had been weeks instead of three days.

He reached for her hand, a bit mortified at how his was shaking.

Behind him, his mother said, "We don't begin to understand what she did or why it's affected her so. What we do understand is that Jem was willing to kill herself to save you. That's love, Thane."

His gaze on the still form, his tone contemplative, he said, "I was hired to find a cold, heartless killer. What I found was a warm, wary, humorous woman, whose eyes were filled with mystery and secrets. Although, she does have a serious knife skill," he added with a wan smile.

"Which we can be doubly thankful for."

That particular skill had saved his life on Pappia and his grandfather's here on Midgard.

"When things went to hell and I learned some of those secrets…I couldn't walk away. I *had* to help and then somewhere…" his thumb gently stroked the back of her hand "wanting to help her turned into wanting her. But she always kept her distance. Never indicated she felt anything past friendship for me. Jem has always put the safety of others first. It's why she drifted, why she didn't form friendships or let anyone get close. She was afraid they'd be hurt or used against her."

"Until Pappia."

"Until Pappia." *Until that kiss.* "That fear will ride her even harder now, knowing her abilities are filtering out to others. And we *were* used…hurt." His defenses crumbled and he turned bleak eyes to his mother. "I'm afraid, Mom. Afraid this will drive her away to protect us."

Reyna snorted. "Remind you of a certain Tracker who wouldn't come home?"

Thane flushed. Yeah, he was guilty of that too.

"Running doesn't solve problems, Thane. It simply pushes them off into the future where they sneak up and whack you upside the head, usually at the worst possible time. And, no, what's happening now doesn't count, so get that my-fault-look off your face. You didn't duck a problem, we've become targeted by a psychopath. As for Jem…" Reyna regarded the silent form for a moment. "The family is honored to stand by her and we don't give two farts about the misconceptions of others. Jem Wilmont is a decent, wonderful person. Granted, with a few unusual talents. Unique talents she has the integrity and honor to not abuse."

"Unique. That's what I keep telling her. She sees herself as a freak."

"We are often our own harshest critics. Take heed." Reyna poked Thane softly in the shoulder. "Humans are not meant to live in an emotional void—psychopaths excluded. It can damage one's psyche and how they perceive themselves. Circumstances and a couple of bastards forced Jem into that for several years. Andi says she is gradually opening up, becoming more trusting.

"Give her time, Thane. She has a lot to unlearn, doors to unlock. But," Reyna said gently, "there may always be a part of her closed off."

"I don't care."

"And neither do we." Reyna swept the monitors with a careful eye. "She's sleeping, Thane, and you need to be back in bed." She turned the chair around. "Then we'll have a talk. You need to know what's about to happen."

Chapter 40

"This is Glen McWilliams, reporting live this evening from the Azusa Memorial Hospital where there appears to be some sort of standoff on the ninth floor between Stohlass security guards, Federal Law Enforcement Agents and a couple of military members. I understand General Sergi Kowalski, himself, is present. He arrived a short time ago, accompanied by several more Stohlass guards and their Head of Security, Nicholas O'Daniel. Can't miss him folks, he's over seven feet tall.

"That floor contains the ICU, which has seen a lot of recent activity due to the attacks on the Stohlass family. Thane Baron is its current visitor. Miss Jem Wilmont, who apparently was caught up in the latest attack three days ago, is also in residence. Whatever is going on this evening has to be—what?"

The reporter touched his earpiece. "You're sure? How reliable…. Ladies and gentlemen, a military transport has landed at the airport and a squad of Marines is headed for the hospital. This is getting serious and—*oh wow*, that's FLEA Director Vanderbilt getting out of that car. Quick, turn the camera."

Vanderbilt's thunderous face came into focus after a dizzying kaleidoscope of images. He was surrounded by several serious-faced men. More climbed out of a second car behind them.

"Holy shit, they're armed! Uh, sorry folks. Whatever's happening up there is serious. Maybe I can get—crap. They just stormed through the main entrance."

"Is there any way we can get in there? Grab an orderly or something?"

Hand on his earpiece, he was obviously addressing someone across the link. "Hell, no I'm not going anywhere. What? Oh." He dropped his hand and faced the camera. "My apologies to viewers again about the language. Guess you can tell I'm a bit excited. We'll have to wait and see what happens next."

He did a quick recap of the recent attacks on Thane Baron and members of his family. Then he summarized Jem Wilmont's history, the known, the rumors, and the speculation.

"I guess the obvious question is, who is the focus of this situation? Thane Baron? Jem Wilmont? Both of them? *Aaaaannnd* the ICU ward is about to get even more crowded. The Marines have arrived."

The camera zoomed around again to show a large cargo-type van pulling up. Four uniformed and armed men disappeared through the hospital entrance. Two more, one male and one female, stood by their vehicle. Their poised, alert attention underscored the seriousness of the situation.

Three more vehicles pulled into the parking lot, but remained further back.

The reporter had the camera scan over them. "And now we have Azusa Law Enforcement on site. Are they watching or participating? For which side?" The video centered back on him. "Folks, we have sailed way past serious here. Whatever storm is brewing inside, at least they won't have to go far for medical attention if it breaks hard."

Minutes passed. Ten. Fifteen.

McWilliams filled it with recaps of everything that had happened that evening, previous assaults on the Stohlass family, of Jem Wilmont, and whatever he could think of to stretch the time while keeping an eye on the building.

"Quick, turn the camera," he said when several men suddenly exited the hospital. "Those are Federal Agents…they're in a glare-off with the two soldiers…hands dropping to weapons—oh boy, it appears we have another standoff. Azusa Enforcers are bailing out of their cars. Are they going to referee or take sides in—I am *not* getting closer." He shot a glare off to the side. "You don't pay me enough to get in the middle of three armed and hostile groups.

"Okay, referee it is. Anyone recognize the Azusa officer? He appears to have defused the situation. Hands are dropping away from—Director Vanderbilt has exited the building with, I'm assuming, the rest of his people. They're getting into their cars and leaving. Well, guess we know who won the standoff inside. Oh. Looks as if the Azusa referee and a couple of other LE are heading into the hospital. Probably to check on the ninth floor.

"Folks, I'm going to see if I can get someone to talk to me. Maybe even that brave Azusa officer. Please keep check with our news link for updates to this unprecedented situation. This is Glen McWilliams for Network Two, live from a very interesting evening at Azusa Memorial Hospital."

* * * * *

This is Glen McWilliams for Network Two, live from a very interesting evening at Azusa Memorial Hospital.

Ahrymani turned the viewscreen off as the in-studio newscaster came on. She didn't need someone to parrot what she'd already seen.

Katherine rolled into the suite, a wide smile on her face.

Huh. Not her usual reaction after a visit with her aunt. "Good news, I take it?"

"Very good news. Did you see the hospital's live video?"

"Yes. It appears Wilmont has a problem. That stunt of hers has the Feds and military fighting over her. Looks as if the military has won, at least for now."

"That's what I figured. This latest attack on Thane, along with that very public standoff and a whole general feeling of uncertainty has finally got Helga hesitating. She even canceled tomorrow's meeting with Gwen Williams. Helga is beginning to wonder if bringing Baron Financials to Midgard might be the death of it. *Finally.*" Katherine threw her hands up. "After all, what investors want to be associated with a company surrounded by such disastrous occurrences?"

"Or exploded by, maybe literally."

Katherine laughed. "Visiting the office, attending a sponsored event, or simply being around them could be hazardous to their health."

Ahrymani's own smile grew wider. "Then we should reinforce that. Target a few of their entertainment arcades. Increase the fear and uncertainty. If we make Baron's family and anything connected to them a risk…"

"Helga will cancel all plans concerning my cousin, Midgard and Baron Financials," Katherine finished. "Which means the living inheritance will be off the table too."

"This works better for us. Targeting Thane or his sister—any family member for that fact is extremely risky now. Unless a golden opportunity comes up, we shouldn't have to. Too bad. I'd hate to waste the little surprise I've got prepped and waiting."

"Once my aunt withdraws her offer, we can go back to our life on Milania and my cousin can go back to his glamorous life of criminal-chasing. I can wipe my hands of all of them."

"No. Not at first. If the attacks suddenly stop, someone could get suspicious and start nosing around. We've been careful, but if someone peels away all the misdirection and casts a wide-enough look? BF becomes a very good motive. Also, Helga's already changed her mind once. She could do so again, especially after Katrina gets older—I hear she's going to make it. A few years of experience on top of her business degree? I can see your aunt considering it."

"So can I," Katherine agreed, her mood turning sour. "Which means my dear aunt needs to die in the near future. With the company's restructure in limbo, or dead, it won't raise any suspicions when I take over. But, to continue the attacks, you'll have to keep coming back. We can't afford you being spotted."

"Doesn't have to be me. We can hire mercenaries or port lowlifes to target either individuals or property every so often. After five years or so, we should be good."

Chapter 41

Jem ignored whoever had entered the room, too miserable to care what machine they'd fiddle with or what stupid question they'd ask. Instead, she heard a chair being rolled up beside her bed. After a minute or so of silence, she nudged her eyelids up a bit. In the dim light she could make out a figure sitting with arms crossed across the armless chair's top. Male, then. She pushed her eyelids up further and squinted. Oh, him. Let them drop back down. She'd expected him after hearing last night's vitriol-laced arguments outside her room.

"I'm really not up for an interrogation, General."

"I don't doubt it. I've seen the hospital parking lot security video."

Her eyes flew open. How many had seen it?

"It's been confiscated," Kowalski assured her, "along with another one from a nearby building that also caught your arrival. Dr. Blackwood has also provided me with a summary of your current condition."

How do you summarize a head that wants to split open so your brains can dance on your shoulders? Or share its wealth in spikes down your spine and limbs? The bouts of vertigo seemed to have stopped, although she could feel the bedpan a nurse had judiciously left beside her.

"That evidence, along with Baron and Stuart's reports, made it possible for me to override Director Vanderbilt's authority under the Planetary Defense and Security Act. You and all knowledgeable aspects of the aforementioned evidence have been sealed under the same Act. Those already exposed have been briefed and will be held accountable for any leaks."

"Thank you. I don't believe I'd fare well under Vanderbilt." What was in store for her under the military?

"I understand Director Vanderbilt's point of view," he told her bluntly. "Being able to negate *every* aspect of security makes you an unprecedented threat, from economic institutions to military installations. I disagree—vehemently—with his resolution. I'm pretty sure it entailed drugs. If anything, attacking or running roughshod over you could very well turn you into the thing he fears most. Like others we won't mention, he fails to realize you'll only be a threat if you choose to be. Or pushed into it."

Others? What others?

Then the General ruined his official-ness.

"Well, hell." He plopped his chin on his arms and gave Jem a rueful smile. "I have greatly admired the restraint you've displayed since you came to our attention. Now?" Kowalski shook his head. "I'm absolutely in awe. Most people would have succumbed to temptation. What am I going to do with you? Scratch that. What *can* I do with you?"

Jem shrugged, and immediately regretted it. Pain surged down her spine. Her left arm's spasm knocked the pan sideways.

"I'll get the doctor." Kowalski rose, concern filling his voice.

"No," Jem said, fighting the pain. "Give me a moment." It was actually minute or two before the pain level dropped to a bearable level. She gave the closely watching general a nod.

"I'll keep the rest short. What I've done has put us both in a very precarious position. You're a private citizen with all the rights and etcetera. Placing you under the Defense and Security Act also makes you a military asset. You did once offer to help out as needed, so I'm assuming we'd have probably ended up in this position eventually."

"I had hoped to keep it a little bit more low-key."

"Vanderbilt's fault," he said, his irritation showing. "The man should have known better. I've already warned him about any further public displays. Do you know why it affected you so severely this time? Was it the distance?"

"I don't know. This was the first time I did it." May it also be the last.

Startled, Kowalski said, "You have never done this before? This is not how you've been bypassing security measures?"

"No, sir." Guess it didn't matter now. "Ask Thane or Seth about—" His hand motion stopped her.

"We're not in a properly secure area. Say nothing explicit."

"Oh. Okay. Ask them about the method we call ghost-mode."

"I'll do that."

A long silence stretched between them. Jem picked at her blanket, aware of his assessing gaze. She rested her head back on the pillow as the throb behind her eyelids intensified. Whatever he was pondering about, could he go do it somewhere else? She needed some of those wonderful drugs. Ah, maybe he was telepathic. He was rolling the chair back against the wall.

"My guards are posted in the hallway to keep out reporters and federal riffraff. You'll be taken to a secure place when you leave here. We'll be able to discuss things more in depth there. Do I have your word you'll stay put until we figure things out? Come to terms?"

She gave him a crooked smile. "Where would I go?"

*   *   *   *   *

"No!" Thane lurched up from his chair. "She nearly died, Kowalski. And you want her to do it again?"

"I'm aware of the risks." Kowalski understood completely what he was asking. He also knew he'd need the family's support in this. "In case you haven't noticed, Jem Wilmont renders all current security and defensive plans obsolete." And wasn't that a kicker? Although, after teleportation, learning about the invisibility was almost anticlimactic.

"Believe me," Nicholas O'Daniel said, "we noticed."

Thane glared at Kowalski, unable to refute the claim. He literally fell back into his seat when his trembling legs gave out.

"You do that again," Reyna said, finger jabbing angrily, "and I will tie you into that chair. Stay off your feet."

"While the circumstances are themselves unique, what she did isn't," Gwen said. "Documented cases of people being able to do the inconceivable under intense stress goes back centuries. Yes, it usually involves someone they care about being in extreme danger. No, it was never repeatable." She gave the general a pointed look.

Kowalski sighed. His intent to only speak to Thane, Seth and the two Stohlass security men had been sunk as soon as he and his aide walked through their front door. Given the close-knit reputation the family had, he shouldn't have been surprised. At least they were in a conference room that O'Daniel assured him was as secure as the one they'd used for a meeting at Stohlass Enterprises a year ago.

"True," Lt. Corrigan said, "except the circumstances *are* unique. Is this a one-time happenstance or a permanent result of Miss Wilmont's mutation? Which is not a natural one, according to Mr. Baron. Therefore, historical rules may not hold."

Andi make a rude noise. "She's certainly breaking a lot of scientific rules."

Understatement of the century, Kowalski thought sourly. "While we will continue to limit the knowledge as much as possible, others *are* going to learn of it. Exposed to it in one manner or another. While her invisibility is impressive, it can be blocked. Teleportation is what's going to give people the most fits. Knowing the distance she can teleport is crucial. It'll help alleviate fears if she can't teleport just anywhere. Say, from orbit into a place on the planetary surface."

"I'd say that's pretty obvious," Gordon said, his tone cutting.

"Even if she could," Thane said, "she won't be in any shape to do anything when she gets there. You saw the hospital video."

Keeping this on a friendly basis wasn't working, so Kowalski let the General out.

"This was her *first* teleport experience, Baron. Will the aftereffects diminish and her distance increase over time? How often can she do it? Does it only affect her and not someone she takes with her—who's conscious? Can she transport more than one at time? How many?" His voice was a ruthless whip. "Potentially, she could transport multiple operatives to multiple locations at various distances. But, why bother? Jem Wilmont is a one-person commando team. If we don't learn what her boundaries are, others will keep pushing for more."

The room went silent. Kowalski exchanged a headshake with his aide, amazed the roomful of otherwise intelligent people had overlooked the obvious. Maybe because they were civilians. Maybe they were simply too emotionally close to the source. Maybe they didn't want to think about it.

"Jem is not a weapon to aim and fire," Thane finally said, his eyes a cold, steel-gray.

"To you and me, no." Kowalski relaxed his tone a bit. "Others undoubtedly will see her as exactly that. Starting with my superiors. By placing Wilmont herself—not just the knowledge about her—under the Defense Act, I made her a military asset. And, truthfully, she can be of great benefit to the Republic. We're not the only fish in the galactic sea anymore. There are two other…entities?" Kowalski shook his head. "Hell, what do we call them, other than a royal pain in the butt? Mark my words, there will be more. Political intrigue and spying will be the least of our future worries."

"What of Jem's future?"

The general rubbed his neck tiredly. "I'm not the enemy here, Baron, and, truly, I am trying to help. I don't want to see Wilmont exploited any more than you do. I'm walking a fine line here, myself. This is not a storm we can avoid. We either meet it head on, or get swamped. By knowing Wilmont's limits…by understanding exactly what she can and cannot do, we can prevent her from being arbitrarily tasked something that puts her unknowingly at risk."

Sarcastically, Seth asked if they could get that in writing.

Corrigan leaned over and whispered something in Kowalski's ear. He shot her a look of surprise and nodded. He turned to Gordon. "Your firm handles all of her legal needs, yes? Could you produce a Jaguide-clad contract safe-guarding her interests and detailing the military's obligations and limitations? With severe penalties if breached?"

Two very feral smiles were his answer.

Chapter 42

Jem set on the edge of her hospital bed, dressed and waiting to be released. Tired, depressed, and a bit headachy. The lingering remnants of what she'd done. She still couldn't believe it. She'd shifted to save Thane's life. Then, somehow, she'd shifted through that out-of-phase-with-the-universe nothingness to the hospital. The pain of those seconds had been as real as the first time, when the Myerstone Lab's malfunctioning experiment had dragged her from that UPMS hanger and started her down this path.

Just when she was learning to live with one freakiness, this had to happen. She was a freak, squared. Her dream of a new life, of a real home...*so close*, she thought bitterly. But Thane was alive, which made whatever came worth it.

Dr. Blackwood pushed the door open. "How do you feel?"

"Tired. A bit of a headache."

"Not surprised, considered you arrived almost as dead as Baron. Nobody will tell me what happened to you. The extreme exhaustion was part of it and I'm told the other part is classified. I don't care about classification, security levels and such. What I care about is my patient's health, and it's hard to treat someone when you don't have all the details. I have found quite a bit of information about you, none of it pertaining to your condition and most of it is hawk droppings. Don't people have better things to gossip about?"

Jem's cheeks flamed warm.

"I'm going to assume the information about your security adroitness is correct or the authorities wouldn't be so flustered. Based on recent events, something happened that has 'raised the stakes,' as they say, and why you're now under the military's aegis. By the way, I approve of General Kowalski and can't abide Director Vanderbilt."

The door opened and a female guard stepped in. "We're ready to leave now."

"Well, I'm not," Blackwood snapped. "Step back outside."

The guard opened her mouth, closed it and did as the doctor ordered.

He turned back to Jem. "My advice? Ignore the crap. My prescription is the same I gave Baron. You need rest, good solid food and more rest. Unfortunately, you don't have a mother I can put into hover-mode."

Oh, boy. She could picture Thane's glare.

"Ordinary painkillers should be sufficient now. If not, or if the pain suddenly spikes, let me know. In fact, put me at the top of your call list." He threw a sharp look at the door. "I have a sneaky hunch that whatever happened six days ago may be repeated."

Unease skittered along still-tender nerve endings. "I'll keep what you said in mind. Thank you for everything."

He gave her a fatherly pat on the shoulder and left. His voice came almost immediately back through the slowly closing door. *"I'm holding you accountable. Don't you dare…"*

The door muffled the rest and whatever response. It sounded as if he was chewing someone out. That someone turned out to be General Kowalski when he stalked through the door wearing an irritated look. Lieutenant Corrigan wore an amused one. She flashed Jem a warm smile and a wink.

"Ready?" Kowalski asked. "I'll go out front and do a song-and-dance to keep the reporters busy. We'll join you later."

They took her down the back way to the service entrance where she and her guards climbed into an enclosed van. Jem slumped back and closed her eyes as it pulled smoothly away. They were probably heading to the airport. Despondency was a dark cloud settling over her. Would her life ever be her own? Her every move not under somebody's scrutiny?

She trusted Kowalski, truly believed he had her best interests at heart. He was also a soldier with a strong sense of duty and superiors. They would expect something in return for their protection. Well, she had offered even before this and she did owe him. She had expected to manage it a bit better, though. Management and control, wasn't that her mantra? *Management and control…management and control…* she chanted silently as the van stopped, started, and swayed around corners.

Yes, dammit, she *would* take control. This was a setback, nothing more.

Energized resolve snuffed out the cloud and she straightened, flashing a smile at the guard across from her. She got a wary look in return. She would insist on a few terms herself, such as living in Azusa. And if they got too demanding, the terms too unacceptable? Well, they just might find those rapids a little difficult to navigate.

How about that? She was thinking like a true Midgarder.

The van turned another corner, slowed to a stop. Too quiet to be the airport. Jem stepped out, chin up and back straight. Then blinked. This wasn't the expected military compound or safe house. She was standing in front of Gordon and Gwen's home. And there was Nicholas, coming out the doorway and giving her a grin almost as big as him.

"What? Expecting to be put up in some uncomfortable military barracks?"

"Something like that."

"Our barracks are quite comfortable," the guard beside her said with a bit of asperity.

Nicholas took her arm. "Come on inside. Everyone's waiting."

Expecting to be taken to the War Room—a.k.a. Gordon's library, she found herself in a small, well-appointed conference room. A crowded one. Reyna, Gwen, and Andi gave her hugs. Gordon and Seth opted for shoulder squeezes while Stuart simply nodded. Then Thane's arms were around her and the sense of safety enveloped her again.

Oh, dear Universe. Do I get to keep this?

"Okay, Baron. Let her up for air."

Wait. Was that…? Jem turned as the arms released her. "Boyd?" Then she was the one doing the hugging. "What are you doing here? When did you arrive?"

"I left Pappia. Thought I'd swing by and see how you were doing before heading home. Got here last night to find you in the hospital and everything crazy."

"You quit your job with the Euphrates Mining Company?"

"It was either that or become a Euphrates citizen. You heard about that? Since Pappia is their mining colony, it followed—kicking and screaming. All EMC personnel and us Independents had forty days to decide. There's a lot of unhappy people there since most couldn't afford to leave and hunt new jobs. Those working under a contract will have to choose when it expires."

"What about Margo?"

"Margo and her sig-ner were mulling it over when I left."

"She settled down?" Jem's face split with a happy grin. They'd both been Pounding J bartenders and she'd eventually become friends with the vivacious woman who had no filter on what came out of her mouth. Conversations with her could be hilarious or embarrassing. Often both.

"How about we all sit down and let the two invalids get off their feet," Gwen said.

Jem looked around the room at all the smiles. This was a way better reception than she'd expected, despite the nervous undercurrent she could sense. Well, she had rocked their world. Thane walked her over to a comfortable-looking chair at one end of the table. Story time coming up. Hers. The oblong style would make it easier for everyone to see her, as well as each other.

Thane sat on her left, Boyd on her right. Jem noticed no one took the seats opposite them. "Are we waiting on someone?"

"We're waiting for—here they are now," Gordon said, as Lee escorted Kowalski and Corrigan into the room.

The general had said they'd be joining her. *And he just spotted Boyd.*

"Who is this? He'll have to leave. This will be a highly classified meeting."

"You can try and make me," the heavy-worlder drawled, to several snickers.

Lee closed and locked the door, formally announced "Room secured," then plopped down next to Reyna.

"Relax, General," Thane said. "Boyd here already knows a bit about Jem from Pappia. You can read him into the Act for the other later."

Boyd gave Thane the stink-eye. "Read me into what act for what *other*?"

"Planetary Defense and Security Act, of course," Thane said.

"So we can talk in front of you about Jem teleporting," Seth added.

Jem watch Boyd's expression go from suspicious, to worried, to astonished. Yep, he had a lot of catching up to do. And, yeah, guess it would have appeared to them as though she had teleported. Huh. Was Kaleb clairvoyant?

"Boyd, is it?" Kowalski and his aide took their seats. "Don't leave without talking to me. Now, Miss Wilmont—"

"Jem," she interjected. Might as well get rid of the formality.

"Jem," Kowalski acknowledged. "You said this was the first time you teleported."

"Yes, sir. I can't explain it other than being desperate. I can't hold a shift for more than an hour, tops. Not enough time for Stuart to get to the hospital with me tagging along in ghost-mode. The door on the hospital's east side was the one we'd always used when we visited, so that was my clearest image. I focused on it. Hard. Kind of a mental grab-and-hold-for-dear-life thing." Thane's life, in this case. "I was determined to keep that hold for however long it took, for whatever it took. Suddenly things went black and..." she couldn't stop the shudder "we were there." It was as terrible as the first time. At least the aftereffects only lasted a couple of days instead of months as the lab accident had.

There was a short, fraught silence.

"I know you don't want to hear this but, can you repeat the teleport? Without the life-or-death impetus?" Kowalski said.

"I don't know and I don't want to try. Is this one of the terms for your continued protection?"

"No. That is yours regardless. This involves a different matter. I understand how—"

"No, you don't," she shot back. "You have no idea what it's like. It's…It's…" she shook her head, unable to come up with anything close to adequate.

"If she doesn't want to do it, then she doesn't," Boyd said, cool determination in his voice.

"Who did you say you were?"

"Her friend." His glare ran around the table. "Am I the only one who cares about *her*, not what she can do?"

"Now see here—"

"That's uncalled for!"

"You have no idea—"

"*Silence!*" Kowalski's voice sliced through the babble and the room became a silent tomb. He leaned forward. "You have the misconception that what you think matters. Let me lay it out for everyone at this table. None of *us* matters."

The tension became almost palpable.

He continued, his voice hard and unyielding. "There are powerful people who have one directive driving their lives: protect. Whether it's the Republic in general or their corner of it, they will do whatever they feel *has* to be done to ensure it. They don't like unknowns. They don't like mysteries. They don't like anything that jeopardizes the status quo.

"Jem Wilmont is all the above and more. She is a flashing red light for these individuals. Unless we can answer their questions, unless we eliminate the unknowns, they will move to eliminate her. That obviously won't be easy, so they'll use whatever method," he paused, "whatever ruthless ploy will work."

They will strike at me through them. Jem's pulse spiked. What she had always feared was coming true. Except it wouldn't be one or two psychos this time, it'd be an organized, concerted effort backed by Republic resources. She needed to leave, to break all contact. *Tonight, I'll*—a warm hand folded itself around hers.

"Running doesn't solve anything," Thane said quietly. "It simply pushes things into the future."

"He's right. This needs to be dealt with now, before things go bad. And yes," Kowalski shot Boyd a scathing look, "we do care. We're all on Jem's side. That's why we're here. But to help you manage what's to come, Jem, we have to know your capabilities and limitations," Kowalski told her. "By having the answers to the questions and de-mystifying what you can and cannot do, well…they still won't be happy but it should keep the scales from tipping over."

A chorus of "*Should?*" ran relay around the table.

"Yes, especially if we can offer additional assurances in writing. Jem, your lawyers are working on a contract to provide that as well as to protect you. It will identify what you will and will not do, as well as controlling what others can and cannot ask of you. And, yes, you can count on requests."

A contract sounded good. Management and control. Yep. Good. Another baby step.

"To all those ends, you'll need to run trials. Experiment. I promise you, we'll take it slow," Kowalski said. "We'll start by trying very short distances."

He was right but, going through it again…she swallowed.

"We'll start by bringing a qualified doctor on board," Reyna said tartly.

"Dr. Blackwood," Jem and Thane said in unison.

"Wait. Just how does this affect her?"

"Any volunteers for showing the irritated heavy-worlder the hospital video?" Thane said.

***

Post-supper pills had reduced a pounding headache to a dull throb. Jem leaned back against the headboard, tired, happy, worried, and not yet ready for sleep. She was in one of the family's guest suites, as this was deemed the safest reporter-free place for now. Thane and the others had caught her up on events and they rambled now through her drowsy mind.

Susi had decided to rebuild their home. In the meantime, she and her family were taking up residence in the Twin Clift Apartments, which Nicholas said had top-notch security. Janice would report back to duty after seeing them settled in. Security precautions on Copenhagen had been heightened around

Dane's and his sister's family.

Katrina was healing. It was now ninety-eight percent certain Dr. Giovannelli's procedure would return her hand to full use, although it remained to be seen how much permanent damage her arm would have. They'd started bone regeneration treatments on her other injuries, feeling her progress advanced enough to be safe. A guard stood at her door to keep the rest of her safe.

Safe. *Such a fleeting concept*, Jem thought. An illusion that comforts people and keeps them from becoming babbling idiots. Her blinders had been ripped off years ago. The Stohlass family's illusion had been shattered in about as horrible a way as possible. Now, they have to be wondering how to protect themselves from a teleporter.

After an enthusiastic—on Andi's part—discussion, she'd grudgingly acquiesced to the term. As Andi had put it, the technical mechanics behind what she did was immaterial, it was the result achieved that was being defined. Jem stared off into space. Teleporter. How many would opt to take Vanderbilt's stance? How many of Kowalski's *others* would believe the threat she posed outweighed her usefulness? The good she could do?

They'd agreed at the meeting's end to wait until she was fully recovered before running any tests. Could she drag it out, pretend weakness or headache? *No.* Why delay the inevitable? Jem scrunched down under the covers as exhaustion crept over her. She appreciated the way the general had used *we* and *us* in their meeting. He really was on her side.

Despite keeping the afternoon's attitudes and conversations light, Jem had once again sensed the underlying tension. No wonder, considering everything they were dealing with. Her problems aside, Patricia Keegan was their foremost worry. And then there was Helga Baron, who appeared to be backing away from her commitment.

When she'd asked about Baron Financials, Gwen had tried to hide her concern behind a disdainful sniff. *The woman needs to make up her mind*, Gwen had said. Well, Jem wondered with a yawn, had Katherine's wheelchair's tires gone flat from her bouncing all over the place? In fact, she'd bet the woman was constantly regaling her aunt with this latest evidence of how unsuitable Thane was to head Baron Financials.

Again, something teased. Danced in the shadows just out of reach.

Another yawn, bigger than the first, drove everything else away and replaced it with the hilarity high point of the evening. Holding Sam—never Sammy, his father had instructed them all firmly—she'd commented to Reyna about his not-so-little newborn size. Reyna had replied that Lee forgot to mention he was the runt of the family.

His response?

I believe I've already proven I'm not small at all. Lee's bobbing eyebrows had elicited groans, blushes, laughter and a quick change of subject.

Jem drifted off to sleep, taking the image of Thane's mortified expression behind a double face-palm with her.

Chapter 43

Rutherford yawned and closed the last trainee's file. Most of the new recruits were shaping up well. There were two that might want to consider a different career field. He'd give them another week. Time to go home.

Starting to log off his computer, a soft chime signaled a new message.

After a short debate, he decided to see if it was important or could wait until tomorrow. Opening his mail, the system automatically highlighted the two new ones. Looks like they came in on the latest UPMS mail pod and—*sonovabitch.*

One text, one video, and both from Vanderbilt.

He glared at the file IDs. The Midgard Fed Director was becoming even more obsessed about Wilmont than him. Frankly, the man's demands for news and progress reports were reaching paranoia level. If that vid-message was nothing more than a rant, he was going to log a formal complaint.

He was not ruining his evening with that man's crap.

He logged off, grabbed his jacket and headed for the door. Whatever it was, it could wait until morning. The scotch and the woman pouring it wouldn't.

Chapter 44

Her aches lasted three days. After another two wonderfully bland days, Jem announced herself as healed at the breakfast table. To her dismay, Gwen immediately let Dr. Blackwood know. Jem found herself scheduled for a full medical exam the next morning.

She gave Gwen a grumpy look and went back to her bacon and eggs.

Dr. Blackwood had taken learning about her skillset rather calmly, simply raising one eyebrow and commenting "It would've been nice to know sooner." His insistence of having a base-line of her medical status was sound. She refused to dwell on the why.

Boyd had stayed at her apartment, since there was no sense in him renting a room when her place was available. She grinned, thinking of the reception several foolish reporters got when they knocked on the door. She and Thane had seen him off yesterday evening. His home world of Brisbane, Anatolia Three, was the *Constance Bell's* third stop. She'd spent one happy evening getting updated on Pappia, including learning that Saul, Pounding J's bouncer, was Margo's significant partner. Her friend's guy had a steady, easy-going nature, the perfect counterbalance for the exuberant woman.

Jem scraped her plate clean, half listening to Reyna and Gwen finishing up plans for the return-to-duty dinner tomorrow night. Janice Stohlass was leaving in two days and everyone wanted to see her off. She was dishing up a second helping from the sideboard when Andi came flying in.

Plopping down in a chair, she announced, "They found another one."

"Where?" Gwen demanded.

"Same place as the first one—Will-lass Entertainment Arcade on Nordic Avenue."

Another bomb. The third one. *Shit, damn, crap.* She collapsed back in her chair, her plate forgotten. "Found before it went off?"

Andi nodded. "Nicholas believes with security around the family so tight, Keegan is now targeting our properties."

"She's doing more than that," Gwen said. "Bombs will drive away customers. Who wants to risk their family if the next one isn't found in time?"

"The woman is determined to take the whole family down." Reyna waved her fork. "We have *nothing* on her. How do you catch a frigging ghost?" Her mouth made an O and she turned to Jem. "Sorry, I didn't mean to malign you."

Jem grinned. Being able to openly talk about it was both refreshing and wonderful. "A ghost might be needed to catch another one. However," she added on seeing the women all perk up, "I'd have to know where and when to keep watch. There's a time limit, remember?"

Andi grunted. "Security will have to be tightened at all our arcades, even if we close them. We'd need it to keep the damage and cost down."

Worried, Jem asked, "Do you have other properties besides the arcades? Are they known?"

Gwen nodded. "There are several business complexes and one apartment building we have invested in. How well known?" She shrugged. "Publicly, not much. Researching business or finance databases will find the information."

"Tax records?"

"No," Reyna said. "The records list the owners of record, not their silent partners. Still…it wouldn't hurt to contact them. Warn them."

"I think they're already aware, my dear," Gwen said. "As soon as this new one hits the news, I predict we'll be the ones getting contacted."

Van materialized in the doorway. "Ms. Williams? Mr. Owens from Ridge Bay Apartments is calling for you on your office line."

"What did I tell you? Though it's a bit faster than I expected. Excuse me, please." Gwen took her coffee cup with her.

"Where are all the menfolk?"

"Lee is doing a post-feeding burp and cuddle bonding." A happy smile lit up Reyna's face.

Andi gave a lopsided grin. "Thane and Granddad were on the terrace, unfortunately."

"Unfortunately?" Jem repeated.

"Yes, they saw Nick running out, heard what happened, and insisted on going…either with him or in another vehicle when he objected."

"Uh-oh," Jem and Reyna said together.

"Yeah. Nick was pissed. He ordered one gate guard into the car and took the other's weapon. Which," Andi winced, "he threw at Thane. It's a good thing my cousin has fast reflexes."

* * * * *

It was several hours later when Nicholas stormed into the house, Thane and Gordon stalking in behind him. He'd kept his temper while going over the situation at the Will-lass Arcade. Everyone there undoubtedly assumed his bad attitude was due to the attempted bombing. It wasn't.

He was *PISSED!*

Screw waiting to reach his office. He wheeled around, there in the middle of the formal front room and not caring who the frigging hell heard, and let it explode. "Your ass did *not* need to be at the arcade."

"Yes, it did." Gordon matched him in both glare and volume. "It and its workers are our responsibility and we need to show the world we are taking these threats seriously. I will not let that…that psychopathic piece of shit destroy this family and all we stand for."

"Am I head of security or not?"

"Yes, which means you work for me."

"Well, *Boss*, you gave Keegan a perfect opportunity today," Nicholas ground out. "Three *key* family members in public and in one place." His status as Security Head and an in-law made him doubly so. You," he jabbed a finger at Gordon, "put us and everyone around us at risk."

Gordon gaped in stunned silence.

"You're saying it could have been a trap?" Thane clarified, keeping his tone neutral.

Nicholas gave him his share of glare and noted his hand rested on the stunner he still wore. Did the idiot think he needed it against him?

"Yes. The bomb was meant to be found. A standard security sweep would have found it, much less the more stringent one now in place. Keegan is toying with us. She's watching how we react. The woman is a prime strategist and is building a plan. If Keegan had been ready today with another explosive, a laz-gun or, hell, more darts, at least two of us would be dead."

Gordon's mouth opened and closed.

"Aren't you being a bit harsh?" Gwen stepped out from the group hovering in the doorway.

"No. My *job* is to implement measures that keep everyone safe. To think about and counteract possibilities. I can't do that when my decisions—my orders—are superseded for some political, prideful, ego-coddling grandstanding. You either trust me to do my job, and permit me to do my job, or you can find someone else to be your security flunky. Which will it be, *Boss*?"

Shock filled every expression.

"I wouldn't have believed this if I hadn't seen it." Jem walked into the danger zone. All attention zeroed in on her. "Patricia Keegan is apparently winning in her campaign to destroy this family."

"She's not won anything," Gordon snapped.

"Sure she has, and you're doing her work for her." Jem stuck her hands in her pockets. "She laid the groundwork. You've built the rest on tension, uncertainty, fear, and paranoia. Stress will eventually open fissures in even the strongest families. She doesn't have to do anything more than an occasional poke. Just sit back, toast the viewscreen, and watch the cracks widen as the family destroys itself from the inside out."

Silence.

"You say it was the right thing to do but, seriously, was it?" she asked Gordon. "Did you or Thane have anything to contribute to the investigation or cleanup being performed by experienced and fully qualified personnel? Could not an interview given in the security of your home or office still properly have expressed your feelings and commitment? Could not your support be demonstrated in a short, no-notice visit at a later time? Or was it, indeed, prideful grandstanding? A figurative pounding of the chest and the adult version of 'you can't make me?'"

Nicholas felt the tension slowly bleed from the room in the long, thoughtful silence that followed. Felt his own anger draining away, replaced by tiredness. Jem wasn't wrong. If he was feeling the strain—and that was exactly what had fueled his outburst—it would be even worse for untrained and unprepared civilians. He should have remembered that. Still, his point had to be made.

"Am I head of security or not?" Nicholas asked again, his tone quieter.

"Yes. Yes, you are. And I apologize. I'll try to be more…prudent in the future." Gordon turned, walked to Gwen and took her hand. They left the room together, the servants scattering ahead of them.

Andi walked over to wind her arm around his. "Sorry, big guy," she murmured.

Nicholas looked to Jem. "Thank you for defusing that. Us."

She nodded, giving Thane a shuttered, unreadable look before leaving.

Thane shrugged. "I admit, we weren't thinking and I'm not use to standing around. I apologize also." He took off the stunner and handed it back, saying, "At least I was armed."

Nicholas took it with a grumpy, narrow-eyed look. Then he and Andi were alone.

"Jem is right," Andi said softly, leaning her head against her large husband's arm. "Damage has been done."

"Yes. The wound will heal." He looked in the direction Gordon had vanished in. Would it heal to what it was before?

* * * * *

Jem's next day was a busy one. Dr. Blackwood was pleased with her excruciatingly thorough exam. Some "a bit odd" results he put down as her body adapting to conditions it was never meant to experience. The interrogation that followed did not go as well. He'd already gotten all the details about her teleport, and he now wanted details of the original event. What she'd experienced during and after. After a frustrating half-hour of trying to answer his in-depth questions, she made the mistake of saying she had Dr. Bluethon's files on a hand computer.

Oh, yeah. Big mistake. She hadn't planned on retrieving the hand comp from its safe hiding place until her home's vault was completed. She'd have to sneak out sometime and make a copy of the relevant files to avoid his pestering. Finally escaping Blackwood's attention, she spent several hours in Seth's office as they worked on her proposed contract.

The evening brought Janice's farewell dinner.

Jem sipped her drink and looked around the room. The dinner was buffet style, allowing people to mingle and talk while they munched. They were mingling and munching, but the talking was…stilted. Thane was brooding in a corner, not even trying to be social. Whenever someone mentioned the stiffness permeating the room, the default reply was a bland "It's the tension and stress, naturally."

Understatement of the year.

The household staff was waiting for the next blowup. Everyone involved in the snit-fit yesterday had been avoiding each other or, like tonight, stiffly polite when they couldn't. And she was at the top of the avoidance list. Not even a head nod in her direction since it happened. It had been a foolish move, jumping in the middle of a family squabble like that. But she couldn't stand by and watch the family tear itself apart in front of her. The family she secretly called hers.

Jem's hand tightened almost painfully around her glass. Who was she fooling?

She'd never be one of them now, except on the periphery. Maybe. If she was lucky. Even Andi's matchmaking prods had stopped. Who wanted a freak in the family? So, why was she even here?

Jem tossed back the last of her drink and set the glass down on the nearest flat surface. Saying a brief goodbye and good luck to Janice, she excused herself. In her allotted suite, she packed the few things that were hers. Making a detour to the Security office, she found Stuart occupying the chair instead of

Nicholas.

He glanced at the pack slung over her shoulder. "Weren't you suppose to remain here for the time being?"

"Am I under guard?"

"No. Has someone given you that impression?"

"I have a few things to take care of." Files to copy. Plans to make.

"What about the trials?"

Jem's stomach clenched. "In two days, last I heard. We've decided on the Stohlass vacation island. It's isolated and the house has a small med-room Dr. Blackwood can use if needed. I'll meet you here. Send me a text if anything changes." She turned and headed for the side door the security people used for quick access.

She heard Thane call her name as she reached the door. She didn't pause or turn around, but continued on out. Jem strolled across the yard, a guard dog getting a quick pat on the head. Once out the back gate, she started walking. Blindly. Not caring where.

Chapter 45

The pounding on Reis's door turned out to be Jennifer Gaines, his partner. Ex-partner.

"We've got to do something about Vanderbilt," she said, brushing past him.

He shoved the door closed. "Not me. He's your problem now."

She stopped pacing and faced him. "What do you mean?"

He sprawled on the couch. "Haven't you heard? I've been terminated."

"What? When?"

"I got the text a couple of hours ago. Really spiced up my breakfast."

Shock turned into fury. "The bastard terminated you by *text*? Without a formal review?"

"Uh-huh." Reis stared, fascinated. He didn't know Gaines knew that many cuss words.

Winding down, she spit out, "Perfect. He can't order you to stand down."

What? "Is that why you're here?"

"Yes. We have to stop them. Vanderbilt and Rutherford are—"

"Rutherford? He's back?" His foot smacked the floor as he straightened. "What do you know?"

Reis simply stared at her after she told him. He couldn't believe it. Yes, he could. He'd watched the Director spiral into zealot-fueled paranoia. His current unemployment was due to him protesting several orders.

Gaines plopped down next to him. Head in hands, she said, "I don't know what to do."

He reached for his phone and called up his list of numbers. Found the one he wanted. He gave her an encouraging smile while waiting for the call to connect.

"Hello, Sergi? We have a problem developing around Jem Wilmont."

Gaines's eyes widened and she mouthed, *"General Kowalski?"*

"Yes, sir. I'm passing the phone to someone who has the information." He held out the phone.

Gaines gulped and took it. "Sir? I'm Federal Agent Gaines. This morning Director Vanderbilt…"

Chapter 46

Jem stared at the convoy of vehicles lined up in the Stohlass driveway. Spotting Dr. Blackwood, she hurried over. "Hi, Doc. How big a boat are we going to need?" They'd be leaving from the private marina the family had recently leased.

"Morning, Miss Wilmont. Nothing large. You, me, Stuart and a couple of guards to watch the boat while we're busy."

She waved toward the vehicles and ignored the twinge of disappointment the lack of a certain name caused.

"Ah. Mr. O'Daniel is going with Ms. Sullivan to her first prenatal checkup. Ms. Williams and Mr. Baron are going to ambush the elder Ms. Baron since she's refusing any meetings. Ms. Stohlass and Mr. Twobears are going to visit with Katrina. Oh! Did you know she's conscious?"

Jem shook her head. Maybe she should have answered one of those phone calls.

"They brought her out of the healing coma, um, yesterday I believe. Her healing has progressed far enough to do the brachial plexus surgery, plus they wanted to rescan for any brain impairment. Is Stuart the man's first or last name?"

"That's good news about Katrina. As for Stuart, that's all I've ever heard him called. My guess? He doesn't like whatever the other one is. And call me Jem, please."

People began exiting the house. Catching sight of Thane, Jem asked the doctor which car was theirs and climbed into its back seat. The doctor sat next to her as a driver and Stuart settled into the front.

The gates opened and the convoy exited. Cars peeled off in various directions. Stuart let them know the one directly behind had the guards accompanying them to the island. Jem stared out the window, mentally bracing herself for what was to come.

* * * * *

Thane waited until they were back in the privacy of their car before giving vent to frustration. "That was a perfectly bad waste of time, Grandmother."

Their driver maneuvered them out of the hotel's parking garage.

"I admit, it did not go as I'd hoped," Gwen said. "Especially with Katherine there. It was rather unfortunate timing for her to visit her aunt."

"Too unfortunate, if you ask me. I wouldn't be surprised if she's bribed a couple of hotel workers to keep tabs on her aunt's visitors."

"Hmmm. Me either. Katherine would do about anything to keep her aunt from restarting things."

"You mean those constant barbs about how we couldn't project a stable business image if we didn't have a stable personal one?" Thane's sarcasm leaned on the heavy side.

"She does have a valid point from a business perspective. Stability is one of the prime factors investors look for. At least Helga never believed those drug charges on Random Two. That's why she sent that lawyer to get you out of it. Idiot that he was, trying to bribe Law Enforcers."

Thane watched the passing scenery out his window. That had been unexpected. When Katherine had made a sarcastic comment alluding to the charges, Helga herself had rebuked her niece.

The family is known for honor, integrity and business sense, Katherine. He himself is a well-reputed Tracker. If he needed money and didn't want to go to the family for some reason, he wouldn't have turned down a very lucrative CEO position.

There had been a flash of intense emotion across Katherine's face after Helga turned away. He was pretty sure it'd been hate.

228

"Katherine hates her aunt," Gwen said. "Are the roots of it from before Helga's decision favoring you, or did it start there?"

Yep, grandmother had seen it, too. "We never have heard why I'm preferred over her niece. You'd think she would be the one in line of succession, especially since she's already a VP and involved in the company."

"That's something we've all wondered about. I did some discreet checking when we were in New Zagreb and nobody knows. Or, more likely, they're not admitting to it." She absently tapped her chin. "There was an undercurrent I didn't care for whenever I brought up her name while there."

"Dislike? Disdain?" Her tapping finger drew Thane's gaze. *Something tapping…*

"Fear."

* * * * *

In the grayness of non-existence, Jem stared at the door. It was a nice door. Very distinctive, very inviting, and about three meters away. Definitely going short for this first test. Could she do it? Without someone's life at stake?

"It's been a couple of minutes. Think she's all right?" Dr. Blackwood shifted on his feet.

Jem glanced over. Stuart and the doctor stood off to the side. One of the doctor's two large medical bags had been placed in the med-room. The other one was at his feet for immediate access. Which made her stomach knots tighten further.

"Not as if we can do anything until she pops back out," Stuart said.

Jem grinned. She really did like the man's practicality.

"She's bracing herself or it's not working," Stuart added.

That gave her pause. A credible excuse she could use? No. She was tired of lies. And they were right; she did need to know. It could make a life-or-death difference in the future. Okay, no more stalling.

She focused on her goal, grabbing it with mental hands. *I can do this…imagine walking up to it, reaching for the knob…I can*—pain, blackness…and she was in front of the door. *Still in ghost-mode*, one part of her pounding brain supplied. Which was a good thing. Her nose was practically in the door. So, it wasn't an automatic release. As long as she wasn't overwhelmed like that first time, she could control it.

Taking a step back before releasing the shift, she wavered unsteadily as the hammers found a few more nails in her head to pound on.

* * * * *

"Now," Gwen said. "Why did you come with me today? You have no interest in the company or meeting with Helga Baron."

Thane glanced out the car window. Shrugged. "I thought it was time I did."

"Hawk snot," Gwen retorted. "I would have thought you'd go to the island with Jem. You're avoiding her. Why?"

"Between the latest attack and everything else that's happened, I…needed time to think."

"Try again."

"She's ignoring us," he burst out. "She just walked out and disappeared. No one knows where she's been for the past two days and yes, I tried to call. She never returned them. Same for Andi." And she'd done it again this morning. He *knew* she'd seen him. Instead of even saying 'hi,' she'd climbed into a car.

"So, in a moment of childish pique, you decided to ignore her. Despite the fact that Jem has a small mountain of stuff to think about? Despite the fact that she almost died to save you?"

Thane remained silent. *Well, put that way...*

"Why are you and Granddad?" he countered, seeing the quick flash of guilt.

"Jem was right in what she said the other day. We were embarrassed by the truth she made us see about ourselves. I guess we can be…arrogant at times," Gwen said, staring out her window. She turned back. "We hurt her, Thane. That's why she left. While we were all selfishly thrashing about in our own misery, no one talked to her. No one asked how she was dealing with *her* problems. *We* ignored her, giving her the equivalent of a cold shoulder. Can you blame her for thinking we resented her for calling us all to task?"

Thane stared, appalled. Was that it? Why hadn't he realized—*because I was too wound up in my own problems*. He was an idiot. Again. How many mistakes could he make with Jem?

Gwen broke the silence as the car turned into the Stohlass gates.

"A number of apologies need to be made," she said. "Why don't you start us off? Stuart will call to let us know when they start back and whether or not Jem will need anything. Yes, I know, I hope not, too. You could meet them at the marina and take her somewhere quiet. Have a private chat."

Thane climbed out of the car. "I've screwed up, Grandmother. I've made a huge ass of myself. Think she can forgive me?"

"Don't worry, Thane. Men usually do both and we usually forgive them." Gwen patted him on the shoulder. "After we let them grovel for a bit."

Thane shared a bemused look with a guard as she sailed into the house. "Guess that puts us in our place."

* * * * *

Jem dropped to her knees, her jaw clenched against the pain. It coursed down her spine, lightning bolts slamming into vertebrae. A firestorm engulfed both legs. Her skull felt as if it was trying to crack open and vertigo spun everything in three different directions. Someone grabbed her arm and the nausea overwhelmed her.

Sorry. Sorry.

A prick in her arm. Needle. Giving her something.

Blackwood's voice said, "Med-room. Quick."

Arms closed around her, lifted her. Not Thane's. Thane was mad at her. Tears trickled down her cheeks. *Hurts, hurts.* A wave of blackness…the arms were gone. Lying flat. Another prick, and this time the blackness kept her.

Chapter 47

It was late afternoon before the call everyone was waiting on came. They were sitting on the terrace, idly talking between bouts of staring off into the distance. His mom had gone in—babies needed feeding often—when Nicholas joined them.

"Stuart called. They're leaving now. Jem is…okay."

Okay did not sound good.

"That can be widely interpreted," his grandmother said. "What, exactly, did he say?"

"They did three tests with breaks in between them. Three, fifty, and one hundred meters. All successful, though the last one took a lot out of her."

"Meaning she collapsed in agony," Thane said. A hundred meters? So much for keeping it short. The others hadn't been too bad or she'd recovered enough to continue. Jem had told him that intense pain inhibited a shift.

"Do we need to make any arrangements?" Gwen asked.

Nicholas shook his head. "Dr. Blackwood monitored her in the med-room for three hours. According to Stuart, Jem is mobile, though pretty exhausted."

"She'll really need our support now," Andi said absently, starting off into the distance.

"Huh?"

"Why?"

"Three successful tests." Andi looked around. "What will be the general attitude—not to mention expectations—now she's a *confirmed* teleporter?"

Thane sucked in a sharp breath. "I believe Jem's favorite expression says it best—shit, damn, crap." He pushed out of his seat. "I'll meet them at the marina and bring her here."

Gwen rose. "I'll see her room is readied and have a light supper prepared."

Thane walked briskly inside. It'd take them about two hours to get back, depending on speed. Plenty of time to come up with a good grovel.

***

He stood on the dock, watching *Stohlass Three's* approach. Thane glanced over as the guard on duty stepped out of his booth. Thane didn't recognize him. That was a hazard of being the newbie—you got the less glamorous jobs, like watching boats rock. They were posted here twenty-six hours a day to prevent any tampering. Even so, he knew a below-water check was performed before a boat was used. Just two of the changes Patricia Keegan had forced on the family.

A swirling motion between two boats briefly drew his attention. A large shard must be feeding on barnacles. Maintenance would appreciate that, having fewer to scrape off themselves. *Three* was slowing now, its engine a muted putter as it drew closer.

Thane stepped up and grabbed the bow lines one of the guards tossed him as Stuart expertly nudged it into its slip. The engine shut off as he secured the boat. A second guard jumped out to tie off the stern ropes.

He turned, and there she was. Pale, tired-looking, the doctor steadying her as she prepared to step out of the boat. Three quick strides and he was taking her hands, drawing her up onto the stable dock.

She gave him a long, searching look. "You're not mad anymore?"

"I never was. There's been a miscommunication and we need to talk." His gaze met and held hers.

A smile bloomed across her face.

"Ah-hem," Blackwood said. "Jem needs food and rest. In that order."

Stuart clapped him on the shoulder. "Later, Thane."

Thane felt his ear tips heat up. He dropped one of her hands, keeping hold

233

of the other. "Supper is waiting at the house and Jem's room is being prepped. Dr. Blackwood, you're welcome to join us and stay the night if you feel you should."

Blackwood studied Jem for a moment, switched to Thane. "I'll take you up on the supper, but I don't believe I need to stay." He picked up the med-bag Stuart had deposited at his feet and walked off.

"Any problems while we were gone?" Stuart asked, as they followed the doctor.

They stepped onto solid ground. Thane shook his head. "I don't know whether to be grateful or worried."

"Try both." Stuart's attention swiveled to the on-duty guard. "Thane," he said sotto voce, "I don't know him."

Thane casually dropped Jem's hand. Stuart just as casually reached up to rub the back of his head, hiding a specific hand signal to the two guards behind them. They didn't have time for anything else.

* * * * *

Z-ping. Z-ping-ping. Stun shots dropped everyone around her. A thump-tingle smacked her back. Another, more painful shot had her wheeling around to see Rutherford's astonished face.

Crap. Too late to drop and pretend. She did the next best thing. Jem *poofed.* She counted six men. No seven. Vanderbilt was coming out of the boat house.

"Unbelievable. I hit her twice and she didn't even stumble," Rutherford said. "We need to go before she returns with help. Probably that giant security guy they have."

Yes, why don't you do that?

Instead, Vanderbilt walked up to Thane and pointed a laz-gun at his head. "Jem Wilmont," he called out loudly, "I doubt you've gone far. You will return, now, or I will put a large hole in Baron's head."

Rutherford gaped at Vanderbilt.

"*Wilmont.* Decide fast."

"You can't do this," Rutherford protested angrily. "And you don't know for sure she's nearby."

Jem chewed on her lip. What to do? Vanderbilt was too far warped to be trusted.

Rutherford swung his stunner toward Vanderbilt. "Put the laz-gun down, dammit. You can't shoot—*Z-ping*." He tumbled to the ground, zapped by the false guard.

"You've got another minute," Vanderbilt yelled.

Jem carefully straddled Thane's body. If she didn't do this right, it would cost Thane's life. She positioned her left hand next to the weapon's barrel and curled her right into a fist.

"Time's—" Even trained, experienced Enforcers need a second or two when someone suddenly materializes in front of them.

Jem knocked the laz-gun sideways in that brief second. An intense laser bolt went into the ground as her anger-driven punch sent him staggering backward.

The laz-gun swung back, centered on her. "You're a freak. You're too dangerous to live."

His emotionless tone was chilling. There'd be no negotiating with him. No compromise.

"So, your opinion justifies six murders? Everyone in agreement?" Jem asked, her contemptuous gaze raking the men around them. The two that did appear uncomfortable went to stand by Rutherford, one of them kneeling to check him. They must be Rutherford's men. Maybe one of them would at least dig up some integrity later and report what happened here.

"The others support you, protect you. No doubt they'll use you for their own gain."

"Personal gain? That's all you can think about? What about the good—"

"Not worth it," Vanderbilt interjected.

"Put your weapons down and your hands up!"

The order was blared out in commanding tones. A half-dozen or more commando-outfitted individuals appeared around them, and two wet-suited ones rolled onto the dock. All had weapons pointed.

She watched Vanderbilt's men complying from her peripheral vision. She didn't dare take her attention off the zealot in front of her.

"Put the gun down, Vanderbilt."

Oh, thank God. That was General Kowalski's voice. His was the only authority outranking this nutbag.

"She's too dangerous to live, Kowalski. She compromises every security protocol. Once knowledge of her ability leaks out, it'll be a race to see who controls her."

"I'd say you're doing a fine job of that yourself," the general said, stopping several feet away. "Because of your actions, the number of people who *do* know have increased exponentially. Your people. My people. Rutherford's people. All the people who've watched *the classified video you sent to Westmoreland*. For Odin's sake, do you know what you've done?

"I intended to keep this knowledge low-keyed, as limited and localized to Midgard for as long as possible. You have blown that clean out of the stratosphere. I now have to alert Military Command to the situation since I don't have the authority to wipe another system's computers. Everyone will require in-briefing. The ones we can find, that is. There is no way to contain this anymore and you can bet your paranoid, boneheaded, unemployed ass that the leaks you are afraid of *and you caused* have already started."

"Then I need to make sure it doesn't matter."

Jem shifted before he finished his sentence, Vanderbilt's intent clear. The laser bolt sailed 'through' her phased chest. He crumpled to the ground, hit with at least two stun shots. She watched Kowalski walk up to him and nudge him with his foot. He shook his head. It was probably for the best she couldn't hear what he muttered.

Kowalski looked around. "Jem? You here?"

She carefully stepped back and rematerialized. She faced him across Thane's unconscious body. "Where do we go from here?"

He looked around at the bodies, then at the men wearing various states of disbelief. He rubbed both hands across his face and said, "Somewhere we didn't want to go."

* * * * *

"Sit down, Thane, before you wear a trench in the floor."

Thane turned, his retort swallowed at the sight of his grandfather's peevish expression. "It's been four hours. Where's Kowalski?"

"Vanderbilt's mess can't be cleaned up in an hour and your pacing won't get him here any faster."

Kowalski's people had escorted them home after everyone became conscious. He'd promised to come give them a report—and get theirs—after he interviewed the Federal agents and Rutherford's men. Dr. Blackwood had checked everyone out, gave Jem several pills, and went home. Nicholas sent a replacement for the real marina guard, who they'd found tied up in the boathouse. They were waiting now in Gordon's library for Kowalski.

Thane looked over at Jem. She was sleeping on the small sofa, face turned inward and her feet dangling off the end. He was pretty sure one of those pills hadn't been for pain.

The door opened and Gwen brought in a cart. "Everybody picked at their supper. We'll deal with things better if our stomachs aren't growling."

She parked it beside Gordon's desk. It bore plates of sandwiches, cookies, and sliced fruit. Water and Pounding J's Aspric whisky rounded out the offerings.

"Three bottles of whisky?" Gordon said, amused.

Gwen shrugged. "It's that kind of night."

"I'll second that," Thane said, moving toward the cart.

Gwen swatted his hand aside. "After you've eaten something first."

They filled plates with food and glasses with whisky. Andi poured herself water from the pitcher. They munched, spoke occasionally, and generally fretted the next hour away. Lee joined them shortly before Nicholas's phone pinged.

"General Kowalski is here." He rose, returning with the tired-looking general.

Kowalski plopped down in a chair and leaned his head back. Closing his eyes, he gave a deep sigh and simply said, "Damn."

Gwen cleared her throat after a minute or so of silence. "Would you care for something to eat or drink, General?"

"If you don't mind, I could stand a drink," Kowalski said, straightening.

"Will Lieutenant Corrigan be joining us?" Andi asked.

"No. She's dealing with all the paperwork. One of the advantages of having an aide." He accepted the glass Gwen handed him and swallowed half of it in one shot. His hand froze, his eyes widened, and he blinked. Blinked again and looked down at his glass. He threw back the rest in another single swallow.

He held the glass out. "Another one, please?"

There were several laughs and a few comments. The room's tension mellowed, albeit didn't go away.

"Right. This is how it stands now." Kowalski cradled his refilled glass. "Azusa's Federal Bureau is in an upheaval. The Director, Assistant Director, and five of their men are sitting in jail. Three are senior agents. They have all been fired, effective immediately, and are facing a number of both civil and Federal charges."

"Did Vanderbilt actually think he'd get away with murder?" Gwen said coldly.

Kowalski nodded. "As one of the top FLEA Directors, he justified it as eliminating a serious *Republic* threat."

Everyone glanced over at the sofa. The Republic's serious threat slept on, oblivious.

"Rutherford is sitting next door to Vanderbilt and is culpable to a lesser degree. He and his two men planned to disable Jem, then use drugs to maintain compliance while sneaking her off Midgard to stand trial for theft on Westmoreland. Someone can explain that later. Baron can explain something else right now."

He tilted his head and gave Thane a probing look. "Rutherford said Jem took *two* stun shots and didn't even flinch."

"Oh, yeah. Sorry." Thane rubbed his nose. "She did mention that, way back when I first learned about her. Kind of forgot about it. Jem says it tingles, tickles—whichever, due to her change."

"Anything *else* you've forgotten?"

Thane shook his head.

Returning his attention to the room at large, Kowalski said, "Vanderbilt did not inform Rutherford that Jem's information had been classified under the Defense Act, nor was Rutherford aware of his full plans. According to what I've learned tonight, Jem would have left Midgard alive but be dead on reaching Jaguide Three. A slow acting poison would be administered at some point before they left."

"So, Vanderbilt used Rutherford. By having her die in their custody, he could disavow any responsibility." Gordon's voice was glacial.

Kowalski nodded, limiting himself to a small sip.

"I'm grateful you showed up. How did you know?" Thane said.

"Agent Gaines, overheard them—at least the first part. She didn't know what to do or who to trust. She went to Reis—who'd just been fired—and told him. He called me."

"You knew and you waited? Almost getting Thane and Jem killed?" Lee said.

Kowalski scowled at the scowls aimed at him. "I didn't get the phone call until almost noon *today*. I had to make plans, pull together a team, and get here from Odinheim. We went straight to the marina, barely making it in time. Baron was already waiting on the dock. I sent two in underwater."

"Ah. That was the water disturbance. I thought it was shard feeding."

"I was waiting outside the marina to grab them after they grabbed Jem. That would provide all the evidence I needed for charges. We moved in when we saw things escalate."

The general took another swallow and looked over at Stuart.

"I've read your technical report and Dr. Blackwood's medical one on Jem's trials." His sudden grin wiped away the tired lines. "The doctor is a spitfire when he wants to be. His very opinionated summary about the trials almost melted my hand comp." He glanced at the form on the couch. "I'll get Jem's testimony tomorrow of what went down at the marina. You were lucky, Baron. That move Jem made—attacking Vanderbilt?—nearly gave me a heart attack. It could have gone so wrong. I don't know why she didn't just shove him aside or smack him with a rock *before* she reappeared."

"Couldn't. Can't touch anything here when I'm there."

Everyone turned. Jem lay face-out on the sofa, her eyes about three-quarters open.

"Rock's too dangerous anyway. Not sure what would happen when I dropped it," Jem said drowsily.

"Dropped where? His foot?" Lee said. "Only danger there is to his toes."

"Hand. Or head. Could cause spasms, finger jerking…zapping Thane."

Nicholas frowned. "Yeah, hitting Vanderbilt could have been problematic."

"Can't hit when there. Drop," Jem murmured, her eyelids drooping a bit more.

"Okay, I'm confused. Anyone?" Kowalski looked at the others for enlightenment.

"You awake there, Jem?" Gwen said, amused.

"I think the doctor slipped me something. I'm having trouble keeping my eyes open." As if to prove it, they closed.

"Certainly sounds like he did," Andi said, grinning.

"We were in the middle of the marina—no nearby buildings. What's this talk about dropping a rock on Vanderbilt's head?" Kowalski said, sounding more frustrated than confused.

Her eyelashes fluttered and they opened partway for a moment. "In. Not on."

After a brief silence, Kowalski carefully asked, "And how would you do that?"

"Hmmm? Just let go."

"Will somebody give her a glass of this whisky?" Kowalski demanded. "I need her cognitive for five minutes."

"Not on top of those pills she took," Gwen said. "Thane, can you get her semi-coherent?"

Thane slid her legs to the floor and pushed her up so he could sit beside her. She snuggled into his side and gave a contented sigh. "Jem…Jem. Wake up for a couple of minutes, please? It's important." All he got was some muttering and her arm thrown around his waist. If it hadn't been for the circumstances, it would've made him happy. "Jem? Wake up."

* * * * *

Thane's voice penetrated Jem's brain fog. She blinked her eyes open and belatedly realized she was cuddled up against Thane. Oops. Nice oops.

Jem straightened, took in the expressions around her. "What?"

"Could you explain the difference of hitting someone on the head with a rock versus dropping it…*in* the head?" Kowalski asked.

"I…" The last of the fog shredded as her brain helpfully replayed their conversation. Crap. Okay. She could brush this off. The lie was on her tongue: *just rambling and bad phrasing caused by the drugs*. Then came a light squeeze around her shoulders. The edge of Thane's lips curled slightly as she looked up. The lie dissolved under the simple display of support. No, no more lies. To Thane. To these people who had supported her from the beginning. It was time she lived up to their trust, and screw the consequences.

She straightened, Thane's arm falling away as she turned to the general. A quick glance verified the door was closed. "I need first to admit that what I did the other day wasn't teleportation. I, um, somehow phased through the interdimensional line. Which I need to explain." The wide-eyed bobbing heads said *YES!*

"Thane has evidently explained what happened at the Myerstone lab on Earth. At least, what he knows or I've led him to believe."

"You mean all those holes in your story I could fly the *Lone Tracker* through?"

She flashed Thane an apologetic smile. "Invisibility was the simplest way to explain it at the time. What I'm really doing," she took a deep breath, "is shifting out-of-phase with our reality. I, uh, no longer exist in this universe when I shift and *please* don't ask me to explain *that*." The multiple dropped jaws was almost comical.

"You physically go outside our dimension?" Andi was almost bouncing in her seat. "I've got so many questions—which will have to wait. Continue, please."

"I can still see and hear what's going on around me, but that's all. No physical touching."

Thane nodded slowly. "She used it to save our butts on Pappia. Their voices were kind of flat and muffled. Visually, it was like watching one of those very old movies: no color and fuzzy around the edges."

"So. Back to Myerstone. I wasn't between the lab and their test site. I was out past it. When their experiment went haywire, the energy field punched through the distant test site and latched onto the first O-engine in a direct line with it…which was a UPMS pod about two hundred kilometers away that I happened to be inside reconfiguring for a courier. I was dragged *to* the lab by the O-field through whatever medium it uses."

She kept her focus on her clasped hands as she described the hanger's destruction, of the deaths of her friend and the courier. She glossed over the aftereffects and her recovery. "It felt as if I had been turned inside out. Who knows? Maybe I was, then put back together when it spit me out."

"It would explain why you were affected so drastically." Andi's words tumbled out in her enthusiasm. "Especially at the DNA level. In fact—I know, I know. But this is *soooo* exciting," she told her shushing neighbors.

Jem described the stasis effect and of walking 'between the atoms of the physical universe back here,' which was the only way she could describe it. When Nicholas jabbed a finger at her, she nodded. Yes, that's how she did it. Finished, she fell silent, drained yet feeling lighter. The weight of carrying all of that was gone, even if they now knew just how much a freak she was.

"Two hundred kilometers…wow. For what it's worth, the lab succeeded in their goal of instantaneous transfer. If we theorize—*mmph*." Andi glared at Nicholas, his large hand covering everything below her nose.

"Your genius brain can theorize later, my dear wife. *Ouch!*" He yanked his hand away.

"So," Kowalski said, his gaze laser-focused beneath drawn eyebrows. "You saved Thane by shifting into this phased-out stasis condition that inhibited the poison. Then, while in that condition, you somehow 'shifted' to the hospital. *Okaaaaay*…how does this tie in with dropping a rock?"

Jem swallowed. This was it. The last reveal. Before she could answer, Andi did it for her.

"It's the dimensional interface she experiences. Jem's occupying the same physical space as other objects, except they're on two different planes." Andi's voice was excited, her hands in motion as she spoke. "In fact, it's possible to postulate there could be multiple 'things' all occupying the same point in a space-time relationship but—yes, yes, getting to my point. Jem is providing the mechanics of the shift, so when she lets go of anything she's carrying it theoretically—and apparently—returns to its original plane of existence and at the point of release. If something is already there, then—wow—I'm not sure. A merging at the atomic level? A ripping or explosive re-entry?"

"Oh, my, God."

Jem winced at the horror in Gwen's voice. A sideways glance showed a thoughtful Thane. Kowalski's face was blank. Was that an ashen undertone to his skin? *The general is running all sorts of possible scenarios.*

Might as well get it all out there. She squared her shoulders and met Kowalski's gaze. "Yes, I can do all kinds of damage without leaving my ghostly safety. A bomb, an incriminating document, poison in a glass...or directly into their stomach."

Utter silence. Even from Andi.

"The ultimate weapon," Kowalski said flatly.

"The unstoppable assassin," Lee said.

Thane glared at both of them. "Do not call her that."

"Got news for you, Thane," Lee said, his tone brusque. "That's exactly how people will think of her."

Kowalski drained his glass, set it on a side table and stood. "Tomorrow I get a full briefing—on everything. None of this leaves this room." He flung open the door and strode swiftly out, not waiting to be escorted.

Nicholas hurried after him.

Gordon grabbed the unopened bottle of whisky and handed it to Stuart. "For the general."

"Yeah, we could all use a good shot or two," Lee muttered. He looked at Jem, shook his head and left.

Gwen cleared her throat. "I need to return the cart to the kitchen."

Jem couldn't blame them for scattering. She was destruction and death.

"That's how you tampered with those engines," Andi said, then pointed a finger at Thane. "She dropped dirt or metal shavings or something inside them. I told you those engines were tamper-proof. Well, from the outside," she added, before following her husband out.

Jem gave Gordon a sad smile and pushed unsteadily to her feet. No need to make the man bolt from his own library. "If you'll excuse me, I think there's a bed calling me."

"I'll see she gets to her room," Thane said.

Relief flooded her when he unhesitatingly took her arm. He wasn't afraid. They hadn't gotten to the door before Gordon stopped them.

"Jem," he said solemnly and gave her a half-smile, "give us time. We were still getting comfortable with invisibility and teleportation. We'll adjust."

Would they? Their reality had already been warped, now it lay in tattered ruins around them.

"Thank you, sir." Weary resignation settled over her. "But I wouldn't be a bit surprised if, right now, General Kowalski is secretly wishing Vanderbilt had succeeded."

"I admit, General Kowalski is under a lot of pressure. He has to chart a path through unknown waters. He's a good man and I honestly believe he will do what's right."

"And if what's right for Midgard and the Republic, and what's right for me are polar opposites?"

Gordon remained silent. A haunted look crept into his eyes.

Jem nodded. That's what she thought.

Chapter 48

Jem had a lonely late-morning brunch. She'd lingered in bed until she couldn't put off facing them any longer. A smidgen of hurt mingled with relief on finding they'd all found something to do. According to Merle, Gwen had gone to visit Katrina, Gordon had gone to confer with a client, and Nicholas was overseeing damages caused by an explosion at their law office. Andi and Thane were around…somewhere.

Well, she had overloaded their mental circuit breakers last night.

She found Thane on the terrace, leaning against one of the posts and staring out across the yard. Jem studied him for several minutes. The long, lean body, the powerful arms, longish black hair gently stirred by the breeze. The sag of his shoulders? That was so unlike him.

"Bored?" Jem asked, stepping out.

"Yes. I'm not used to not doing anything," he said, his voice moody.

Yes, he needed to be out working. Tracking.

"You could take a job. I'm sure Thor has several…" His head was shaking *no*.

"You heard about this morning's explosion?" Bitterness joined moody.

She took a step toward him. Stopped the hand wanting to touch, to offer comfort. It balled instead. "I heard." It had closed him up again. "You can't keep doing this, Thane."

He looked over his shoulder. "Doing what?"

"Blaming yourself. Waiting, doing nothing. Staying stuck in neutral."

Something flickered across his face. "Partly from dealing with grief. Mostly due to fear for your family. With prudent changes, everyone has resumed their lives except for you. Your grandfather said it best, 'The Stohlass family is not cowering.'"

He was facing her by the time she finished, a scowl darkening his features.

"Is that what you think I'm doing? Cowering?"

"Hell, no. As I said, you're stuck in neutral, a self-imposed limbo. Will Keegan strike at them if you leave? Will they become collateral casualties if you stay? Do you protect the family best by staying or leaving?"

His lip curled. "Yeah? And which way does your wisdom-ness recommend?"

She shrugged. "Doesn't make a difference. Keegan will strike whenever, wherever, she can. Tomorrow. Next week. Two years from now after everyone relaxes their guard. It won't matter if you're here or on the other side of the galaxy."

His face was blank now. Her traitorous feet took another step forward.

"There is no guarantee against this kind of depravity, Thane. All we can do is keep watch, remain on guard, and keep hunting her. Trust your family. Trust yourself. It'll frustrate the hell out of Keegan and, one day, she'll make a mistake."

Thane's gaze bored into hers for a long, long minute. His shoulders straightened. The empty, bitter look in his eyes faded. In its place was the focused, very much alive look she loved. She smiled. Her Thane was back.

"Come with me."

Her smile faltered. Before she could reply, the terrace door behind her slid open and Stuart stepped out.

"Jem, General Kowalski would like to see you at his temporary office in the Federal Building. I'm your driver."

"I'm going with her."

Jem looked down at her disheveled, two-day old clothes. "I need to go by my apartment."

"I'll let him know we're on our way."

***

They walked into the Azusa Federal Building.

"I'm sorry," the worried looking receptionist said, "General Kowalski has only cleared Miss Wilmont up to his office."

Jem gave him a level stare. "It's all or none."

After a brief call, they were escorted to a small conference room on the eleventh floor. The door next to it still had Director Vanderbilt's name on it. Jem stopped in surprise to find Seth Sullivan already sitting at the table.

"Do I need a lawyer?"

"Specifically, no," Seth said. "Although it's always a good idea when dealing with government officials. We'll also be going over your contract today. I've compiled both General Kowalski's and your inputs."

General Kowalski and Lt. Corrigan entered through a connecting door and took their places on the other side of the table.

* * * * *

Ahrymani approached the hotel briskly. The two-hour workout at a local gym had been almost as enjoyable as the report on the breakroom's vid-screen about the latest bombing. *Well, hell. That's Helga Baron walking out of the hotel.* Ahrymani slowed her steps. The woman hadn't left the hotel since she checked in. Was she leaving? There was no sign of baggage or aides as Helga disappeared into the back seat of a luxury sedan. So, not the airport.

Where was Katherine's arrogant, condescending aunt going?

Helga didn't do shopping, that's what her aides were for. The woman was also turning down all meeting requests from Gwen Williams. Too worried about being collateral damage? *If only,* was Ahrymani's amused thought as she entered the hotel's lobby.

"Katherine," she called out on reaching their suite. "I saw Helga leaving in a car. Do you know where she's going?"

"Yes," was voiced in Katherine's usual aunt-induced sour tone. "She's off to visit with her granddaughter."

"At the hospital? She's awake?"

"Awake. Aware. And seeing visitors."

"Is that so?" Ahrymani flashed her lover a jaunty grin. *Helllloooo, golden opportunity!* Good thing she'd automatically scanned the car's ID plates as it pulled away from the curb.

* * * * *

"I'd like to clarify two issues before we begin the interview, Miss Wilmont," Kowalski said. "First, the Jaguide theft. Mr. Sullivan has provided Mr. Rutherford and myself with the circumstances surrounding it. Rutherford acknowledges you were in an untenable situation."

"I think the correct term is flabbergasted," Seth said, getting an annoyed look from the general. "They had narrowed the theft to the timeframe you were 'missing' with the pirates, and for some inane reason he never considered coercion."

"Is there anything else about that event and/or circumstances you have not shared with *anyone*?"

Jem took a minute to think it over. "No, sir."

"Second item. You are immune to stun shots per both Rutherford and Baron."

Thane shrugged when she glanced over. "He's annoyed we forgot to mention it."

"I apologize, General. It's not as if I think about getting shot every day. I don't think immune is the right word as I do feel them," she said. "My reaction to Rutherford's second shot was stronger, more painful than the first." Same as on Stromli Four. "It's possible that I've simply acquired a much higher tolerance and a series of them in quick succession would take me down."

Thane shot the general a dark look. "We are not going to do trials on that."

Seth agreed. "No telling what the cumulative effect would be."

The general glanced sideways at his aide.

"I've noted the unproven but possible condition of high tolerance, sir."

Kowalski fixed a piercing look on Jem. "Is there anything *else*, Miss Wilmont?"

The general's cool tone indicated he wouldn't tolerate any more surprises. However, the military did not need to know about a potentially powerful weapon. Stuart and Thane's blank-faced silence beside her was an unspoken agreement. And since it also happened to be a totally separate issue from her, she had no problem telling him *nope*.

Then she added, a bit caustic, "That I know of. I'll be sure and let you know of any new tingles."

Kowalski grunted and looked over at Seth. "I want that in writing. Now, Miss Wilmont, please provide your testimony of what happened at the marina yesterday, starting from the time of your arrival until the events terminated."

"I'm not sure the exact time we arrived, but it wasn't dark yet," Jem started, using the same cool tone. "We pulled into the slip, then…."

* * * * *

Ahrymani waited, parked and patient, at the entrance to a small alley a block down from the hospital. It was close enough for her to observe vehicles leaving, yet far enough to escape their security's scrutiny. She leaned over in her seat, pretending to check something, when a couple of men walked past. She wore her favorite assassin disguise of short black hair, cap, sunglasses and fake boobs. Still, she didn't want to risk them getting a good look at her face.

This was risky enough, so close to the hospital, but the payoff would be worth it. Helga's death would solve all of their problems. She began killing time—pun intended—by mentally compiling a list of things she'd buy once she got access to all that credit.

She gave her timepiece another check. It had been over an hour now. How long… She squinted at a sedan pulling up to the exit. Yes! That was her car.

Ahrymani's pulse quickened as she started up the engine on her big, commercial truck. Her old trainer's voice echoed: *Focus on the target. Keep your breathing even.* She slipped the face mask into place. Wait. Wait. *Now!* She accelerated sharply out of the alley. Horns blared, vehicles sheared away. Her truck rammed her target, crumpling the doors inward. She continued to accelerate, pushing the vehicle off the road, up on the curb, and slamming it into the side of a building. The car was pinned.

Ahrymani jumped out, ignoring the screams and shouts. Running, punching a guy that tried to grab her. She needed distance.

Five meters…ten meters.

She dodged another grabber. Stumbled. *Damn leg.*

Seconds later and about twenty meters away, she whipped around and shoved her hand in her pocket. Several people were trying to pry open the sedan's doors or restart the truck. Too bad for them. She pressed the remote button and dodged around the corner.

The blast from the bomb hidden behind the truck's grill was heard four blocks away.

* * * * *

"…your men escorted us to the house and Dr. Blackwood checked everyone over." Jem paused, and asked politely, "Is that sufficient or do you need me to continue?" She licked dry lips, wishing someone had thought to bring water.

"Yes, that's sufficient for now." Kowalski tapped the tabletop twice and looked to his aide. "Anything?" She shook her head. "Mr. Sullivan, I believe you have a preliminary draft for us?"

Seth nodded and picked up the hand comp laying in front of him. "I've outlined the main points and we'll add all the legalese later. So…" he scrolled down for a couple of seconds, "the contract is between Jem Seaborne Wilmont of Midgard and the office of Midgard Planetary Defense, with its Commander—currently General Sergi Harmon Kowalski—being its one and *only* representative."

Seth looked up. "This keeps Military Command from sliding in and taking over."

Kowalski frowned. "I need to be able to appoint an alternate for when I'm not available or incapacitated in some manner."

"That is provided for in a subpoint with the caveat that the Alternate *cannot* reappoint someone else. If the unfortunate happens where both of you are unavailable, the contract falls into abeyance until the Command position is filled. A second sub-point states the term 'Commander' shall represent both Commander and Alternate from this point on."

Kowalski nodded.

"Second main point. The Commander shall not force or coerce Wilmont in any manner to accept a task she believes is, but is not limited to, improper, immoral, beyond her capabilities or that someone else can perform adequately." Seth didn't bother looking up for his approval. That point was nonnegotiable. It also left open the option of her voluntarily accepting such a task for whatever reason.

"Third. The Commander shall not arbitrarily revoke, suspend, or violate Wilmont's civilian rights in any manner for any reason."

"Accepted."

"Fourth. The Commander shall pay Wilmont standard contractor pay from acceptance of a task to its completion. Oops. I'm changing 'completion' to 'termination.'"

"Wise," Thane muttered. "There could be a difference of opinion on when it's done."

"Who determines whether or not it is?" Jem's question stumped them for a moment.

"How about having completion criteria stated as part of the task parameters?"

"Is Lt. Corrigan's suggestion acceptable to both parties? Excellent, I'll add that as a subpoint." A few key strokes later, Seth said, "An additional subpoint states bonus and hazard pay will be commensurate with the level of a specific task."

Jem hid her grin at the 'say what?' look Kowalski gave Seth. Ghost-mode was pretty risk-free.

"There is risk involved in what she does and in performing the, uh, physical aspects of a task," Seth said. "She is still susceptible to lasers, drugs, explosions, and falling off cliffs."

The last item got a weird look from the general, but he said "Understood and accepted."

"Fifth point. Wilmont shall evaluate and accept a reasonable number of tasks during the lifetime of this contract. She shall not be expected to take on every task requested, even if it does not violate Point Two."

No working me to death, Jem thought, as she and Kowalski acknowledged acceptance.

"Sixth. Wilmont shall have the option to accept, at her discretion, requests made through the Commander for tasks that are not normally within his jurisdiction, both on and external to Midgard."

"There may be times when your skills are needed—perhaps essential—elsewhere in the Republic," Kowalski explained. "It also serves to appease Military Command's stance about me hogging you."

"Military Command and Federal Agencies can't sidestep you?" Jem asked, worried they would try it.

"No, they will have to go through my office. Even if some admiral orders me to make the request, it's still your option."

"Okay, no problem then. I accept."

Uh-oh. Seth just shot me a warning look.

"Seventh. Wilmont shall provide the Commander with the times she will be unavailable for tasks, in as much as possible and if known in advance."

Well, that was understandable, Jem thought as she nodded her acceptance.

"Eighth. Wilmont shall remain in constant communication with the Commander and keep him informed of her physical location at all times."

"No." Jem said.

"Hell, no," Thane said.

"I'll agree to remain communicative with the Commander, meaning I can be reached within a reasonable timeframe in regards to my location. I may be off-planet. But I am not a dog and will not be kept on a leash." She gave the general a warning look. "The Commander can accept I have a life outside his purview or we can drop this whole thing now. In fact, you can damn well caveat that. I will not be leashed in any shape or form."

The argument she was expecting didn't happen. In fact, the twitch on Kowalski's face looked suspiciously similar to an aborted smile. Had he expected that demand to be refused? If so, why bother in the first place?

Kowalski was nodding. "Understandable and accepted."

Seth was eyeballing him, too. He had undoubtedly argued the point, so having Kowalski so agreeable and with no argument now? Then she caught Corrigan's wink. Yeah, something fishy going on.

They waited silently as Seth's fingers flew across his hand comp.

"Eighth point changed to 'The Commander shall be able to contact Wilmont within a reasonable timeframe commensurate to her location.' I've also inserted a new ninth point that Wilmont shall not be restrained, impeded or tracked in any way or form."

Kowalski raised a finger. "There may be times we need to track her. Depending on circumstances, we may need to know her location for retrieval of supporting team members or if she's become incapacitated."

Meaning I've collapsed or burned out.

Seth looked at Jem. "Split them?"

Jem gave him a nod and said, "Add 'with my express consent.'"

"I'll also add 'and only for the duration specified by the task' to it," Seth said. "Okay, hang on a minute…'tracked' is removed from nine, moved to a new ten with the two additions."

"Accepted." Kowalski said briskly.

"Accepted," Jem echoed.

"Next item," Seth said, foregoing a number. "Wilmont shall not leave Midgard, except for extenuating circumstances, for a period of five Midgard years from activation of contract."

"And we're back to hell, no," Jem said flatly.

"Consider this, please," Kowalski said. "Uproar is a mild description of what's going on in Military Command. They, and any other Federal Agencies, have to adjust to you and what you represent."

"A tool or a threat."

"Unfortunately, yes. A number of protocols will have to be changed, probably a few new ones instituted. It will take time, though things will eventually drop back down to a simmer. And it keeps something…untoward from happening as you wander the Republic."

"That could happen here as well," Stuart said. "Nearly did."

"Yes, but we at least have better control of events here. Not the least of which is Ms. Wilmont's home in Spine Ridge Fjord. That's a perfect solution. Isolated, limited access, secure, and easily defended."

Kowalski's argument was valid. Jem shared a long look with Thane. Saw the disappointment and regret in his lopsided grin. No.

"One year, General, no more. If things can't be settled by then, they never will be. There's always going to be someone new being briefed in and then flipping out."

He gave a small laugh. "You're right. Agreed."

"Next item. Violation of any of the above points shall, but not necessarily, constitute a contract breach. Unless both parties agree the circumstances surrounding the violation are unavoidable and provisionally acceptable, the contract shall be rendered null and void."

"Accepted," Kowalski and Jem chorused together.

"Last item. If the contract is rendered null and void due to an unacceptable violation, the guilty party shall pay a penalty of one billion credits—a hundred million dollars—to the other party."

Kowalski stared at Seth for several seconds. "I guess I did say heavy penalty. What if the party can't pay, or refuses to?"

Seth shrugged. "Then your office had better have a better lawyer than us."

Jem and Thane both laughed. Seth was telling the general he expected any violation to be on his side.

They waited. It was a pretty hefty penalty the General was committing to.

Seth's eyebrow crept up. "General?"

"Agreed," Kowalski said, a bit surly. He added, "Where's the addendum about any new tingles?"

"You weren't joking?"

"No."

"Jem?" Seth looked at her.

She chewed her lip. "I don't know."

"Why? What's the problem?" Kowalski asked, alert.

"Well, people have trouble enough with me now. If I develop something else—believe me, I hope not—what will the reactions be then? More constraints? More paranoia and fear?"

Thane gave the general a hard stare. "And all that may lead to some more stupid decisions."

There was a long, tense silence as everyone waited for Kowalski's decision. If he insisted, the contract would fail because Jem would not agree.

Corrigan cleared her throat. "How about something along the lines of Miss Wilmont agreeing to report new developments that complement an existing ability or could be beneficial in some other manner? At her discretion?"

"Same problem," Thane said, shaking his head.

"I will agree," Jem said slowly, "to report to the Commander any changes to my physical or mental condition that may affect my performance. After all, I could lose as well as gain a skill sometime in the future. I could also become disabled or an invalid due to illness or accident." *Or non-accident.*

"That doesn't address the issue." Kowalski said, fingers tapping the table.

"No, sir, it doesn't. I hope not to have any more surprises hiding inside me. If one does pop out…we'll have to wing it."

"Military Command does not like winging it."

Stuart snorted. "My first commander excelled at it."

"Your first commander was an idiot, which is why I replaced Captain DeJohn after she was given a position they felt she could handle. But…I'll accept the performance statement," Kowalski told Seth.

"I'll add it as a subpoint under seven—the one about availability."

"How soon can you have the final ready for signing?" Kowalski asked.

"Probably take a couple of days. In case you haven't heard, our office building was targeted this morning. We'll need to temporarily work—"

"You can work here. The Assistant Director's office is two doors down and currently empty. The JAG officer I brought with me will assist you. He will need to review the document before I can sign it, so that will cut down on time. Which we don't have a lot of. It needs to be finalized and signed, as in hours."

"What's going on?" Seth asked sharply.

"An Admiral and a full Commando Unit are headed this way in a troop ship. They should arrive by this evening, at the latest. Technically, we're the same rank. But as a representative of Military Command, he has a little bit more sway."

Seth's jaw set. "He would demand changes to the contract?"

Kowalski grimaced. "Count on it. Including who is the second party in the contract."

"Or refuse a contract completely," Lt. Corrigan said. "Leaving everything open."

"Wait a minute." Thane held up a hand. "How long is the contract good for? Was that the five-year, now one-year timeframe?"

Seth frowned. "It was. Now…General? Jem?"

"Short of secretly tucking you away somewhere, Jem, this is the best protection I can give you," Kowalski said, dropping formality.

Jem's gaze met his. The soldier was gone, leaving the man behind. A man who was doing his best in a volatile situation. She could do no less. At least this way, if things went nova, they could say they tried. She gave the general a thank-you smile and said, "Five Midgard years, Seth."

"Please remain available for signing as soon as it's ready. Mr. Sullivan, I'll send Captain Chandler your way."

Kowalski and Corrigan disappeared through the same door they entered through. Seth left for his temp office.

"How much crap are they aiming at our fan?" Stuart asked.

"Four commando teams?" Thane was disgusted. "A frigging lot. That's how many make up a full Unit," he added, seeing Jem's puzzled look.

Jem's mouth formed a silent O as both Thane and Stuart's phones sounded the 'Don't-ignore-me' ping.

Thane read his display and then angled it over so Jem could read it.

Explosion one block from hospital. Gwen not involved. Nicholas.

"Okay, that's good to know." Thane put his phone away. "There's a cafeteria on the first floor. Let's get something to eat and drink while we wait."

They took their munchies and drinks to a corner table and spent the next two hours watching people come and go. Some of them took their food and left after spotting them. Thane and Stuart made a game of it.

"The woman getting the sandwich and cake? She's going to stay," Stuart said of the Federal agent approaching the cashier.

"Guy behind her isn't," Thane said. "He keeps flicking glances this way."

"You'd think we've got some kind of contagious disease, the way they're avoiding us," Jem said.

"That's anger in his face," Thane said, "not fear. He's pissed. We're responsible for Vanderbilt and the others being in trouble."

"And the fact of *why* they're in trouble doesn't bother him?" Jem was appalled.

"I'm sure it does. But right now, we're an easy target for the anger."

"It's a bit more than that," Stuart said, wadding up his third bag of chips. "Every agent assigned under Vanderbilt is facing intense scrutiny. Background checks, interviews, etcetera. It will be worse than their initial hiring checks since the investigators will be digging for anything that resembles Vanderbilt's taint. Which means a few other incidentals might be uncovered."

"Huh." Thane pondered that for a moment. "If the whole Azusa Federal Bureau is under suspicion, who's going to do the checking? The military?"

"Nope. They'll have to bring in Federal Agents from the other districts. Maybe even from off-planet."

"Incoming," Jem murmured, recognizing the stone-faced woman making a straight line for their table.

"If you'll come with me, please," Agent Gaines said, "they're ready for you upstairs." She dropped formality once they were in the elevator. "Thank Odin, you're all okay."

"Yes, thanks to you and Reis," Jem said.

"I had trouble believing what the man had planned. And to learn it was even worse?" Her shoulders sagged. "He used to be a good Director. I don't know where or when he went wrong."

Gaines escorted them to the same conference room as before without entering herself. Kowalski and Seth were already seated. From the legalese displayed on the large vid-screen, it was the first page of her contract.

"Do I have to wade through that?" Jem asked, horrified.

A young man with captain's bars sitting in front of the computer chuckled. "No. Mr. Sullivan and I have already agreed on the fancy wording. You and General Kowalski will be reviewing the main points to verify their meaning and intent hasn't changed before signing. Everyone ready? Good.

"Please direct your attention to the screen. This contract is between Jem Seaborne Wilmont of Midgard and the Midgard Planetary Defense office…

They were on the fourth point when Lieutenant Corrigan rushed in.

"Sir, Admiral Hawthorne is in orbit. They're using military protocol to land here, at the Azusa Port."

"Captain Chandler, you've verified the contract points are all that I've agreed to?" Kowalski barked out.

"Yes, sir."

"Mr. Sullivan, you've verified the same for Miss Wilmont?"

"Yes, sir."

"Move, Captain." Taking the man's seat, Kowalski scrolled down to the bottom of the document. Reaching the appropriate line, he typed in his name. Moving the cursor to the empty block beside it, he inserted his index finger into the egg-shaped reader plugged into the computer's external port. His fingerprint image from one side of the fingernail to the other appeared in the block.

"Miss Wilmont." The general motioned her into the chair.

Jem entered her name on the line beneath the general's and added her fingerprint.

Captain Chandler retook his seat and filled in the line and block as first witness. "We need a second witness. No," he said, when Thane moved to take the seat. "You're too close to Miss Wilmont. We're going to get enough flack as it is. Stuart."

Stuart looked unhappy, but he sat. His name and fingerprint appeared on the vid-screen.

Well, that explained why he went by his last name.

Thane cleared his throat. "Isn't there a 'u' in Claus?"

Jem couldn't keep her grin hidden as *Claas* Karagiannis Stuart shot him a dirty look.

"Want me to erase it?"

"*No!*" both Chandler and Kowalski shouted.

"Move," Chandler instructed sharply. Sitting, he began striking keys furiously. "General, I'm sending a copy to our offices in Odinheim. Sullivan and Wilmont, I need your email addresses."

They rattled them off to the captain, with Seth adding Gordon's to the list.

Chandler cleared the comp screen and turned the vid-screen off. He leaned back. "Done." He ran a hand across a tense face and looked up at the General. "Good luck, sir."

Chapter 49

They left right after the signing. Thane felt sorry for the general. The Admiral's briefing on the latest events would not go well.

Gordon met him and Jem at the front door. Stuart would park the car and go in the Security side door.

"Seth?" Gordon had sent a text message requesting he come to the main house with them.

"Behind us," Thane said, noting his grandfather's tension.

The car pulled in. Seth's guard in the front passenger seat got out, pausing and blocking Seth's door for a moment as he automatically scanned the area before letting Seth exit it.

Seth rolled his eyes. "Really? We're inside—"

"Deal with it," Gordon snapped. "Come. We're meeting in the family room."

Okay, something was definitely up. And why were they meeting in the family room instead of his library or the conference room?

The reason why was sitting in a comfortable chair between Gwen and Reyna. Helga Baron. *Really*? The woman was here after refusing to meet with them for days? No one was wearing a happy look, so the acquisition of BF must be off. No, that's not it. The woman would have simply called and left.

Thane leaned over from the chair next to Jem and in a low voice said, "She's a bit pale. Think something happened to Katherine?"

"If so, your relatives' faces probably wouldn't be quite so glum," Jem whispered back.

Thane flashed her a grin.

"You heard about that explosion near the hospital?" Gordon said, taking the chair next to Gwen.

"Nicholas sent a text letting us know Grandmother wasn't in it." Thane sent a sharp look at Helga. "Katherine?"

"No. It was my car. My driver and security guard were killed. If I…" She paused. "I had accepted Miss Williams offer to accompany her back here to discuss BF. We were preparing to leave the building in her car when it happened."

"It was deliberate? Keegan?"

Gordon gave a sharp nod. "Witnesses described the same woman from the alley—black hair and boobs. She was wearing a mask this time, undoubtedly knowing she couldn't escape unseen. She used a large truck to ram their vehicle into a building, then ran. The truck exploded seconds later, killing and injuring a number of people along with the car's occupants. Law Enforcers have already collected nearby security videos showing the attack. Nicholas is acquiring copies for us."

"Have you informed Katherine you're okay? Does she even know?" Jem asked.

"Yes. I called her as soon as we knew my vehicle was involved." A small smile crossed her face. "It's one of the few times I've known her to be speechless."

Thane snorted. *Bet that didn't last long.*

"How long did it take her to start trashing us?" his mother asked, making a rude sound herself.

The smile disappeared. "Trashing you? No. That we disassociate, yes. She's not wrong. Being connected to this family in any manner currently carries risk. After today, very much so. The attacks are no longer limited to your immediate family members. It doesn't even have to be a person, just something connected *to* you. You've had fires and explosions at your properties. She could have driven that bomb-laden truck into one of your arcades filled with families. This Keegan person has no regard for human life—collateral damage, I believe it's called."

Helga gave Gwen a pointed look. "I was undoubtedly targeted today as it's well-known in financial circles I'm establishing a Baron Financials office through your family here. She is targeting you personally and financially. Why?"

The whole room sighed. Several eyes shifted to Thane.

"We don't know." He started to leave it at that, but his conscience poked him. She deserved an explanation now. "Keegan was behind that attempted drug frame years ago on Random. I've now been targeted three times and she's expanded it to my family. As you've seen splashed all over the news."

"We haven't been able to figure out why," Reyna said, her worry evident.

"The end-goal of any action must be, at minimum, commensurate with the level of effort to achieve it," Helga said. "What does she gain by attacking Thane directly, or indirectly through his family or family business connections?"

"Well, she's sure getting one hell of a revenge for something," Thane said. "I've twisted my brain and I can't come up with anyone that I've hurt or ruined in some manner. The only relationship I've ever had ended with her dumping me."

"Did you dissolve the prenup listing her as your beneficiary?"

"No prenup," Thane said. "It lasted less than six weeks."

"A competitor you've driven out of business?" Helga persisted.

"No. I had two competitors take up other careers because they couldn't provide results. Nobody would hire them."

"You said you didn't ruin anyone. How about ruining someone's plans? As a Tracker, you've undoubtedly caught a number of criminals over the years."

Jem pulled out her vibrating phone and glanced down at the screen. "Excuse me," she said before leaving the room.

"Helga has a point," Gordon said. "Law Enforcement may issue the warrants, but it's you that tracks them down and brings them in. It would be safer to go after you than Law Enforcement."

"We looked through all my records, back on Milania, remember?" Thane said, getting irritated all over again. "We came up with three possibilities and they were all male. The New Zagreb detectives were going to check them out. Lieutenant Wheeler said they'd requested all of their information. Has anyone heard what they found out?"

"I think we'd have heard if they have a suspect. It's also possible Keegan was a partner or close family member of one of them. I'll get in touch with the Lieutenant to find out for sure and ask how thorough their checking was," Gordon promised.

Seth rose. "Excuse me."

Twisting around, Thane saw Jem standing in the doorway, her raised hand indicating she'd just motioned to Seth. The set to her shoulders underscored the angry glint in her eyes. She said something to him low-voiced.

Seth shook his head, turned and motioned to Gordon. His granddad joined them and they all disappeared down the hallway.

Dammit, now what? The Admiral?

Thane kept glancing at the empty doorway until they managed to politely divest themselves of Helga Baron. Two of their guards would drive her to her hotel and to ensure she was safe before leaving. He scrambled through the house, finally finding the three of them in the Security office. All were wearing tense, unhappy expressions. It was Nicholas's coiled, tense posture that drew him up short. Leaning stiffly against his desk and wearing a stunner? The man was primed to erupt into whatever action was needed.

"What's wrong?"

"General Kowalski, Admiral Hawthorne and one Commando Team will be arriving shortly," Nicholas all but growled out.

"Are we being invaded?"

"Officially? No. Unofficially, it's an intimidation tactic." Gordon waved at Jem. "She turned down their 'request' to meet with them in the Federal Building."

"Request?" Jem's angry glint burned hotter. "The Admiral's aide is a snotty, arrogant bully who ordered me to immediately *present* myself to the Admiral. I told him I was tired and would visit with them tomorrow. After he finished sputtering, he demanded to know my location and hung up."

"I received a text message from the general a few moments ago," Seth said. "He let me know who and how many were on their way here and wanted to ensure Jem had representation. Oh, the Admiral is as yet unaware of their contract."

"Think the Admiral is afraid Jem might vanish before tomorrow?" Stuart said.

"Who knows?" Gordon's mouth set in a grim line. "What do we do about having a military team at our gate? Without a warrant, we can refuse them, except it'll generate problems."

"Already started," Nicholas said. "Andi called me a few minutes ago. The troop ship made the news. Add them on top of everything that's gone down in the past two weeks and the speculation is getting pretty wild."

"I'm sorry. I didn't want to bring this into your home."

"You didn't," Gordon said. "It's the asshole wearing admiral stars."

Jem laughed. "Admiral Asshole. I approve."

"A news crew with a live-feed drone has planted themselves out front," Stuart said, watching a bank of video feeds.

Gordon bit out a curse. "They are going to have to make an official statement soon. Something to cover all aspects without giving away what we don't want public."

"In the meantime," Seth said, "I suggest we remain polite but firm. Jem's contract is in place and it protects her to a great extent."

"And if Admiral Asshole decides to ignore the contract? Ignore her rights?"

"There's not too much we can do if he does, Thane." Gordon's eyes turned the same steel-gray he'd passed down to his grandson. "We'll make him regret it, though. Seriously regret it. Nicholas. Have your men escort their vehicle to the side entrance, out of view. I will allow the commando leader to accompany the Admiral—we wouldn't want him to feel threatened. The rest of his team will remain in their vehicle. I'm sure a couple of your men wouldn't mind loitering outside in this nice weather. The General and his guests will be escorted to the conference room where Jem and Seth will be waiting."

"And me!"

"No, Thane. Jem has to face them on her own. She has to prove *she* is capable of dealing with them and that she'll not put up with their bullshit. Otherwise, they may assume she needs someone—us—to prop her up and will try all sorts of intimidation tactics."

Thane's jaw flexed. His grandfather must have read his mind.

"None of us is putting up with it either. Which is why Nicholas will be their escort."

A grin flashed across Nicholas's face. It didn't reach his eyes.

* * * * *

Jem and Seth didn't stand when their visitors were shown into the conference room. Jem kept the cool, non-hostile look Seth had advised her to wear. *Let them be the ones to start the fireworks,* Seth had said. *That puts them at fault, especially if he tries to void your contract.*

The Admiral, naturally, took the seat on the end. Was that to prop up his authority or his ego? His aide sat on one side of him, Kowalski on the other. Where was Kowalski's aide?

"Miss Wilmont, Mr. Sullivan, this is Admiral Rashid Hawthorne and his aide, Lieutenant Paul Jordon. I believe you know Major Elijah Markowitz."

She smiled at the man sitting on the other side of Kowalski. "Despite the circumstances, I'm happy to see you again, Major. I was impressed by the level of competency and practicality you displayed last time we met. We may have need of it again."

Markowitz simply gave her a brief grin and a head-dip of acknowledgement.

Right. He was here to support the admiral. Can't be friendly with the enemy. Which probably also accounted for the general's blank expression. She did find it interesting that the major chose to sit next to Kowalski and not the admiral's aide. Seeing as how the lieutenant's expression matched his snotty voice, she wouldn't want to sit beside him either.

The admiral's mouth opened, but Seth was quicker.

"Miss Wilmont offered to meet with you tomorrow. Is there any particular reason this meeting couldn't have waited until then?"

"I expected General Kowalski to either have Wilmont available when I arrived or know her location. He had neither."

Jem caught the slight curl of the general's lip. Oh. That explained that odd point and why Kowalski had expected it to be rejected. He'd been ordered to leash her. He could honestly say he tried and it was soundly rejected. Well done.

"My client is not at the beck and call of the military. She had things to take care of that did not include standing around waiting for you to arrive since it was unclear when you would."

"General Kowalski has briefed me on the unfortunate actions taken by Director Vanderbilt. A technical team will be sent to Jaguide Three to purge all traces of the unsanctioned video from computers and impress on those knowledgeable to maintain their silence."

"Or else they'll be purged?" Jem couldn't help saying. The Admiral ignored it, although the lieutenant gave her a disgusted nose-curl. Really? He looked older than five.

"General Kowalski's report and attending evidence of your…ability is impressive and, honestly, hard to believe. Teleportation?"

"It would explain how she consistently got past my team," Markowitz said. "All the other reports—"

"Yes, yes," the admiral interrupted, waving a hand. "We've all read the dossier on her."

I have a dossier? "You doubt General Kowalski's word?"

"Military Command has tasked me to confirm his report. I expect a demonstration to do so. In the meantime, I had to ascertain your current location and to ensure the viability of maintaining your location at all times."

Jem managed to keep her voice civil. "That's going to be kind of hard to do, Admiral." Yep, fireworks coming up.

"Not at all," Hawthorne said. "A long-range tracker band will provide a continuous update of your location."

Jem glanced at the general. He returned her look impassively. Okay. Apparently the general hadn't shared all his latest news. He'd know a tracker wouldn't work when she shifted.

"I've brought the band with me. The major will ensure it fits comfortably."

Jem glanced at the major this time. Another impassive expression, although she got the impression he wasn't happy. The lieutenant's smirk said he was very happy.

"No tracker," Jem told Admiral Asshole coldly. "I am not a dog and I will not be leashed as one."

"You will put it on. That's an order."

"Excuse me? Did I miss my induction into the military?"

"Yes." Hawthorne's non-friendly smile was all teeth. "When General Kowalski put you under the Defense Act."

"Incorrect." Seth's voice was even colder than Jem's. "Being a military asset means she works *with* and *for* the military, it does not mean she joined them."

Lt. Jordon raised a finger. "Wilmont was identified as a highly dangerous person even before Kowalski's report. Her threat level is now rated as Cosmic."

That's a threat level? Must be, from that flash of surprise across Kowalski's face.

"Are Major Markowitz and his team wearing trackers?" Jem asked straight-faced. "After all, they are a highly dangerous group. They're trained to infiltrate and destroy and cause all kinds of mayhem. Why, they could do almost as much damage as me."

Markowitz's gaze narrowed, his affronted demeanor saying *Almost?*

"That's ridiculous," the admiral said.

"Is it? Half the mercenaries on Palmyra Two are former military. Evidence indicates the woman currently targeting Thane and his family is military-trained. One of the men you brought with you could decide to go freelance—he's conveniently on-site—by accepting a commission to blow up something or shoot someone."

"Impossible. The men under my command are honorable."

Even Markowitz gave Hawthorne the side-eye in the silence that followed.

"What has given you the impression that I'm not?" Jem said, her voice coated in ice.

"Miss Wilmont's actions and non-actions have proven her adherence and commitment to the Republic and its citizens' overall well-being," Kowalski said, his voice as hard as the Elbow.

The lieutenant snagged Jem's attention. He was fiddling with his phone below the table level.

"Her potential is catastrophic," the admiral said, his tone dismissive. "There must be some form of control. The tracker is non-negotiable."

Now Markowitz was leaning back and frowning downward. Silent-mode phone? Was this some kind of phone tag?

"Potential doesn't count. Intent and actions do," Kowalski rebutted. "Besides, it's already been negotiated and rejected."

Okay, Markowitz just sent a short text. What was—*oh, wow.* He was giving the lieutenant one of the dirtiest looks *ever*. Seth did a light shoulder bump. Yep, he saw it.

Kowalski didn't, his attention locked on the Admiral. "Your insistence of Miss Wilmont wearing a tracker violates her contract."

"What? Contract?" A vein throbbed in Hawthorne's temple.

"The contract I was going to inform you of, except you insisted on rushing over here. Miss Wilmont has signed a five-year contract with the Midgard Planetary Defense office. She will provide assistance on an as-needed basis for tasks that meet specified criteria."

The Admiral's mouth opened and closed several times. The lieutenant's hung open.

Jem couldn't resist. "Is the Admiral prone to apoplexy, General?" *Oooo. Good thing I'm not flammable.*

"I want to see this contract."

"Certainly. Captain Chandler will assist you when we return to the office I'm using locally. As he reviewed the contract prior to signing, per protocol, he can answer any questions you may have."

The Admiral stomped out of the room, trailed by his aide and the major. Kowalski stopped briefly in the doorway to say he'd be in touch.

"Admiral Asshole is going to cause trouble," Seth said, crossing his arms. "Hopefully, General Kowalski can keep him in line."

"Maybe. Unfortunately, they're equal in rank and the admiral's used to getting his way." Anger drained away, leaving Jem tired and discouraged.

Seth cast her a sympathetic look. "We'll deal with them."

What about the next ones? And the ones after that? This was her life now, and she was already so tired of it. Yes, she was having a pity party. Everyone pull up a chair. She felt the tears building and pushed away from the table.

"I need to leave. Just for a while," she added when a worried look scrunched his brow. Bitterness followed her out of the room. Even her lawyer wasn't sure of her.

* * * * *

Thane leaned against his grandfather's desk. Nicholas had reported their guests leaving several minutes ago. Knowing Seth, he would be having some kind of post-meeting talk with Jem. Maybe once he finished, he could finally get Jem to himself. They needed to talk.

When Seth did walk in, Jem was not behind him.

Dammit. "Where's Jem?"

Seth shrugged. "She took off, didn't say where. I'm guessing she needs some time to herself. The meeting did not go well, which we expected. The Admiral is a four-star asshole."

Gordon smirked. "That's almost verbatim what Captain Chandler said. I spoke with him while you were occupied and got a rundown on Hawthorne. He's a senior Admiral that nobody seems to like. Also, according to Chandler, he was 'highly incensed,' quote-unquote, when he was passed over as Supreme Commander to deal with Beckett's pirates."

"Thank God for that," Seth muttered.

"So, how bad did the Admiral do?" Thane asked.

Thane's anger deepened as Seth relayed the meeting's content. That boneheaded, over-inflated, manipulative, paranoid bastard.

"We'll have to wait and see what the Admiral's next move is." Gordon rubbed his neck "I don't care for this one bit. Why did he bring four commando teams? That reeks of preplanning."

"It could simply be caution," Seth said. "He didn't know what to expect and with Kowalski's report—oh! Evidently the general hasn't told him about the out-of-phase bit."

"Which is why the admiral thought the tracker band would work. Interesting." After a moment, Gordon added, "Think it was intentional or an oversight?"

"I'd say no opportunity at first, then intentional." Seth's grimaced. "Think how paranoid the Admiral would react on learning that tidbit."

"Great. Another Vanderbilt." Thane straightened and headed for the door. He needed to find Jem.

Twenty frustrating minutes later, he stepped into the Security office. Stuart was manning the chair.

"Have you seen Jem?"

"She signed out one of our jet packs. She's most likely gone to the fjord."

"Thanks." Thane wheeled around, only for Stuart to call him back.

"She looked beat, Thane. Jem's had to deal with a lot these last couple of years. For a quiet, half-introvert like her, the notoriety and loss of privacy is the worst of it."

Yeah. He knew. "If anyone asks, I'm taking the *Stohlass Three* to the fjord."

Stuart smirked. "Jet pack will get you there faster."

Who told Stuart about his avoidance of jet packs? Scowling, Thane said, "No, thank you, *Claas*." Leaving Stuart with a scowl of his own, he hurried out to his car.

Chapter 50

Kowalski seethed quietly on his side of the van. Across the narrow isle from him sat a boneheaded imbecile who was about to undo all the work he'd done. He'd tried to keep things calm. After all, Admiral Hawthorne was the Military Command's representative. But he'd had enough of the man's arrogance and as soon as he got the jackass back to his office—

"What the hell are you thinking, making a contract with Wilmont?"

Well, if the jackass wanted to argue in front of subordinates…

"You are an ego-bloated idiot," Kowalski snapped. "Your hard-fisted, insulting arrogance may cost us a contract that will provide us with an unparalleled advantage in numerous situations. Jem Wilmont is a civilian. She should be treated with respect, not with the same disdain and condensation as you do your aide."

Lt. Jordon's head drew back.

"Respect?" Hawthorne sneered.

"This woman has not used her ability for her own advantage. She has not used it for all the wrong things it could be." If this idiot knew about her shifting, he'd go the same way as Vanderbilt.

"She's a freak with unparalleled power that needs to be controlled. She's a human Delgado."

Freak, huh? That had Kowalski's back teeth grinding. To some extent, unfortunately, he wasn't wrong in equating her to a weapon of mass destruction. What a Delgado didn't destroy with its initial explosion, the devastating firestorm it generated would. In space, not even a Jaguide-hardened battleship could survive one. It was the Republic's ultimate weapon.

Emphasis on *was*. Jem had just taken that distinction.

"In that case, Admiral," Markowitz drawled from his seat next to Kowalski, "I'd say she damn well needs to be treated with respect. You go thumping on a bomb, it might blow up in your face."

Kowalski grinned and glanced sideways. He noted the barely hidden hostile looks all the commandos were giving the admiral. Right. These men had worked with Wilmont last year. They obviously had a good opinion of her and resented the Admiral's.

"How do you expect to control her? Drugs? Threats against her friends? Miss Wilmont wants to cooperate with us. She even took a contract to do so. It outlines the obligations of both parties. And if you violate her civilian rights, if you try subjugating her, the bomb will blow up and I'll make sure Military Command knows it was your fault."

Kowalski leaned forward and pinned Hawthorne with a hard, cold stare. "First, she'll disappear. How do you expect to find her, much less apprehend her? Ask them." He jerked his head sideways. That produced a number of snorts and *good lucks*.

"Second," Kowalski continued, "the Stohlass family is a financial and legal powerhouse that considers her one of them. If you pull any adverse stunts with her, the resulting firestorm will burn both you and Military Command. Publicly and as badly as they can."

"Ridiculous," Hawthorne said, his tone haughty. "They might be big on Midgard, but trying to fight Military Command? They'll behave."

How had he lasted long enough to make Admiral? "The military is here to protect our people, not run roughshod over them whenever it's convenient or suits some agenda."

"We must be prepared to handle extenuating circumstances, however unsavory."

Shock held Kowalski immobile for a moment. *Did the man actually mean what that implied?* Yes, yes he did, going by that smug countenance. The major and his men weren't liking it either. Kowalski made a mental note to send a message off to Command. Did they share the Admiral's attitude and belief? Were they aware of his plans? If they were in agreement, well…*shit*.

"Gordon Stohlass," mused a commando on his left. "Wasn't he the lawyer who won that major multi-system lawsuit about a decade or two ago? I don't remember the company names."

Kowalski nodded. "It took two-years and they even invented a few dirty tricks. But Mr. Stohlass won and the three large corporations involved were dissolved. Nobody remembers them, except as a case study in law courses. My JAG officer regaled me with it one boring evening."

"I've met several members of that family." Markowitz crossed his arms. "I was impressed with their intelligence, loyalty, and obstinacy. Underestimate them at your own risk."

Several of his men gave agreeing nods.

"And for the record," Markowitz said, his tone still pleasant, "the next time your aide tries to give an order to my men, I'll break his balls."

The aide in question blanched, his gaze jerking toward the Admiral.

"Lieutenant Jordon was following my instructions. If Wilmont proved obstinate, he was to order the team to enter and restrain her."

Kowalski's eyes narrowed. *How did he expect them to restrain her?*

"Which they should have followed. They had no business requesting confirmation from you." Hawthorne shot a glare down the van then turned it on the major. "Or of you countermanding his text."

Evidently the Admiral didn't have prior experience with the hierarchy of commando teams.

"Then the Admiral can expect to share his aide's treatment," Markowitz said. Pleasantness disappeared. The battle-hardened veteran dropped into place with the finesse of a titanium-vault door. "Nobody gives my men orders but me."

The rest of the ride was made in silence.

Chapter 51

Thane tied the cabin cruiser to Jem's dock. Looking up, he could see the late afternoon sun glinting on glass. The windows were installed. The large entrance yawned open. Its door would be hung last to accommodate the last stages of construction. Inside, he was relieved to find a jet pack and helmet stacked next to the elevator. There had always been the possibility she'd gone elsewhere. He walked down the short hallway and up the steps. At the top, he found its door had been hung. It opened silently.

She was curled in a corner next to the terrace windows, her face buried in the arms wrapped around her knees. He scooted down the wall to sit beside her. Minutes passed before he noticed the wet streaks down her pants legs. Reaching under her arms, he gently tipped her head up until tear-drenched eyes met his.

"It's all a tangled mess. Nothing is going the way I want," she said.

"What is it you're wanting?"

"A normal life." Sniff. "I want to *be* normal. I want…" her voice dropped to a whisper. "I want to be with you."

His pulse sped up. "Could you settle for one out of three?"

Jem searched his face for several seconds before lunging forward. Thane caught her in his arms and dragged her onto his lap. His arms enclosed her and they held each other tightly.

"I'm afraid," she mumbled into his shoulder.

"Of what?"

"Of the trouble I bring, linked to your family as I am. Of what else that damn lab may have done to me."

"The family has been linked with you for months. In case you haven't noticed, they don't give a damn. Trouble? *Hmmm*. Would that be something like what we're currently experiencing that *I* somehow brought?" He felt her wince.

Thane's gaze wandered to the lengthening shadows outside. This, he thought, was the perfect spot. Her home in the beautiful fjord they both loved. No one to interrupt. He gently tipped her head up again.

"I love you."

And since those words were so inadequate, he flung open the shutters to his soul and let what dwelt there shine through his eyes.

Their eyes locked. Hers widened.

He watched the hard-built walls fall, one by one, until nothing stood between them. His Jem was a bright, glowing blaze that would warm him for years. Her eyes spoke to his, her soul to his. And her next words bound him to her.

"I love you."

He smiled and kissed the top of her hair. "We're always going to be tangled up in idiots, assholes and opportunists. There'll be surprises, both good and bad. Whatever comes, we'll ride that raft together."

Jem snuggled back into his shoulder and he heard her whispered *"Together."*

He sat silent, content, as the daylight slowly bled away.

***

They spent the night in the cabin cruiser. Sometimes they talked, sometimes they didn't. They even got a few hours of sleep. It was mid-day before they loaded the jet pack onboard, fired up the engine, and turned the bow toward the sea.

"They're probably wondering where we are," Jem said from the seat beside him.

"Oh, they know where we are. They're just wondering when we'll surface." Thane's wicked grin vanished, seeing the worry on her face. Keeping one hand on the wheel, he used the other one to take her hand. He squeezed it gently.

Jem squeezed back. She lifted her head and stared forward.

Their phones started ringing as soon as they cleared the fjord.

"We have got to get a relay installed," Jem muttered.

An hour and a half later they puttered gently toward the dock and a not-so-small party waiting for them.

"Should we be worried?" Jem chewed a lip. "I see Nicholas and…I'm guessing those are all his people. I recognize a few of them."

"See either Seth or Gordon?" Thane's attention bounced between the group and the approaching dock. "No? Then we should be okay."

Thane killed the engine and let the boat coast gently into its slip. Nicholas and one of the guards caught the ropes and tied the boat up. They stepped out onto the dock.

Thane eyed the group warily. "Okay, let's have it. Why do we have such a large welcoming party?"

Nicholas's lips quivered, then broke into a broad smile. "We're here to verify Jackson's win." He jerked his thumb over his shoulder.

A guard wearing an even larger smile waved.

"What did he win?" Thane asked.

Nicholas snorted. "A very large pot. We had to start the betting over several times, so the kitty kept growing."

"Uh…I'm probably going to regret asking. What was the wager?"

"Did you think we were all rooting for you and Jem out of the goodness of our matchmaking hearts?" Nicholas's eyebrow cocked upward. "There were a lot of bets hanging on when you two would finally get together."

Thane shook his head. Jem hid her red face on his arm. "Ready to head home?" he said.

"I'll get the jet pack." Jem scurried away.

Thane's smile dimmed. "Any other reasons for the number of men?"

The tall security guard's gaze flicked in Jem's direction and back. "Gordon wanted to make sure you both made it home."

"Admiral or Keegan?"

"Take your pick."

Jem rejoined them. Happy-guard Jackson relieved her of the jet pack as they headed for the small convoy of vehicles.

"Jem needs to go by her apartment to pack a bag. She's moving in," Thane said matter-of-factly.

Nicholas nodded. "It would be safer at the moment. I'll call Gwen to get her room ready."

Thane spotted his sly grin. Glancing over, Jem caught his eye and then rolled hers. They were in for several rounds of ribbing…and his grin told her he couldn't be happier.

Jem didn't need long to pack the few things she needed. When they were back in the car, Thane asked if there had been any more problems.

"No further incidents from Keegan but several demands from the Admiral," Nicholas said. "The first is a worry, the latter is an annoyance. Lieutenant Wheeler gave Gordon and Seth the usual 'can't disclose information on an open case.' She did say that of the three names you provided as possibilities, two are dead and the other one is in an asylum."

They turned into the gates.

"That would be the cultist?" Thane guessed.

"Yes, and family members of all three were cleared. They'd just as soon forget they're related to them. Wheeler also provided copies of several security videos involving Keegan, including the one with Helga Baron's car. She's hoping we might catch something they missed."

"Their people are pretty thorough," Jem said from the back seat.

"True." Nicholas brought the car to a stop at the side security entrance. "But they might pass over someone or something as normal where we would say 'what the hell?' Don't worry about your bag, I'll see it's taken to your room. Lunch is waiting for you in the small dining room."

Thane took Jem's hand, felt the slight tension in it. "You already know they approve of you, so let's get the ribbing over with."

Jem laughed and the tension fled. They walked in together.

Surprisingly, several dishes of excellent food were the only things waiting for them. Thane had expected to find it accompanied by a large serving of family. "What do you think?" he said, filling his plate.

"They're letting us relax, get settled, then they'll ambush us." Jem spooned up a large serving of fruit compote.

"Sounds about right."

* * * * *

Fortified with lunch, they wandered toward the family room where the ambushers waited. Impatiently, Jem figured. She could picture Andi bouncing in her chair. That was going to be hilarious in her third trimester.

Laughter, hugs, and one 'it's about damn time' filled the next several minutes. Gordon and Seth even joined in, emerging from the library they were using until their offices were repaired. Jem beamed, a deep warmth filling her at this unfettered welcome to the family. Thane pulled her down on the small sofa and tucked her into his side. *This will never get old.*

Thane asked which asshole they should ask about first.

"Admiral Asshole is a bit perturbed," Gordon said. "He's not happy about the contract, not happy he can't find you, and very unhappy that you haven't presented yourself to the Fed Building for a demonstration of *alleged* abilities."

"How insulted is General Kowalski?" Jem asked, peeved all over again at the arrogance.

"Considering he thinks the man is a moron, he doesn't care," Gordon said. "He's more pissed at his behavior. He and his aide are throwing orders and insults around like confetti. They are singlehandedly destroying any rapport between Military Command and Midgard, and that includes both military and law enforcement branches."

Seth flashed a triumphant smile. "On the plus side, they have driven pretty much everyone to your side. They'll do anything to obstruct the two morons."

Gwen shook her head. "How did this man make Admiral?"

"You'll be happy to hear the Jaguide issue has been resolved, Jem," Seth told her. "Rutherford is being released, no charges due to Vanderbilt's misrepresentation and shenanigans. In return, he will close his case as 'coercion under extreme circumstances,' and keep silent on what he's learned. He's in a hurry to get home since there's no telling how much data they've lost from the techs' wiping."

"I should feel sorry for him," Jem said. If he'd gone about it differently, she would have. "He was just doing his job and it was a bad situation all around."

"Yeah, well, that's one less thing to worry about," Thane said. "What about Keegan? Anything new?"

"No," Gordon said flatly.

"How are things with Helga Baron? Have things restarted?" Jem asked, curious and knowing Thane didn't care enough to ask.

Reyna shook her head. "Still on hold. She was unusually friendly the other day, though. Think it was shock?" she asked her mom.

"No," Gwen said. "I got to observe her at the hospital, talking with Katrina. The woman knows she made a mistake—several mistakes, and is too proud to come out and admit it. She's trying to make up for it and reconnect with her grandchildren in the only way she knows how. That's why she's giving away a no-strings-attached trillion-dollar corporation."

Thane's jaw dropped. "*Trillion*?"

"I believe so, even with the investors that moved their accounts. It'd be even larger if the woman had established satellite branches in other systems. Which is what we will be doing."

"You've never mentioned how much the company is worth," Reyna said.

"Did you forget how to access financial databases?"

Reyna flushed. "No. I didn't care."

"Katherine cares. Which is why she is so intent on derailing the transfer." Disdainfully, Gwen added, "I wouldn't be a bit surprised if she's secretly rooting for Keegan to succeed."

Whatever comment Gordon was going to make never materialized. His mouth slowly closed as his face took on a thoughtful look.

"She would benefit the most from Thane's death," Seth said after a long silence.

More silence.

"You don't think—no, she couldn't be. Not in that wheelchair," Reyna said.

But the thought had been planted. What had Helga said? The gain had to be equal to the effort? Trillions, huh? Jem had known people who'd kill all their relatives for that amount. Everyone was thinking the same from their thoughtful expressions. Thane's concentrated frown was one she recognized. He was trying to puzzle something out.

"You said you had more videos? Why don't we go through them?" Jem gave a vague hand motion. "The more people watching, the better chance one of us might catch something."

Everyone congregated in the conference room except Reyna and Lee. It was feeding and snuggling time again. Nicholas commandeered the computer terminal. As he was pulling up the files, Jem's phone rang.

The ID displayed soured her mood. "What do you want, Lieutenant?"

"This is Admiral Hawthorne."

Even worse. "Do you usually use your aide's phone? It's real simple to get your own number. You go to a kiosk there at the airport—you know, the place your ship landed at—and link your phone to it. I'm sure you can afford the charge on an Admiral's pay. But if you're overextended, I'm sure the lieutenant won't mind giving you an advance."

Across from her, Gwen was holding a hand over her mouth. She could see Thane's shoulders shaking in her peripheral vision.

"Maybe you can charge it to the military since you're on a mission," Jem added.

"Very amusing. You were to have come to the Federal Building today." The Admiral's voice was frost-coated.

"Nope. I offered to come today and you pressed to have the meeting yesterday."

"You will come to the Federal Building and provide a demonstration."

"If you can learn to ask—a snotty one will do—I will consider it tomorrow. In the meantime, I have something more important to do this afternoon than put up with your hubris."

She hung up and looked to Seth. "How far do you think I can push?"

"Honestly? I don't know." Seth pinched his nose. "We're walking a fine line here in military jurisdiction. Admiral Hawthorne could declare the contract null and void. It would be a legal battle from there."

And she'd be on the run again. No way would she put up with that dictatorial ass.

"Maria Jorgenson's husband," Gwen said, naming her friend of over thirty years. "He was a military lawyer. He might be able to advise us."

Gordon smacked his forehead. "We should have thought of him sooner. I'll contact him and see if he's willing to consult with us."

* * * * *

Admiral Hawthorne threw the phone. Lt. Jordon managed to snag it after a couple of mid-air fumbles. He glared at the man standing in the doorway.

"You said this *contract* was supposed to control her, Kowalski. I don't see any control. The woman does what she wants and totally ignores us."

"I said nothing about control." Kowalski's words were coated with contempt. "The contract is a means of mutual respect and cooperation. Two words you don't appear to comprehend. You're an Admiral, for Odin's sake. You're supposed to be representing Military Command, not acting like some rank-heady ensign that just graduated from the Academy."

Hawthorne's face was a splotchy red-purple as he rose slowly behind the desk.

Lieutenant Jordon took a step back.

Major Markowitz took a step forward.

Chapter 52

"I've got the first one ready," Nicholas said, as the frozen image of a street appeared on the viewscreen.

Gordon squinted. "That's not the first one. That's here, outside the Azusa hospital."

"Stuart is on a security sweep. I want to wait until he finishes and can join us since he was with you on Milania. I'm starting us with the attack on Helga Baron's car because it provides the first real view we get of Keegan. The video is from a retail store across the street from the attack and starts about thirty seconds prior."

The video began playing. Helga's car came into view. A truck suddenly shot forward from the left and slammed into it. They watched the car pushed into a building, a figure jumping from the cab and running. Others ran toward the smashed vehicle. There came a brilliant flash, flying debris, and the video went black."

"The camera was destroyed by debris," Nicholas said. "The next video is from farther down the street and gives us Keegan running away."

Jem stared at the screen with a stony expression. "How many people were killed? She had to know it'd happen."

"Oh, yeah," Seth said darkly. "That was a major city block. That's why she wore a mask."

"One of the ones killed was Doctor Wilhelm Laurenston, a leading neurologist," Gwen said sadly. "He was on his way home after performing surgery and stopped to help the victims."

Nicholas looked up from the computer. "You do realize that method of attack had to be already prepped and ready to go at the first opportunity. It was intended for one of us."

The look Nicholas gave his pregnant wife wasn't the only worried one around the table.

How many others were waiting in the wings? How much carnage was this psycho willing to do?

The second video started. This one showed Keegan running, turning, and then the flash and flying debris from the right side. She ran into a side street.

"Nick, can you restart it?" Andi said. "Zoom in and focus on her running."

"Were they able to track her past this point?" Thane asked.

Gordon shook his head. "She ran into Stony Point Park, which is a block down that street. The areas north and west of the park are private homes and streets. No cameras. She probably had a change of clothes and a disguise preplaced in the park. Change, walk out, whistling or something, and nobody pays attention."

"Ready." Nicholas restarted the enhanced video.

Keegan ran, stumbled, ran, turned, and disappeared down the side street.

"Okay, those boobs are part of her disguise because they're fake," Andi said. "Not a single jiggle the whole time she was running."

"You're right." Gwen tapped her chin. "The black hair has to be too. She'd want to keep it different from her usual style and color to prevent an enforcer from taking a second look."

"She kept the remote detonator in her pocket," Nicholas said, eyeing the screen. "That prevented her from losing it while running. Dropped, or maybe knocked from her hand."

"Nicholas," Jem said, "play it again and do a zoom-freeze on her face when she turns around."

Jem squinted at the enlarged image. Everything was covered except the eyes and below the nose. "Thought so. The mask she's wearing is from Milania. I spotted them in almost every retail store. Several versions of feline, like that one, seemed the most popular. There was a three-day holiday coming up that would be filled with parties and carnivals. I'm pretty sure it's based on an old Earth festival."

"Well, that puts her as the assailant there," Gordon said. "She probably picked one up as a potential disguise."

"*Noooo*," Jem said, thinking about it. "I think she was hoping for a second try at Thane. On the festival's first day, which is always a Friday, *everyone* wears a mask. Even to work."

Thane grimaced. "She could have walked right up and done a Seth bump-and-stab. We left before she got the chance and kept the mask. Although…" He studied the image for a moment longer. "Maybe she already had it."

Gordon's attention swiveled to him. "The one she was wearing when you first met with her?"

Thane nodded. "It covered her face, same as that one. I'm pretty sure it was a cat of some kind, too."

"This confirms the link to your Random frame, Patricia Keegan, and the current attacks," Nicholas said.

"Does this mean Keegan is from Milania?" Jem asked.

"No," Gordon said. "Only that she's been to Milania or received the mask as a gift."

Jem knew they were all back to wondering about Katherine and Keegan. *Katherine and Keegan.* But…wheelchair. A paid mercenary maybe? According to Milhann, there'd been no contract. At least, not a general up-for-grab one.

They watched two more security videos. The one of the recent bombing of the Stohlass law office was interesting. With one-hundred percent coverage, there wasn't any way to get close without being seen and recorded. What did Keegan do? She flew a drone at the building and pulled the nose up in a sharp ninety-degree bank right before it impacted a window. And stuck. Then she simply detonated its payload, all the while staying annoyingly out of sight.

Stuart had joined them by then and he shook his head. "That woman is a tactical genius. I'd never have thought of that."

"Okay, last video is of the car bombing in New Zagreb." Nicholas accessed the file and it flashed on the screen.

It was the first time Jem had seen it and she watched it closely. "*Freeze it.*"

Startled, Nicholas did.

Jem rose and went closer to the screen. "Back it up. Restart at where she's walking away from the car."

The video restarted. The person rose from 'dropping' her phone and walked casually away from the rental car. Passing a line of parked vehicles, she made a sharp turn to the right and continued on until out of the camera's range. The video froze.

Jem turned, momentarily taken aback at their focused intensity. "The woman has a prosthetic right leg. You can see the slight hitch when she turns."

"Run it again," Thane demanded.

"Zoom in and run it in slow motion," Gordon added.

They scrutinized the woman as she made a slight, almost military pivot around a car's fender. The hitch in her stride was now obvious. The video froze again.

"That's not noted in any of the reports," Stuart said, frowning.

"Do you know how many people have prosthetic right legs?" Seth said. "Gender, age, and military training will narrow the list down, but it's still a lot."

"Ahrymani Carpenter has one." Jem walked back to her seat beside Thane. "I watched her walk out of a restaurant not too long ago. She had that same hitch."

There was a collective inhale.

"I did not run a background check on any of the Barons' aides," Nicholas said stiffly, staring at the screen. "I assumed they would have done so before hiring them. Carpenter has all the indications of military training and—*son of a bitch!*" His fist slammed on the table and he spit out a stream of curses.

Andi put a hand on her husband's shoulder. "Nick. We don't know for sure it is her. And you would expect a high-profile family to verify their employees. We sure do."

He wasn't mollified. "I shouldn't have assumed. Especially after the attacks started here. Dammit, I should have accounted for the possibility of her sliding in under our radar and double-checked everyone. *Everyone*. I screwed up."

"We all screwed up," Stuart said. "None of us suspected Carpenter."

"And it's still only a suspicion," Gordon cautioned, his fingers drumming on the table. "All we have is supposition and circumstances that any decent lawyer would get thrown out. If she is Keegan, we need to have proof."

"She's not Keegan."

* * * * *

Everything crystalized as his hindbrain smacked his frontal lobe with the information that had been dancing just out of reach. Thane raised his gaze from his grandfather's drumming fingers.

"It's Katherine Baron." He held up a hand to stop the storm of questions and demands. "How am I sure?" He stared three years into the past.

"I couldn't see her face at all, between the mask, the hood, and the dim lighting. When I heard what the job was—a basic ransom payoff and pickup of the item—I declined. Told her she could get someone a lot cheaper to do that. Maybe a friend or family member. She became agitated. Said she couldn't trust anyone else with the cash card and needed someone who could handle the thief if he became violent and tried to keep both. I finally agreed and we know what happened.

"I didn't pay attention to it at the time, but my brain must have stored it. When she thought I wasn't going to accept, her hand was doing this odd tapping thing on the table. Remember when we went to see Helga, Grandmother, and Katherine showed up?"

"Yes. She was her usual irritating self."

"Did you see what her hand was doing after Helga rebuked her?"

Her forehead furrowed in concentrated thought. "No, not—yes. She was doing…that." She pointed to his hand, his thumb and pinky rocking on the table.

Silence until Gordon said, "We're back to circumstantial. A lawyer would argue it's a habit any number of people could have."

"Damn lawyers," Andi muttered. When her brother gave her an affronted look she added, "Company excluded, of course."

"Even if it was her back then, it can't be her now," Seth said.

Thane leaned forward, his voice hard. "That's where Carpenter comes in. They're reusing the old alias."

Babble filled the room. Questions, comments, curses.

Gordon rapped the table until it grew quiet again. "All right everyone. Let's look at the timeline and work the facts with the supposition Katherine Baron is Keegan the First."

"It's her."

"I happen to agree with you, Thane, but we have to come up with solid proof to take to Law Enforcement. Okay? Great. Now…" Gordon rubbed his chin. "Stephen Baron, Helga's other son, and his family is killed. Katherine moves into the company, anticipating being the new heir. Then Helga tries to recruit Thane for CEO. He keeps refusing, but Katherine sets up the frame on Random Two as a precaution. Which explains how she was able to inform her aunt about it. I was completely unaware you were in trouble until I received your message."

Jem jerked. "That's it! How she knew. I knew we were overlooking something, but I couldn't figure out what."

"The frame fails," Seth said, taking up the thread. "He publicly renounces the CEO position and Katherine relaxes, thinking everything's good. After a two-year gap, two things happen and probably close together. Katherine learns her aunt is re-courting Thane and becomes a paraplegic after an accident."

Thane frowned. "Helen Brinkman said she went, uh, somewhere for evaluation and treatment."

"Orion Two," his grandmother said. "I asked Helga about her condition."

Stuart leaned back and crossed his arms. "Orion Two handles a large percentage of the military's medical needs. If her injury was military related— I'll lay odds it was—that's where Carpenter would have been sent for treatment and fitted for her leg."

Thane kept his voice professional when he said, "They meet and somewhere along the line they form a partnership. Katherine commits to removing me permanently this time. Ahrymani Carpenter is her weapon and the first strike is the fjord laser attack."

The relief was overwhelming. It was all about greed. He had not brought this on his family.

"I'm pretty sure they're lovers, too," Gwen said. "Katherine never replaced her personal aide after the one she brought with her quit. That leaves Ahrymani Carpenter—who is supposed to be her business aide—to take care of whatever Katherine can't do on her own."

Seth's head tilted. "When did the aide quit?"

"Right after they went to Odinheim."

"That's suspiciously convenient. She can't verify whether or not Carpenter disappeared for a day or two," Nicholas said, his words clipped.

"And her absence allows them to freely talk and plan as needed," Stuart added.

The room's angry tension ratcheted up another notch.

"The second attack also fails—in that Thane wasn't killed," Gordon said, tight-lipped. "They pay someone to watch the family, then show up on Midgard where Carpenter can observe and validate his information." His jaw flexed. "She already had it planned out…the mercenaries hired before they arrived."

"But why so…" his grandmother's voice trailed off and she simply waved vaguely at Seth.

Bile burned in his throat. "Because Katrina also stands between Katherine and Baron Financials. My sister was the prime target that day. The others were simply meant as distraction. Misdirection."

"They had to make it look as if it was a vendetta of some sort," Jem said, reaching for Thane's hand. "If just he and Katrina were targeted, Katherine Baron would have become the prime suspect. Her hostility, the impending loss of a trillion-dollar company—she wouldn't be the first to hire a killer…or offer to share it."

Thane swore silently, viciously. His grandmother's face was buried in her hands. His grandfather's arm was around her, his expression one of utter sadness. Seth was staring off into space while Nicholas and Stuart sat grim-faced. Jem sat quietly supportive beside him, their hands linked.

The silence remained unbroken for several minutes.

When his grandmother's hands dropped, her eyes were red, dry, and furious. "Let's get those bitches."

Gordon gave her a squeeze and turned to the room. "Everything after that stays true to their plans of killing Thane while making it appear to be a vendetta. Katrina survived the attack, but they undoubtedly counted on her dying from her injuries. The attacks on our properties, the poison dart attack—how did she know Thane went to the Fjord?"

His grandmother made a sour face. "That may have been my fault. We were having another meeting with Helga. She wanted to know why Thane wasn't attending and I mentioned he was going there. One of her aides must be compromised or they have her room bugged."

"Makes sense. They'll need to keep track of her visitors and her plans," Thane said.

Stuart gave Jem a hard look. "They are aware of what you can do."

Seth snorted. "They can't do much with the knowledge, as it would bring up the question of how they knew it."

"Yeah, and what do you think would happen if they slip that tidbit—anonymously—to the news?" Jem said sourly. "Reporters are still nosing around, trying to find out what the fiasco at the hospital was about."

Thane tensed and turned to Nicholas. "We need to accelerate her home's construction. We can probably count on General Kowalski adding a bit of push."

"That leaves one item," Gordon said. "Yesterday's attack. Given what we know now, it's obvious they were looking to resolve the whole problem by taking Helga Baron out. With her dead, everything would go on hold and Katherine would have immediately stepped in and taken over."

"And shot us the finger," Andi said. "Literally."

"Instead, it diverted the focus and brought a new set of questions into the investigation."

"They have made their first big mistake," Seth said.

"No," Jem said coldly, "their first and biggest mistake was attacking this family."

Chapter 53

Ahrymani leaned back in the overstuffed chair, keeping her face blank and her fists folded under her arms. She'd been just as shocked as Katherine to learn Helga was alive. But this ranting rampage the woman had been on since yesterday… If she heard 'dead' one more time…

"My aunt should be dead. They should all be dead. Dead. Dead. *Dead*."

Katherine's wheelchair had rolled from one side of the room to the other till it ran out of power and she was forced to roll it manually. She parked at the end of the couch. "Thane Baron's alive. Katrina Baron's alive. Helga Baron's alive. *Why the hell won't they die?*" Her arms waved in circles.

Nails digging into her palms, Ahrymani rose and poured herself a whisky.

"Fix me one."

Katherine's demanding tone scrapped across Ahrymani's tight nerves. Setting her jaw, she poured a second glass and handed it over wordlessly. Katherine was right about one thing, that family had the universe's luck. She took a large swallow. It was time to be realistic and pull the plug on this operation.

"I think it's time we leave."

"What? Why?"

"Even without Wilmont's teleporting, the odds of a successful hit against any of them now is low and the risk of *us* being caught extremely high." If she went down, so would her whiny lover. "We need to take what we can and move on. Whether or not you establish your own company, you've got your income from Baron Properties. We can—"

"*No.* I want Baron Financials."

"Well, you're not going to get it," Ahrymani snapped. "Helga appears ready to restart everything."

"If you hadn't screwed up yesterday, she—"

Ahrymani's glass slammed down on the table, the contents sloshing out. "I did not screw up," she said, stalking to Katherine's wheelchair. The woman shrunk back, her eyes wide as Ahrymani leaned over her, griping the chair arms. "I made my target," she enunciated carefully and coldly. "Would you care to tell me how *you* would have known Helga wasn't in that car? Would you care to tell me how *you* would have known Helga did a three-sixty from her previous behavior by leaving with Williams?"

Katherine's face went pale and her throat bobbed.

Yes, be afraid.

"I'm through risking my neck while you sit here grousing about Helga, Thane, and the universe. I'm going to the gym." She shoved back from the chair. "I'll be back when I don't have the urge to snap your whiny neck."

* * * * *

Katherine sat mute, watching Ahrymani storm out of their suite with her gym bag. She took a shaky swallow of whisky. Everything was falling apart. Ahrymani was falling apart. It was not supposed to go this way.

She'd felt drawn to Ahrymani Carpenter from their first meeting at the Hunter Advance Medical Center. They'd both been in wheelchairs, the other woman being fitted for her prosthetic leg. Soon, they were spending all their free time together.

One evening, when she was doped up on medication and Ahrymani was halfway through a bottle of whisky, they found themselves venting. She on her aunt and her plan to bring her cousin on board Baron Financials and the potential of him inheriting it. Ahrymani on the training accident that wouldn't have happened if she'd been the one at the shuttle controls. Katherine had admitted to her attempt to frame Thane and wishing he was dead. Ahrymani had revealed that the crash didn't kill the stupid pilot. The blow to her head shortly afterwards and before the rescue team arrived had.

Somewhere during the night, a suggestion was made—Katherine wasn't sure by which of them. Probably in jest at the start, it had evolved into a solid goal by the time Ahrymani left Hunter ahead of her. Ahrymani would go to Midgard, take care of Thane, and meet her afterwards.

Ahrymani's military training and natural flair for planning made it all seem so perfect. Everything was falling into place to clench her inheritance of BF. And now it was going so wrong. Just how big a lucky streak did her cousin have?

And now he had a teleporter. A real-life, pop-his-fucking-ass-to-the-hospital teleporter.

She downed the rest of her drink and went to get another. Attacking her aunt had been a mistake. She was sure of it. And counting so heavily on Ahrymani Carpenter was another one. Stuck in this wheelchair, she'd felt—no, she'd taken the easy way. She'd allowed Ahrymani to take the lead in making as well as implementing plans, counting on her expertise. She hadn't even known about the truck bomb until Ahrymani used it. She must have built it during one of her 'shopping' trips.

She'd been taking a lot of those trips lately, Kathrine observed sourly. And to the gym.

What else had Ahrymani done or arranged without her knowledge? It hit Katherine hard, realizing she'd not only lost control of their partnership but also their relationship, if Ahrymani's threatening behavior earlier was any indication.

She took a large swallow of whisky, relishing the fire burning its way down.

All right, time to retake control. Time to stop taking the easy way.

Looking back, Katherine saw a whole string of mistakes. Becoming complacent and confident of her inheritance were the first two. Her aunt and cousin both should have had accidents before now. She shouldn't have stopped after the frame failed, as either one of them could have changed their minds. Which had happened.

Her biggest mistake? Ahrymani Vargas Carpenter.

Ahrymani's plans had become bolder, riskier. Like yesterday. Middle of the day, multiple witnesses, and unknown number of casualties. Stupid, stupid, stupid. Even with the mask and disguise. Had Ahrymani made any errors in her rush to get away? Were there clues that could lead determined Law Enforcers to Ahrymani, and then to her?

That wasn't the only risk she now faced, Katherine fumed. The attack against her aunt would have someone pondering its connection to the string of attacks against Thane and his family. That someone might look more closely at Helga, Thane, and Katrina Baron and what connected *them*. Just as she had feared.

Everyone knew of her opposition to her aunt's plans.

Everyone knew *she* wanted Baron Financials.

Katherine gave vent to a long string of curses. Thanks to Ahrymani, this had become a colossal mess. She saw only one way to survive it. By the time she reached the bottom of her glass, she was running as hot as Ahrymani had been cold.

Anger that her lover had turned on her.

Rage that she wasn't going to inherit Baron Financials.

And a boiling, bubbling hate for her cousin and the aunt that preferred him over her.

Chapter 54

Breakfast the next morning was subdued, both his grandparents looking as tired as he felt. Thane doubted anyone had slept well. He hadn't and neither had Jem. They'd simply held each other, too emotionally drained from the evening's revelations for anything else. It was well past midnight before he'd felt her muscles relax in sleep. Another hour or so before he finally followed.

They had decided, unanimously, to keep the information limited to their group. Not even other family members would be told. It was too volatile. Too painful. Nicholas would even include several other names with Ahrymani Carpenter's in his request for background checks. Thane had seen a lot in his years as a Tracker, had witnessed the horror of the Branson Hotel Fire and Beckett's devastation on Magnus. He still found it hard to understand someone like Katherine and Ahrymani.

He shook his head. Maybe they really were psycho magnets.

"We most certainly are *not* psycho magnets," his grandmother retorted.

"What? Oh, sorry. I didn't realize I'd said that out loud."

"What we have is a conflux of events," Gordon said.

Thane coughed. "Conflux? How about a deluge."

"It has been a bit overwhelming at times," Gwen said, poking at her fried shard.

Thane caught Jem's shoulders hunching in his peripheral vision. He pointed his fork at her. "That does not include you."

"No, I didn't mean…" Gwen said, flustered. She squared her shoulders.

"Learning about your, uh, skills has been more flabbergasting than overwhelming. And yes, there's a difference," she added, seeing Jem's amusement.

The house steward appeared in the doorway. "Major Markowitz is at the front gate. He wishes to speak with Mr. Baron and Ms. Wilmont."

Mr. Baron and Ms. Wilmont exchanged worried glances.

"Is he alone?" Getting a nod, Thane told him to show the major in here. No reason to miss breakfast.

Jem had finished getting a second helping of eggs and bacon when Van escorted him in.

"Major, have you had breakfast?" Gwen asked politely. "You're welcome to help yourself."

His gaze landed on the sideboard. "Thank you, I think I will."

Thane's brows lifted when the major set his plate in front of an empty chair. It held a thick pile of both bacon and shard topped with eggs. He exchanged amused glances with the others as the major went back for bread and coffee.

They politely waited, continuing their own breakfast as the major plowed through his food. He leaned back in his chair, took a sip of coffee, and gave a sigh of pleasure. "That was excellent. Thank your cook for me."

Gwen smiled. "I'll let Merle know. They run out of food where you're staying? Should we expect the rest of your team?"

"If they knew how good this was, yeah, they'd be over. Breakfast isn't why I'm here."

"We kind of figured that," Thane said. "We can guess what the Admiral wants."

Markowitz sipped his coffee. "I'm here on behalf of General Kowalski, not the Admiral."

Thane blinked. Shared another blink with Jem.

"Yesterday, the General and the Admiral almost came to blows. As entertaining as that might have been," the major said dryly, "it would not have been productive. The general approached me this morning and asked for a favor." He looked to Jem. "From Miss Wilmont."

"Which is?" Jem asked cautiously.

"The General would take it as a great personal favor if you would come to the Federal Building, answer—as much as possible—the admiral's questions, and give him a small demonstration so, quote, he can get the bastard off his planet. Unquote."

"Well, I have to agree with the general's sentiment."

"Doesn't hurt to be owed a favor by the Planetary Defense Commander, either," Gordon said.

Jem looked to Thane. "Didn't we have something planned for today?"

She was asking him about the psycho lovers and the plan they'd come up with. None of them had any qualms about Jem using ghost-mode to spy on them after what they'd done. He looked to his grandparents, then back at Jem, aware of the Major's watchful gaze. "We can postpone our fun till this evening. I'm all for getting the Admiral off our planet."

Jem nodded. "Major, you can have the general inform Admiral Asshole I will 'present' myself in, say, two hours."

"*We* will be there in two hours," Thane said. He was not letting her walk in there alone.

Markowitz finished his coffee and stood. "Thank you. Sorry to interrupt your breakfast," he said, giving them a not-really wink. "See you in two hours. I'll see myself out."

* * * * *

Jem managed to keep her answers civil, mostly, during the Admiral's questioning. They were back in the same conference room as previous. Kowalski was watching the proceedings like a hawk, and she'd bet Lt. Corrigan's hand comp laying innocently on the table was recording. Hah! They distrusted the asshole even more than she did.

The Admiral had obviously read General Kowalski's reports concerning her teleporting trials. Oddly, he hadn't asked about invisibility or phasing. While the Admiral conferred low-voiced with his aide, she slanted a sideways look at the general, sitting stiffly at his end of the table. Had he intentionally left that out of his reports? Catching Thane's gaze, he tilted his head in the general's direction as if questioning. Yeah, he was wondering the same thing.

The Admiral turned back to her. "Now, for the demonstration. You've examined the director's office next door? Good."

Jem eyed him skeptically. Prepared to insist on a short demo, supposedly to reduce the debilitating aftereffects, they'd been surprised at his ready agreement. They'd expected him to want to test her limits, without regard of how she'd be affected. It was…odd.

"Major Markowitz is awaiting you there," Hawthorne continued. "You will teleport in; the major will verify and report to us. Please," he added with a non-friendly smile.

Okay, something was plainly up. Jem didn't know if it was his 'please' or Lt. Jordon's smirk that set off her alarm bells. She gave Thane a long look under her lashes as she pushed up from the table. His crossed arms and blank face said *not trusting him.*

Jem stepped back into a clear space, gave Thane a nod, the Admiral a scowl, and shifted. She raced toward the director's office in ghost-mode. Faking it was their plan. Using invisibility and simply phasing through the walls would give the same impression of teleporting and without the physical problems.

Whoa! Jem came to a stumbling halt after entering the office. The Major's whole team was here. While not in full combat gear, it was close. And that was a frigging hypodermic in the major's hand. It was an ambush. Anger flooded her at the major's betrayal.

"Well, do you have her," snapped Jordon's voice from a phone.

Wasn't that an interesting way to phrase the question? Not, 'do you see her?'

"No, sir," the soldier behind Markowitz said unhappily into his phone. The major's face was hard, his gaze furious as it darted around the room.

Oh! They were under orders. Jem dashed back into the conference room. Huh. No shortage of angry glares and accusing tones here.

"Where did she go? Did you plan on her disappearing?" Hawthorne split his glare between Thane and Kowalski.

"What the hell did you mean by 'have her?'" Kowalski demanded.

Jem shifted back, taking a moment to enjoy Hawthorne and Jordon's shock.

"He meant to ambush me. The major's full team is next door with a hypodermic needle ready."

"*Markowitz!*" Hawthorne's yell brought the commandos bursting into the room.

Thane knocked his chair backward as he jumped up and took position in front of her. Kowalski also jumped up. Corrigan, Jem noticed, remained seated. Yep, she was recording.

"He obviously intended to catch me off guard," Jem said. "Drugging me and using an armed team to prevent any interference."

"Stun Baron and get Wilmont," Hawthorne ordered.

Hesitantly, several commandos raised their stunners but looked to Markowitz. Before one of them could comply, Kowalski was also standing in front of her.

"Up to shooting a Planetary Commander, son?" Kowalski asked one young man.

The Admiral screamed, "Shoot them! I order you to shoot them!"

The conflict in Markowitz's face was telling. She resolved the issue by grabbing Thane's arm and then *poofed* them both into ghost-mode.

Kowalski turned to Hawthorne and in a glacially cold tone said, "You duplicitous, dishonorable, maggot-infested, boneheaded spash." What followed was in an Old Tongue.

Norwegian, maybe Danish? Whichever, there was no mistaking its virulent content. *I have got to learn that.*

"What the bloody hell is going on here?" said a new voice, interrupting Kowalski. "Point those weapons down, *now.*"

Everyone turned to the authoritative-sounding newcomer standing in the open doorway. Markowitz and his team snapped to attention.

Holy crap. It was Supreme Admiral Anton Gleason.

The man had been raised to the Republic's highest rank a year ago in a bid to eradicate the pirates. He had authority over every military asset, whether space-borne or planet-bound. He wore that authority quietly, confidently, and angrily into the room.

The commandos split a path open for him as Admiral Gleason walked forward. Another man—a Lt. Commander from his rank—walked behind him, hand resting on a weapon as he passed warily between the armed men on either side.

Admiral Gleason stopped beside Kowalski, gave him an at-ease command and faced Admiral Hawthorne. Lt. Jordan had also sprung up into attention, while Hawthorne had merely stood. Was that a breach of protocol since Hawthorne was outranked? Maybe Admirals went by different rules.

"Hawthorne, would you care to explain why these men were pointing weapons at General Kowalski?"

No title for the admiral. Jem and Thane exchanged grins. *This is going to be good.*

"Sir," Hawthorne said in a barely civil tone, "my men weren't aiming at Kowalski."

Admiral Gleason turned to his aide. "Commander Johnson, am I mistaken?"

"No, sir. Weapons were definitely pointed at General Kowalski."

Jem nodded at Thane's hand motion and released their shift after moving them safely aside.

Johnson gave a startled jerk and Gleason did a double take when they reappeared.

"Wow. Jem Wilmont and Thane Baron?" Gleason said, his voice a bit awe-struck.

"Yes, sir," Jem said.

"General Kowalski's report was explicit, but actually seeing it…amazing." Gleason blew out a breath. "The current situation has something to do with you?"

"General Kowalski was providing coverage for me. They—"

"The Admiral set a trap and planned to drug her," Thane interjected, his chin jutting toward the commandos.

Admiral Gleason turned. "Major…Markowitz is it? What were your orders?"

"Sir. I was to drug Miss Wilmont when she appeared while performing a teleporting test as requested by Admiral Hawthorne. We were then to take her to our ship for transport to Military Command. Sir."

"Thank you. At ease." Gleason waved a hand at the commandos. Lt. Jordon evidently took that as permission for him also.

"Then what, Hawthorne? I left Military Command yesterday and there was no plan of hosting Miss Wilmont that I am aware of."

He'd come by UPMS courier pod or a small scout craft to get here that fast.

"Well?" Gleason's voice turned ominous.

"I was going to make arrangements," Hawthorne replied sullenly.

"What kind of arrangements require a Commando Unit?"

Getting no reply, Gleason pivoted. "Major, are you the Unit's ranking senior? Good. You and your men will return to your quarters, wherever they are. Inform the other teams that the Unit is now under my direct command and none of you will take *any* other orders. Understood?"

"Yes, sir," the team chorused.

"The local population, including Miss Wilmont, is to be treated with respect at all times. I will be in touch. Dismissed."

After another chorus of "Yes, sir," accompanied by sharp salutes, the commandos vanished.

Wow. Their own version of poofing.

"Ms. Wilmont, Mr. Baron, you are free to leave. I would like to confer with you later, if you don't mind."

Jem gave him a more-than-happy-to smile. "General Kowalski has our phone numbers, or you can call the Stohlass home."

"Thank you. Please close the door behind you."

As the elevator dropped them toward the lobby, Thane rubbed his nose and said, "I think we can strike Admiral Hawthorne off our problem list."

"I think we can safely mark Military Command off it, too," Jem said, beaming happily.

* * * * *

They were in the family room, having been driven inside by a late afternoon rain storm. His grandmother, mother and Lee had gone off to organize a welcome party for Sam, when the gate guard announced General Kowalski's presence. A few minutes later Stuart escorted both him and Admiral Gleason in.

Thane couldn't help straightening a bit.

"Good evening," the Admiral said. "Mr. Stohlass, thank you for inviting us into your home."

"You are most welcome, Supreme Admiral," Gordon said. "Would you care for a drink?"

Gleason smiled. "Simply Admiral or Gleason will do. A drink sounds delightful. Perhaps after our meeting. Ms. Wilmont, I understand the house has a secure room. May we go there for a private chat?"

Jem motioned. "This way, sir."

Thane watched them disappear down the hallway. This Admiral was way better than the asshole. "We're lucky Admiral Gleason decided to personally check things out."

Kowalski snorted. "Luck, my ass. I sent a priority message detailing Hawthorne's attitude and a copy of our contract. The Admiral and I served a cadet semester on the same ship and became friends. We've kept in touch. He knew I wouldn't have sent that message unless the situation was about to go fubar. I knew Hawthorne was going to pull something, just not what."

Thane shook his head. It had come perilously close to being messed up beyond repair. "Then he most certainly didn't appreciate seeing those weapons pointed at you. What happened after we left?" He motioned Kowalski over to a chair.

"Can you stand a drink, General?" Gordon asked.

"Most definitely. Same as last time, if you have it." Accepting the glass, Kowalski took a small sip. "Excellent." He took a second sip. "What happened? Admiral Gleason was not very pleased, especially after Lt. Corrigan played back her recording. I think it was hearing Hawthorne screaming 'shoot them' that really fired the Admiral up. I have never enjoyed the smell of burning boot laces so much."

Stuart started laughing. "Sorry. I haven't heard that one since I was in uniform. It's a very old Earth military saying," he said, seeing the puzzled looks around him. "It means someone is getting an epic dressing down. One so hot they're scorched all the way down to smoldering stumps in their boots."

Thane laughed with the others, even as he cast a worried look toward the hallway.

"Anton—Admiral Gleason—is a good guy, Baron," Kowalski said. "One of the best."

"How many other Hawthornes and Vanderbilts are there? How often will Jem end up having to defend herself?" Thane grumbled.

The General cocked his head. "Off hand, I'd say every so often. It's going to be unavoidable, which I'm sure you're already aware of. All we can do is hope for the best and plan for the worst. Which is why I've left a few things out of my last report."

"So, the Admiral—either one—doesn't know about the phasing?" his grandfather said.

"No. I believe that would be…too much." Tiredness swept across his face.

Thane suddenly realized the weight of responsibility this man was taking on. The choices he was having to make. The general was owed a case of Pounding J whisky. His grandfather must have been thinking along the same lines.

"General, Admiral Gleason is in a unique position to help you. If you trust your friendship, trust the *man*, then tell him."

Kowalski nodded after a moment. "How is Jem's home construction going?"

"Too slow for the circumstances," Thane replied. "We'll need to accelerate it. Stuart and Nicholas have drawn up a security plan."

Kowalski offered advice between insightful questions as they discussed the fjord's security. He also offered military-grade sensors for their use. Stuart called in Nicholas and, by the time Jem and the Admiral reappeared, they were making updates to their plans.

"Okay," Gleason said, settling into a chair, "About that drink?" Gordon handed him a glass and he passed it under his nose, inhaling deeply. "Hmmm. A strong scent."

"They've got a unique blend," Kowalski said, blandly. "It has a great flavor with a bit of bite. A large swallow will get you past the bite and to the flavor."

Before any of them could sound a warning, Admiral Gleason did just that.

Two of the Republic's highest-ranking men regressed into teenagers right in front of Thane. As soon as the Admiral got his lungs back, he proved to have an ear-burning, wise-cracking wit, and the General was firing back at the same hilarious level. By the time the two of them took their leave, Thane's side hurt from laughing so hard. All in all, he decided, it was a good way to spend an afternoon.

* * * * *

In the privacy of his suite, Kowalski told his friend Jem's other secrets. Now, as the minutes crept past, he watched and wondered. Which would emerge from the man's quiet contemplation: friend or Admiral?

"Do not put that information in a report, memo, or note-to-self," Gleason said heavily. "Not anywhere. I agree with your assessment. This phasing has to be on a crisis-need-to-know basis." He took a deep breath and added, "And I appreciate your trust in me, Sergi."

Relieved, he said, "If I couldn't trust you, Anton, who could I?"

"We'll keep everything else limited to teleportation. Limited?" He snorted. "God, can't believe I'm saying that. Who knows about the other?"

"Thane and several members of his family, of course. A couple of their security staff. The loyalty runs deep there, so I don't believe we need to worry about them. For everyone else, awareness of her teleporting is through an incident."

"Which includes this Patricia Keegan."

Sergi grimaced. "And however far it's been spread on Jaguide Three or by Vanderbilt and his followers."

"You'd think a Federal Director would have known better." Anton blew out a heavy breath. "I could sure use some of that whisky. You owe me for that, you know."

"Nope. That was payback for Regulas Two."

Anton squinted at him. "That was, what, twelve years ago?"

"Fourteen," Sergi said cheerfully.

"Right," Anton said dryly. "Not that you've been keeping track."

A comfortable silence stretched for almost ten minutes.

Rubbing his neck, Anton said in a resigned voice, "There will be more incidents from fools like Vanderbilt. More attempts to coerce her as Beckett did. Without Delgados, please."

"A tool to use or a threat to eliminate."

Anton eyed his friend. "That's a quote, isn't it, and a very apropos one at that."

"From Thane…he's been protecting her for a couple of years. For several reasons, I'm sure." Sergi's smile was fleeting. "Wilmont is building herself a fortress in Spine Ridge Fjord. There remains the issue of the vulnerability posed by her friends and family. They will be prime coercion targets."

Sergi exhaled deeply. "What do I do?"

"*We* stand watch and do what we can. You are not alone, my friend."

Chapter 55

At the hotel, Jem waited in ghost-mode.

They'd implemented their plans shortly after the general and the admiral left. She had shifted and gone ahead of Thane and Gwen, who should even now be approaching Helga Baron's hotel room. The plan was for to her watch Katherine and Ahrymani, determine how they were monitoring Helga, and monitor their reactions. She'd taken a position inside their suite door, where she could quickly check the hallway if someone approached that way.

Currently, from the facial expressions and body language, she'd say neither woman was in a good mood. Ahrymani was slouched on a couch, watching a military-themed movie on the viewscreen. Katherine, on the other side of the room, was reading something on her hand comp. Was this due to missing their target again? A lover's spat?

Ahrymani suddenly straightened and her attention left the screen. The motion brought Katherine's head up.

"What?" Katherine said, her voice both sullen and sour.

Only she could pull off a dual tone that way.

"Helga has visitors. Thane and his grandmother." Ahrymani muted the program.

Aha! Bugged.

"Why bother monitoring? It's over."

Ahrymani's head swiveled. "No. I need to stay aware of anything that may affect us."

Even shifted, Jem could sense the hostility radiating off both of them.

"What do you mean, no?" Katherine demanded. "We can't kill either one now. It's—" Ahrymani's hand motion brought her to a stop.

"They're encouraging Helga to continue the startup of Midgard's BF office." Ahrymani's expression turned distant as she concentrated on what she was overhearing. "They're offering the security of their home for meetings and for the remainder of her stay." Pause. "Helga says she'll think about it…asking how Katrina is…" A smile flittered across her face. "Your cousin is muttering something derogatory about you…more general conversation…they're leaving. Helga is ordering supper. Does she ever eat anything besides pasta?"

Ahrymani relaxed back against the couch and returned her attention to the screen where four soldiers were creeping down a corridor. She left it muted.

"Well, is that it?' Katherine said.

"Yes."

Jem watched, intrigued, as Kathrine's hand clenched and unclenched on her chair arm. This was way more than a lover's spat.

"What did Thane say about me?"

From the gleam in Ahrymani's eye, Jem was pretty sure the response of "It was too low to understand" was a lie. Katherine's narrow-eyed glare said she realized it, too.

"What, exactly, did they say to Helga?"

"I'm not a recorder," Ahrymani said, annoyed and without taking her attention from the screen. Soldiers poured into what appeared to be a large hanger from several corridors. "I gave you the main points of the conversation."

"Did you?" Katherine's tone was caustic. "You've left off informing me of other things."

Ahrymani turned from the screen. Jem's neck hairs would be standing on end if she wasn't in ghost-mode at the look on her face. This woman was *dangerous*.

"You never cared about the technical aspects," Ahrymani said. "You only cared about them becoming dead and you in control of Baron Financials."

Well, now we know for sure, Jem thought grimly. The silent, full-blown battle on the screen was a perfect backdrop for the one taking place in the hotel room.

"Leaving all the details to you has cost me both." Anger boiled off Katherine. "There's been too much violence centered on them. No way can I inherit now without facing heavy suspicion. The Midgard office will probably happen. Then, in a couple of months, she'll enact the living inheritance. I'm going home to nothing. Three years of work, of putting up with the bitch, all for nothing."

"There's still time for your aunt to die and you inherit."

Katherine made an angry slashing motion. "Only if her death can be proven as natural and I'm in no way responsible. Even if Helga discontinues her plans and we return to Milania, there will be watchers. Suspicion. I cannot make any move against her now."

"Fine. Establish your own company. There's the income from your properties, plus whatever your aunt leaves you from her personal estate. We'll still be well-off."

"*I* will be well-off," Katherine said. "We're done."

Jem stared in alarm as Ahrymani rose slowly from the couch.

Katherine gazed at her. "I realize you expected to profit from this partnership. Even though you've failed to meet my goal, I'll see you're compensated as soon as we return to New Zagreb."

Ahrymani hands were balled fists. "I did the planning. I executed those plans. I put up with your whining and temper tantrums. Compensated? You're damn right I will be. I want fifty percent of your income from Baron Properties for the next five years."

"You will get thirty percent and for one year."

"Fifty, for three years and expenses for continuing the attacks. They can't just stop without risk of suspicion directed *our* way."

Katherine glared. "Fine. Three years, but you'll fund those attacks from your *thirty* percent. Personally, I don't care. They can't do anything without proof and I have no intention of returning to this miserable planet. The air here is as heavy as the gravity."

Ahrymani stalked over to the wheelchair. Rage shimmered in the air around her.

Jem watched warily. Should she interfere? Should she let Ahrymani exact revenge for all of them?

Katherine's chin rose haughtily. "If anything happens to me, you'll get nothing. You can't turn me into law enforcement without incriminating yourself. As you said, you did the planning and execution." Katherine's eyes glittered with malice. "In fact, I could weave a credible story where I have no idea of your outside activities and that *you*, secretly Patricia Keegan, were using me to hide behind while gaining access to your targets. Yes, I like that."

Katherine rotated her chair and added, "I'm going down to the restaurant. I expect your things moved to another bedroom when I get back."

Ahrymani jerked her foot back to keep it from being run over. The look aimed at the door closing behind Katherine wasn't dangerous anymore, it was deadly.

Jem didn't know which impressed her more, Katherine's bravado or her stupidity. The woman might think she had the upper hand, but someone of Ahrymani's nature was going to get payback. One way or another. From the calculating look that had replaced her rage, Ahrymani was already plotting.

Shit, damn, crap. This was not good. Ahrymani was now a wild card. There was no telling which way, or at whom, she'd strike. Jem felt the tug telling her she was nearing the end of her phasing limit. It was time to leave.

By the time Jem hurried out of the hotel, the tug had become a hard pull. She made it to their rendezvous and into the enclosed van before the shift gave way. Stuart and Gwen both gave a small jump as she stumbled into view.

Thane drew her down onto the bench next to him and wrapped an arm around her. "We were getting worried. You were gone almost ninety minutes."

That long? Teleporting must have increased her tolerance.

"Well, there's a lot to be worried about." Jem gave them a quick summary of what she'd seen and heard. Silence fell after she finished.

Stuart started up the van and began the drive home.

"If they're disbanding, how do we catch them?" Thane said. "We can't set a trap and we don't have any physical proof. Would Jem's testimony be enough? Especially when their lawyer will contest how she heard it?"

"That," Gwen said tersely, "is a question for your grandfather."

An hour later, they were waiting for his answer.

Comfortably seated in Gordon's library, Jem had repeated her information. Gordon, Nicholas, Seth, and Lee all wore various expressions of thoughtful contemplation. Well, Nicholas's was more one of contemplating mayhem, Jem thought. Confirmation of Ahrymani as the assassin, which he blamed himself for overlooking, was sitting hard on him.

"Jem's testimony might indeed be a problem, legally," Gordon finally said. "The defense would insist on prosecution explaining how she overheard the damning conversation, since it supposedly took place in a private suite and they certainly wouldn't have done so in front of a witness."

"Trying to use the classified argument to hide it won't work," Seth said. "The defense will argue that, given the charges' severe penalties if convicted, there must be absolute confirmation of every piece of evidence."

"We could say we snuck a bug of our own in," Thane said.

"They'd want to know who, when, and how the bug was placed," Lee said. "And why isn't there a recording."

Thane shrugged. "So, we make up something."

Gordon gave Thane a puzzled look. "You're suggesting that several people, including Jem, perjure themselves?"

"Just me," Thane replied. "I'll say I installed it. All Jem has to truthfully say is she *heard* them."

He would do it. Jem stared as he calmly sat in the center of their silent scrutiny. This was so different from the by-the-book Tracker she'd first met. How far would each of them go to protect her? How far would she let them?

"They would have a federal trial since the acts were across multiple Systems, right?" At Gordon's nod, Jem said, "Couldn't the Feds, backed by General Kowalski's office, insist on a closed, private trial? Use Planetary Security as the reason?"

"She might have something," Seth said thoughtfully. "There is substantial precedence for having a high-risk witness testify anonymously—undercover agent and such. But I can't think of a single case where the Federal trial itself was completely closed from the public. Military trials can and do. I'll get in touch with Bill tomorrow and get more details on them."

"Bill?" Thane and Lee both said.

"William MacAllister, Maria Jorgenson's husband and ex-JAG lawyer. He was more than happy to consult with us. We spent the afternoon reviewing Jem's contract and he said it was tightly written. Bill said it would take something extraordinary to force a Republic military office or officer to break it." Seth grinned. "He was a bit curious about some of the points, but didn't ask. I let the 'she's very stealthy' gossip stand."

"If we can go that route…" Gordon was tapping his desk again, "they'd have to swear all participants to secrecy. They'd keep the number limited for that reason."

"Still, how do we prove invisible testimony?" Seth said. "How do we prove she was in the room and heard what she did? That it's not being made up? It'll come down to Jem's word—a reputed assassin—against theirs. Their lawyers will insist her testimony be thrown out on those grounds."

"Is it time to bring in Lieutenant Wheeler and her partner?" Jem asked.

"They'll demand proof too," Lee warned.

Gordon shook his head. "Not yet. Let's wait until Seth talks with Bill. We may need to consult with General Kowalski's JAG officer. Hell, maybe we should go straight to him anyway."

"Let's get their asses in jail first," Nicholas drawled. "Then we can argue how to try them."

***

Jem lay in Thane's arms. She felt the steady rise and fall of his chest and worried. Worried they couldn't prove who their enemy was. Worried they would strike again. Worried they would get away with death and destruction. Worried they would live their lives freely, while Thane and his family lived with fear and uncertainty and stress.

Worried there'd be no justice.

Worried she might choose to cross her own boundaries.

Chapter 56

The next day dawned sunny and breezy, a typical May day. Lt. Corrigan called mid-morning with updates. Admiral Gleason would be returning to Earth on the troopship with Admiral Hawthorne, where Hawthorne would be immediately retiring. Two commando teams were being temporarily attached to Midgard Planetary Defense for training and adaptation to higher gravity. Since the troopship would now have room and plenty of guards, the Admiral was also taking Vanderbilt and his wayward followers with him. Their trials would be held by a Federal court on Earth.

Jem had shared an *uh-huh* look with Thane on the higher gravity training news. As if the military wouldn't think to use a gravity grid like the *Lone Tracker's*. Nor had she noticed Major Markowitz's team having any difficulties in their movements.

"I think we need to contact Lieutenant Wheeler about Ahrymani," Jem said after the call with Corrigan had ended.

Gordon frowned. "We don't have anything to give them other than your say-so."

"Then let's give them that. Let the Azusa enforcers do their job," Jem urged. "If they have something specific to look for, they should be able to dig something up. A clue that supports it…someone who saw something. Anything to tie it to them. Or maybe one of them will get nervous at the sudden attention and make an *oops*."

After a pause, she added. "The family deserves justice."

Gordon studied her for a moment. "I have to be in court this afternoon—final arguments on a case. Seth will be here after talking to Bill. Hear what he has to say and talk it over, the three of you. If you all agree…then contact the Lieutenant. Give her what you know, and we'll hope for the best."

* * * * *

Seth's information was both good and bad.

"According to Bill, a closed military trial is possible, given the circumstances and those involved. However, he feels—and I agree—it would generate a lot of speculation and only increase the rumors swirling about Jem."

"That won't be the only thing swirling," Thane said darkly. "Reporters."

Their debate was short and unanimous.

* * * * *

"And how did you happen to hear this?" Lieutenant Wheeler asked in a hard voice.

"I'm stealthy." Jem gave her a cheeky grin.

"Not buying it. Not in a hotel room," Wheeler said, crossing her arms.

"Ahrymani Carpenter isn't the only one who can plant a bug," Thane said.

"Uh-huh. Did you?"

Thane opened his mouth and got Jem's elbow in his ribs.

"No. We were pretty sure Helga Baron's room was bugged but needed proof. I used my stealthy feet to get into their suite. It does have multiple rooms, you know. I was there, they just didn't see me. Once I was in position, Thane and his grandmother went in to talk to Helga. Ahrymani evidently wears an earpiece for constant monitoring and summarized the conversation she was hearing in Helga's room to Katherine. Once that conversation ended, the one in my current location started and rapidly devolved. Katherine left for the hotel restaurant. Ahrymani went into the bedroom for her things and I sneaky-footed it out."

Jem was proud of that story. All true and without giving away anything.

"Why didn't you record it?" Detective Minsky asked, eyeing her as suspiciously as his partner was.

"Didn't take one. I was only looking to verify the bugging. Overhearing

312

their fall-out was unexpected." Both enforcers wore dissatisfied looks. They probably believed she had recorded it, but was withholding it for some reason.

"So, Ahrymani Carpenter is Patricia Keegan, which was originally Katherine Baron." Wheeler got three head-nods. "And the whole purpose behind these attacks is so Katherine Baron can inherit a trillion-dollar company?" More head nods. Wheeler huffed out a breath. "Now we have to prove it."

Minsky rubbed his chin. "That falling out could work in our favor. We can push a little there. Interview each one separately. Ask open-ended questions, implying we know more. Which we do."

Seth shook his head. "I don't see either one turning on the other. They've gone too far, done too much."

"Katherine could easily pull her frigging 'I didn't know' routine, too," Jem said crossly. "She only needs to mention something that incriminates Ahrymani and walk—roll away scot-free."

"That will happen anyway unless Carpenter herself has proof of Katherine's willing participation. Otherwise, it would be her word against the wheelchair-bound VP of Baron Financials," Wheeler said. "Your evidence is heavy, but circumstantial. A judge and jury will want positive proof."

"Yeah, Seth said that too," Thane admitted, getting a told-you-so look from his cousin.

"The truck was stolen eight days before the hospital attack," Wheeler said, tugging on an ear. "She had to have had some place to keep it and build the bomb. Officers are currently canvassing the city now. If we can find it and we're lucky, she left fingerprints or DNA."

"She's used explosives on her latest strikes. I'll start checking sales, both here and in surrounding towns." Minsky looked at his partner. "Carpenter will be disguised, but we can narrow down the possibilities by body type."

"Okay, now we need to make sure our suspects stay here. How soon did Katherine Baron say they were leaving?"

"She didn't really say. My guess? It depends on what her aunt decides to do. Ahrymani might even bail sooner."

"We offered to host both Helga and the meetings here for security," Thane said. "That was the excuse we used to see her and determine if her room was bugged. The offer was real, though. She hasn't accepted, yet, that I know of."

"Can you verify whether or not she has with your grandmother?"

"Sure."

After Thane disappeared, Wheeler turned a speculative look on Jem. "You *really* didn't record that conversation?"

"I really didn't."

"Too bad. So, there's a rumor going around that the Spine Ridge Fjord construction is yours."

"We're trying to keep that information limited as long as possible," Seth said as Jem nodded. "Please do not provide confirmation."

"I draw a lot of attention when I'm out in public. I wanted a quiet, peaceful place away from prying eyes and wagging tongues."

"And from flaps similar to the ones between General Kowalski and ex-Director Vanderbilt?"

"Especially those, Detective Minsky." Jem glanced at her lawyer, then back. "I have signed a contract with the Planetary Defense Office to work with them on an as-needed basis." Both detectives' attention sharpened. "I expect there will be other flaps in the future."

"Why?" Wheeler said.

"Jem," Seth said warningly.

"There may be others who cannot handle knowing my stealthy secret. Or want to take advantage of it."

"That's classified and on a need-to-know basis," Seth said, testily.

"Did I say anything classified? Those are frigging *proven* facts. Things aren't going to stay classified forever, Seth. It can't. We lucked out at the hospital. The first time I—"

"*Jem!*"

If he'd let her finish… "The first time I provide support in a situation in a non-contained environment *with witnesses*, Enforcers such as these," she jerked her thumb at the detectives, "will have to deal with them and any fallout."

"They're *hom*icide," Seth said, "not crowd control."

"How far were Kurzvall, Beckett, and Richardson willing to go?"

Tension crackled in the silence.

Wheeler looked between the two of them. "Okay, I don't fully understand what you're saying—and that bothers me—but I get the gist of what you're not. And that worries me. Thank you, Miss Wilmont, for your honesty. I'll pass your warning up the line." She gave Seth the stink-eye. "Maybe you should get a more supportive lawyer."

Before Seth could reply, Thane returned with his grandmother in tow.

Thane took in all the bad-tempered expressions. "What did I miss?"

"I'll fill you in later," Jem told him as he retook his seat beside her.

"In answer to your question," Gwen said, "Helga Baron has not yet replied to our offer. Either yes or no."

"Can you keep the negotiations on hold?" Wheeler asked. "If that's what's keeping her niece and Carpenter on Midgard, it needs to be stretched while we investigate."

"They can still up and leave at any time, regardless."

"Understood. We'll work on that and try to come up with something," Wheeler said. "In the meantime, can you keep things on hold?"

* * * * *

"I'm glad you understand," Gwen said. She'd managed to coax Helga Baron out of her bugged hotel room and to a nearby restaurant.

"Do the Enforcers know when she will strike?" Helga asked.

"No, only that the indications are it will occur around our home," Gwen lied. She hoped it was a lie, what with Ahrymani becoming unpredictable. "You and your aides will be safer staying in your suite. So, as much as I obviously hate it, postponing the resumption of the startup is best. We're hoping it won't be too long before they either catch this despicable person or, at least, confirm our home is safe."

Helga nodded and surprised Gwen by saying, "You've never asked me why I chose Thane over Kathrine, since she has been involved with the company for several years."

Gwen shrugged. "We figured you had finally come to your senses and

315

were trying to make it up to him."

"I deserve that. And you're half right." Helga stared off into the distance. "Greg was a quiet, stubborn child. No arguing, no tantrums. He simply listened and then did what he wanted. He majored in Geology against my preference. He joined the Survey Corps against my will. He married a different woman from the one I thought was more suitable."

Gwen's eyebrow arched.

"The last communique I received from him said he was resigning from Survey and taking up residence on Midgard. I was furious." Helga's gaze met hers. "And then he was gone."

Pain seared Gwen's lungs. For a brief moment, they were simply two women who'd endured the devastating loss of a child.

"When Reyna failed to conform to my wishes—no, my demands, I threw my own tantrum."

"Twenty years is a long time to pitch a fit."

Helga nodded. "In wisdom's hindsight of old age, I was an arrogant fool. I was used to getting what I wanted. Always. And it has cost me. You do not know how much I regret what I've lost," she said quietly.

Gwen tamped down her emotions. While she was surprised by the woman's sudden openness, she did not want to feel sorry for her. Helga Baron was reaping what her hubris had sowed. "You said I was half right."

The silence stretched, then, "It was fairly well known my brother was born with a blood disorder. But there was also something…broken in Ezra. A coldness. The full extent of which was kept within the family. Ezra even managed a fairly normal public image and marriage for a while."

"Is that why BF passed to you?"

"Yes. Father felt Baron Properties would be less taxing for him. As the years passed, things…worsened. Finally, Natalie moved out of the house and initiated divorce proceedings, except he died before they could be completed."

Uh-huh. The office gossip she'd heard during the audit said the woman had suffered a nasty fall down a staircase prior to her moving out. Coincidence?

"Did you seek any medical help for him?"

"Of course not," Helga said, affronted. "I would not have that stain on the family name. The blood disorder, which Katherine's two sisters inherited, was bad enough. By her teen years it was obvious Katherine had inherited Ezra's coldness instead."

Coldness? Try sociopathy.

Such an arrogant, prideful fool. "That didn't keep you from making her a Vice President."

"An unemotional coolness can be beneficial at the corporate level. Katherine relishes the prestige and political power that comes with Baron Financials." Helga paused. "She also enjoys living in high comfort. Her share of income from Baron Properties barely covers her expenses."

"Well. That explains her fight to keep her BF income." *And she'll eventually sell the company for its credits.*

Helga ignored that. "I had hoped being involved in the company would keep her balanced. It hasn't. I see Ezra when I look at her. Katherine intentionally antagonizes subordinates or makes unreasonable demands on their time and tasks. She is indifferent to them. My niece has become," Helga paused, "cruel."

"It became fairly obvious during our audit that Katherine was not popular. You believe she'll get worse, as did your brother." Gwen didn't make it a question. Could sociopathy mature into psychopathy?

"The postponement isn't necessary. We can continue the meetings by conference call."

If only they could. Gwen didn't need to hide her reluctance as she said, "Thank you, but my attention is going to be on our current troubles. We will resume as soon as possible. Please be patient." Gwen cleared her throat. "In the meantime, please allow everyone to think you're undecided on, well, everything. I'm sure Katherine will take advantage of it."

The other woman's expression sharpened, then turned thoughtful. Had she given too much away? Helga Baron was not a stupid woman.

Chapter 57

Jem and the others spent the next two days trying to come up with a plan to catch the two women. In the meantime, Admiral Gleason and his party left for Earth. Kowalski returned to Odinheim and Major Markowitz and Captain Tagawa's commando teams took up residence on an unused Sea Patrol base on a mid-sized island southeast of Azusa. Katherine Baron and Ahrymani Carpenter were interviewed, separately, in regards to the perceived attack against Helga Baron.

Lieutenant Wheeler called her afterwards.

"Yep, Baron is setting up Carpenter. She managed to include a snide comment or two about not being able to get out and about as often as Ahrymani, who 'disappears for long stretches.' Unquote. I almost asked why she hadn't taken on a new personal aide, especially with her disability."

"That would have made her suspicious that you were suspicious," Jem said.

"Uh-huh. I refrained. I waited until the interview with Ms. Carpenter was pretty much over, and then casually asked how she liked Azusa shopping. Ms. Baron had mentioned she was gone a lot." Wheeler chuckled. "Carpenter hid her irritation pretty good, but it was there."

"Katherine had better be careful. Ahrymani is not as tightly leashed as she believes," Jem said.

"Won't happen," Wheeler said. "At least, not until after she gets her money."

"Ahrymani has found an alternate source of income." Jem coughed. "Me. I received an extortion message last night from a temp kiosk number. I'm to set up a separate account and move ten million dollars into it by close of business today. She won't contact me again unless there's a problem."

"Dammit, we need to get that boy's suggestion implemented. She knows you have the funds—hell, all of Midgard knows you're ultra-rich. The threat?"

"To pass my secret—which she stumbled upon—to every news service on Midgard."

After a short pause, Wheeler said, "That must be one hellacious secret." Another pause. "Damn, that's smart. No way to set up some kind of trap. Plug a cash card in anywhere and withdraw funds whenever she wants."

"And demand a refill later," Jem said glumly.

"*Wellll*, you did say it was going to come out eventually anyway. If you were to go ahead and release the information yourself…"

Jem grinned. The woman hated not knowing. "I'll let you ask General Kowalski that." She could practically feel Wheeler's wince through the phone.

After a few more exchanges, they ended the call. There had to be some way to set a trap.

***

Her phone pinged. Finally. Jem read the text out loud. "Where's my account?"

She quoted as she typed. "*Account name is J. S. Wilmont. Number 23900222AJ89-8. Password is ImAfriggingBITCH.*"

Gordon and Gwen laughed. Thane merely grinned, already aware of it.

Ping. "Why didn't you use the info I gave you?" Jem read to the others. "You bet I'll tell her why." She typed furiously and sent it off.

"What did you tell her?" Gordon asked.

"That I'd be taking my money back after we put her ass in jail. I can't see her turning it down. She'll have—" *Ping.*

Jem glanced down at her phone. One eyebrow tilted upward. "Skipping the first part, she says that will cost me another five million. Moved into the account in the next two hours. She'll check."

Thane bit out several cuss words that were remarkably similar to the first part of Ahrymani's message.

"She's going to keep bleeding you," Gordon said, his voice furious.

"That's the nature of extortion," Jem said absently, her mind working furiously. "I think…I know how to trap her," she said. "It's risky and could backfire."

"We'll deal with it," Thane assured her.

"We'll *all* deal with it," Gordon said, Gwen nodding in agreement.

Jem's smile was a blaze of sunshine. "First, I need to lock the account. Hand comp. Who's got—thank you Gwen."

Then, she again quoted as she typed. *"Listen up bitch. I've locked the account. It will stay locked for one week. That's seven days. Use both hands to count it. If you do as threatened, you lose it. If you threaten me again, I'll go to the news services myself and you lose it. At the end of the week, and if you've been a good girl, I'll release the lock. You can check on the balance. I'll contact you at this number at this same time next week."*

Jem's phone remained silent. "What do you think?" Jem said after a couple of tense minutes.

"I think she's doing some heavy cussing," Thane said.

"I think she's salivating at all that money, frustrated she can't get to it, and plotting how to pay you back without losing any of it," Gordon said.

"I think we need to hear Jem's plan," Gwen said.

* * * * *

Ahrymani breathed in, breathed out, and silently cursed Wilmont and the Barons—all three of them—as she fought to gain control of her raging emotions. First Katherine and now Wilmont. Acting so superior. Handing out orders and disdain as if she—Ahrymani Vargas Carpenter—was nothing but a lowly dirt-pounder.

It had all seemed so simple. Hit a couple of quick targets that would set her for life with endless credits. When her second attempt had failed so spectacularly, she should have taken it as a sign and walked away. But the payoff…the challenge. The adrenaline rush that made her feel so alive.

Her pulse steadied and her breathing evened out.

Stepping out of the shadowed doorway she'd been messaging Wilmont from, she kept her face a calm mask and her stride brisk as she headed back toward the hotel. She stopped at a small restaurant for supper. She had quit drinking or eating anything in their suite unless she personally watched room service deliver it. She had no intention of finding out the hard way if Katherine had more poison.

Her instincts went on alert as soon as she entered their suite. Katherine wore a self-satisfied smirk. "What?" she asked cautiously.

"My dear aunt paid me a visit."

"Here? Helga Baron came *here*?"

"She's conceded she should have paid more attention to my warnings." Her voice was smugly satisfied. "Helga is thinking seriously of canceling everything altogether and returning home."

"Why the sudden change?"

"The luncheon she had the other day with Gwen Williams? Evidently she pressed Helga pretty hard to restart everything. Helga says she's fed up with the family's snobby and dictatorial attitude. Not to mention, how their current problems will affect the company. It appears I may win after all."

"Win what?" Ahrymani scoffed. "Decades of bowing and scraping and trying to please a woman who is never pleased? Waiting for her to die?"

"I'm sure you can find an unobtrusive way to assist her along."

Ahrymani threw back her head and laughed. "You've used me, thrown me away, and now you're setting me up as a scapegoat." Her face hardened. "No. What's more, you still owe me."

Katherine glowered at her. Ahrymani could see her trying to figure a way out of it. Nor did she like the idea of being dangled for three years. Well, she had the perfect solution.

"Listen up, bitch." Yes, that had a nice ring. "I want a cash payout. I want, oh, ten million dollars is a nice number. I don't care how you do it or where you steal it from, but you'd better start figuring it out now. I want it when we get back to Milania."

"That's, that's impossible," Katherine sputtered.

Ahrymani's smile was predatory. "Consider it an advance on your inheritance. Consider it the challenge of your *life*." Leaving her ex-lover, ex-partner sitting in shocked silence, she went into her bedroom. Closing the door, she leaned back against it and enjoyed the extremely satisfying feeling of being back in control.

Now, how to deal with Wilmont?

Chapter 58

The countdown started. Seven days of tension and feverish activity.

Days one and two. Jem's plan was gone over repeatedly, scoured for weak points.

Day three. Based on a warning from Lieutenant Wheeler, they revised security.

Day four. Azusa Detective George Heimann was arrested for multiple murders.

Day five. Ahrymani Carpenter's plan to teach Jem Wilmont a lesson was in place.

Day six. Katherine Baron was found comatose in her bedroom.

Day seven…

Chapter 59

Jem was propped against a wall, staring out from the terrace. Thane came up behind her, folded his arms around her, and rested his chin on her head.

"That's a serious thinking face."

Jem leaned back against him. "These last few days have me wondering about people. How they can do some of the things we've seen. From Grathen blowing up the Myerstone Lab to Kurzvall to psychopathic monsters that now include Ahrymani Carpenter and Katherine—did you hear about her?"

"I heard she died this morning from multiple organ failure. Yes, there are bad people out there, mostly in the minority."

"Yeah, well, that minority can do a lot of damage. I can't believe an Azusa detective, a seasoned Law Enforcer, would turn on his own people. He killed Lieutenant Lundgren and all those other Enforcers. That's why Detective Minsky was brought in from Ord. Kelding and Wheeler needed someone they could trust while they investigated.

Thane shrugged. "Envy, frustrated ambitions, and plain ol' greed. Not to mention stupidity. I can't believe the idiot was continuing to send messages to Kurzvall. That's what finally got him caught." He gave her a quick squeeze. "There's a lot of good out there. Margo and Boyd, Curtis and Kahn, Reis and Gaines, Wheeler and Kelding."

"All the good here, in this family," she said softly. "I was so lost—"

"*Shhhh.* That's the past. We have the future, once we finish this tonight. You should eat something."

"I'm not hungry. Guess I'm too wound up." She had managed some breakfast, but failed to get a single bite down for lunch. So much was riding on their plans.

Andi stepped out onto the terrace. "You and Thane could always go somewhere and *unwind*."

Jem turned and hid her flushed face in Thane's chest. He found it funny.

"Not a bad idea. I've found a relaxed Jem to be a better—*oof*," Thane said, as Jem's fist found his stomach.

Now Andi was the one laughing and Jem just knew her face was as red as the other woman's hair.

"Captain Kelding called," Andi said. "They've finished checking the last of our Azusa properties and no explosives found. Maybe Carpenter doesn't plan on using them until after tonight, except the conniving bitch won't get the chance because she'll be in jail."

"May we be so lucky," Jem murmured. She had thwarted Carpenter. The woman would want payback. Why else buy all those explosives now that her original plan was dead?

Lieutenant Wheeler had passed the warning to them several days ago. A woman they believed to be Carpenter in disguise had purchased a large quantity of explosives from three stores across two days. Anticipating an attack, the family had closed all five Azusa Stohlass Entertainment Arcades last night. For safety, Suzi and Seth had taken their families to the vacation island this morning, along with a contingent of guards. Eric's family had "battened down their hatches," as he put it.

"Anything from Wheeler?" Thane asked.

"No, and that would be a good thing," Nicholas said, joining them. He slipped an arm around his wife. "Means no change in plans or a problem that's cropped up. They should be spreading out around Ahrymani's hotel in the next hour or so."

"That soon?" Jem said, surprised. "It's what? A little after 1600? Contact isn't supposed to be for another three hours."

"Captain Kelding has had someone watching all the exits since this morning. There's nothing to prevent Carpenter from leaving the hotel early."

True. "Think Ahrymani will spot them?" Jem chewed her lip. The background report Nicholas had finally received listed advanced military training up until the crash that ended it. "She knows what to look for."

"Captain Kelding's plan is top-notch. Instead of trying to tail her—which Carpenter probably would catch—she'll be sprinkling her people in the surrounding area. Some are hidden, others will be part of the normal background. She'll shift people around once we know the direction Carpenter is moving."

"Think she'll use a disguise?" Andi asked.

"Not from the hotel. Carpenter has to be keeping them elsewhere in case her room is searched or accidently found by maid service."

Gwen popped her head out. "Merle has sandwiches and soup ready for an early supper. Let's eat. That's not a suggestion."

Nicholas kissed the top of Andi's head. "Can you handle food?"

"I'm feeling perfectly fine, Nicholas Delvarias O'Daniel."

They trooped into the dining room, where the delightful odor of shard chowder met them.

"Boy, does that smell good," Thane said, inhaling deeply

Jem's stomach agreed, sending out a loud rumble. Okay, maybe she could eat a bit.

"I…I'll get something later." Andi turned and bolted out the door.

Nicholas sighed. "Well, 'perfectly fine' didn't last long."

Gwen looked thoughtful. "You know, Nicholas, I think it's the fish. Its odor seems to set her off more than others."

"Huh. Maybe my kid is going to hate fishing."

"Be taking after his-or-her father then," Thane said to bursts of laughter.

At 1700, their phones *pinged* with a group message from Kelding. "*Target on the move.*"

Jem sucked in a breath. It'd started.

Kelding's people kept them informed of Ahrymani's movements.

Dressy Ahrymani entered an apartment building several blocks away from the hotel. Fifteen minutes later, sloppy Ahrymani emerged wearing short black hair, worn jeans with a faded brown shirt tucked half-in-half-out, and scuffed boots. Her disguise was broadcast via text to all participants.

Target heading southeast on Temple Drive came a watcher's text.

* * * * *

Ahrymani strolled casually for a block and turned left. She passed a couple politely arguing over someone named Albert. An office worker striding briskly from the opposite direction disappeared into a store. Turning right several blocks down, she saw two women waiting in a transportation booth, one of them impatiently tapping her arm. A man enjoying a drink at an outside café table gave her the eye as she sauntered pass. She gave him a not-interested smile and continued on.

Finally reaching her destination, Ahrymani leaned against the banking kiosk, hands in her pockets and glanced around. It was primarily office buildings along this street, and most of them emptied out by this time. Exactly why she'd chosen this spot. She'd spent almost thirty minutes wandering the streets, watching for signs of surveillance. There hadn't been any.

Wilmont thought she was so smart. Let's see how she feels after tonight.

She pulled out her phone and glanced at it. 1758. Almost time.

A guy came up to the kiosk, paused. "Not working?"

"Just waiting," she replied with a smile. "My boyfriend is working late. Go ahead." She politely moved away, pretending to watch a lighted window in a building across the street. The machine beeped several times.

The man gave her a smile and said, "Hope you don't have to wait much longer," before heading down the street.

1804 read her phone timestamp. She pulled up Jem's number. *"Unlock it now"* she texted.

"Why?"

"Because I've been a good girl," Ahrymani typed, sneering at the words. Just wait an hour, you bitch. *"Is there a reason you need to wait another hour?"*

A minute passed. Two. Then, *"Unlocked. Don't call me again."* The connection broke.

Ahrymani accessed the account. Yes! She moved most of it into an account she'd set up under an alias. She'd transfer it again once she got off-planet. The last one hundred thousand credits she downloaded into a cash card. Ten thousand dollars would do for now. She also had her pay from her employment as Katherine's aide.

She headed back to the apartment.

Her cover was gone now, along with Katherine's funds. Damn woman, up and dying that way. Strange, she hadn't appeared to be having any problems. Could Wilmont have popped in and poisoned her? Got rid of the pain in everyone's ass and ensured Thane's inheritance? Either way, that bit of bad luck was her ticket off Midgard. One of Helga's aides had already instructed her to gather up Katherine's things and return them to New Zagreb. Her employment would terminate once that was completed.

Ahrymani climbed the stairs to the second floor. She'd send a vacating message to the rental management office after she left tonight. Destroy the disguises tonight or take them with her? Take them, she decided. She'd bundle them in with Katherine's things. Nobody would think to search a dead woman's baggage. She'd destroy them later…or not.

She unlocked the door to the apartment. Wilmont was right. Once her secret was out, they'd be no more payments. Ten million plus what else she could squeeze out wouldn't last long in the lifestyle she intended to have. The disguises would come in handy. She'd make an excellent mercenary. Hmmm. What name would she use? Certainly not Keegan.

*　*　*　*　*

In ghost-mode, Jem followed Ahrymani into the apartment.

She had sent Gwen the code to unlock the extortion account after getting Ahrymani's demand. They'd all agreed the apartment was the perfect place to set their trap. She'd waited for Ahrymani in the lobby, shifting when one of Kelding's spies reported her approach outside.

Jem had hoped to find explosives. Nope, none. No obvious booby traps either.

With Ahrymani in the bedroom, Jem poofed back and quickly texted *'room 209, am in, no booms'* to Thane. Captain Kelding was probably going to learn a few new cuss words.

Jem put her phone away and leaned back against the door. Listened to some banging from the bedroom. Ahrymani walked out, bag in hand, and froze at the sight of her.

"Did you think I wouldn't find you?"

Ahrymani's eyes flashed to the locked door behind her. "No need to ask how you got in."

"Nope."

There was a loud pounding on the door. "Azusa Law Enforcement. Open the door."

"That will be Captain Kelding and her Enforcers," Jem said helpfully.

Ahrymani dashed back into the bedroom and slammed the door.

Jem unlocked the door and slipped to the side before flinging it open.

Kelding and a host of Enforcers poured in. Thane was right behind them.

"Bedroom," Jem told them, pointing.

An Enforcer started to force open the door. A laser bolt flashed through the door. He fell back, his arm singed and unnecessarily yelling "laz-gun." Another Enforcer pulled him to the side as Kelding motioned everyone back. Before she could say anything else, more laser shots punched through the door and down the wall. First up high, then low. Where someone might be standing, or dropped to avoid the high shots.

"Is the idiot looking to get killed?" Wheeler said.

"This is Captain Kelding of Azusa Law Enforcement." The shots stopped. "I'm sure you've spotted the officers outside the windows, and I have more with me out here. Surrender now before you kill someone and it gets a whole lot worse."

"Really?" came the derisive reply.

"Sure. Thane Baron is itching to assist us in taking you into custody."

Thane's teeth flashed in a feral grin. "Love to," he said loudly.

After a moment, the door cracked open a couple of inches. A laz-gun came sliding out. "Hands on head," Wheeler ordered, snatching it up.

The door opened fully and Ahrymani stepped out, hands on head.

It was over. Relief flooded Jem as she watched Ahrymani searched and cuffed. Only one thing left. "The explosives. Where are they?"

Ahrymani gave Jem and Thane a cold stare. "Wouldn't you like to know? By the way, what time is it?"

"1847," Wheeler said, warily.

"She's set them for 1900," Jem said, giving Ahrymani a stone-cold look of her own. "That was our original contact time and why she moved the payoff up."

When Ahrymani shrugged, Jem knew she was right. "Where are they?"

Ahrymani's answering smile sent a cold chill up Jem's spine. "You and the Stohlass family will find out soon enough."

Kelding slammed Ahrymani against the wall. "Where are the explosives, you psychotic piece of shit."

Jem wasn't surprised at the captain's reaction. Her family had died in the horrible Branson Fire that had been planned and set by a psychopath.

Ahrymani shrugged again. "I was going to blow up your fjord place. There were too many workers about to plant explosives, so I took my next best option." A maniacal light lit her face. "Then you made it so much better."

Jem blanched. "The island." She grabbed Thane's arm. "She's rigged your vacation home."

"Oh, yeah." Ahrymani gave a cruel laugh.

Wheeler swore. "We didn't think to check properties outside of Azusa." She looked at her time piece. "It's 1852. We can warn them, but there's no time to evacuate."

Jem pushed Kelding aside, grabbed Ahrymani by the throat, and re-slammed her against the wall. "Where's the bomb?"

Ahrymani sneered at her. "What else can you do to me? I'm already going to get life. Beat me up? Kill me? I'd prefer that, actually."

"How about me teleporting *half* of you into this wall. How's that going to look? How's that going to feel? Pain as one half tries to process being merged with the wall? Maybe cut in half. Maybe your insides will explode where the two halves join. Why don't I start with one leg? The real one."

Ahrymani's face was a frozen mask of horror.

"Six minutes," Thane said, his voice taunt.

"*Where is the bomb?*" Jem didn't even recognize the harsh voice as hers.

"Primary in the med-room. Six places, hidden. A-A-Accelerants too."

"Any on the dock?"

Ahrymani shook her head, sliding down the wall when Jem released her.

"Teleport?" Kelding said, disbelief on her face.

"Call General Kowalski. Let him know you've all breached classified. Thane…"

He stepped to her side. "Can you do it?"

"I have to." They had only minutes.

Grabbing him around the waist, Jem shifted them into ghost-mode. Ignoring the shocked faces around them, she focused attention inward and pictured the door ingrained in her memory from her tests. And reached.

Pain, blackness, disorientation.

They were there. People laughed and talked around them. Unaware.

She released the shift, sagging against Thane as the pain surged through her. *Explosives*, she heard him yelling, telling everyone to get to the dock. Then he scooped her up and was running for the med-room. Would they make it in time? She gritted her teeth as knives competed to see which could carve out the most of her spine.

There. An innocent-looking med-bag tucked into a corner. "Phone," she said to Thane as he put her down. "Call when you're all out." Dropping on top of the bag and wrapping her arms around it, she tried to shift. Nothing. She screamed mentally: *SHIFFFFFFFTT!* Something gave, and pain followed her into the shift. It wouldn't go off now. Shouldn't.

She closed her eyes, only needing ears to hear the phone Thane had left on the floor. Instead of fighting the agony, she simply rode it, following it down her legs and arms. Blackness danced at the rim of her awareness, seductive in its numbness. *No, not yet,* she told it. Finally, after an eon, the phone rang. She pushed up to her knees, rocked a couple of times, and shoved herself away from the bag. Watched it solidify out of ghost-mode.

…eight, nine… Was her brain was counting for the bomb? How much longer she could stay shifted? *…fifty-six, fifty-seven, fifty*—the bomb exploded.

How do you describe a supernova from the inside?

Beautiful. Deadly. A blinding white incandesce that would have reduced her to atoms if she'd been there. Not here. Somewhere. She needed to figure out where she was when here. Wherever here was. *Am I babbling?* Yep, babbling.

The blast zone was rimmed in a flaming dance of destruction and death. The accelerants would have torched the rest of the home. It could be rebuilt. The family was safe. *Her* family was safe.

She couldn't hold the shift much longer. She tried to move away, but her body refused to obey her. The blackness waved and slithered toward her.

Thane would be on the dock. Safe. Safe. She could see it, see Thane.

The pain began to fade, draining away. How she wished they'd had more time. *Thane*, her soul cried out and blackness swamped her.

* * * * *

The dock was crowded. Silent. The only sounds came from the waves slapping against the pylons and boats and the crackling roar of the inferno raging above them on the hillside.

Thane stared at it from the edge of the dock, Susi's phone clutched in his hand. *Jem was safe. Jem was safe*, he chanted silently. Nothing could touch her in ghost-mode. So where was she?

Susi touched his shoulder. "Thane, I'm so, so sorry," she said, tears running down her cheeks.

She didn't know about the phasing. Then his hindbrain reminded him Jem had teleported them here, even farther than before…which had nearly killed her. Thane sucked in a breath. For the first time in a long time, he asked the Universe for a favor. *Please, please, let her live.*

A sudden commotion broke out behind him. Shouts. Turning, he spied Jem. On hands and knees. *Alive.* Tossing the phone to Susi, he launched himself toward her. Sliding to his knees, he grabbed Jem as she collapsed and hugged her to his chest.

Her eyes half opened, met his. A smile touched her lips. Then those gorgeous eyes closed and her head rolled to the side.

Chapter 60

"May I join you?" Gwen Williams asked politely, stepping into the hospital's small, non-denominational chapel. She settled into a chair two seats over from Helga Baron and stared at the waterfall cascading down the back wall. It burbled gently into a narrow basin.

"The people of Midgard have built their lives around water. I've heard numerous metaphors and idioms related to water, the sea, or sailing."

"Water, in all its forms, can be soothing," Gwen replied without looking over.

"Yes, it is."

"I wish to express my condolences for your niece."

"Thank you. How is Miss Wilmont?"

"We don't know. Dr. Blackwood is with her now. I understand you're making arrangements to return home."

"Yes. They are releasing the—Katherine shortly."

"Does her mother and sisters know?"

"I sent word. They'll meet me in New Zagreb for the memorial."

Gwen studied the waterfall for a moment. "Have they found out why Katherine's organs failed?"

"No."

"Your brother died the same way, I believe? Sudden multiple organ failure?"

"Yes."

"I guess Katherine took after her father more than was thought." Gwen flicked a quick glance sideways. "The blood disorder, of course."

"Yes," Helga said, her gaze on the water. "The underlying cause must be the same."

"Were you able to spend any time with your niece before she became…ill?"

The water tinkled softly into the basin.

"I visited with her, yes. Spoke with her in the manner we discussed. Katherine was happy to hear I was thinking of canceling things." Helga paused. "We even had conciliatory drinks together."

Did you now?

Helga looked over. "I understand Ahrymani Carpenter is in custody. She was the one attacking your family."

Interesting how that was stated, not asked. "She's been charged on all counts, including the deaths of your driver and guard."

Helga nodded "Good. It's over. The monster has been caught. I hope this puts an end to some malicious gossip I've heard, as it will be dealt with severely. I will not have the Baron name and reputation smeared."

Gwen stared, nonplussed. Did she truly believe she could sweep it all aside? "I can't help wondering where the line between sanity and psychopathy is. Is there some way to tell when the line has been crossed?"

"That's what makes them monsters. They rarely show their true colors until it's too late." Helga rose. "I will contact you when I'm ready to resume Midgard's startup." She turned and marched off.

Gwen pondered the empty doorway for several moments, then returned her attention to the waterfall. Its quiet murmur soothed the aches inside her, though the holes would never fully close. She mourned the loss of so many lives in an arrogant pursuit of greed and power. And she wished Helga Baron well, an overly prideful woman who bore the weight of monsters and of her own ruthless choices.

She made a mental note to ensure the family never ate or drank anything served by Helga Baron's hand.

Chapter 61

It took several tries before Jem could get her eyelids fully raised. Hospital decorations beeped beside her. She must be alive. *Fire. Flames.* She raised her head, the dim lighting and fuzzy vision making it hard to see. Relief surged. No burn marks. How long had it been?

The door opened. "Naturally, you wait until I had to step out." Thane's hand cupped hers as he settled into the chair beside the bed. "Welcome back."

She blinked. Blinked again, but his blurred features didn't clear up. "I'm alive."

"Yes. Don't ever do that again. These last weeks have been hell."

Weeks? "How long has it been?"

"Three weeks and six days."

Four weeks. "I'm kind of surprised I'm alive," she said, giving a small laugh.

Thane shook his head. "You wouldn't be if you hadn't teleported out to the dock."

"I did?" A hazy memory, of thinking about Thane and how he'd be safe on the dock.

"Not surprised you don't remember. You collapsed right afterwards." His face turned serious. "We used CPR until the med-vac arrived and airlifted you to the hospital. On top of everything else, you had a brain bleed. A type of hemorrhage. Dr. Blackwood treated it and then all we could do was watch and wait."

That explained the four weeks. "You haven't been sitting here all that time, have you?"

"No. You woke up briefly last night. Called the night nurse 'Marion.'"

Jem frowned. "I don't remember that either." Dr. Marion Bluethon had been the mother-hen at the Myerstone Lab.

"The doctors believed it was a good sign that you'd wake up again today. So yes, I've been here since morning." He raised her hand and kissed it. "I didn't want to miss this."

Jem's eyelids lowered briefly. Wow. Four weeks and still tired. She forced them open. Squinted. Still fuzzy. "How is everyone? What's happened?"

"Let's see, best news first. Katrina came home three days ago, pretty much healed. She'll need to do a hand-soak for a month or so in Dr. Giovannelli's solution, and Mom has her scheduled in with a physical therapist for her arm. The family is back to as normal as we can be." He grinned. "Especially with a teleporter in the family. You thoroughly awed the family, shocked a bunch of Enforcers, and thoroughly irritated General Kowalski."

Jem's mouth opened, closed when Thane raised a hand.

"The irritation comes from all the paperwork in having to in-brief a large number of people. He fully understands the why of it. And he's the one who irritated our new FLEA Director."

"Seriously?"

"Very. Director Ankara Raine transferred in from Helsinki's Eastern District—she was the Assistant Director there. She was a bit miffed on finding two military guards on your door. Director Raine says she doesn't know what set Vanderbilt off—no, she's not been in-briefed—and that, quote, 'I am not Vanderbilt and you would do well to remember that in the future,' unquote."

"Ouch. We don't need another Fed war. Is it Markowitz's people?"

"That'd be using a sledge hammer to kill a granite beetle. The general has been rotating teams in from Odinheim and Spine Point Sea Patrol."

Jem gave him a puzzled look. Odinheim she could understand. But the Spine Point SP was based on the furthest island in the Spine Island chain.

"He wanted to make sure there weren't any ties to Azusa's current problems. Director Raine has been busy smoothing over those problems and getting things reorganized. Reis has been re-instated and is now the Assistant Director of Oslo's Western FLEA district. Director Raine has also made an offer to Lee Twobears. He's waiting until Mom can talk with you before deciding."

Jem's thought processes weren't fully awake and it took a minute for the reason why to hit her. "Talk about a long-distance marriage," she said. "I trust Reyna's judgement. Tell her to go ahead and look for a new Foundation manager. She'd probably be happier here with Katrina and the rest of you anyway." She'd moved to Earth to be with Lee.

"Actually…Mom wants to move the Foundation here. She says using Baron Financials as its investment resource will keep it funded, even without any outside donations."

Jem blinked. "I never thought about that. I set it up on Earth because I used my account there to kick it off. Tell her I approve and thank her. What about Ahrymani and Helga?"

Thane's jaw set. "Ahrymani Carpenter pled guilty at her pre-trial hearing and left last week on a prison ship to Hellspawn, the Fed-Pen planet they should have sent Beckett to. It pisses me off," he said scowling. "All the lifers go there and he sure as hell isn't going free again."

Seth's comment came back to her. "Maybe he negotiated staying on Skewed in exchange for revealing whoever helped steal the Delgados." Jem's pulse spiked at a sudden thought. "Is Ahrymani talking about me?" Trying to negotiate her own deal?

"Nope. Ahrymani's been kept in isolation since her arrest. She's also been warned against even hinting anything about you." He rubbed his nose. "I got the impression that if she's not careful, she might end up in one of Hellspawn's lava pools instead of a cell. Accidently, of course."

Of course. "Helga?"

"Helga Baron took Katherine's ashes home. Midgard's Baron Financials office officially opens next week. She'll return and grace us with her offensive presence at the official ceremony."

Jem grinned. Thane would never do more than tolerate the woman.

"This last item should make you happy." Thane patted her arm. "Boyd is here. Permanently. He's even taken it on himself to oversee the interior outfitting of your home. The man has taught our supply people a thing or two. Fortunately, you'd already discussed most of what you wanted with the architect and, well, I supplied a few ideas."

"You do know me pretty well." Besides, it was also going to be his home now. Then she added with a mischievous grin, "It can always be ripped out and redone." They both laughed.

Quiet descended and they simply held hands. Jem didn't know what the future held and found she didn't care. Her life was full now, so different from the lonely, bleak one she'd been existing in. She had friends and allies. She had Thane. The Kurzvalls, Vanderbilts and Hawthornes of the universe were so outclassed.

After a while, Jem dozed off.

Titles by R. D. Chapman

<u>Blurring Reality Series</u>

Shattered Reality

Blurring Reality

Tangled Reality

Reality Kicked

<u>D'Accio Investigations Series</u>

At Any Cost

About the Author

R. D. Chapman has been an avid reader all her life. A retired empty-nester living quietly in Nebraska with her husband, she draws on a lifetime of experience ranging from cook to software developer to craft characters and stories. She writes in a blend of SF&F, urban fantasy, and mystery with a smidgen of humor and romance. When not writing, she loves spending time with the three Rs: Reading, cRocheting, and Relaxing.

* * * * *

Thank you for reading *Tangled Reality*. If you have enjoyed this book, please consider leaving a review, as they are essential to expanding my sales and readership. Even a few simple lines will help. Thanks!